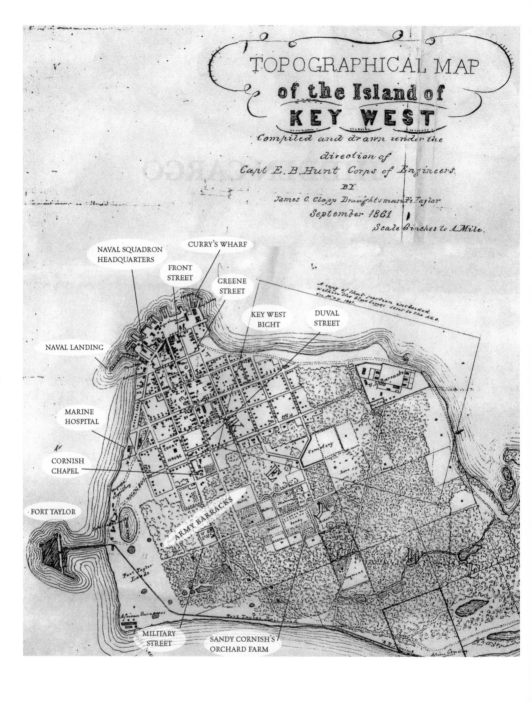

TOPOGRAPHICAL MAP
of the Island of
KEY WEST

Compiled and drawn under the

direction of

Capt E. B. Hunt Corps of Engineers.

BY

James C. Clapp Draughtsman Ft Taylor

September 1861

Scale 6 inches to 1 Mile.

NAVAL SQUADRON
HEADQUARTERS

CURRY'S WHARF

FRONT
STREET

GREENE
STREET

KEY WEST
BIGHT

DUVAL
STREET

NAVAL LANDING

MARINE
HOSPITAL

CORNISH
CHAPEL

FORT TAYLOR

ARMY BARRACKS

MILITARY
STREET

SANDY CORNISH'S
ORCHARD FARM

Old Havana Bay

EL MORRO FORTRESS

ENTRANCE TO HARBOR

LA CABAÑA FORTRESS

LA PUNTA FORTRESS

CASA BLANCA

PASEO DEL
PRADO

OLD CITY

PLAZA DE
SAN FRANCISCO

CAMPO DE
MARTE

CAMPO DE
PEÑALVER

CASA DE
RECÓGIDAS

REGLA

EL CERRO

Also by Robin Lloyd

Rough Passage to London: A Sea Captain's Tale
Harbor of Spies: A Novel of Historic Havana

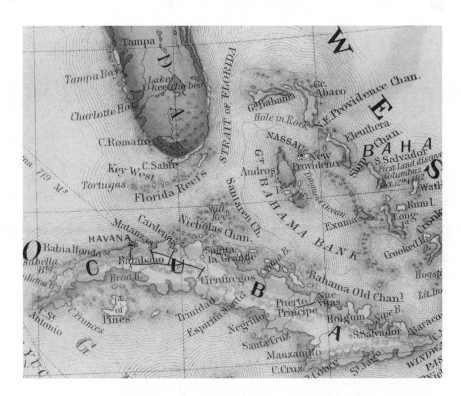

HIDDEN CARGO

A Novel

ROBIN LLOYD

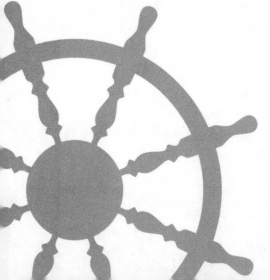

Essex, Connecticut

An imprint of Globe Pequot, the trade division of
The Rowman & Littlefield Publishing Group, Inc.
4501 Forbes Blvd., Ste. 200
Lanham, MD 20706
www.rowman.com

Distributed by NATIONAL BOOK NETWORK

Book cover: Colored lithograph by Frédéric Mialhe. Courtesy of Cuban Heritage
Collection, University of Miami.
Topographical map of Key West (1861): Courtesy of Monroe County Public Library,
Florida Keys History Center, Key West, Online Photo Collection.
Nineteenth-century map of Old Havana Bay: Courtesy of Harvard Map Collection,
Harvard Library.
Title page: "Map of Mexico, Central America and the West Indies" (1868) by Augustus
Mitchell, cropped. Courtesy of Harvard Map Collection, Harvard Library.
Image from Part I: Lithograph courtesy of Monroe County Public Library, Florida Keys
History Center, Key West, Online Photo Collection
Image from Part II: Lithograph by Frédéric Mialhe. Courtesy of Cuban Heritage
Collection, University of Miami.
Image from Part III: Lithograph by Eduardo Laplante. Courtesy of Cuban Heritage
Collection, University of Miami.

British Library Cataloguing in Publication Information Available

Library of Congress Cataloging-in-Publication Data

Names: Lloyd, Robin, 1950- author.
Title: Hidden cargo : a novel / Robin Lloyd.
Description: Essex, Connecticut : Lyons Press, [2023] | Summary: "A new
  seafaring novel by the author of Rough Passage to London and Harbor of
  Spies"—Provided by publisher.
Identifiers: LCCN 2022054489 (print) | LCCN 2022054490 (ebook) | ISBN
  9781493072316 (cloth : alk. paper) | ISBN 9781493072323 (epub)
Classification: LCC PS3612.L69 H54 2023 (print) | LCC PS3612.L69 (ebook)
  | DDC 813/.6—dc23
LC record available at https://lccn.loc.gov/2022054489
LC ebook record available at https://lccn.loc.gov/2022054490

∞™ The paper used in this publication meets the minimum requirements of
American National Standard for Information Sciences—Permanence of Paper
for Printed Library Materials, ANSI/NISO Z39.48-1992.

For Tamara, Marisa, and Samantha

"I was free; but there was no one to welcome me to the land of freedom. I was a stranger in a strange land."

—Harriet Tubman, "Scenes in the Life of Harriet Tubman"
by Sarah Hopkins Bradford, 1869

Preface

This novel is a work of fiction. Most of the characters are invented, as are all of the situations. While the story is a product of my imagination, it should be noted that some historical events mentioned in the book are real, such as the hurricane that struck Key West in 1865. Some of the military officials and individuals residing in Key West in the months following the end of the Civil War are actual historical figures as is the US Consul General in Havana. Many of the details surrounding the reports of kidnappings along the Gulf Coast and Florida are based on research from US Army records, congressional records, newspaper accounts, and consular dispatches sent from Cuba to Washington. These combined sources of information helped to inspire this novel.

FORT JEFFERSON

Part One

"I look where the ship helplessly heads end on. I hear the burst as she strikes. I hear the howls of dismay. They grow fainter and fainter. . . . I can but rush to the surf and let it drench me and freeze upon me."

—Walt Whitman,
"The Sleepers"

1

October 22, 1865

A strange stillness hung over the calm water surrounding the walls of the sea fortress. The young Navy lieutenant breathed in deeply as he looked out at the ghostly pewter sky and the unusually flat sea. The morning air had a different feel to it, heavy and jagged like a saw's edge. Everett Townsend turned to walk down the fort's granite spiral staircase to a gun casement window. He squared his unshaven jaw and looked out at the horizon again as a touch of foreboding shivered through him. Windless weather and pungent air signaled a storm.

A sudden squeal of iron-rimmed wheels on stone broke the silence. A steady stream of military prisoners all dressed in the same drab prison clothes stumbled out from inside the walls, some of them pulling four-wheeled drays. Townsend watched the shabby patchwork of snarls and sneers, a long line of misery, suffering, and sickness. Another workday had begun at the military prison at Fort Jefferson in the Dry Tortugas.

With the war over, prisoners from both sides were being sent to the Dry Tortugas for all kinds of crimes. Desertion, murder, theft, conspiracy. The prison fortress had come to be called Devil's Island. Scores of inmates had died in these walls from breakbone fever and its more deadly companion, yellow fever. No prisoners wanted to hear that they were being sent to the Dry Tortugas.

Since the end of hostilities six months ago, Townsend's gunboat schooner, the USS *Rebecca*, had become a dispatch and supply vessel. There were five hundred soldiers at Fort Jefferson and five hundred prisoners, all dependent on supplies from Key West. It was dull routine, but it was a better assignment than the steamboat sailors who were scrubbing decks on their ships at anchor, or the sailors assigned to replace channel buoys that the Confederate saboteurs had destroyed. Wartime danger had been replaced by peacetime boredom.

Gone were the big gunships with their smoky funnels that had defined the Navy's blockade in the Gulf of Mexico. By now, almost all of the thirty ships that made up the East Gulf Naval Squadron had been sent north to be decommissioned and sold. Townsend was one of only a handful of Naval officers still stationed in Key West. He'd served for two years, and he was restless to get on with his life.

A rapid-fire drum roll echoed through the Fort's parade ground. Townsend pulled out his watch. It was eight a.m. He needed to get clearance from the post quartermaster before they could leave. They would have to weigh anchor soon if they were going to get back to Key West, some sixty-five miles away, before nightfall. But there was no wind, and the USS *Rebecca* was going nowhere without wind. He heard the familiar hum and whine in his ears, and he slapped his face. "Damn mosquitos." He shook his head. *Nothing those man-eating buggers like more than dead air.*

A line of Black soldiers with their brass-buttoned blue uniforms and shining rifles marched by to take their positions. *So much pride and hope in those faces,* he thought to himself. He knew these men were with the 82nd Colored Infantry, some of whom had run away from plantations to enlist, and who now probably wanted to be discharged just as much as he did. The Navy lieutenant had tried hard to put the war behind him, but the sight of these soldiers brought the memories back, unbidden and unwanted.

The crack of shots ringing out from the dark jungle. His friend bleeding, eyes dark with fear. Clyde Hendricks had clutched his hand. Townsend had tried to staunch the bleeding, but there were too many wounds. As his superior officer, he had put Hendricks in danger's way, and for that he would always punish himself. Townsend had even convinced him that fighting against the Southern Rebellion was his cause, a struggle for emancipation even though Hendricks was a Bahamian. And now his friend had died for that cause.

A slight breeze on his face and the scratchy wisp of rustling palm fronds pulled him back to the present. The wind was coming up, and he felt his spirits rise. Four heavily guarded prisoners, cursing and sneering, shuffled out of the sally port in leg irons and chains ahead of him. His eyes hardened. The dirty faces simmering with resentment were familiar. The four accomplices to Lincoln's assassin, John Wilkes Booth. They had been convicted a little over three months earlier by a military court in Washington and had been sent to the Dry Tortugas in July. The infamous names of Spangler, Arnold, O'Laughlen, and Samuel Mudd, the doctor who had tended to Booth's broken ankle. All but Spangler were given life sentences.

"Don't worry Lieutenant, they won't be escaping anytime soon."

He'd been looking for the post quartermaster, but the officer had found him first.

"How did you catch him?"

Townsend had heard about Mudd's attempted escape from prison a few weeks earlier on board one of the transport ships, but he didn't know the details.

"One of the sailors recognized him and hauled him out of the cargo hold. We put him in solitary. Said he was scared of what these Black soldiers might do to him. Justice comes in many ways, don't it?"

The officer chuckled at himself, but Townsend only nodded as he watched the four men stumble off to begin another day of hard labor.

The post quartermaster handed Townsend the signed papers confirming the delivery of barreled meats, bags of flour, sacks of vegetables, and crates of canned goods.

"By the way, Lieutenant, there was one item missing."

Townsend shot the post quartermaster a worried glance.

"What would that be? I don't think . . ."

"No, not to worry Lieutenant, you delivered what was listed. But next time bring some of those *habanos* with you. I hear you can get a heavy stack of a hundred cigars for four dollars in Key West. This is a lonely place without a good Cuban cigar."

Townsend saluted. "I will be sure to do that." He handed the post quartermaster one of the cigars he routinely kept in his jacket. "Try this one. It's real Havana tobacco rolled by Cubans in Key West."

The officer wiped the sweat off his face with a crumpled bandana and nodded appreciatively.

"Good luck on the way back. You may need it. Big storm's brewing." He pointed up to the fort's flagpole where the American flag fluttered ever so slightly. Underneath a half-blue half-yellow triangular signal quivered a warning of worsening weather. "Barometer is falling like a Canada goose full of lead buckshot."

Townsend needed no warning. He'd seen the signs himself. Even the high-flying frigate birds that normally glided overhead were nowhere to be seen.

A soldier with the duty boat was ready at the pier to row Townsend out to his ship. The USS *Rebecca*, a seventy-one-foot-long centerboard schooner, with her two raked back masts and long bowsprit, had a signature profile that was easy to find in any harbor.

"Pretty ship you got there, Lieutenant. Must be one of them Confederate boats the Navy acquired during the war."

Townsend nodded.

"She was a former blockade runner. The Navy captured her coming out of the Steinhatchee River with a full load of Confederate cotton."

Townsend looked at the schooner. She was a bigger version of one of the Maryland-built schooners the watermen around the Chesapeake Bay called square-sterned bugeyes, but with higher freeboard. The bottom half was built out of roughly hewn thick logs, so with the centerboard raised, the boat could be run ashore with little damage to the hull. As a former Maryland boy, Townsend was quite familiar with the rig. His father, who owned cargo schooners in the Bay, had made sure of that.

"Almost like she was designed for carrying out raids into Florida's swampy hideaways," the private said. "I reckon you made good use of that twelve-pounder gun up there by the bow? Kill a lot of them butternut rebels, did ya?"

The Navy lieutenant didn't reply.

The small rowboat banged up against the schooner's hull with a dull thud, and Townsend grabbed hold of the outboard stays to pull himself on board. The bosun and the three other seamen in the crew had mustered into line. Townsend saw the brooms, holystones, and buckets so he knew the crew had been scrubbing the decks as requested. He acknowledged them and then waved them off to get the cleaning equipment put away, raise the sails, and haul up the anchor. Townsend hardly knew any of these men. They were all strangers to each other, sailors tossed from one Navy ship to another like flotsam in the aftermath of a storm.

Amid the clicking of mast hoops and the squealing of blocks, the crew began hauling up the sails. They were so shorthanded the bosun had to join them. On the voyage over from Key West, Townsend had recognized the skills of the bosun, who was a little older than he was. Ezra Metcalf was a Penobscot River sailor from Maine, a big, square-faced hulk of a man with a thick black beard that hung down below his chin like a well-cropped hedgehog. Townsend thought he was about twenty-five years old, but he seemed much older.

With the sails flapping back and forth, the crew started pulling up the anchor. First the thick hemp anchor line, and then the heavy chain crept through the hawsepipe.

"Anchor's hove short, Cap'n," shouted the Black sailor standing in the bow. Townsend could see the near vertical anchor chain.

"Break her out then," he yelled out. "Back the staysail. We'll pay off on the port tack."

"Port tack it is, Cap'n," the Black sailor replied.

The man's name was Josiah Tollman, but he answered to Stumpie. He was the only Black man on board. He got his nickname because he was so wide-shouldered and stocky he had to turn sideways to go down the companionway into the cabin. Townsend knew he was from northern Florida and had served as a coal heaver on a Navy gunboat, but he didn't know much more than that. He was someone who preferred to say little, especially about his own life.

The boat fell off on the port tack, and the men eased the sails. Slowly at first and then surprisingly quickly, the schooner began to gather headway. Townsend could see the anchor emerge from the foamy white water at the bow.

"Anchor's broken out, Cap'n."

"Bear away. Ease the sheets more," Townsend shouted to the two other men standing amidships. The young one was a Cuban from Key West named Joaquín de la Cruz, small, thin, and agile. He couldn't have been more than seventeen years old. He'd tried to join the 47th Pennsylvania Infantry in Key West early in the war, but they wouldn't take him because he was too young. The Navy had been his only alternative.

The other sailor was a silent, brooding man with speckled gray hair and a small beard jutting out from a narrow jaw. Townsend guessed he was about forty years old. Charles Langworth was his name. All Townsend knew about him was that early on in the war he had briefly served in the Confederate militia, but switched sides when the Confederate forces in Florida started a ruthless conscription drive. It seemed he had no love for the Confederacy, but no real loyalty to the Union either. Townsend had decided the man also had a close relationship with silence.

With the anchor now tied down to the cathead, the schooner slipped away from its anchorage and soon was out in the middle of the Northwest Channel. Townsend looked over at the endless shallows and imagined the explorer Ponce de Leon sailing through these waters in 1513 in his search for gold and a fountain of youth, and naming this sprinkling of barren islands for the only thing of value he'd found there. *Las Tortugas*. The place of turtles.

Townsend lit a cigar, something he did routinely to clear his mind. The overcast skies made Fort Jefferson appear to rise out of the sea like some formidable citadel from a lost underwater world. He wondered what that Spanish explorer would think if he could see this fortress and the surrounding islands. Where once there were just nesting turtles, there were now massive brick walls and a lighthouse as well as an island where the dead were buried.

The wind was building in intensity, filling the schooner's sails, but it wasn't stormy yet.

"She seems to stand it very well," the bosun said.

"No need to shorten sail yet," Townsend replied.

"Aye, aye, Cap'n."

Townsend handed off the wheel to the bosun and went below to the captain's cabin set against the ship's transom where he had a small table with only an overhead hatch to provide daylight. This was his sanctuary. He pulled out the latest US Coast Survey chart that covered the Tortugas Keys and the western end of the Florida reefs.

The Navy lieutenant caught his own eyes in the small mirror by his desk. They were like dark pools staring back at him. He ran his hands through his black curly hair as he took careful measure of himself. His face was mahogany brown, dry and leathery from the sun. He thought he looked older than his twenty-two years. He knew the war had changed him. Doubts continuously swept over him like an incoming tide. The sight of those he'd seen die were always with him as were the ghostly voices in the darkness along the river-banks and swampy inlets where he'd carried out raids. They called it the jungle coast. The west coast of Florida was wild country, an inhospitable land where it was hard to tell who was a rebel and who was a refugee—who needed saving and who needed killing.

His thoughts turned to his family. Both his parents had died during the war. His younger brother had fought for the Confederacy and been killed at Antietam. His closest remaining relative was his Spanish grandmother who lived in Cuba. She was immensely proud of her heritage and her ancestors. He shuffled through papers and looked at the last letter he had received from her. He'd responded to several of her letters over the past two years, always addressing her as *Abuela*, which she seemed happy to accept. She'd written from the family sugar plantation in Matanzas province. With her fine neat handwriting, she described the upcoming harvest, how it should be a record year, and how much she wished he could be there to see the beauty of the lush cane fields. It was clear she wanted him to come to Cuba when he was discharged from the Navy. He was her closest living relative.

Mi querido Everett,

No te imaginas cuanto significas para mí . . .

She had written how important he was to her, and that when she thought of him, she thought of his mother, her darling Esperanza, the light of her life, who now was in the other world. Townsend put his elbows on his desk and placed his hands under his chin. He imagined his grandmother at her desk, her thin face, dark eyes, and her black hair streaked with gray.

He shook his head. He knew his grandmother was sincere, but she was living in a dream. In reality, his mother had hated his grandmother and had run away from Cuba to get away from her. He'd visited the family plantation. He could understand his mother's aversion to the place. He also felt a sense of dread at the thought of once again coming face to face with his family's close ties to slavery. He put his grandmother's letter down with a sigh.

Far more pressing to him now were thoughts of Emma. *Emma Carpenter Lozada, the woman he had hoped he would spend his life with.* He felt his stomach tighten. He had driven her away. He didn't know why he had refused to make a commitment to her. It was the war, he told himself. The long absences, the intensity of patrolling up those rivers, the trauma of the yellow fever outbreak, all had taken their toll. He picked up a piece of paper and began to write. Perhaps too late to patch things up, but he still held a faint hope. He began writing down some of his feelings for her.

Dear Emma,

I thought you should know I am still in the Navy, awaiting discharge. I wonder how you're faring now that you are back in Havana. I find myself thinking about you constantly. I see you on the terrace of your mother's boarding house painting the ships in the harbor. I hear you playing a Mozart sonata with your violin. . . . I miss you so much . . .

Townsend abruptly crumpled up the letter and threw it on the floor. The boat heeled suddenly, reminding him of why he'd come down to his cabin. He made some quick calculations at the chart table and looked around the cabin to make sure the kitchen table and chairs were all secured to the floor. If they were lucky, they could reach Key West before dark, but as he surfaced on deck, one look at the cresting whitecaps told him they might not be so fortunate.

2

By noon, sea and sky had come together, emptied of all color in an endless canvas of black and gray. This was no ordinary storm. The topmasts were soon bending like coachwhips, and Townsend ordered the men to drop the topsails, reef all sails and run lifelines from bow to stern, tie the jolly boat down, secure the water barrels, and tightly close the hatches and portholes. He looked behind him to the south. He could barely make out the lighthouse on Loggerhead Key that gave him a visual bearing.

"I reckon we're in for a real blow," Metcalf said in his distinctive lilting accent. He pointed to the waves with the cresting whitecaps. "What's our course to be?"

"We'll stand on a north, northeast course for now until we get the first bands of squally weather," Townsend replied, trying to sound assured. "Then turn southeast and try to reach the light marking the channel into Key West."

"Why not heave to?" the bosun asked. "Ride out this storm out in open water?"

"We need to make Key West by nightfall."

"Don't mean to question your thinking, Cap'n," Metcalf said, a stubborn edge in his voice. "I don't believe we can reach Key West before dark. This ain't no run-of-the-mill, mackerel sky storm we got comin'. This could be one of them hurricanes."

"We need to get back and make a report to Naval headquarters," Townsend snapped back with a glare. "The commander will want us back in port." He looked away. Townsend knew the bosun was right. There was no need to be reckless. But the war had made him more willing to take a risk. It had left him skeptical and suspicious of other men's advice, less trusting of others. It had hardened him, making him even more stubborn than he was before. But there was another reason he wanted to get back as soon as possible. He wanted to see if he could find out any news about Emma. She had left Key West months ago to sail to Havana, leaving behind many of her belongings at her sister's house where she had lived during the war. Her sister's husband had confided to him that Emma might be coming back to collect her possessions. He thought he could leave a letter with her sister and find out more about Emma's plans.

They were about twenty miles out into the Gulf when the first line of sharp squalls struck them, and the unruly winds suddenly switched to the northeast. One look at Metcalf's sullen face told him that the man was watching him. He brought the ship to windward causing the sails to crack like gunshots. He then gave the orders to drop the mainsail, leaving them with a tightly reefed foresail and a small storm trysail. For the next three hours, the winds picked up dramatically while the steadily falling barometer told Townsend there was a lot more storm coming.

Mounting waves rose along her lee quarter, leaping over the side. The strong gusts of wind and the stinging rain began to unnerve him. This storm was descending on them more quickly than he had expected. Metcalf had been right. They were being knocked down further to the southwest, away from the Key West channel buoy toward the shoaly areas. Night would soon fall, and the weather was worsening.

Before Townsend had time to think of an alternate plan, a solid black cloud rose up into the eastern sky and dropped on top of them with a sudden fury, almost instantly turning day into night. The winds burst onto the ship with a howling roar and a deluge of water, rain, and spray. The *Rebecca* went over onto her side and the crew found themselves sliding down the near-vertical deck into foaming ocean water.

Townsend clutched the wheel and tried to hold on even as he felt his feet slipping. He forced his knees between the spokes to try to control the kicking wheel. It was a constant fight for him to hold the schooner steady. Water poured over the gunwales into the cabin. He called out to Langworth to start pumping. The other two crew members were caught in a swirl of foaming water covering the deck that would have pulled them overboard if not for the lifelines. Townsend feared the masts would give way. It was Metcalf who saved the day by taking the ax from the side of the wheelhouse and cutting away sections of the bulwarks on the lee side so that the water could more quickly drain off.

Townsend stood rigidly still. Soaked and shivering, he shielded his eyes as he looked at the bucking bow of the schooner and the lines thrashing about the deck. The ship tossed about, shaking furiously, running blindly. His mind became jumbled. He imagined Hendricks, calm as ever, looking at him in that same quiet manner with those oddly mismatched eyes, one hopeful, the other sad. Townsend looked to him for some kind of signal, but none came.

It was Metcalf who snapped him out of his paralysis. Clutching the wind-ward stays, the bosun, his eyes large and haggard, pointed to a dark clump off to the southwest.

"Mangroves," he cried out. "Sharp on the starboard bow. Must be Marquesas Keys."

Townsend could just make out the low shadowy line on the starboard side. During the war, he'd once pursued a small Confederate sloop into a narrow channel on the southeast side of this circular archipelago of mangrove islands. He'd followed behind and discovered a wide shallow lagoon where you could find shelter. He'd always heard that there was no better way for a boat to ride out a hurricane than tucked inside one of these heavily forested mangrove hideaways.

Leaning back against the powerful northeast wind, Townsend grabbed the wheel with more purpose. He knew there was plenty of deep water if he stayed in the Boca Grande channel on a southerly course, keeping a mile to two miles away from the Marquesas. Over the noise of the wind, he told Metcalf his plan and had the bosun inform de la Cruz to look out for a peninsula on their starboard side.

Water and wind churned around him. Townsend wiped his face as they approached the northern edge of the Marquesas. He thought he saw a ship. He wondered if his eyes were playing tricks on him. A shiver of suspense shot down his back. He turned his head quickly toward the mangrove shoreline and caught another glimpse, but then it was gone, swallowed by the sea. Townsend looked again and this time he saw it. A big schooner had run hard aground in the Marquesas shallows, the hull leaning to one side. Townsend watched mesmerized as four small ghostly figures attempted to climb into one of the ship's yawl boats even as white rollers swept over the deck, exploding in bursts of spray.

"Look, Metcalf. A shipwreck. Do you see it? Over there."

The bosun turned, but at that moment a huge wave blocked his view. He shook his head.

"Did you see it? A wreck!" Townsend screamed, but his words were lost in the howl of the wind. Metcalf just kept shaking his head. When Townsend looked back, the shipwreck was lost into the spray and darkness behind them.

From the bow, de la Cruz quickly signaled that they'd passed the peninsula he'd been told to look for. Townsend began turning the helm to starboard even as he caught sight of a giant wave looming above them. Every spar and part of the rigging seemed to quiver as the boat rode up the side of this mountainous wave that seemed to grow bigger and bigger.

When they reached the crest, Townsend signaled to Metcalf to help him and together the two men pulled the spokes of the wheel hard to starboard. The schooner began hurtling down the other side of the wave. He could now just barely make out the narrow entrance framed by a low line of mangroves. He yelled to Langworth to raise the centerboard, and then turned the boat toward the break in the shadows.

Moments later, the *Rebecca* shot into an unmarked channel with extreme shallows on either side. Townsend kept the boat pointed directly at the break in the wall of mangroves ahead of him. He knew his timing had to be perfect. There was deep water right up to the mangroves, but then it shallowed out quickly. If he went too far, the schooner would go hard aground in the most exposed part of the lagoon, where the waves would swallow them.

As soon as they reached the tree line, he rounded the ship up into the wind. He heard the sails explode and the rigging shake and snap. The bosun threw out the stern anchor as a big swell hit them broadside, causing the schooner to career over to one side, but then the anchor line drew taut, slowing the boat's forward progress. The thick hull hit the sandy bottom with a jarring thud, and then the schooner's bow shot forward with tremendous force, twisting and scraping into the noisy embrace of the mangrove forest.

In the black hole of the ship's hull, Townsend and the four others huddled together in the darkness, curled up against the bulkhead. There was no sleep to be had that night. He had no sense of what time it was. Hour after hour the storm continued to rage. He couldn't see the other men. All he heard above the howl of the wind and the creaking of the ship were occasional curses. Townsend couldn't get the sight of that shipwreck out of his mind, and the figures he'd seen struggling on deck. He wondered whether those men were dead. *They must have drowned.* Townsend placed his hands over his head to block out the deafening noise. He wasn't even totally sure that the shipwreck was real. Maybe he imagined it?

De la Cruz crawled into one of the berths and began praying in Spanish. "*Santa María, Madre de Dios ruega por nosotros, pecadores ahora y en la hora de nuestra muerte . . .*" Townsend was fluent in Spanish, so he was well aware of the words, a prayer to the Virgin Mary.

A rolling wave smashed against the ship's hull. Townsend could now feel the boat being rocked back and forth and then the jarring thump and the thud of the thick hull hitting the sandy bottom. Townsend braced himself for the moment when the wood below his feet would finally surrender to the battering of the waves.

Sometime in the middle of the night, the winds died down. Townsend guessed it must have been around midnight. He allowed himself to think that perhaps the worst was over, and he prepared himself to go outside. But then the fury of the storm began all over again.

Townsend heard a voice in the dark.

"Tide's rising, Captain. Winds have changed direction. Storm surge coming in from the west."

"I know Metcalf . . . I know . . ."

The flood of water now rushing in was inundating the low-lying land and the mangroves of the Marquesas, raising the boat higher and higher. The spiderweb of lines they'd run through the mangroves and secured to the stilted roots could soon give way due to the tremendous force being exerted on them by wind and the sea. Townsend imagined the boat being carried away by the wind and the current, hijacked by the storm surge onto the first rocks or sandbars they ran into.

"Grab that line, Bosun."

Townsend was already tying one end of a thick half-inch line around his waist, securing it with a bowline.

"Are we going outside, Cap'n?"

"I am. You're staying, Metcalf. Just secure your end of the line to the base of the main mast and slacken ever so slowly. Tollman, you help him. Feed the line to me and take up slack as needed."

Townsend crawled his way in the dark to the companionway and climbed up the steps. Slowly, he opened the hatch and immediately wished he hadn't. A sudden blast of wind filled with rain and sea spray burst into the enclosed cabin.

"Keep that rope tight, Metcalf," Townsend yelled as he wiggled outside onto the deck. The wind immediately stung and burned his face. Its unrelenting howl was more intense and louder than he had imagined. He had been under fire during the war and had heard cannonballs flying at close range. The only way he could describe the sound he heard now was imagining hundreds of cannonballs roaring by.

The Navy lieutenant put his hands over his ears and covered his face with his arm. It was dark, but his eyes had grown used to the blackness. He clung to the slippery deck like a lizard on a wall, crawling and clawing his way over to the windward side of the boat where he grabbed the lifeline with one hand. There at the rail he could see the cresting waves steadily rolling in and then bursting onto the deck, exploding on top of him in a deluge of foam and spray.

He was alone now, alone with the storm. He conjured up the image of a crouching cat, the storm stalking its prey, looking out over the horizon. He saw a body lying in repose, and realized he was looking at himself. Townsend shook his head to try to regain his focus. He felt the extreme strain and pressure on the hemp lines holding the boat. There was no way he could loosen or slack them. A voice inside his head spoke to him, a calm and resonant voice, with a soft Bahamian lilt. It was Hendricks. They'd been through so much danger together. He knew he could trust this voice.

"You ain' got no choice. Cut de lines," the voice said.

Clinging to the shrouds to brace himself, he got up on his knees and pulled out his ship's knife. He began slicing the lines from the cleats and bitts. One by one he cut them. The boat sprang upwards, tasting freedom like a captive bird, and then groaned as a separate set of lines restrained it. When they'd run the schooner into the dense foliage in the lagoon and tied it down to the mangroves, he had insisted that the crew set up a separate protective set of lines with more slack, just in case something like this storm surge happened.

Once safely back inside the dark cabin, Townsend threw himself down on the cabin sole shivering with exhaustion. All he could do was pray that the second set of lines would hold. Only Metcalf and Tollman seemed to understand what he'd done. The two others were either asleep or lost in another world. Townsend closed his eyes. He was cold and wet. His mouth was salty, giving him a sudden thirst. He wrapped his arms protectively around his body as he listened to the gale outside, allowing himself to fall into his own dark thoughts.

Strangely, he kept thinking about writing a letter home, but then he realized there was no home. He thought of his father's last letter. His familiar scrawling handwriting was shaky, the lettering faint and wobbly. He knew something was wrong, but he never thought it was a farewell letter. He never thought he was dying. He'd written the Admiral requesting an emergency forty-day leave to see his father, but the fighting in Florida was intense then, and his request had been denied. He should have tried harder, but he hadn't. With his father, mother, and brother all dead now, he was alone. At least his poor father had died knowing that his only remaining son had managed to become a Navy lieutenant even after suffering the disgrace of being kicked out of the Naval Academy for unruly behavior two years earlier.

His troubled mind wandered back to the ambush on the Suwannee River. He remembered rowing down river after attacking a band of Confederates herding cattle north for the rebel armies, and then hearing the cry of a panther. The rustling of leaves had whispered the only warning. Then the scream of bullets. Cries everywhere. Through the smoke from the ship's howitzer, he could see the shadowy gray figures on the banks firing at the boat through the black stands of trees. The sound of Confederate cavalry thundering down toward them. A man in a dark gray cavalry greatcoat shouted. "Show them no quarter!" They were aiming at the Black seaman in Navy blue, the man he'd ordered to climb to the top of the mast to pilot them down the river.

The waves pounding against the hull now seemed to him like sea creatures gnawing at the sides of the boat, demanding to be let in. He imagined the seawater creeping in through the planking, rising steadily, dark and salty. The overhanging mangrove branches scraped against the hull, snapping and cracking in the air, whipping the sides of the ship like a cat-o'-nine-tails. *Death comes to us all.* He tried to imagine what was waiting for him on the other side. The fates would decide. He accepted that. He bowed his head and readied himself for whatever lay ahead.

Townsend must have dropped off to sleep because the next thing he heard was a man's voice telling him to wake up. It was dawn, and the winds had died down considerably. Townsend opened his eyes to the faint light and the sound of the halyards slapping against the mast. *Whop. Whop.* He shook himself awake. A shadowy, bearded figure with a heavy neck and broad shoulders was talking to him. It was Metcalf.

"I'm guessin' the better part of last night's mischief be over now, Cap'n," the bosun said to him.

Townsend jumped up, telling Metcalf to wake the others as he staggered toward the companionway.

3

Filled with trepidation, and uncertain at what he would find, Townsend slid open the hatch. As his head emerged from the companionway, his lungs filled with a warm blast of tangy salt air mixed with the earthy ripeness of the mangroves. He looked around at a scene of complete destruction. The once lush Marquesas looked like a place that nature had decided to abandon. Miraculously, the hull was intact, and they hadn't lost the jolly boat overboard as he had feared they might. Piles of twisted rigging were strewn around the deck along with broken branches, sand, and mud.

It was early afternoon when they finished making essential repairs—replacing and tightening the stays for the two masts, and jury rigging a new headsail. Fortunately, the mainsail that had remained furled during the storm and had been tightly secured was undamaged. They used a kedge anchor to pull themselves out of the snarl and tangle of the mangrove forest and then with the winds now switching more southerly, sailed out of the channel away from the Marquesas lagoon. The sky and the ocean were still a ghostly gray. The winds had died down considerably, but the swells were still huge.

Townsend handed the helm to Metcalf while he continued to survey the damage to the boat. Down below, he could see that water was coming in through the centerboard trunk, so he ordered Langworth to take the first turn at manning the hand pumps. Then he told Tollman to use the draw bucket to scoop up seawater and clean away the mud and debris still on the decks.

Townsend gave out these orders even though he was in a trance. The constant battering flashed before him in a jumble of images. He was still not certain how they had survived. He couldn't get the haunting sight of that wreck out of his mind. At first, he didn't want to say anything. He thought no one would believe him, but then he decided to tell the crew what he'd seen. They looked back at him, their eyes large and haggard.

"Was I the only one who saw it?" he asked.

No one spoke. Finally, Metcalf asked each sailor. They all shook their heads. No one else had spotted anything like that, but they all agreed it was their duty to investigate it.

As they approached the northern edge of the Marquesas, the scars from the storm were everywhere. Leafless trees, stumped and bent over, twisted and broken branches. The bosun pointed out several bales of cotton mysteriously floating in the shallows near the channel. An eerie sight, as there was no sign of where they'd come from. Both men knew what the other was thinking. A long line of white-headed pelicans crossed in front of them, flying through the pewter sky like a wobbling kite's tail.

De la Cruz from up in the crosstrees, shouted, "*Los mástiles de una goleta. Allá.*"

He pointed off to the north and said he could see a ship's spars jutting out of the water not far from where the pelicans were flying.

Carefully and slowly, Townsend climbed the shaky ratlines and with his telescope caught a glimpse of a lead-gray hull with broken topmasts. It was the ship he'd seen—a large schooner, nearly twice the size of the *Rebecca*. It was canted off to one side in a dangerous area of shoals surrounded by outlying clumps of mangroves. The westerly waves had moved it into slightly deeper water, where the incoming breakers kept up a continual assault on the hull.

Once back on deck, Townsend took the helm and steered as close as he dared to get a better look, remaining about a mile away in the deeper water of the channel. He guessed that the ship might have been coming from New Orleans, perhaps headed for New York or Boston. There was no sign of any movement. He scanned the horizon looking for survivors, but there was nothing to see. No sign of life.

"We'll have to file a report," Townsend said to Metcalf. "We need to search that boat, check for survivors."

"Aye, aye, Cap'n."

"Heave to!" Metcalf shouted to the foredeck sailors.

The crew backed the storm jib to windward while keeping the reefed mainsail loosely trimmed on the other side. With these swells, Townsend calculated that the *Rebecca* would stay in place with little to no motion, forward or backward.

Townsend decided to go himself to inspect the ship, and he chose Toll-man to go with him. He'd seen that Langworth and the Black sailor had not worked well together and he wanted no trouble. They lowered the jolly boat and began rowing toward the wreck. The big schooner was in four to five feet of water, solidly aground on grassy sand. The ship's rigging was twisted and shredded like a tangle of forest vines. The cargo was strewn all around, caught in clumps of mangroves along the shoreline. Dozens of cotton bales and rough-hewn sections of lumber were being tossed around in the shallows like bobbing pelicans.

The schooner's lead-gray color made Townsend curious about whether it was a former Confederate blockade runner. One of the two yawl boats was still on board. Not a good omen. He could read the ship's name on the stern. *Hard Times*, out of New Orleans. With the ship's sharp bow, raking transom, and flat bottom, Townsend's skilled eye told him the ship was probably a Gulf Coast schooner built in Biloxi or Appalachicola.

The southerly waves were battering one side of the ship, so they rowed around to the protected side, where they tied a painter to the shrouds. They'd brought along a flask of water and a canvas bag with a coil of rope, a knife, a hammer, and an ax in case they needed to open any doors or cut any ropes. Townsend knew the ship would break apart soon. With each incoming swell, the ship's wooden beams groaned in agony. They climbed aboard and care-fully pulled themselves from one part of the slanted deck to the next, grab-bing onto whatever they could to keep their balance. The planking cracked and creaked with each step they made.

Townsend opened the hatchway that led to the cabin and began to walk down the companionway steps. He could see there was at least three feet of seawater inside. A large skylight overhead provided enough light to make out shapes of objects. Just below the water level, he could make out the black outline of the wood-burning stove and the kitchen table where the crew had sat. A salted fish of some kind hung from a nail behind the stove. There were several berths made of rough-hewn oak planks and gimbaled turpentine lanterns attached to the bulkheads. It was clear the crew had left in a hurry. Tar-stained ditty bags stuffed with sailors' clothes and sewing kits were still hanging on hooks.

Townsend spotted a bookshelf above one of the berths, and he stepped down into the water to reach it. There was a navigation book on Florida and Cuba with a secession insignia on it. He waded as far as he could go, but then swam back to the stern of the ship. In the captain's cabin, where there was a lingering scent of tobacco smoke, he found a collection of pipes and pack-ages of Virginia Belle chewing tobacco perched on a small cabinet. He smiled when he read the label on the matches: "Lucifers. To Be Kept Dry." What surprised him was a package of Cuban cigars, *Flor de Tabacos de Partagás*. He knew the brand. It was some of the finest tobacco grown on the island of Cuba, all from the *Vuelta Abajo* region. There were bottles of opium powder and jimsonweed. Townsend wondered what these men wanted jimsonweed for. It was a poison—at least that's what he'd been told.

Toward the bow, the two men heard thuds. Something was crashing against the bulkhead that divided the cabin from the cargo hold. Tollman, who had followed cautiously behind Townsend, looked over at him with alarm.

"What dah be, Cap'n?"

"I reckon we'll find out, Tollman," Townsend replied tersely.

"Sounds like someone bangin' on de wall," the sailor said. "Could be evil spirits. Haints, we call 'em. Tryin' to escape."

Townsend ignored that remark. He took one last look around. He noticed that the navigation book had a heavily worn Spanish nautical chart of Cuba folded inside and a small sketch book. He opened the notebook and was surprised at some of the detailed pencil drawings of islands and one river that had more twists and unusual bends than he'd ever seen before. It looked like a long rawhide whip whistling through the air. On a whim, he threw all the charts, the navigation book, and the sketch book in his canvas bag. The two men climbed out of the cabin and crawled underneath some of the fallen wreckage to get to the center of the ship. They reached the cargo hold hatch on hands and knees.

"Dis ain' just toggl'd down—it nailed shut," said Tollman.

The two men began to pry open the hatch with the knife and the hammer. They pulled out nail after nail until they could lift the large cover and look down inside. The smell of turpentine and moldy, wet wood assaulted their noses. Townsend could just barely make out the barrels of turpentine and the shadowy stacks of bales of cotton on one end. Some pieces of lumber had come loose in the water and were banging against the other side of the hold.

"Looks like your haints are carved out of wood, Tollman," Townsend said. He reached down into the water and grabbed something. He pulled up a man's floppy hat. The Black sailor recoiled. With fresh urgency, Townsend handed Tollman one end of the rope they'd brought and lowered himself inside the hold. He splashed around inside the dark space, listening to the echoes, trying to get used to the darkness. His feet touched something heavy but soft. He thought it moved, and he wondered if it could be a fish. He jerked away, but then something else pushed up from underneath him, caus-ing him to swim away.

"What in tarnation?"

Townsend felt a shirt and pulled on it. A large object bumped up against him. He reached down and grabbed it, gasping as he realized what it was. He surfaced in an explosion of splashing, yelling to Tollman.

"Wha' happen? What you see, Cap'n?"

"A hand! A man's hand!"

"Oh, Moses! Sweet heavenly Moses!" cried Tollman.

Then something else floated to the surface. Townsend turned to look at what it was and found himself staring at a man's grayish black face. The mouth was wide open, and the sightless, dulled eyes stared up at him.

"There's a dead man. Right here!" Townsend yelled as he splashed about in the water.

"Oh Lawd! Sweet land of love and mercy!" Tollman cried out as he jumped back.

"Throw me a line, damn it to hell!" Townsend shouted. He now knew what was bumping up against him. He shivered. There were bodies of dead men floating all around him. He felt nauseous. All he wanted to do was get out of there. Trembling from head to toe, he grabbed the line that Tollman threw him and took deep breaths to calm himself. It was then that he heard a faint noise from one corner of the cargo hold. Something was moving. His heart felt like it had climbed into his throat.

"Somebody here? Who's that?" Townsend cried out. He heard a groan. Some rustling. Townsend was too shocked to say anything. The noise came from the top of the cotton bales which were above the water level. Then he heard a weak voice stammer.

"Help me. . . . I need help."

"Tarnation to hell! There's someone alive down here, Tollman," Townsend shouted. "A survivor. He's injured."

Townsend grabbed one of the floating pieces of lumber inside the hold and began swimming with it over to where the voice came from. He could now see the shape of a man looking down at him.

"Hold on. I'm coming. We'll get you out of there."

"*Ma tête*. My head," the faltering voice cracked. "Hurt bad."

"We will get you help," Townsend replied, but the man just groaned. "Who are you?" Townsend asked. He noticed the mixture of French and English.

The figure in the shadows didn't respond, and Townsend knew he had to get the man out into the open air quickly. Slowly, he tied the rope around the man's waist and lowered him gingerly onto the board. He took care to keep his head above water as he pushed the rough-hewn log over toward the cargo hold entrance. He could now see the man was a young Black man, dressed in simple homespun clothes. He'd been hit on the head by some blunt object and had lost a lot of blood.

Tollman made good use of his broad shoulders and grabbed the man's collar, giving one tremendous yank and pulling the injured man up through the hole, all the time talking to himself about Moses and Abraham and sweet salvation. Once Townsend got out of the hold and looked down at the man lying face up on the deck, he knew there wasn't much they could do for him. He was struggling for breath.

"We're losing him, Tollman," Townsend said as he nudged the man's shoulders. "Give me the flask."

Townsend tried to get the man to take a drink, opening his lips to let the water trickle into his mouth. He sputtered and then swallowed. Townsend loosened the man's shirt. In the bright sun, his dark skin shone like polished mahogany, revealing the raised welts from previous whippings. The man's eyes seemed to be looking past Townsend into the sky above.

"Help me raise his head, Tollman. We need to give him more water."

Tollman cradled the man's head while Townsend held the flask to his lips.

"Your name . . . What's your name?" Townsend asked, leaning close to hear if the man replied.

"Thaddeus. Thaddeus Burrell," the man breathed out, struggling to speak.

"Where did you come from?"

The man's eyes blinked and then closed. His lips moved, but no sound came out.

"What happened?"

The dying man reached to grab Townsend's shirt.

"Buckra man," he whispered. "Take us from Fannie Place plantation near New Orleans to the ship on de river. Dey lock us up. Ten of us."

"Where?" Townsend asked as he leaned in closer. "Where were you being taken?"

The man didn't reply. His hand fell to the side. Townsend repeated the question.

All he heard was the man say, "Thaddeus free now. A free man. *Libéré.*"

Townsend shook the man, but to no avail.

"Taint no use, Cap'n. He deh in the hands of the Lawd now."

Townsend sat back trying to catch his breath and absorb what had just happened. The man had said there were nine others with him. The hatch had been nailed tightly shut. They had been left to die there. He didn't know how, but he knew the guilty ones were most likely those four men he'd seen escaping from the ship in the storm.

Tollman was the one who broke the silence. "Looks lak Lucifer himself bin heah. Brought in a whole mess of hell and evil with dat storm."

The dead man's face stared up at Townsend. The eyes were no longer moist, but dry and flat like sunbaked mud.

"I don't know, Tollman. I'm not sure about Lucifer, but I think you're right about hell and evil."

Once they returned to the deck of the USS *Rebecca*, Townsend and the other members of the crew watched the water sweep over the wreck, the waves and current slowly dragging the wooden hull through the sandy shallows into deeper water. Townsend stood there, silent and awestruck, listening to the ship's timbers groan like a dying sea creature in agony. He felt guilty that they were unable to recover the bodies, but it was too dangerous. He and Tollman had been forced to leave quickly. He thought about the war and the cause he had fought for—the freedom of the enslaved. Was it coming undone already?

He heard the harsh squawk of a great heron and spotted the tall, white bird partially hidden inside a large clump of mangroves next to a few snowy white egrets. Then there was a frenzy of splashing from a school of fish. Dozens of dark cormorants swooped by the schooner and began diving into the water for their morning meal. The silhouette of an osprey looked down at this drama from a leafless tree like an expectant vulture. He thought to himself with sadness that this spot next to the mangroves was the only marker these men would have.

4

October 24, 1865

The smudgy gray of early morning found the USS *Rebecca* to the north of the northwest channel buoy about twelve miles from Key West. The battered schooner was still leaking, and the crew were taking turns at the hand pumps. Townsend looked around at the deck at the unsmiling, gaunt faces covered in salt spray. There were no broken bones, but all of the men had sustained cuts and bruises. He could tell they were spent, their haunted eyes sunken. They had worked as only men did when they needed to save their lives. He knew they were lucky to be alive. They had all looked death in the eye, and death had looked back at them—sparing them this time. They knew the boatman would come for them soon enough. This had been a dress rehearsal.

Due to the big swells and the danger of running aground, Townsend had decided to stay well offshore the previous night. It had been the right decision. Overnight the winds died down, signaling the end of the stormy weather, and now a moderate breeze from the south rippled across the surface of the water. A cold shiver ran through him as he once again saw the dead men in that cargo hold, their unseeing ghostly eyes staring up at him with a look of fearful resignation. These people had been locked up and left to drown. He needed to inform the military authorities about what he'd seen. To him, it looked like a cold-blooded killing.

The sun soon began peeking out of the clouds on the horizon, giving a reddish-orange tinge to the sky. Townsend's spirits lifted. He raised his head to the rising sun and felt its warm touch on his forehead. The rosy fingered dawn, he murmured to himself with a smile. He loved the sound of those words. He'd been required to read Homer's *Odyssey* and *Iliad* in his English and Ethics class when he was at the Naval Academy, and for some reason those words now came back to him.

Townsend thought of Emma and allowed himself to imagine that they were together again. Like Odysseus had returned to Penelope. The two thousand dollars of prize money he had won during the war by capturing Confederate blockade runners would be enough to buy them a small house in Key West. He pictured himself slipping a ring on her finger and feeling the warm glow of her smile, the softness of her touch.

"*Cayo Hueso*. I can see it!" de la Cruz shouted from high atop the schooner's main mast, interrupting Townsend's reverie. The Navy lieutenant whispered the name to himself, the Spanish name for Key West. *Cayo Hueso* meant Bone Key. Some said the Spanish had found piles of bones there, but others thought the name came from the bleached limestone and pieces of dead coral along the shoreline, which may have looked like bones to the Spanish.

The tropical sun now exploded into view with a blast of bright light. Townsend could make out the silhouetted rooftop observatories of the Tift, Filor, and O'Hara buildings along Key West's waterfront, the church steeples behind them and the brown walls of Fort Taylor off to the right. Metcalf climbed the shrouds with the telescope.

"Looks like the harbor didn't fare so well, Cap'n. Most of the ships are underwater or run up on land. The wharves all smashed to pieces."

There was a deathly silence on board the schooner as the storm-battered ship sailed into port. The harbor normally congested with Navy gunboats, big merchant ships, and fishing sloops was now a graveyard of listing and overturned hulls. Some of the piers and dockside shacks were nothing but splintered planks, twisted and contorted by the storm's winds and punishing waves.

Just four days earlier, Townsend had watched flotillas of Bahamian sloops with their baggy white mainsails coming in from a morning on the reef, selling their live pompano and mackerel to the large Havana-bound schooners. The sun-filled harbor with its peculiar blend of copper green and turquoise water had been full of boats. A Navy troop transport paddle steamer had crossed in front of the *Rebecca* on its way out of the harbor. Hundreds of soldiers were waving their hats and singing. They were going home. *Lucky devils*, he remembered thinking. But now he wondered if that hurricane had caught up with that Navy steamer somewhere out in the open ocean. Maybe they weren't the lucky ones?

Townsend pondered the dark hand of fate as he looked at the destruction all around him. Many of the boats used for salvaging wrecks off the Florida reefs had been pushed ashore. The cruel irony of that sight didn't escape him. As a Navy officer, he knew that fortunes had been made in Key West from others' losses. Now this town of profiteering from shipwrecks had become a victim of the sea as well.

Metcalf pointed over toward Curry's wharf where there was plenty of deep water, and Townsend told him to drop anchor just north of there in the Key West Bight. He rowed ashore in the jolly boat, eager to get to Naval head-quarters. If those four men he'd seen had survived, he was almost certain they would surface in Key West. There was no other logical place for them to go in a small open boat. He tried to imagine the terror that those ten men had experienced, locked in a dark cargo hold, listening to the thundering waves and the howling wind as seawater poured into what would become their cof-fin. He wanted justice for those freedmen, and he wanted the men who had locked them in there to be held accountable for their cruelty.

Once ashore, Townsend walked toward the Naval Landing, sloshing his way through floating debris and renegade pieces of lumber. The town seemed eerily empty, with hardly a person to be seen. He cut through some alleys because Front Street was flooded. A large painted sign for the Key West Fish Company creaked and groaned as it dangled precariously from the side of a boatshed. The winds had torn off window shutters and roofs. A rooster crowed from the safety of his perch on a rooftop. A donkey brayed from behind a house. He headed south toward Caroline Street which was higher ground. He could hear an ax chopping, hammers banging, and men shouting. He was surprised to see some men clearing the debris from downed coconut and gumbo limbo trees so they could repair a porch.

"Hey, you there! Come on over here and lend a hand, will you."

The man shouting at him was a thin man with a badger-like face and a shiny bald head. Townsend thought he recognized him as one of the return-ing wharf rats from the war, an ex-Confederate who still walked around in a soiled gray coat. He'd met embittered Confederate veterans like this before.

The man placed himself in Townsend's path and was soon joined by an-other man, more finely dressed in a linen coat. He had a bull mastiff mongrel on a leash, a big dog with a square head like a lion and powerful neck and chest muscles. Dogs like this were used in Cuba to catch runaway slaves.

brindle-colored, probably a mix between bloodhound and bull mastiff. They were bred in Cuba to follow a scent for miles and then attack. He was surprised to see such a dog like that in Key West, but he soon put that thought out of his mind.

"I *said* I needed a hand," the bald man snorted, his wild eyes gleaming with resentment. He came closer and Townsend could see that he had tobacco stains in his teeth and a cloven lip under his moustache.

"We ain' got no slaves no more in Key West so it's jus' us white folks now. Ain't that right Don Pancho? We need to clear away these trees to fix our porch."

The man with the dog approached Townsend. His face was pointed with a sharp nose, his body thin as a coiled whip. His curly black hair and black eyes made him look Spanish. He was also chewing tobacco, and Townsend could see he was making no effort to hide a Bowie knife attached to his belt.

"Now that the war is over, we Southern veterans need some federal assistance, officer," the man said in a cynical voice. "Just like you bluebellies give the slaves."

"Or maybe you think we're jus' two worthless crackers?" the bald man chimed in.

"Sorry, I can't help you," Townsend replied, trying not to recoil at the unwashed, vinegar-like smell of these two men. "I've got pressing duties to attend to. I need to get to Naval headquarters."

"Oh, too important to help out, are you?" the bald man said as he spat a wad of black liquid down to one side of Townsend's feet. He looked like he was going to grab Townsend, but his companion with the dog restrained him. A low growl came from the animal that now seemed much more threatening than it had before. "*Quieto, Macho, Quieto.*"

Townsend didn't let on that he knew Spanish. The dog's name meant tough guy. Not wanting further confrontation with a couple of drunken Confederate hotheads, he quickly brushed past the men who were muttering about Yankee law not applying to Florida.

The Navy lieutenant quickened his pace, kept his eyes down at the chalky, white-shelled road. He was not going to get into an argument about the war and slavery because of his uniform. Key West may have been in the hands of the North during the war, but with the war over, it was increasingly clear that the town was only half Yankee at best.

Key West was in fact a town of many different worlds, separate worlds, a place where people had worn masks during the war. He'd spent time with Emma's sister and her husband, Emilio, who had lived in Key West for many years. They had told him how many of the locals, who called themselves

Conchs, kept their views to themselves as they read about victories of the North in the pro-Union island newspaper. Emilio said many of his fellow Cubans were the same, hiding where their true sympathies lay.

When he reached the corner of Whitehead and Front Street, Townsend could see there were lines of people outside the Navy Office building. There was a crowd clamoring to talk with the Naval commander, wanting information about the arrival of ships. One of the companies of the Second US Colored Regiment, who were encamped in the Lighthouse barracks near Fort Taylor, had marched into position. Townsend caught the sidelong glances and sneering faces of a small group of locals toward the Negro soldiers.

"Go home!"

"We don't want ya here. The war's over."

"Yer nothing but an occupying army."

Townsend ignored the noisy fracas as he muscled his way through the crowd of hecklers. A group of lanky, horse-faced temperance church women were handing out pamphlets outside the Naval building. One of them, with a toothless smile, dressed in a high collar, tried to give him one. "Repent young man. Behold the manifestation of God's wrath on this city of sin!"

Townsend pushed his way past her and hurried up the stairs to the commander's office on the second floor. He told the chief yeoman in the waiting room that he was here to give a full report on the USS *Rebecca*'s return voyage from the Tortugas. The officer ushered him into the commander's office just as two other Navy captains left. Neither had a pleasant look about him.

Commander George Ransom, in his long blue Navy coat, had his back to Townsend and the chief yeoman. He paced back and forth, rubbing and pulling his formidable foot-long black beard as he walked. He stopped beside a telescope that looked out at the harbor while he spoke to several formally dressed men. Townsend thought he recognized some of the town's leading businessmen, a few of whom had been ardent Confederate sympathizers, but were now following the smell of federal money in the air. From some snatches of the conversation, Townsend could tell they were demanding that the Navy get more supply ships. The wharves in Key West needed to be repaired immediately so that steamships could dock.

The Naval commander looked like he was losing his patience, but he promised these men he was doing all he could, given how many shipwrecks there were up and down the Florida coast. Ransom was an experienced Naval officer, a war hero who had fought with Farragut in the Mississippi campaign and had captured three Confederate steamers trying to run into Wilmington with arms. He was a career Navy man, who knew he did not want to make enemies out of these powerful and rich local men.

Townsend nervously shifted his weight back and forth as he waited with barely restrained tension. Ransom still hadn't noticed him. Townsend respected his commander, but he knew the feeling wasn't mutual. His commanding officer saw him as a troublemaking young officer who didn't follow orders; the commander was also aware that Townsend had an unusual past association with the Confederacy as a blockade runner from Havana.

Ransom had told Townsend he wanted to discharge him, but his superiors wouldn't hear of it. With the Navy downsizing so rapidly, the top Naval officials in Pensacola and New Orleans had argued that Townsend's skills and knowledge of the murky rivers on the Gulf Coast would make him hard to replace. There was also a policy to use sailing ships when possible to save coal.

The disgruntled merchants were just leaving when a young Navy officer burst into the room, saluting sharply. "Beg yer pardon sir. Don' mean to interrupt, but two merchant ships jus' come into port with news of several shipwrecks up the west coast of Florida. Some wreckers jus' arrived. They say there is a steamer under water near Sombrero Cay, and more wrecks off the Florida reef."

Ransom still hadn't noticed Townsend standing there. His brow furrowed, the Navy commander began dictating to the petty officer, who was taking down notes. "Write Admiral Thatcher that we have no ships. We need help from Pensacola. There could be many lives lost. Dismissed."

The young Naval officer hurried away. The chief yeoman took that moment to announce Townsend.

"Uh hum. Excuse me, sir. Acting Volunteer Lieutenant Everett Townsend of the USS *Rebecca* is here with news about Fort Jefferson."

Commander Ransom immediately wheeled around.

"Ah, Lieutenant. I hope you bring good news. How did Fort Jefferson fare? What were the damages?"

"Don't know, sir. We set sail before the hurricane hit. I fear it was bad. We barely made it back."

Ransom grimaced, then glared at Townsend.

"Can the USS *Rebecca* make sail?" he barked.

"No, sir, the ship is leaking badly. Two of our sails are shredded. It's a mess down below. All our provisions are soaked through. The ship needs major repairs. I fear that parts of the hull planking may have cracked. We were lucky to survive the storm."

Ransom cursed and proceeded to pace around the room, shaking his long beard as if that would help him get rid of these problems. Townsend could see the strain in the man's face. He knew how frustrated he must be. He was a local commander with almost no ships ready to go to sea.

"Sir, I have a shipwreck to report. Just off the Marquesas. We discovered ten bodies inside the ship. They were all freedmen. They'd been locked up. Trapped in the hold. I suspect foul play."

Distracted and troubled, Ransom didn't reply.

"It was a former blockade runner, sir. Lead colored. Name of *Hard Times* out of New Orleans. Four men escaped. And from the looks of what they left behind down below in the cabin I'd say they were ex-Confederates. I thought it was important to notify you immediately, as those men most likely will come here if they survived the storm."

With his formidable beard, deep-set eyes, and thick eyebrows, the Naval commander turned to stare directly at Townsend with a sudden intensity.

"Don't misunderstand me, Townsend. I recognize what you saw must have been disturbing. But right now, I'm more concerned about finding and rescuing survivors than I am about some freedmen who died in the storm."

"Yes, sir, I understand how serious the situation is, but I thought this was something important—"

"Dadblame it, Townsend!" he banged his fist on the table, causing everyone in the room to turn in their direction.

"Not a single wharf or ship in this harbor made it through unscathed in one way or another. As you've heard I've got shipwrecks up and down the Florida coast and more damaged ships coming into this harbor as we speak. Our priorities are clear."

"Beg your pardon, sir, but in my humble opinion this was murder of the cruelest kind. I felt compelled as a matter of urgency . . ."

Ransom's face turned red, and Townsend thought he would explode, but instead the commander controlled himself.

"There is no proof of murder, Townsend. But go ahead and make a report with the Army's Provost Marshal. In the meantime, I want you to get your ship up on the rails, make the necessary repairs, and then report to the chief yeoman for further orders."

"Aye, aye, sir."

"You're dismissed."

As he left, Townsend could hear Ransom cursing at one of the petty officers.

"I've got no damn ships—and no officers worth a damn!"

5

As he walked by the gun casements in Fort Taylor, Townsend listened to the heavy stomp and thud of boots and the gruff voice of the drill sergeant in the parade ground. A slow breeze brought some relief from the hot sun. There were four companies with the Second Infantry regiment still garrisoned in Fort Taylor, and six others in barracks and tents, all waiting to be sent home to Virginia, Massachusetts, and New York. Throughout the summer, the War Department had been disbanding regiments, but many of the Colored regiments in Florida still remained in uniform. Townsend watched as a company of Black soldiers marched in place following the drill sergeant's commands and felt a common cause with these men.

An astonished regimental commander looked up from his desk when Townsend was ushered into his office. Townsend was also surprised. He'd expected someone less senior. Unlike Commander Ransom, the colonel had a high regard for him.

"Lieutenant Townsend, what a surprise," said the colonel as he wiped his brow with a handkerchief. "Hot as the hinges of hell in this place, I'd say."

"Yes, sir."

"Like a bloody furnace. But then the views are nice, aren't they?" he added with a sardonic grin.

Townsend chuckled. The older man seemed pleased to have this interruption. Townsend had come to know Colonel Benjamin Townsend when they were both stationed at the military staging area of Depot Key at Cedar Keys during the summer of 1864. Townsend had ferried Black infantrymen from the colonel's regiment along with a group of Florida backwoodsmen and rebel deserters with the Second Florida Cavalry into the dangerous Confederate-held interior.

Like many of the senior white officers commanding Black regiments, the colonel was a staunch abolitionist. He was tall and thin, battered but not broken by the war despite the horrors he'd witnessed at Bull Run and at Antietam. Townsend wasn't sure why, but the colonel had taken a liking to him—maybe because they shared the same last name or a similar wry sense of humor. He had joked that they might be distant lost cousins.

"I'm glad to see the Navy hasn't discharged you yet."

Townsend smiled back at his superior even as he shuffled his feet.

"No discharge as yet, Colonel."

"With funding for coal so diminished now, I imagine your superiors are under orders to use sailboat captains as much as possible. Besides, with all your wartime success, you're too valuable to let go, I should imagine."

Townsend nodded appreciatively. As a result of several successful raids near Clay's Landing and further up the Suwannee River, the colonel had written a hearty endorsement to the Navy recommending Townsend's promotion from acting master to acting volunteer lieutenant. Townsend's habit of making quick decisions had served him well in that no man's riverine wilderness.

"What brings a swamp sailor like you to Fort Taylor? Missing Useppa Island? Maybe you've come to request a commission to the US Army?" The officer openly chuckled. He knew Townsend was a volunteer like he was and was anxious to be discharged.

The Navy lieutenant shook his head politely. "No, sir, I believe I am still a seaman at heart."

The colonel cocked a bushy eyebrow with an inquiring slant and stroked his large drooping moustache and bearded chin.

"Something to do with that hell-fired hurricane that knocked us from here to kingdom come then? What's it like in town?"

"Quite a lot of damage, Colonel."

"Doesn't surprise me. Overturned our barracks. Some of the old-timers here tell me it's the worst hurricane to visit these latitudes since the great gale of '46. That's when the old lighthouse at Whitehead Point was washed away."

Careful to preface his remarks by saying Commander Ransom had suggested he come to speak with a senior US Army officer, Townsend immediately related the events of the shipwreck and what he'd seen out on the Marquesas. He then gave his opinion that these men, whom he'd seen escaping from the wreck, were probably ex-Confederates and would undoubtedly make their way to Key West. He was fully expecting a reaction like the one he'd received from Commander Ransom. Instead, the Army commander showed considerable interest, his face taking on a more somber expression as he wrote notes.

"They were locked up? That's what the dying man told you?"

"Yes, sir. That ship's cargo hold hatch was nailed shut tighter than a hangman's knot. It was like a jail cell. He said he and the nine others were picked up at some plantation called Fannie Place. The man I spoke with had a French accent. Spoke that patois like they do in parts of Louisiana."

"What was the name of the ship?"

"*Hard Times* out of New Orleans."

"And he gave no indication where they were being taken to?"

"No, sir."

The colonel continued writing notes, finally putting his fountain pen down and looking up at Townsend.

"You should know, Lieutenant, the Army has heard of similar reports of freedmen disappearing in the Gulf area. The latest was from Clark County in Alabama where unfortunately we have no federal troops, so we haven't been able to confirm anything. We've also had reports from Marianna to Tampa Bay of ex-Confederates roving across the land, stealing livestock and provisions, and taking the law into their own hands. Seems as if some Southerners are reluctant to accept the war's verdict. They carry a grudge like dogs carry a bone. Half the population in the state of Florida is Black. These white people want revenge, and they're taking it out on the Negro. As bad as it is now, it no doubt will be worse if the Army withdraws."

"If I may ask, Colonel, where does the Army think these freedmen are being taken?"

"We don't know. Most likely some swampy wilderness where there's timber to be cut. The fighting may be over, but there's still a powder keg of unfinished business in Florida. For a Black man, it's a dangerous place."

"What about the ones who left those men in the hold to drown like they were cattle? Can the Army Provost Marshall assist . . . ?"

Colonel Townsend grimaced, his brow furrowing.

"Rest assured, Townsend, we'll find these criminals if they surface here in Key West. My guess is they've departed this godforsaken world. The chances of them surviving that hurricane in an open boat are slim. But I certainly intend to find out more about this ship, *Hard Times*. I'll be in touch with the Bureau of Military Information in New Orleans. Given all the reports of groups of freedmen disappearing in the Gulf, they may send an investigator down here. In that case, they will want to interview you."

The colonel paused, his stare lingering on Townsend's face.

"Before you head back to the docks, I might suggest you talk to Old Sandy Cornish. You must know him, that old Negro gentleman with the farm not far from here. He knows just about everything that's going on in Blacktown here in Key West. He's a lay preacher who has just finished building his own church, Cornish Chapel. With all these freedmen coming down here to seek the Army's protection and search for jobs or federal aid, I would bet my last dollar that word of any foul dealings would come with them."

"Yes, sir."

"Anything else to report?"

"No, sir."

"Then I wish you a good day. It was nice to see you again, Lieutenant. I'm sure with all the shipwrecks, you have plenty to do as well."

The sun beat down unmercifully as Townsend walked along the one-thousand-foot-long wooden causeway that connected the brick fort to the island. The sun glitter on the water was so intense he couldn't see. He breathed in deeply and smelled the air thick with salt, squinting out toward the shoreline with the gliding pelicans and waving palms. A light breeze rippled across the water, filling the sails of some incoming sailboats and setting his mind in motion.

The thought of going to Old Sandy's orchard farm made him think of Emma. A visit to Old Sandy's was a diversion for many Navy officers when they had liberty. They could get a plate of fresh tropical fruit for just fifty cents. On several occasions, he had brought Emma with him to the farm to see the goats and sheep and taste some of the sweet oranges, mangoes, and sapodillas there.

They had given Old Sandy the black cat called Look-Out they'd brought from Cuba. She'd turned out to be an excellent rat hunter and had produced a litter of kittens, all double pawed with six toes. Emma was a favorite of Sandy's wife, Lillah, whom everyone called Auntie. Townsend knew she would be disappointed not to see Emma. He gulped as he thought about what he would have to tell Auntie if she asked about her.

On the rough country road where the soldiers marched regularly, Townsend found himself slipping and sliding though thick layers of mud.

Old Sandy's farm was on the eastern outskirts of the town. Before he even reached the farm, Townsend could hear one of Old Sandy's donkeys braying a welcome, followed by a discordant symphony of goats bleating. Townsend looked at the devastation from the hurricane all around the twenty-acre farm. The fruit orchards that Sandy was so proud of were now a labyrinth of broken branches and leafless trees.

From behind a small clapboard house, the large gray head of a Black man emerged. It was Sandy Cornish, unmistakable with his barrel chest and muscular shoulders. He was propping up a piece of wood next to one of the columns of his beloved porch, which the hurricane had partially knocked down. Townsend smiled and waved. Old Sandy smiled back.

As Townsend stretched out his hand, he took quiet measure of the old man. With his shirt unbuttoned, he looked like a prize fighter even though he was seventy-five years old. His thick gray hair rose up like a lion's mane, but the large inquiring eyes and the broad smile framed by a thick well-trimmed beard gave him an air of distinction. Townsend had always felt a tie to the older man. He was like a grandfather he never had. They were both from Maryland, and Townsend had told Old Sandy about his parents' involvement in helping runaway slaves escape up the Susquehanna River.

"Bring sum tea, no, Auntie," the man cried out to his wife. "I told Auntie we won't be havin' any fancy balls heah for sum time. Taint no use 'till I can repair dis stately piazza for our Southun mansion." His laugh was deep and rich.

Townsend's eyes were drawn to the man's scarred fingerless hand, but he quickly averted his glance. Sandy Cornish's dramatic story of being kidnapped was well-known in Key West. Before the war, he had been a free man working on the railroad in northern Florida when six white men assaulted and seized him. They were taking him to New Orleans to sell him on the auction block. He escaped and, to avoid being re-enslaved, he plunged a knife into his hip joint, severing his ankle as well. He then took an ax and chopped off the fingers of his left hand. With pools of blood all around him, he had invited the gaping onlookers to put him to work as a slave.

Old Sandy's wife appeared with two glasses of tea. He stood up and greeted her. She was younger than he was, probably in her fifties, and much shorter. But what she lacked in stature, she compensated with true grit and toughness. It was generally known that she had helped Sandy buy his freedom. People say after he took a knife to himself, he would have died from all his injuries if not for Lillah. She nursed him back to health over many months.

"And how is Emma?" Lillah asked. "Such a fine young woman with a big heart. So kind and so pretty. You a lucky man, ya know. When you gwine to get married?"

Townsend nodded but didn't say anything. The older woman paused and looked at Townsend closely as if she could see the guilt on his face.

"Where is she now?"

"I'm not entirely sure. I think she's in Havana with her mother."

"Was it yellow fevah dat chase her away?" Lillah asked.

Townsend shook his head even as he averted his eyes from her steady stare. He wanted to say yes. There had been dozens of deaths over the past two years in Key West from yellow fever, including the Colored regiment's previous commanding officer. During the worst months in the heat of summer, ships had been unwilling to drop supplies or pick up mail from the island, scared off by the large yellow flag flying from the Squadron's signal mast. Navy ships had been ordered to anchor well offshore, keeping watch over the island like grim and silent prison guards.

Emma not only had not left the island during that fateful summer, but she had volunteered as a nurse at the Marine Hospital. Townsend had only been there once. All he remembered was the smell of urine and medicine and the constant moaning of men in pain down the corridors. He'd asked her to stop working there because it was too dangerous. She had replied she couldn't stop with all these people suffering. They'd argued.

"No, it wasn't the fever," Townsend gulped. "Mercifully she survived the outbreak. She just wanted to go home to Havana to help her mother with the inn."

Lillah Cornish raised her eyebrow.

"How long since you las' seen her?"

"I suppose several months."

Lillah shot him a fiery look and then dropped the tray with the glasses of tea.

"Oh, Lawd, what stupidness! I dun' spilled the tea and broke de glasses," she cried out as she glared at Townsend. "I'll go see if we have more. I'm 'fraid dat gon' be de last of it."

When she reached the house, she let the door slam behind her. Eager for a distraction, Townsend stooped to pick up the pieces of broken glass as he told Old Sandy about the latest reports from the US Army.

"That's why I came here. With all the refugees who have arrived recently, I wondered if you had heard any stories concerning freedmen disappearing on board ships?"

"Disappearin'? Doesn't surprise me. Nothin' but trouble and hardship up in cotton country now. All dem rebels taking away de Black man's rights with guns and whips as quickly as de federal soldiers explainin' what dose rights be. So if freedmen disappearin' on boats it deh for a reason. Dey tryin' to escape from de plantations. Dey lookin' for safety. Dey want to be near whar de federal soldiers be, for protection. Das why dey come heah."

"Yes, I understand." Townsend said, "but what the Army is describing sounds more like foul play of some kind."

Sandy Cornish raised his eyebrows.

Townsend then told him about the sunken ship he'd encountered, and the dead freedmen in the cargo hold. "The dying man I spoke with was from a plantation, probably near New Orleans. He made it sound like they'd all been kidnapped. Have you heard any stories like that?"

"Kidnapped?" The old man grimaced as he raised his head. "Kidnappin', you say. No, I ain' heard dat. Lawd a'mussy. I hope das not true."

Sandy Cornish shook his gray head back and forth as if he were trying to rid himself of a sadness. "I can't belive ahm hearin' dis. We jus' passed through de inferno of slavery, and dese people still see de Black man as der property to do wid as dey please. If dey kidnappin' freedmen, I hate to think for what reason. Das whut happen to me, you know, all dem years ago. I was free, a free man, but sum men tried to sell me off as a slave." The old man slumped down in his chair and continued to shake his head.

Out of respect, Townsend didn't say anything at first, but then when Old Sandy looked up, he continued.

"I think these men on the shipwreck were being taken somewhere against their will and that's why they were all locked in that cargo hold. The worst part is that they were left to die."

"Hard to believe dis old monster comin' back already," Old Sandy said as he looked at Townsend with eyes that no longer glistened but glowered with defiance. He yelled out to a young Black child who was helping him clean up the debris.

"Juni, cum heah."

The boy named Juni ran over.

"Yes suh, Mistah Cornish."

"Juni, dat man Jacobs still stayin' in de milk shed?"

The boy shook his head and said that Mister Jacobs had left to go to town and would be staying in the chapel. Old Sandy nodded and turned to Townsend.

"You should talk wid dis man. Levi Jacobs. He's a new arrival. A Navy man jus' like you. Been discharged. Tol' me his two sons were taken from a

New Orleans plantation shortly after de war ended. Jus' like you described. Left on a ship and dey never came back."

"Why is he here in Key West?"

"Lookin' for any trace of his two sons. Like so many freedmen now, he's lookin' for family. I believe he wuz given de name of a ship captain who comes heah fairly regular," Old Sandy replied. "He thinks dat captain might know whar dey are."

Townsend leaned toward Sandy.

"Where can I find Levi Jacobs?"

"He comin' to de Cornish Chapel for de service dis Sunday," Old Sandy said, his wide face beaming with pride. "We jus' finished building dis new chapel, you know. De first proper church for us Colored here in Key West. Sacred ground. I gwine to be preachin' dis week, and Jacobs speakin' as well. You should cum. Perhaps he could tell you more."

"I might be intruding, no?"

"Not at all. You deh welcome. It's my chapel and ahm invitin' you. I gwine to tell Jacobs about you if ah see him. Maybe you gwine to help each other?"

Just then, three men arrived carrying musical instruments. There were two violinists and a banjo player.

"I'll be on my way. Thank you for the invitation on Sunday."

"God speed, young man. De Lord will provide."

As the Navy lieutenant left, he could hear the faint twang of a banjo and the quiver of a fiddle, and the refrain from an old Union song about the fall of Charleston. Above all the instruments he could hear Old Sandy's commanding voice as clear as a bell.

> "Oh have you heard the glorious news? Is the cry from every mouth,
> Charleston is taken, and the rebels put to rout
> With a whack row-di-dow, Babylon has fallen
> Whack row-di-dow, the end is drawing near."

6

October 27, 1865

A prolonged roar quickly followed by several cannon blasts from Fort Taylor startled Townsend, making him jump. The cannons were signaling that a large Navy ship was coming into port. He quickly climbed up Tift's observation tower and took out his telescope. He could see the ship, powering its way through the southwest channel, belching out clouds of black smoke down by Whitehead Point. The ship was a screw-propelled brigantine steamship, probably part of the former blockading fleet up north.

Townsend was under orders to write up a report on the number of shipwrecks and survivors, so he had spent the previous two days at the docks. Reports of casualties from the storm continued to increase. He had heard from a captain of the Army tug just back from the Tortugas that the post quartermaster at Fort Jefferson had been killed in the hurricane. A building had collapsed on him. Townsend realized he didn't even know the man's name.

Survivors were still arriving along with mountains of recovered cargo piled up on the decks of incoming salvage ships. The shoreline was lined with horse-drawn wagons backed down into the shallows, ready to be loaded up with the spoils. The talk on the docks was that the rescued cargo from this hurricane might be worth nearly two million dollars, and that most of the profits from the auction sales would end up in the hands of the local merchant William Curry, or "Rich Bill" as he was called by some in town.

To get to the Naval landing more quickly, Townsend took a shortcut through some alleys filled with one story raw-board shanties wedged together. A dog growled and barked, and he whirled around as he remembered that ex-Confederate with the bull mastiff. But there was nothing to be seen. The only ones watching him as he climbed over a fence into someone's backyard was a crowing rooster and a hog grunting with pleasure at some scraps the animal had discovered.

The ship was just coming into the landing at the Naval dock when Townsend began pushing his way through a dense cluster of workmen, sailors, and peddlers with donkey carts. It was a blur of rum-soaked faces and rheumy eyes so common in Key West. The ship was the USS *New Berne* from New York, now on its way to the Naval yard in Pensacola.

As soon as it was docked, Townsend climbed the steep gangway toward the ship's deck. Some sharp-elbowed reporters from the New York and New Orleans newspapers, their notepads already in hand, plowed ahead of him, eager to get interviews with the survivors. "Step aside for the news," they yelled. "Make way for the press." Townsend heard someone next to him shout back, "Feeding off other people's miseries! You're no better than the salvage wreckers! Bunch of leeches."

When he reached the deck, one of the reporters was interviewing a sobbing woman with two small children. She'd been on a ship from New Orleans headed for Liverpool and had lost all her possessions. He turned and spotted the *New York Herald* reporter whom he knew because his offices over Hick's store were adjacent to the Naval yard. He was talking with a small group of men clustered together who were strangely quiet. Their legs were swollen. The skin on their faces was blistered red. Someone had given them clothes that didn't fit. They were a sorry sight.

Townsend moved closer to hear what they had to say. The men were found floating on a raft and had been there for four days, much of that time without water. Everyone else had died on board their ship, which was named the *Mersey*, bound for Cork with a full load of mahogany from Mexico. Two other reporters suddenly arrived.

"Is it true that you survived by sucking the blood of one of the other sailors?" one asked.

"How did that make you feel?" inquired another reporter. "Tell us what it was like."

Townsend shook his head. *Leeches indeed*, he thought.

At that moment, he spotted the captain with his long blue coat, a large middle-aged man with bushy winged-tip sideburns. He walked over and quickly introduced himself. The ship captain, whose name was Acting Master Robert Holley, gave him a full report. He'd stopped to rescue survivors from four ships, but they'd seen several others just east of Sombrero Light halfway up the Keys surrounded by wreckers.

"Didn't hear anyone aboard mention a ship called the *Hard Times*, did you, Captain?" Townsend asked.

"No, can't say as I have. Why do you ask?"

"She's out of New Orleans. Sank about thirty-five miles from here out by the Marquesas. I thought you might have heard something."

The man smirked. "*Hard Times* you say? And she sank in the hurricane? Well then I guess she was aptly named."

Before Townsend could ask him another question, he heard a man shouting. "*Stop, thief! Stop them!*"

A group of men were shoving people to one side, triggering a litany of curses. A man fell back onto Townsend, who grabbed hold of the ship's rail to stay upright. Four men hurtled by. Hardened, blistered faces burned by the sun. Scraggly beards and ragged clothes. They had the look of flea-bitten dogs with dirty, frizzled hair. The one in front was a tall, thin man with sandy hair. Townsend noticed his pale blue eyes when he turned to look behind him before hurtling down the gangway.

The captain immediately called for the Marines on board to pursue them. Townsend rushed over to the side of the boat to look at where these men had gone, but they'd lost themselves in the crowd of people on the landing.

An older man with a finely brushed silk hat and an eye-catching mustard-colored waistcoat emerged from inside the cabin house waving his fist and shouting to stop the thieves.

"May I ask what happened, Mr. Browning?" the captain asked with concern.

Townsend was surprised by his deferential tone.

"Desperados they were. My wife and I returned to our stateroom to find them rifling through our possessions. One of them pulled a Bowie knife right out of his boot and held it to my throat. Called me a scalawag and said the War of Northern Aggression was not over. Took all our gold coins. They grabbed my wife's string of pearls right off her neck."

"I assure you, Mr. Browning, the Marines will catch these villains and your jewelry will be returned."

"I should hope so. Secretary Wells will not be pleased that this has happened to us, not at all."

Townsend raised his eyebrows. The man's mention of the Secretary of the Navy accounted for his status on board ship. From the snatches of conversation, he gathered Mr. and Mrs. Effingham Browning were on their way to New Orleans to look for some new financial opportunities in the Old

South. The reporters had heard the exchange too and quickly surrounded the couple, allowing Townsend to pull the captain aside.

"Who were those men, Cap'n?"

Captain Holley breathed in deeply and then fondled the winged tips of his sideburns.

"I believe we picked them up from an open rowboat early this morning. I never got any details. But the first mate would know. He interviewed them."

The captain called the first officer over and asked for the names of those men.

"They were a dodgy bunch, Captain. Unreconstructed rebels, if you ask me. They kept changing their names and their story. I didn't have time to properly interview them. Nearest I could tell their ship went down around the Marquesas. They were the only survivors. They lost everything. They abandoned ship in the yawl boat and run up on a beach on one of the Mule Keys. Kept alive with some brackish water they found there."

From the officer's visible discomfort in his face, Townsend knew he must be worried that he would be given the blame for this incident.

"They were trying to row island to island to Key West. Only the current proved too strong for them. They were lucky we spotted them. They were drifting out into the Florida Stream. They were in such bad shape I didn't fully interview them. I just gave them food and water. They were desperate. I had no idea . . ."

"What was the name of their ship? Did they say?" Townsend asked excitedly.

"*Hard* something. Maybe *Hard Work . . . Hard Luck?*"

"*Hard Times?*" Townsend asked.

"Yeah, that's it. Out of New Orleans. They said they had a load of cotton and lumber. Don't know what port they were headed to?"

After some bickering with the chief yeoman, who criticized Townsend for his ill-mannered persistence, the Navy lieutenant was ushered in to see Commander Ransom. The commander was clearly involved in a serious conversation with a tall, brown-haired man dressed in a tailored suit. Townsend had been expecting a cool reception from his superior officer, but to his surprise the commander seemed eager to see him.

"Townsend, I was just about to send for you. Come in. Come in. This is Major J.K. Hutchinson, Bureau of Military Information. He has only just arrived from New Orleans. He's been telling me about his intelligence work during the war. He went on scouting missions in rebel-held territory up the Mississippi. Quite a brave man. He's from the good state of Ohio. Works under Brigadier General Sherman and collaborates with Colonel Thomas Osborne of the Freedmen's Bureau in Florida."

"I see," Townsend said, not sure how he was supposed to reply. The Army officer nodded to Townsend, who took quick measure of him. He was a handsome man with a large moustache, stubbly beard, and a chiseled nose. He had a muscular body with a strong jaw and carried himself with a military air, as if he'd just been awarded a medal.

Ransom urged them both to have a seat in the comfortable mahogany and rattan Campeche chairs by the window.

"It seems Major Hutchinson is quite eager to talk to you, Townsend. Your report on that shipwreck has caused quite a stir at Army headquarters in New Orleans."

"Is that so?" he replied, meeting Major Hutchinson's ever-present smile.

"Lieutenant Townsend, my team of agents on the New Orleans docks knows all about the ship you found."

"The *Hard Times?*"

"Yes, we've had that ship under surveillance for over a month, along with several others. What I'm about to tell you is under the strictest confidence. Intelligence information. The men on board are cotton thieves, ex-Confederates. We know they and some other smugglers have been stealing federally owned cotton placed under the control of Treasury agents on the banks of the Mississippi. The troublesome fact is, that's not all we're concerned about."

The major paused to light his cigar. Townsend wanted to blurt out that he'd seen the men, but he could not speak out of turn among superior officers.

"We have heard rumors that the *Hard Times* has been picking up refugees, freedmen, enticing them on board."

"And taking them where?" Townsend asked. "The dying man said he and the others had been locked inside the cargo hold. Could they have been kidnapped?"

"We don't know, Lieutenant. That's why I was sent down here. To get more information. At this point, all we have are rumors."

"You must have heard some details?"

"There is talk that the *Hard Times* might have been making trips to the West Indies."

"The West Indies," Townsend gulped. "You mean Cuba. Any freedmen taken to Cuba will be sold into slavery." He was thinking of the charts on board the shipwreck—the notebook with penciled sketches of the coast, marked in bays and inlets. He had brought all of that with him.

"We are well aware of that, Lieutenant," the major snapped. "We know Cuba is still very much a slave island. Even so, Colonel Osborne of the Freedmen's Bureau and some of the Army officers in New Orleans and Florida remain skeptical that this is happening. At this point, it is just hearsay."

Hearsay? Townsend opened his mouth, but Commander Ransom spoke first.

"I had no inkling about any of this," Ransom said. "If it's true, that's nothing less than treasonous."

"That's why I'm down here, Commander. We greatly—"

Townsend could not stop himself. "Sir, I have something important I need to report. I . . ."

"Don't interrupt, Lieutenant," Commander Ransom barked. "Your superior officer is speaking."

Hutchinson turned his head and cast a critical glance at Townsend as he puffed on his cigar. "Tell me, Lieutenant, did the freedman you spoke with—that Thaddeus Burrell—did he say anything about Cuba?"

"No, sir."

"Anything about the men on board that ship?"

Townsend shook his head. "He just called them buckra men and said they'd been locked up."

"Nothing more?"

"No, sir."

Hutchinson's voice was pleasant yet firm. "Is it possible these freedmen were hired workers who were just being disciplined when they were put below in the cargo hold?"

"I suppose it's possible." Townsend sniffed. He began to suspect that this Army officer was trying to cast doubt on his version of events.

"Understand, as an investigator, I have to consider all options, and one of them is that these freedmen accepted a job offer to be part of a lumber crew somewhere in Florida, and then these freedmen had second thoughts and tried to take over the ship, resulting in them being locked in the cargo hold. Isn't that possible?"

"Yes, sir. I suppose it's possible," Townsend retorted. The Navy lieutenant kept his face still as he reached into his bag and produced the marked-up charts and notebook with the sketches of the coastline. "I took these from the *Hard Times* before I discovered the men locked in the cargo hold. I think you'll agree that this points to more than just mere *hearsay*—at least as far as the ship's destination is concerned."

Hutchinson flipped thought the notebook, his eyes lingering on each sketch.

"An excellent find indeed, Lieutenant. I am pleased to have this evidence. Thank you for providing it. I will include this in my report."

The Army officer cleared his throat and had a sip of coffee. He appeared thoughtful as he puffed on his cigar, blowing out clouds of smoke into the room.

"Lieutenant, you know these waters. It's impossible to survive that weather in an open boat. Don't you think it's quite likely that these men you saw are dead?"

Townsend sat up taller.

"Not only are they not dead, Major, they're alive, and they're here in Key West!" he blurted out. "They were picked up by the Navy steamship in port now. They were rescued in an open rowboat."

"What!" said Hutchinson, leaning forward.

Commander Ransom's eyebrows rose. "The ship that just docked? The USS *New Berne?*"

The Army officer sucked in air, his face and nose becoming more pinched. "Are they still on the ship?" he asked in a hushed whisper.

"No. They robbed an older couple after the ship docked—it seems friends of Secretary Wells—and then ran off."

"You saw them?" Hutchinson's smile had evaporated. His face tensed up. "What did they look like?"

Townsend described them. He watched Hutchinson's cheeks twitch, his eyes darting back and forth. It was clear this description matched whatever the intelligence officer knew about these men. Hutchinson got up from his chair and began pacing the room, puffing on his cigar. Townsend thought he looked as taut as a bow string. Hutchinson looked over at Townsend and seemed to catch himself. He almost immediately restored his smile and his controlled composure.

"We must find these men, Commander Ransom. I will need your help."

"Naturally, Major. You can count on our support."

"Do you know these men, Major Hutchinson?" Townsend asked, trying to keep the accusation out of his voice. "You seem to know what they look like."

"Yes, I know them." The major paused. "For the last month I've been downing whiskies with these varmints at a saloon and boarding house on Basin Street owned by a woman named Jenny King. Place is swarming with ex-Confederates. They know me as a plantation owner, a former Confederate officer just arrived from Cuba where I had been since the surrender of General Lee."

Hutchinson looked squarely at Townsend and Ransom. "What I am about to tell you is sensitive information that should not be repeated." He did not continue until each man nodded.

"We have a small team within the Bureau of Military Information and the Provost Marshal's office who are infiltrating different ex-Confederate groups in New Orleans and Mobile. These unreconstructed rebels are full of daring-do talk." He began waving his cigar around. "Some say they are going to Mexico to join up with Shelby and Maximilian's army to have another crack at the Yankees. Others go on about emigrating to Brazil to restore the Old South, and others like to brag that they're selling Negroes to Cuba." He tapped his ash in the tray on Ransom's desk. "This captain and his men onboard that ship, the *Hard Times*, are some of the biggest talkers. He likes to brag to Jenny King he's gonna bring her ten thousand dollars of gold doubloons from Havana and spend it all in her establishment. Most likely pure poppycock."

"What's this man's name?" Townsend asked.

"Hodge is the ship captain. Ezekiel Hodge. Do you know something about him, Lieutenant?" asked the major, his eyes lingering on Townsend.

The Navy lieutenant shook his head.

Hutchinson put down his cigar, took out a plug of tobacco, and began vigorously chewing it. "To be quite honest, I was not expecting to find these men alive, but now that we know Hodge and his men are here in Key West, we need to be careful how we proceed."

"So what does that mean? You don't want to arrest him?" Townsend blurted out.

Hutchinson shot a stern look at Townsend, his lips tight.

"Lieutenant, any charge of kidnapping or murder is *complete* conjecture. But assuming your suspicions are correct, this matter carries far more importance than perhaps you realize. This is an issue of national security. This man, Hodge, is more valuable if he can lead us to his business associates."

"So are you proposing to just let him escape?"

"I didn't say that. I need to find him, talk with him, and use some friendly persuasion about the possible prison time he might face. We know he's a cotton thief and smuggler. We don't know much else. You might say I would like to recruit him—use him to spread the breadcrumbs, Lieutenant, and see what larger rodents come out of their hiding places in New Orleans, where I expect he's now headed. Understood?"

"Yes, sir."

There was silence in the room. Townsend tried not to think of the faces of the drowned men—their killers getting away with it. Commander Ransom spoke first.

"You can be assured, Major, that the Navy will provide you with the full attention and support you require regarding this matter."

"I'm pleased to hear that Commander Ransom." Hutchinson then turned to face Townsend. "You've seen these men, Lieutenant. If you find them, have the Provost Marshal or the Navy shore patrol bring them to me. I would suggest that you leave behind your Navy attire. As I said, you don't want to scare them off."

Ransom called for the petty officer to take charge of conducting a search of all boats in the harbor, and he told Townsend to check all the boarding houses in town, high and low.

7

October 28, 1865

It was Sunday and the town's church bells were clanging their call for the morning service. Stray shafts of light pierced the tall canopy of sturdy mahogany trees, revealing a funeral procession underway, further evidence of the hurricane's human toll. As the small group of mourners slowly turned onto Fleming Street on the way to the cemetery, the Navy lieutenant took off his hat as a way of paying his respects. He knew after what he and his men had been through, there but for the Grace of God went his coffin.

Townsend focused his thoughts to the task at hand. He knew it was unlikely he'd find Hodge and his men in any boarding house, but he hadn't expressed his skepticism to Commander Ransom and Major Hutchinson. The town had close to three thousand people and scores of abandoned buildings. These men could be holed up in any one of those ramshackle buildings. He'd been instructed to go to all the rooming establishments in Key West, high and low, and he intended to follow those orders.

By mid-morning Townsend had already been to three boarding houses in the area around the docks and the Bight where rooms went for a dollar a night. He'd dressed in civilian clothes as he'd been ordered to. He'd gotten used to keeping a safe distance from the flea-ridden beds with sheets that looked like they hadn't been washed since the beginning of the war.

At one two-story frame house near Greene Street, the owner met him at the door, unshaven, barefoot with red puffy eyes after a night of too much whiskey. Townsend had walked into a small living room with calico curtains, bare floors, and two rickety old chairs. He'd asked the man if he'd had any recent arrivals. Any shipwrecked survivors? The innkeeper replied with a sneer that he never asked any of his guests for personal information, but even if he did know something, he certainly wouldn't divulge it to the Union Navy. Somehow the man had guessed he was a Navy man even though he wasn't wearing his uniform. Townsend left, shaking his head. He wondered if these divisions in the country would ever heal.

At the more elegant Russell Hotel on Duval Street where the large parlor room was full of talk of shipwrecks and salvage auctions, Townsend made the same inquiries, but found nothing suspicious. As he had suspected from the outset, he had come up empty-handed. He thought Hodge and his men were probably hiding out on a boat or at a house owned by some Confederate veteran. He now headed off to the boarding house which Emma had once called home.

Townsend stood on Simonton Street in front of the two-storied white clapboard house with the wide porch and tall green shutters that he knew so well. The boarding house was a former private home that Emma's sister, Elizabeth, had turned into a small inn when she moved to Key West nearly ten years ago with her husband. She called it The Grove, a reference to a former popular inn in Key West called Cocoanut Grove on Front Street that had been owned by Ellen Mallory, the deceased mother of the Confederacy's Secretary of the Navy.

Townsend felt a tightening in his chest as he looked up at the tall palms shading the second-floor veranda. The dappled morning light mixed with shadows of palm fronds was dancing across the front of the boarding house, revealing a damaged balcony. There were a few broken branches in the yard, but otherwise the house had gotten through the storm virtually unscathed.

He slowly opened the gate and walked toward the house, climbing the steps onto the creaking front porch. He felt like an interloper as he looked around. He wasn't even sure if Emma's sister would welcome him inside. His eyes rested on the two-seater swing where they used to sit together to have tea. They'd both laughed so much in that swing and held each other close in the cool fragrant night air. One night, he'd almost asked her to marry him. He'd grabbed her hand, but the words never came out. He remembered the expectant look on her face, but then the moment was over. He was a coward.

He loved her, but he'd been afraid of the responsibility of being saddled with a wife during a war.

Townsend clutched the letter he'd written, his face pricked with unease. He hoped Elizabeth would agree to send it on to Emma. He thought about what he'd written. He had poured out his heart to try to explain himself. He should have tried to understand the loneliness she was going through. He knew she was homesick and wanted to return to Havana. He should have known how strongly attached she was to the island.

He gulped as he thought about the last paragraph in the letter. After much hesitation, he'd written how sorry he was about an incident at the dance hall that had caused their final break. He'd been drinking too much, and he never should have done what he did. He had thought about saying more, but decided to leave it at that.

Townsend knocked, but there was no answer. He was about to knock again when he suddenly panicked, turning abruptly to leave. He leaned down to place the letter on the porch table when the door opened and Emma's sister appeared. Elizabeth Carpenter de Hernández was a taller woman than Emma, but not nearly as pretty. She wasn't unattractive, just somewhat plain. *More like their formidable mother*, he thought—full figured with a prominent nose.

Just by her cold demeanor, Townsend knew that his breakup with Emma had caused her sister to more decidedly turn against him.

"Why, Mr. Townsend, I thought we'd seen the last of you." She looked him up and down. "I see you're dressed in civilian clothes. Are you out of the Navy now?"

"No, I'm still in the Navy."

"And what may I ask brings you here after these many months?"

"It's a military matter. I've been sent to make inquiries. We're looking for some dangerous men—recent shipwreck survivors—wanted for questioning. Ex-Confederates."

"And you think they are here?" she asked. Her scorn wasn't even thinly veiled.

"We wondered if these men might have—"

"Why would you suppose, I would open my doors to such men?"

"I just thought—"

Townsend gave a quick description, but she cut him off.

"No, I have no new lodgers, and I haven't seen these men, but I'll be sure to let the authorities know if I do."

She was about to close the door when Townsend blurted out. "I hope Emma and your mother, Mrs. Carpenter, are fine?"

Elizabeth raised one eyebrow even as a frown emerged between both eyes. She knew Townsend didn't care much for her mother.

"They are well, thank you. Keeping the boarding house in Havana is a full-time job, and this latest hurricane didn't help."

Townsend shifted his weight from one foot to the next. His heart beat rapidly. He wanted to ask so many things.

"I don't suppose . . . I just wondered, does Emma have any plans to return to Key West?"

Townsend heard something fall inside the house. Elizabeth flinched but paid no attention to the noise. Townsend could tell she was flustered because she didn't say anything. Then a chair scraped, and Elizabeth jumped again suspiciously. Townsend leaned forward to look inside the house. He could see it was dark because a few of the windows were still shuttered from the hurricane.

"I'm sorry, I have guests to attend to," she said nervously. "I think you should go. I still have to fully open up this house."

But Townsend wasn't listening. He knew she was lying. The war had taught him to read people, particularly ones that were hiding something. Intuition told him that Elizabeth was worried, maybe even alarmed. *Could she be in danger?*

"Are you all right?" he asked with concern.

"Yes, I'm fine. Please go."

She waved him away and started to close the door when Townsend's eyes shifted to some movement over her shoulder. Something made the curtains shake. It was just a shadow. He heard rustling, and suddenly his troubled mind was back on patrol on his boat on the Suwannee River. He thought he heard the thundering of hooves and the thud of musket balls hitting wood.

He reacted without thinking, brushing by her as he charged into the room. He saw a figure move back into a dark corner. He grabbed a walking stick leaning against the wall.

"Come forward. Let me see your face!" he cried out, shaking the stick menacingly. A figure stepped out of the shadows. Townsend froze, then took a deep breath, badly shaken. After a long pause, he breathed out her name.

"Emma. How in the world . . . Am I dreaming?"

She didn't say anything and kept looking over at her sister, but even Elizabeth was quiet. There was an awkward silence as no one knew what to say next. Townsend couldn't stop staring at her. He hadn't seen her for more than six months. His eyes darted from her high forehead to her sculpted cheekbones, from her almond-shaped eyes to her long, slender neck. He felt a blinding rush of emotions and an overwhelming desire to run toward her and hold her in his arms, but nothing happened.

"Really Mr. Townsend, you should go," Elizabeth said, as she recovered her composure. "My sister has things to do."

At that moment, Elizabeth's husband Emilio walked in, assessing the situation even as he greeted the Navy lieutenant. Townsend had always gotten along well with the tall, broad-shouldered Cuban, but the end of his relationship with Emma had created a strain. Emilio Hernández was an independent shipowner who sailed back and forth between Havana and Key West. He catered to the wealthy merchants in Key West who wanted a regular supply of fine-quality cigars, Spanish wine and French brandies, as well as tropical fruit. At one point, Townsend thought he would work with him as a ship captain when the Navy discharged him, but now that was clearly no longer an option.

"You can't be here, Everett," Emilio said. "You have to leave."

Emilio moved toward Townsend to show him the door, but Emma held him back.

"No, that's all right, Emilio," Emma said. "It may be a good time for Everett and me to talk."

Elizabeth scowled after them as they walked out on the front porch and sat down on the wooden rocking chairs where they'd sat so many times before. The empty two-seater swing hung motionless. Emma was guarded and distant, her brow furrowed. Townsend kept looking at her and then looking away. He finally broke the silence.

"I wish I'd known you were here."

Emma's eyes blinked rapidly.

"It was a last-minute decision to come. Emilio showed up in Havana unexpectedly, and I decided to go with him on the return trip. What about you? Why did you decide to come back here? I mean . . . was there a reason?"

"I'm investigating a shipwreck I saw during the hurricane. A crime was committed on board, and the men responsible are most likely hiding out in Key West. I've been sent to try to find them."

"I hope you catch them," she said. "It does look like you have your hands full."

"What are your plans?" Townsend asked. "Will you be here for a while?"

"No, I'm going back to Havana as soon as Emilio makes his next trip over to Cuba. I just came to get my clothes and see my sister. The hurricane kept me here longer than I expected."

"So, you're definitely going back . . . I mean, for good?"

"Yes. Cuba is where I want to be. It's not just my mother. Change is going to come to Cuba like it did in this country, and I want to be a part of it. Cubans want freedom from Spain, and women must play a role. The Spanish, with their titles and their government jobs, live like lords and ladies and expect Cubans to serve them. We are like their servants, unable to get jobs in the government, unable to speak out about anything. That must change."

Townsend raised an eyebrow. He knew how serious the Spanish authorities were. In Cuba there can be no public meetings, no publications, no demonstrations that challenge the government. You weren't even allowed to have any religious protestant pamphlets. The punishment could be imprisonment or worse.

"But Emma, have you considered the danger? Why not stay in this country?"

"I may be American, but I am also Cuban, born and raised. *Soy cubana.* You know that. It's my home."

Townsend found himself lost in what seemed to be a forest in her eyes.

"I've missed you," he finally said. "Do you remember the time we sailed to Woman Key, and we had our lunch on the beach. I dove for conch, and you uncovered some turtle eggs in the sand."

"Yes, that was a good day," she said with a smile. "That was when we still laughed a lot."

"Or when we took a walk on Emma Street through a bad part of sailor town, and we joked that we could build a house there? You remember . . . you said you'd prefer to build a house on Everett Street." Townsend looked at her hopefully. "Can't we make a fresh start?"

She sighed. "How would we do that? It's no use, Everett. We seem to be going in different directions. You've changed. You're still fighting the war. Why, you almost killed me with that stick! Were you having hallucinating visions?"

Townsend didn't reply. He knew she was right. He was moody, restless, and quick to anger. His relapses into the shadows came and went like gusts of wind.

"Can you even settle down to a normal life? What will you do when you leave the Navy?"

"I have some ideas, but I'm not sure."

Emma curled her lip, on hearing this. "What about your grandmother in Cuba? What will happen to that plantation? What will happen to her?"

Townsend flinched.

"I don't know."

"You need to find your direction, Everett. I was always told good fortune favors those who believe in what they're doing."

To change the subject, he handed her the letter. "I wrote this because I didn't think I'd see you. I hope you'll read it." He smiled. "I want to be someone you can trust, Emma."

"That's not a word that comes readily to mind when I think of you, Everett. You might say you scuttled that ship."

"I'm sorry." He looked down at his hands. "I can explain. What happened at the dance, it's not what you think."

Emma cut him off. "I know what I saw." She looked at him with a cold stare that seemed to stab him in the eye.

"I did get drunk that night. I'd just come back from a month on patrol. Some of the other Navy officers invited me there. And that girl you saw me with. I don't know who she was. She approached me and then you came in. I'm sorry."

"Were you sorry when you started the bar fight? That Army officer you slugged was a good friend of my sister and Emilio."

Townsend shook his head.

"That was a mistake. I was drunk and not thinking clearly. The truth is, I was jealous when you started dancing together."

"He was just being courteous to me."

"It looked like it was more than that."

Emma glared at him.

"What happened to us, Everett? I told you when we first met that dependability was what mattered to me."

Gone were fragility or vulnerability. Emma had a certain determined fire in her eyes and fixed conviction in her face. Townsend turned away and pretended instead to be watching a man in a donkey cart filled with burlap bags pass by. He felt badly about himself because he still hadn't had the courage to tell her the full truth. He had gone to the dance on his own because he was mad at her. He did approach that girl. Her eyes locked onto his as soon as she walked into that dance hall. He should have turned away, but he didn't. He'd already had too much rum. He still didn't know what happened that night, but he did remember how María Elena had tended his injuries. He thought he remembered her fingers on his face and then those same fingers gently unbuttoning his shirt.

Townsend ran his hand through his hair and turned back to face Emma.

"Will you write?"

"I don't know. I used to think it was fate that brought us together in Havana," she said with a note of sadness as she looked him in the eye. "But now I think fate is as fickle as they say it is. Maybe we're just another casualty of war, Everett."

The clanging of more church bells alerted Townsend that the late morning church service was about to begin. Old Sandy's church, the newly built Cornish Chapel, was just a few blocks away.

"I'm sorry, Emma. I made a commitment to see someone at church. I have to go."

She nodded. "Goodbye, Everett."

There was a firmness in her jaw and a toughness in her eyes that made her more attractive to him. He wanted to hold her, and kiss her gently, but he knew he would be rebuffed. They shared a simple handshake before he walked down the porch steps.

Townsend allowed himself to take a last lingering look at her face, and then turned to walk away out onto Simonton Street without looking back. He felt a knot in his stomach. He wanted to turn around and wave, but he was too proud.

A sudden northerly gust of wind brought him the faint smell of rotting fish from the fish market at the Bight, and his nose twitched with displeasure. He thought of fate. He wondered if it was pre-ordained, or maybe Divine Providence points us in a certain direction like a compass needle, and then our choices dictate how we get there. He felt a heavy sadness descend on him like a tide rising, and he sank down at the base of a large tamarind tree and put his face in his hands. Townsend hit the tree with his fist and cursed himself for being such a stupid fool.

8

The mid-morning sun was slanting in long bars across the row of houses, and Townsend realized he would be late if he didn't hurry. He turned left from Southard Street and soon enough he spotted the chapel at the edge of town on Whitehead Street. He could hear music and the soothing voices of the congregation singing in harmony. He felt physically drained, broken inside from his conversation with Emma, and the rhythmic singing made him feel lighter. He could just make out the words. "We are climbing Jacob's ladder, soldiers of the cross," they sang. He recognized the song as a traditional Negro spiritual about freedom.

The chapel was a two-story, frame building painted white with a bell. Townsend found his dark mood slowly lifting as he walked up the stone steps and peered inside, not certain whether he would be welcome. The voices and the music caused him to stop and watch the congregation as it swayed back and forth in unison. He looked around the small church. It was simple with raw-wood pews—nothing remarkable but the pulpit and a cross to adorn the altar. The large beams reminded Townsend of the keel and frames of a ship's hull.

A quick glance told him he was the only white person there. He felt he was intruding, but one of the church ushers at the door motioned for him to come inside. There must have been seventy-five to one hundred people there—men, women, and children. Some of the men were finely dressed in smooth shirts with cravats and a dark long coat, evidence of how many freedmen in Key West had prospered even before the war. A few just had baggy, loose-fitting work clothes. But what stood out for Townsend were the number of women in the congregation, many of whom were elegantly dressed with ribbons and bows in their hats and dresses. He spotted Old Sandy walking down the center aisle toward the altar.

Townsend couldn't believe this was the same man he knew. He was transformed from farmer to preacher, dressed in a long-tail black suit and satin waistcoat, his thick gray hair combed back. Following a short prayer asking God to ease the earthly burden of the congregation, Preacher Cornish began talking about this new chapel which he and Reverend Strong from the African Methodist Episcopal Zion Church in Hartford had helped build. He nodded his gray head when he caught a glimpse of Townsend in the back corner of the church. He said proudly that the Cornish chapel would be a safe harbor for all who no longer have shelter.

"As many of you know, jus' a little more than a year ago we had no place to go. We gathered outside to worship under a Spanish lime tree not far from heah. Now we have our own chapel, de first church for Colored folks heah in Key West. Dis sanctuary is open to all our brethren, freedmen who come from de cotton fields and rice swamps. I see dem comin'. Thank the Lawd, I see dem comin'."

There were murmurs of amen and hallelujah around the chapel. Old Sandy's voice became softer and more conversational, and he began speaking about the meaning of freedom. He told the story of Jesus and the blind man.

"De Scriptures say dat Jesus was called on to cure a blind man and so he took dat man walkin' over hills and valleys and den at Jesus's command, de man opened his eyes. And to his surprise, he could see. Jesus asked de man what he gwine tuh do now. Would he go back tuh where he'd bin? No, Lawd he replied, I movin' forward. I can see clearly now."

"Glory be to God! Hallelulah!" came a chorus of voices from the front of the chapel.

Old Sandy raised both his arms up to the roof and looked out at the congregation.

"We all deh like dat blind man. We know we need to move forward, liftin' while climbin'. We dun passed through de fiery inferno of slavery. Sum people gwine tuh want tuh tear us down, but we ain' gwine tuh go back. We have to find our way through dis ocean of darkness. Let us all rejoice in our newly gained freedom and find de light in dis weary land. We bin waitin' long time now."

"Lawd a' Mussy," came the response from the front rows.

"De Bible says make a joyful noise," cried out Old Sandy. "Let us unite heart and soul in singin' to de Lawd."

The musicians took that as their cue and the chapel was once again filled with song and the lively mix of piano, tambourine, and the quivering hum of the fiddle. The rhythmic voices and the clapping of hands seemed to make the walls vibrate, and Townsend found himself strangely feeling both sorrow and happiness. He watched the exuberant faces of some women near him who were singing and clapping to the rhythm of the tambourine, and he joined them. When the music stopped, Old Sandy began to tell the story in the Bible about Joseph seeking his brethren.

"Lak Joseph, we too are seekin' our families. We too are searchin' for de kinfolk whom we lost. We all tryin' to heal dese wounds of slavery, de separation of families."

Old Sandy paused and looked over at a bearded Black man who was seated next to his wife. Preacher Cornish asked him to stand beside him and then introduced him simply as a man on a pilgrimage, who was trying to find his two sons. The man had a thin face and wire-rimmed spectacles. He was dressed in dark blue Navy pants, a white shirt, and suspenders.

"Dis man has come from Georgia and Louisiana, down de coast of Florida in search of his chilun. Let us welcome him tuh our midst. He gon' tell us his story."

The churchgoers murmured their support. Townsend knew who the man was before he even stepped up to the pulpit and began speaking.

"My name is Levi Jacobs. I bawn and rais'd a slave in de Sea Islands of Georgia at de Butler plantation. All around us was plenty river and swamp. Rice country. Every mawning before de sun come up we would wake to de sound of a conch shell. Das how we knew anudah day of hardship in de rice fields had begun."

Townsend noted that Jacobs had a slight lilting accent, much like his Bahamian friend Clyde Hendricks, but with a difference. His accent and the way he spoke made Townsend wonder about the man's education and his upbringing. As if he read Townsend's mind, Jacobs offered up the information that his mother had been a slave brought over from the Bahamas several years before freedom arrived there in 1833. He learned his alphabet and his numbers, thanks to a Black lay preacher. He said that man, with the support of Mrs. Butler, the English wife of the plantation owner, had secretly taught him and two other boys without ever telling her husband.

Jacobs said at the Butler plantation they all spoke Geechee, but his mother made sure he spoke like a Bahamian. She would always tell him stories about life in the Bahamas. The fish markets, the donkey races, and the lively Jonkonnu dances around Christmas time. Townsend could tell from the enthusiastic reactions in the pews that there were certainly some Bahamians in the chapel. Jacobs said he used to dream of being free and taking his mother back to the islands, but she had died enslaved in Georgia before the Civil War began. He paused for a moment as if he was paying his respects to the memory of his mother. Then he lifted his head and began to calmly explain how life had changed for him one day when the foreman called the slaves at the Butler plantation together.

"T'aint no easy way to tell you dis story, but I gon' start wid when dey sold all of us. It was March 2, 1859. Sum 440 men, women, and children, we were all told dat everyone gon' be sold. By den, all of us had heard de whisperin' dat Mastah Pierce Butler had dun lost all he family money. Me wife and two childrun along wid all de others had been herded tuhgether into sheds and stalls at Savannah's Tenbroeck Racetrack. Kept dere for four days for inspection by de buyers."

Townsend could see that Jacobs had the full attention of the congregation. He could hear the murmurs and the whispering as he began to relate how field hands, blacksmiths, coopers, housemaids, and dairywomen all went up for sale. Townsend now remembered reading about this auction in an article in the *New York Tribune*. The sale was infamous. Buyers from all over the South had descended on Savannah, looking for bargains.

Jacobs calmly described the auctioneer as an elegant, well-dressed white man with a soft pearl-gray, winged-tip beard and moustache. He said he looked like a kind man, but when he brought Jacob's wife up and put her on the stand, he told the bidders there was good money to be made with this prime Negro wench.

Jacobs paused, and Townsend could sense a simmering bed of deep anger in the man's face.

"She was sold for 1,200 dollars. The price for me was 1,310 dollars 'cause I was both a carriage driver as well as a boatman. Me wife, Lena and I watched our two sons, Caiphus and Henry, be auctioned off like two yearling hosses. They wa' only ten and eight years old. At a bang of de auctioneer's gavel, dey was sold. One thousand dollars for each of dem. Sold to two men from Louisiana wearin' slouch hats, mud-crusted boots, and revolvers on deh hips. I saw me wife, Lena wince. She stood deh, tears fallin' from her face as she watched de frightened faces of our two boys. We watched dem bein' led away. Das the last time we ever saw dem. We came to call dem two days, 'de weeping time.'"

Townsend could hear the creaking of the pews, and a murmur of sympathetic responses. "Lawd a' Mussy." "Amen."

Jacobs went on to describe the journey he and his wife made to the plantation they'd been sold to. They were thrown in the back of a rough wagon with two slave handlers, banging over roads of ruts and roots through Georgia into the pale roads and black forests of northern Florida. They were taken to a large plantation in Suwannee County not too far from Tallahassee cotton country.

"De place was owned by an old Florida Indian fighter, a man dey called de Colonel. To be fair, he was known to be kind to his slaves most times. Treat dem good, he would say, and deh gon' work harder. But dat ol' man, he like his favors, and one day he decide to choose me wife."

Townsend could see how difficult this was for Jacobs as he paused to clear his throat. Words of support rose up from the congregation. Jacobs said the colonel's wife found out about her husband's infidelity. He described how this angry woman ordered the overseer to strip his wife and tie her to the whipping post by her wrists.

"She wa' a jealous woman, a cruel one too. She grab de overseer's bull whip and began lashin' me poor wife like a demon. I couldn't take it no longah. I ran up to dat woman and grab de whip from her. Das when she had de overseer tie me up next to me wife and he whip me good, until me back deh shredded."

A woman near Townsend began crying into her hands. Another woman with a shawl next to him stared vacantly at the altar, like she was lost in a memory. He sensed that each and every one in that congregation could identify with what Jacobs was saying. So many had suffered through some version of this story.

Jacobs went on to describe how he and his wife tried to escape.

"It was early in de mornin' jus' after Mr. Lincoln freed de slaves in January '63. We taught it wa' gon be easy 'cause de overseer and his men still bin celebratin' de new year. Dey all drinkin' whiskey and playin' cards. We each had our satchels full of food and we had our forged travel documents. We wa' gon' take a log raft down de Suwannee River all de way to de Gulf where dem Union Navy blockade boats were anchored. We had heard dis was de quickest road to freedom."

Townsend shook his head in amazement about this story. He'd seen it replayed on that same river dozens of times. He'd rescued so many runaway slaves during the war up the Suwannee, and he knew the odds of escape were never good. The pain twisted across Jacobs' face as he described how his wife fell when they heard the dogs start to bay and howl. In a rush of fear, they went different directions through the cypress swamp toward the river. He said he was already there hiding behind a log when Lena emerged from the woods. She called out his name. That's when he saw the man with the rifle behind the tree. He shot her in the back as she reached the raft.

"I followed down river and I found her. I stayed wid her de whole night, slappin' mosquitoes from bitin' her face. Nuttin' I could do, but hold a rag on de bullet hole. I jus' watched de life bleed out of her on de banks of dat river. She made me promise to find our two boys. 'Find dem Levi,' she said. 'Promise me, you gon' find dem.'"

Jacobs stopped and looked down, wiping his eyes. Townsend could see some people openly crying. Jacobs described how he buried his wife on the banks of the Suwannee River under a cypress tree. He carved her name into the tree with her dates.

"De weepin' time, for sure. Lawd, a'Mussy!" a group of women murmured.

"Before I left dat place, I got down on me knees, and I prayed to God to help me find dem two boys. Wid de end of de fightin', dese past several months I bin travelin' from town to town. Here in Key West, I hope I gon' find a man who I wa told knows whar me sons deh. Dem two boys are all I have left. I pray to God I can find dem."

"Glory be to God, hallelulah," Preacher Cornish shouted, then hugged Levi Jacobs as the congregation burst into song.

The singing was so loud, the small chapel seemed to explode with energy. Townsend found himself mouthing some of the words. He knew the spiritual about hiding the tracks of runaway slaves. "Wade in the water. God gonna trouble these waters." As a boy in Maryland, he would sometimes hear those words coming from the boat shacks on their property. His father would hide runaway slaves there at night before secretly putting them on one of his barge boats that would take them north up the Susquehanna River to freedom.

At the end of the song, Townsend didn't move. He closed his eyes and tried to understand why he felt so drained. He felt the beauty of the voices that seemed to convey the triumph of light over dark. He watched as members of the congregation approached the altar to speak with Jacobs, and he knew he would have to wait his turn to speak with this man and discover more about what had brought him to Key West. His story about what had happened to his two sons seemed all too familiar. He needed to know more about that ship captain whom Old Sandy had said Jacobs was looking for.

9

Townsend finally approached Jacobs and introduced himself as a Navy lieutenant who was friends with Preacher Cornish. Jacobs squinted at him, his suspicion plain of this white man out of uniform claiming to be a Navy officer. Townsend wanted to say how much the church service had touched him in a profound way, and how he felt the pain and sorrow Jacobs had experienced, but he couldn't find the words.

"I just want to thank you for sharing your story. It was so moving."

Jacobs looked at him strangely, making Townsend feel uncomfortable.

"I'm here because Preacher Cornish thought you might be able to help us with an ongoing investigation, a military matter."

Jacobs glared at Townsend and then glanced over at Old Sandy who was still surrounded by members of the congregation. Townsend could see Lillah Cornish by her husband's side.

"Preacher Cornish sent you? Why? He ain' never mention nuttin' to me."

"I wanted to know more about your sons' disappearance. He made it sound like there might have been—"

"Why you want to know?" Jacobs snapped. "I dun me military service. I can tell you sharin' a ship with dem sailors taint feel so different from de hard task masters on de plantation. Coal heavin' down in that furnace room, holyston' de decks. Das all de Navy wanted from me. I dun wid dat."

"Maybe we can help each other?" Townsend said.

"I *dun* me duty," Jacobs repeated. "I dun me service, and now I lookin' for me two sons."

At that point, Old Sandy's towering figure emerged from the cluster of talkative ladies. He walked over toward them.

"Mistah Jacobs, thank you for yo' stirring words. A true inspiration. Yo' journey of faith and resilience sets an example for us all. Let me jus' say I remain confident de Lawd will provide and lead you to yo' two sons. Trust in de Lawd."

Jacobs shuffled his feet back and forth. Old Sandy glanced at Townsend, then put his right hand on Jacobs' shoulder and said he thought Townsend might be able to help him.

"I know ahm askin' a favor from you to help dis man. At least, give him a few moments of yo' time. He is a friend of mine. He jus' might be able to help you."

Townsend tried to keep his face expressionless, open. Jacobs stared at him for several seconds. He took off his glasses and began wiping them with his bandana.

"Alright den, Mistah Navy officer, wha' you need to know?"

"Tell me more about what you found out about your sons," Townsend said. "What happened when you went to the plantation? What did they tell you?"

Jacobs looked up at the rafters as if he were seeking guidance and inspiration and then began talking.

"I went back to de old Butler plantation in Georgia and a minister dere helped me find de plantation whar me two sons had been taken. Sugar cane country near New Orleans. Near as I could tell de war had left a heap of misery along dem banks of de Mississippi. Sum sad lookin' land. Fields gone to bush. De former slaves had no work and no place to go. Many of dem had jus' walked off. I was told by a few of dem who wa still der dat me two sons had been taken by sum buckra men a few months prior, supposedly to cut timber and clear land in Florida."

"Were they kidnapped?"

Jacobs glowered at Townsend.

"I ain' know. One old man I found knew me two boys. He gave me de name of de man who took dem. He said he overheard his name mentioned."

"What was the name?"

"Hodge. Cap'n Ezekiel Hodge. He fought with de rebels." Jacob's eye twitched as he said it.

A jolt of excitement ran through Townsend, but he didn't react. He had hoped Jacobs might have useful information for Hutchinson, but he hadn't allowed himself to believe that he and Jacobs might be looking for the same man.

"Go on."

"I went down to de Basin in New Orleans, askin' bout Ezekiel Hodge. Bunch of buckra men tol' me dem boys nevah comin' back. Dey kept laughin' and tellin' me I could get a job wid Hodge. Fair wage. And dey laughed again. Cap'n Zeke is what dey called him—a Tampa Bay cracker. Maybe I'd find him dere."

"So is that where you went? Tampa Bay?"

"I did. Traveled through de gardens of hell to get der."

Jacobs described a nightmarish, month-long journey, traveling down rivers filled with gators and snakes and then slogging through saw palmetto and swamp grass. At Cedar Key, he talked his way onto a fishing boat bound for Tampa Bay.

"I almos' get kill'd in Tampa. A bunch of dem swamp crackers started to drag me down de dirt street toward an oak tree right in de center of town. Call' me a road walker and a thief. One of dem had a rope. Townspeople never raised a hand to stop 'em. If it weren't for a federal agent of the Freedmen's Bureau comin' by wid sum of dem Black Union soldiers garrisoned there, I would be long ago dead."

"Did that federal agent help you find Hodge?"

"Yes, suh. I tellin' you. Tank de Lawd for dat man. He took me to de place called de Scrub near Fort Brooke whar de Black people live and whar de Freedmen's Bureau handin' out food and tellin' people der rights. No one der had heard of me two sons. But de agent found out dat some of de ex-Confederates runnin' sawmills up de Hillsborough River knew Hodge. Dey told him Hodge has a woman in Key West. She moved here from Tampa wid her family."

Townsend nodded at this new information. *Hodge has got a woman.* It was the lead he was hoping for. "Did you get her name?"

"Ángela. Dem people in Tampa said she lives wid her brother, who fought alongside Hodge up in Tennessee. She's Spanish, I tink. Das what brought me down de coast another two hundred miles to Key West. If I can find her, maybe I can find him."

He paused and raised his eyebrows at Townsend.

"Why you askin' me all dese questions? How is me searchin' for dis man Navy business?"

"Because I believe the man you're looking for is here in Key West right now."

Levi Jacobs sucked in his breath.

"Hodge?" he breathed out. "You found him?"

"He and three others were picked up by a Navy supply ship and brought to the Naval landing. Their schooner was lost in the hurricane. They ran off the Navy ship after robbing a man and are now in hiding."

"So he deh a wanted man now? A wanted criminal?"

Townsend nodded. "I believe so. The provost patrol officers in Key West along with the Army's many informants are looking for Hodge. The Navy is searching the boats in the harbor."

Jacobs bowed his head and prayed. The tears came as if from a bottomless well, a steady flow. The man let his heavy weight collapse on a pew where he began singing softly to himself. Townsend noticed that he was holding onto two small wooden carvings of horses, the kind that children might play with. He was rubbing them back and forth between his thumb and his forefinger.

Townsend just stood there silently listening. He could only imagine the sadness that this man must feel. He'd fought for the Union, and now, like so many other freedmen, he was in a desperate search for the remnants of his family. The end of the war had given him freedom but left him living a nightmare.

Lillah Cornish brought some water to Jacobs, who nodded his thanks. Townsend noticed he put the horse carvings into his breast pocket next to his heart. The man wiped his eyes a final time with his bandana and then looked at Townsend.

"I want to hear all about dis man. What do you know of him?"

"Very little except to say he's not a good man."

"Wha' you mean by dat?"

Townsend told him about the man's ship and what he'd seen on the shipwreck.

"There were dead men in the cargo hold. All freedmen. They'd been locked in there. It looked like some of them had been clubbed on the head, but they probably died during the hurricane by drowning. The only survivor told me before he died that they'd been *taken* from a plantation near New Orleans. I saw Hodge and his men escape in the launch. He left them there to die."

Jacobs showed little emotion until the Navy lieutenant mentioned the name of the plantation near New Orleans the dying man had given him, Fannie's Place. Jacobs flinched. It was like someone had stabbed him. Townsend asked him if he had any other questions, but there was no reply. Jacobs sat there still as a statue, expressionless, empty of words, staring vacantly into the silent chapel. Townsend was worried that he had fallen into a state of shock like some soldiers he'd seen after the heat of battle. He'd seen men close to a breaking point before.

"Jacobs, are you alright?" He couldn't be certain if the man had heard him. Townsend finally shook his shoulders, and Jacobs snapped back, looking up at him with confusion in his eyes. "What is it? Do you want some more water?"

Jacobs shook his head and blinked at Townsend.

"It's de same place. Fannie's Plantation. Das whar me two sons were taken after de auction. It's whar I went to find dem. The east bank of the Mississippi River in Plaquemines Parish." He looked into Townsend's face. "You tink me two boys were on dat ship you found?"

Townsend paused before answering. He wondered if he had made a mistake by telling this man what he'd seen on that ship.

"Not likely. You said your sons were taken months ago. I don't think Hodge would still have had the same men in that hold, all this time."

"Whar would dey have taken dem?"

"I don't know," Townsend replied. "Maybe Jacksonville or St. Augustine. There's a lot of timber cutting in central Florida. It's hard to say. The hurricane could have blown the ship far off course. We won't know until we find Hodge."

"Tell me de truth—do you tink me two sons dead?"

Townsend hesitated for a moment, then shook his head. There was such desperate grief in the man's eyes, he found himself at a loss for words. He almost had mentioned the rumors about Cuba, but he stopped himself. There would be a better time to tell Jacobs about that dire possibility. The fear of their death was enough—he did not want to add the fear that they could have been re-enslaved in Cuba just as they had gained their precious freedom.

The truth was, Townsend didn't really want to think about the Cuban possibility. He had witnessed the particular horrors of slavery in Cuba. He was still struggling to come to terms with these rumors that Hutchinson had reported. He kept trying to tell himself they were probably false, but he hadn't forgotten Hodge's cabin in the shipwreck where he'd found everything from Cuban cigars to maps and sketch books of the Cuban coastline. He closed his eyes, willing away the memories of what he'd seen in the Cuban countryside—on his own family's plantation. He could not think of what he'd seen without feeling the shame.

"Lieutenant, you evah dream of de dead?"

Townsend was surprised to now be called lieutenant, but even more taken aback by this unexpected question.

"I mean your friends, your relatives who dun' left this world for de next? You evah dream of dem?"

"I suppose so," Townsend said slowly. "Why . . . why do you ask?"

At that moment, he thought of his mother, who had always been a moral polestar in his life. Both she and his father had taught him to help the underdog. The last time he saw her, she had been reading Emerson. "Be true to yourself, Everett, and you will never lose your way," she had said. "Be comfortable with who you are. Never lie to yourself."

Jacobs pulled out the carvings of the two little wooden horses.

"I helped me boys carve dem out of driftwood. Dese got left behind. It's all I have from dem. Sometimes I rub dese hosses, and I have happy dreams about me two sons."

"Your boys were fond of horses?"

"Oh yes, from de time dey bin small. I teach dem how to ride, you know. I raised dem to be good stable boys. My wife was so proud of her sons."

Townsend nodded. He felt a sense that this man's fate and his own had been intertwined for some reason. He and Jacobs were linked by those bodies in that shipwreck. In his gut, he knew that Hodge had murdered those men. He just hoped that Jacobs' sons had not met a similar fate.

"How you gon' find dis man, Lieutenant?" Jacobs asked.

"You said Hodge has a woman?"

Jacobs looked up, his eyes still red.

"I been lookin' for her since I got here. I aks around de docks. Sum of dem Spanish fishermen, but dey ain' wan' to help. Das why I appealed to Preacher Cornish."

"I will make inquiries about this Ángela. That's our best lead."

Jacobs nodded and reached out his hand. "Thank you, Lieutenant."

Townsend shook it and put his other hand on the man's shoulder. "We will find your boys, Jacobs, wherever they may be."

Townsend felt the warmth of the sun on his face as he walked past the courthouse on Whitehead Street on his way to Naval headquarters. He had left Jacobs at the Cornish chapel where he was staying. He told him to give him a day or two. He would get back to him as soon as he could locate where this woman Ángela lived. Townsend knew the search would not be easy. Officially there were about one hundred Spanish Cubans in Key West, but that was a low estimate because of the constant ebb and flow of people coming over from Cuba.

The Spanish speakers in Key West were a mixture of fishermen, cigar rollers, sailors, and store owners. It was a small community—Townsend knew that discretion was required. He had thought about going to see the Spanish consul in Key West, but he quickly ruled that out. Likewise, he thought it was too risky to make inquiries around the docks. Word that a Navy lieutenant was asking questions might spread like wildfire and cause Ángela to tip off Hodge.

Townsend thought of Joaquín de la Cruz. The young Cuban seaman in his crew had told him about his grandfather, José de la Cruz, a fisherman who had lived in the Spanish community in Tampa for years before moving to Key West. It was a long shot, but he thought worth the try. Townsend headed to the Naval yard. He would deliver his report on what he had found at the boarding houses and then he would track down de la Cruz from whatever Navy grog house he was in. He decided he would not inform his superiors about Jacobs. Not yet.

10

October 30, 1865

Two days later, with Joaquín de la Cruz leading the way, Townsend and Jacobs walked up the coastal dirt road past the US Army barracks hugging the shoreline. The old man lived near the salt pond at the northeastern end of the island, where he had a small *rancho*. Jacobs had insisted on coming with them even though Townsend had tried to discourage him, telling him he wouldn't be able to understand any of the conversation as de la Cruz's grandfather spoke only Spanish.

They went several miles on a muddy trail through scrub brush and mangroves until they came to a raw-board wooden hut with a palm-thatched roof. There was a small pasture to one side with goats and chickens, and one cow fenced in by posts and rails cut from gumbo limbo trees. A rickety wharf attached to some pilings offered a way for the fisherman to tie up his small boat.

De la Cruz suddenly stopped and pointed to a submerged log in some muddy water, not six feet away from their feet.

"Don't move, Cap'n," de la Cruz whispered. "*Cocodrilo.*"

Townsend froze. He could now see the eye ridges and the narrow shovel snout. He could hear Jacobs gasp behind him. The crocodile had drifted in under the stilt roots of some mangroves next to the path, ready to snatch whatever came his way. Townsend slowly reached for his revolver. Before he could pull it out of the holster, a shot rang out. The water next to his feet exploded in a fury of splashing and thrashing. He jumped back. Another shot, and the crocodile shuddered and rolled over on its stomach.

A thin man wearing a wide-brimmed palm leaf hat holding a long rifle stepped out from behind a leafy palmetto, no more than twenty yards away from them. He was chomping on a moist, chewed-up cigar, his leathery face so lined with furrows and wrinkles that it reminded Townsend of a blistered piece of driftwood. The old man pulled his grandson into a hug, explaining in Spanish that he had heard them coming and thought they were thieves.

"*Cocodrilo maldito*," he said as he pointed to the crocodile and said he could get good money for the skin. Townsend nodded and said in Spanish that he understood the danger to the goats. The old man smiled broadly, revealing a toothless mouth. The young Cuban sailor introduced Townsend to his grandfather and explained that the Navy officer was *su capitán*, and that Jacobs was a Navy veteran.

The old man's face crinkled in an even wider grin, congratulating Townsend and Jacobs on winning the war. He said he hoped the American Navy would now invade Cuba and liberate the island from the Spanish. He pointed to the dead crocodile and said the Spanish were just the same. "*Los españoles son iguales a los cocodrilos, hijos de puta que son. ¡Ladrones y piratas!*" He called them sons of bitches and plunderers and thieves who expect anyone born in Cuba to serve the Spanish crown. They treat the Cuban *criollos* as peasants. That's why he left to come to Florida nearly twenty years ago.

Townsend nodded politely. He took a closer look at his host. With his faded pants and patched shirt, it was clear he was barely making ends meet. His hands were so calloused and cracked they looked like crocodile skin. The old man told his grandson to bring some chairs, instructing him to bring the big one for *el comandante*. Townsend smiled at this sudden promotion, and as a token of goodwill he bought one of the baskets the fisherman was making.

From his time living in Havana, Townsend was quite familiar with Cuban customs including the importance of gifts and compliments. After Townsend's purchase, the old man now insisted he call him Don José and handed him one of his hand-rolled cigars as a token of his appreciation. They talked about the hurricane and then Townsend asked him if he knew a young woman named Ángela. He explained that her family had come to Key West from Tampa and that her brother had fought for the Confederacy.

"*Sí, sí, Angelita Menéndez, como no. Conozco a la chica y a la familia también.*"

To Townsend's surprise, the old man said he knew Ángela and her family. He went on to explain that he had worked for Ángela's father, Rafael

Menéndez, for several years on one of his boats fishing for king mackerel until he found out about the man's past.

"*¿Qué pasó, Don José? ¿Algo serio?*" Townsend asked. He wanted to know what in the man's past would make Don José leave a job after several years.

The old man stopped to take a few puffs of his cigar and stared after the smoke as it drifted away.

"*Ese sinverguenza era negrero,*" replied the old man simply. "*¡Imagínase! Era negrero.*" Jacobs looked over at Townsend for an explanation. Townsend quickly translated.

"He says he worked for Ángela's father for several years on one of his fishing boats until he discovered that the man had been a slave trader, and then he quit."

"Oh, Lawd," Jacobs whispered.

Townsend turned back to the old fisherman and quickly resumed his conversation in Spanish. Don José said that Rafael Menéndez was once one of the favored ship captains for Julián Zulueta and Francisco Marty y Torréns, two of Cuba's biggest slave traders, until he was caught by a British Royal Navy gunboat with five hundred slaves on board and forced to leave Cuba. That was almost fifteen years ago in the early 1850s. Don José explained that the money Menéndez used to set up his fishing business in Tampa Bay all came from his slave trading profits. When he discovered where Menéndez's money came from, he walked off the job. He wanted nothing to do with his dirty money.

"*Dinero sucio,*" he said. "*Ha oído de esos dos piratas—Zulueta y Marty?*" he asked Townsend.

Townsend nodded but said nothing. He felt a wave of guilt sweep over him. Before he joined the Navy when he was in Cuba, he'd met both of those men. Together those two had brought in tens of thousands of African slaves into Cuba over the years. They were actually acquaintances of his grandmother—something he was not about to confess to the de la Cruzes or to Jacobs.

As he puffed on his cigar, de la Cruz went on to tell him how Rafael Menéndez bought a house in Key West just before the war and moved his family there. Unfortunately for him, he and his wife were both struck down by yellow fever. That left Ángela alone until her brother came home from the war.

"Her brother?" Townsend asked.

"*Sí, sí,* Francisco. *Un fanático,*" Don José said, shaking his head. "As a very young boy, he sailed with his father on several of those slave voyages, and then later here in Florida worked for him in the fishing business. That's when

I got to know him. He was always a crazy one. *Un muchacho cruel.* He liked to fight dogs, if I remember. He was part of a group of local *Confederados*, who called themselves the Key West Avengers. They all swore to fight against federal control of the Florida Keys. But the Confederacy wanted infantry men and they sent him and the others north to fight in Tennessee where instead of glory in the Confederate cause, they found starvation and chaos. I understand he's an angry man now. Keeps to himself. They say nowadays he's always sailing to Cuba."

"Cuba?" Townsend interjected. "He goes to Cuba. Any idea why?"

The old man avoided his gaze. *"No lo sé, Comandante."* He stopped himself and shrugged. *"No le podría decir."*

Townsend looked over at Jacobs, who seemed removed. He clearly couldn't follow any of the Spanish.

"¿Y Ángela Menéndez?" Townsend asked Don José, wondering how much the old man might know about her activities. *"¿Qué hace ella?"*

"Es costurera. Trabaja en su casa." A seamstress who works from home, Townsend whispered to himself. He asked for the address, and Don José told him that the Menéndez house was a few blocks from the Bight. The clerk at the ship chandlery on the corner of Caroline and Elisabeth Streets knows the family. He could make inquiries there.

Townsend repeated the directions to Jacobs, who nodded. As they departed, the old man motioned to Townsend and his grandson, and said to them in Spanish that none of what he'd said about the Menéndez family should be linked to him. As they departed, the old man gave them some advice.

"When you go to the house, I'd bring some of your Navy friends. They don't like strangers, and Ángela's brother is quick to anger, eager to pull a knife. *Tenga cuidado.* I'd be careful if I were you."

November 3

Their visit to the Menéndez household was delayed by the official Navy business of getting the *Rebecca* up on dry dock and repaired. Three days later, Townsend went with Jacobs to the address they'd been given by the clerk at the ship chandlery. Don José had asked Townsend not to bring his grandson with him because Menéndez might cause problems for the de la Cruz family.

Townsend agreed. He didn't want Jacobs to come either in case there was trouble, but the Navy veteran had dug in his heels.

"I ain' gon' follow yo' orders, Lieutenant," Jacobs said angrily. "No more bowing and sayin', *yes sah, no sah*. I dun me military time."

"Understood Jacobs. Just do me a favor and stay out of sight. Don José warned us we could get an unfriendly reception."

Townsend was nervous because he'd said nothing to the chief yeoman at Naval headquarters about what he was doing. He'd dressed in civilian clothes as he'd been asked to do before. Rather than make any inquiries to his superiors, he had decided that he would press ahead and continue the search on his own. He wanted to catch Hodge, and he didn't want to be told to stand down. All of that was freelancing. He knew that could get him into hot water with his commander.

As he stood outside the small frame house, Townsend could just barely see Jacobs crouching under a tamarind tree a block away. The house looked strangely familiar to him, but he wasn't sure why. He knocked on the door and almost fell backwards off the porch when he heard the growl of a large dog. The door opened and Townsend found himself staring at a man and a large bull mastiff dog. The brindle-colored dog growled, tugging at the leash, its hackles raised.

"What do you want?"

At the sight of the menacing dog, Townsend suddenly realized why the house was familiar. This was the man with the dog who had confronted him when he stepped ashore after the hurricane. He and another man had been repairing this porch and wanted his help. At first, Townsend thought his cover had been blown, but then he realized from the man's blank stare he hadn't recognized him without his Navy uniform. Townsend was about to ask for Ángela, but then he had a sudden change of plan. He found himself making up a story as he went along, trying to keep the uncertainty and tension out of his voice.

"I'm here from . . . from Curry's Salvage and General Merchandise Company on a matter of some importance. I'm looking for the captain and crew of the schooner *Hard Times*. I was told to come here."

"What!" the man asked, his dark, menacing eyes unable to hide his surprise—and his alarm. "Who told you to come here?"

From another room came a woman's voice.

"*¿Quién es?* Who is it, Pancho?"

Pancho. The name he'd heard that day when he came ashore after the hurricane. A common nickname for Francisco. Townsend was careful not to reveal anything. He just kept talking as he quietly took measure of the man and the dog. *Here is Francisco Menéndez, and the woman inside is probably Ángela.* Like a fisherman with a hook, he knew he needed to use the right bait to lure Hodge to the surface.

"Some sailors down at the docks told me to come here," Townsend said. "We need to find a man by the name of Ezekiel Hodge. Do you know him? He's the captain of the *Hard Times*. Wreckers spotted him coming to this house."

"I don't know anyone by that name," Menéndez said, his eyes blinking rapidly. The man's body was tense, his hands slightly trembling.

"*¡Coño! ¿Quién es este pendejo?*" Menéndez cursed under his breath.

The man had just insulted him and called him a terrible name, but Townsend blinked and pretended not to understand. "This is the Menéndez house, isn't it?" he asked innocently. "I was told you are a friend of Captain Hodge?"

The man's jaw clenched, and he shifted uneasily from one foot to the next as he turned his eyes away from Townsend to look back into the house. The Navy lieutenant knew he needed to plunge ahead with more questions. He didn't wait for an answer.

"Our wrecking boats found the *Hard Times* a couple of days ago, and they've recovered some of the cargo, even some of the personal effects. We need to contact Captain Hodge right away. He may need to make a report to the Navy before he can make a claim. Apparently, there are some serious questions about what they found. . . . Quite serious questions."

Townsend knew he was definitely operating outside his original orders to not tip off Hodge, but he found himself caught up in his assumed role as a salvage wrecker with Curry's, and he couldn't stop. He was enjoying himself.

"Is someone asking for Zeke?" Ángela asked in Spanish from behind the door.

Zeke was Ezekiel Hodge. "Is that your wife?" Townsend asked. "Does she know this man, Hodge?"

The thin man ignored Townsend and rattled off instructions to Ángela in Spanish. He told her to go to the boat right away and tell Zeke they found the *Hard Times*. The Navy wants to talk to him. This could be trouble.

"Maybe your wife knows Captain Hodge? Can you ask her?"

Pancho Menéndez blew up at Townsend, cursing him in Spanish.

"That's my sister, you shit-eating carpetbagger!" He grabbed a rifle from behind the door and pointed it at Townsend's stomach. "Get out of here, and don't come back or I'll let my dog take a piece out of your leg."

As if on cue, the dog lunged at Townsend, its teeth bared. The man yanked at the leash of the growling dog and pulled him back.

"*Quieto, Macho.* Now beat it," he said to Townsend.

Townsend tipped his hat. "I'm sorry to have upset anyone, sir." A plan was beginning to form as he walked away from the house. He glanced back to see if they were watching him. Pancho Menéndez held the rifle over his shoulder. There was a woman by his side. As soon as he rounded the corner at Elisabeth Street, Townsend spotted Jacobs sitting in the shade of a tamarind tree.

"Ángela will be leaving the house soon. She's going to the ship where Hodge is hiding."

Jacobs' face lit up with astonishment. "Hodge is here, in a boat?"

Townsend nodded. "Follow her, but stay back. I'll go a different way to the shoreline road."

As soon as he reached the road along the water, Townsend took cover behind a barnacle-encrusted sponge boat that had been pulled up onto the shore for repairs. He didn't have to wait long. He spotted Jacobs first and then across the street he could see the tall, slim young woman in rustling black, wearing an embroidered white silk blouse that covered her neck and arms. She had a veil over her head, but Townsend could see the dark hair with dangling curls, her jaw set.

Townsend watched as Ángela began waving her hands at the boats anchored offshore. She approached a man who was repairing his fishing nets, who seemed to know her. After a short conversation, the man picked up a conch shell and blew it like a trumpet. Townsend could now see some movement in the fleet of boats. A man on board a large dark green schooner got into an open launch boat and rowed ashore. He embraced Ángela.

Townsend moved closer. He could see the man's face. Sandy hair, a bramble of side whiskers, and a fuzzy beard. It was one of the men he'd seen escaping from the deck of the USS *New Berne*. The one with the blue eyes. It was Ezekiel Hodge. After talking with Ángela, the man began pacing back and forth like a caged tiger.

Crouching behind trees along the shoreline to stay out of sight, Townsend approached Jacobs who was sitting down, pretending to be cracking open a coconut. Townsend nodded in the direction of Ángela and her companion.

"You see that man, with the woman in the veil?"

Jacobs nodded as he stared at the man.

"That's Hodge. I have no doubt." Townsend said. He could see the muscles in Jacobs' jaw and neck tense up even as his eyes gleamed with intensity. Jacobs leapt up, but Townsend managed to pull him down when they spotted some men running toward the couple. One of them was Menéndez with his dog. The other had a shiny bald head and a badger-like face, which

Townsend remembered only too well. He was the other ex-Confederate who had accosted him when he had come ashore.

"Stay hidden," Townsend said. "I'm going to report this to the Naval Squadron headquarters—the Navy shore patrol will come and arrest these men. Watch them so we know where they go. Don't let them see you."

Jacobs nodded, crouching again, but his jaw remained taut and clenched. An hour later Townsend was back with the shore patrol officers. It had taken him a longer time than expected because he had to make a formal request for the shore patrol to the chief yeoman. He was expecting he would find Jacobs where he left him, but to his surprise there was no one there. No sign of Hodge, Ángela, or her brother. He scanned the fleet of boats. The dark green schooner was gone. Finally, he spotted the man on the shoreline whom Ángela had spoken with, and he walked up to him. He was a Cuban fisherman and Townsend spoke to him in Spanish.

"*Buenos días, señor*, I need to ask you a question."

The man ignored him, but then Townsend spoke to him again, this time introducing himself as a Navy officer. "Where did the girl go, the one you were speaking with? Ángela. Where is she? Tell me or these policemen will have to shackle and cuff you."

The fisherman looked past Townsend at the approaching officers of the Navy shore patrol. He hesitated, but when Townsend jingled some coins the man gave him a licentious grin.

"Pretty girl. You like her? *Ángelita es bonita, ¿verdad?*"

"Where is the schooner?" Townsend asked.

"They left," the man said as he waved at the harbor. "They left in Don Pancho's schooner. They sailed to the north toward Fleming's Key, headed for New Orleans."

"The woman too?"

"*Sí.*"

"Anyone else?"

"*Un negro.*"

"What!" Townsend's eyes shot wide. "What did he look like?"

"Thin man, blue pants, white shirt. He wore spectacles."

"What happened? Did they capture him? Was there a fight?"

"No, no fight. He approached them. Looked like he was asking for a job. They hit him around the head, called him some names. He looked scared, but it seemed like he wanted to go with them." The man shrugged.

"*Gracias, señor*," said Townsend, pressing a few coins into the man's hand. He dismissed the patrol officers and cursed under his breath. He grimaced as he began to understand what had happened. He'd let Hodge get away, and now Jacobs was gone. He should have known Jacobs would feel he had no choice but to get on that boat. As he'd said, Hodge was the only one who could help him find his two sons.

Townsend's mind was cluttered with a range of different emotions. He shut his eyes against the guilt. He had never told Jacobs what he feared had happened to his sons. He had never warned him about the Cuban possibility—that his sons, and now he, could be enslaved again. Townsend put that thought out of his mind.

He feared facing Major Hutchinson and Commander Ransom. They would be furious that Hodge and his men had escaped. As he headed to Naval headquarters to make his report, he prepared himself for the worst. To his surprise, he found the building abuzz with the news that the former attorney general of the Confederacy, George Davis, had been arrested in Key West where he'd been hiding out, waiting to escape to the Bahamas. Two other ex-Confederate cabinet members, Breckinridge and Benjamin, had successfully fled from Florida to the Bahamas and Cuba months earlier. The Navy wanted to make sure Davis was sent to prison.

Townsend finally found a moment to inform Commander Ransom that he had information about Hodge and his men. "I regret to report, sir, that Hodge and his men escaped. They slipped away on a dark green schooner headed for New Orleans . . ."

"I suspected as much," the commander replied. "Major Hutchinson told me before he left that he was sure they were already heading back to New Orleans."

"Major Hutchinson has left Key West?"

"Yes, he told me he thought there was inconclusive evidence of kidnapping or murder on that shipwreck you found, and he needed to get back. He assured me they would look for Hodge and his men there."

"But Commander, with due respect, what if Hodge is indeed kidnapping and carrying American freedmen to Cuba? Are we just letting this man escape? We could send one of our ships and try to overtake him. We might catch that green schooner before it gets to—"

"Enough, Lieutenant! Any investigation of that varmint is a matter for the Bureau of Military Information in New Orleans and the Provost Marshal there. I'm sure Major Hutchinson knows what he's doing. Those Army officers may arrest Hodge for stealing and smuggling federal cotton. But as far as this kidnapping to Cuba business is concerned, it's still conjecture. Those men may very well have been bound for some sawmill in Florida. Forget about Mr. Hodge, Townsend. It's not your problem. It's an Army matter. That's an order."

Townsend bit his lip.

"But sir—"

"It's not the Navy's concern, Lieutenant. My priority now is putting that Confederate big wig Davis on the USS *Memphis* when she comes into port. That's going to be your assignment, Townsend. I want that traitor locked up tight in that ship's stink-hole bilges. Understood! Then I want you and your schooner to head back to Fort Jefferson on another resupply mission."

Townsend clenched his jaw. "Aye, aye, Sir."

11

January 9, 1866

There were no windows in the Navy grog house, so the dim light from kerosene lamps spilled out into the smoke-filled room like shafts of moonlight in a moist fog. Townsend pulled out one of the hand-rolled cigars he'd bought in town and lit it with a Lucifer match. He rubbed the scruffy beard that now covered his chin and cheeks. He knew he looked terrible. He hadn't shaved for weeks. *Might as well let it grow*, he mused.

Even though it was still morning, Townsend picked up the bottle of rum on the table and poured himself another glass. He, Langworth, and Metcalf were on liberty after returning to Key West from a lengthy voyage up the eastern coast of Florida. De la Cruz and Tollman had remained on board the ship. His head was swirling in waves, but he didn't care. *Damn the entire coast of Florida with its swarms of skeeters and no-see-ums*. He'd had his fill of Florida's bugs and the oppressive heat.

Ever since the surprise arrest of the former Confederate attorney general in Key West two months ago, the Navy had kept them busy, supplying Fort Jefferson and patrolling up and down the Florida coastline. Townsend had seen how white resentment was growing. The former Confederates wanted revenge. As bad as the situation was, the Army knew it would be worse if their soldiers withdrew. The war was over, the Union saved, but the problems were far from solved.

He and his crew had also continued to pursue persistent reports of freedmen disappearing on board ships. Their most recent assignment had been to sail up to the sparsely settled Indian River area. The federal government had received a letter from a Florida district judge advising them that two loads of American freedmen had already been taken to Cuba. Suspicions centered on a man named Henry Titus, who military authorities called "an avowed unreconstructed rebel." Townsend had found the man and his recently purchased steamship, but he could find nothing to link Titus to kidnapping or Cuba. It was just like with Hodge and his cohort Menéndez, he'd told the crew. There was plenty of smoke everywhere but no fire.

A fast-picking banjo and a lively fiddle startled him from his brooding. Behind the dusky silhouettes of a few bar girls, some newly arrived sailors had launched into a popular sea chantey called "The Hog-Eyed Man." Metcalf, his square face now flush with rum and beer, stood up and began singing. The fiddle picked up tempo and began freewheeling and wailing away. Metcalf went into full cry as he stomped his feet along with the other sailors.

> "Oh, Sally's in the garden sifting sand.
> with her hog-eyed man hand in hand
> Steady on the jig with a hog-eye, oh
> She wants the hog-eyed man."

Townsend smiled and shook his head—a solid dosage of rum had turned the bosun's normally reserved demeanor on its head. He knew that all four seamen on the USS *Rebecca* were increasingly restless and wanted a discharge. The eighteen dollars a month salary was hardly an incentive for any of them to stay in the Navy. The bosun made a little more than that, but not much.

Langworth watched with a pinched face, his scraggily beard and hangdog eyes making him look like unfriendly company. Sailing these past few months with him, Townsend had gained some insight into this strangely quiet man. He had told Townsend he fought for the Union, not because he wanted equal rights for the Black man, but out of hatred for the Confederate zealots. They'd burned his house down and taken his wife to a camp near Tallahassee, all because he refused to serve for three years. When he learned that his wife had died in that camp, he joined the Union Navy. It was all about rendering justice, he'd said.

"Langworth, I'd like your opinion. What do you make of all of these reports of kidnapping? Seems like there's a lot of mud on the wall, don't it?"

"You want mah opinion . . . Cap'n?"

"You're a true Floridian, man. My curiosity is genuine."

Langworth did know the mindset of the crackers and the planters. Early in the war he'd worked as a Florida swamp cowboy running cattle north to feed the Confederate armies. He was from the town of Brooksville, a place that took its name from Preston Brooks, the South Carolina congressman who almost beat to death the abolitionist Senator Charles Sumner with his cane on the Senate floor back in 1856.

"Cap'n, my hometown is alive with angry men. I'm willin' to bet my salvation that thar's plenty of Negro stealin' going on, all the way to the Alabama border. Those people went to war for slavery and still see nuttin' wrong with it."

With a pause in the singing, Metcalf fell heavily into his chair opposite the two men and grabbed the bottle of rum on the table as Langworth continued talking.

"It's just like sellin' cotton—makin' a speculation on Blacks is something these people are accustomed to doing. Simple as that."

Metcalf shot Langworth a piercing look.

"You think it's justified?" the bosun asked Langworth.

"I didn't say *nuttin'* about what's right or wrong," Langworth replied. He put the cigar down, pulled out a plug of Virginia tobacco, and began chewing on it. "Southerners are like cats being picked up by the tail. The federal government dun' freed their slaves and given them no compensation for their loss. The Union armies have seized plantations. Southerners been left with nuttin' but blackened buildings and debt. I will say this—the federals think the dust has settled now and the war is over. Wa'll in my opinion, the dust here in Florida is still pretty thick. There's still a score to settle."

Townsend sighed and downed another glass of the Havana rum he liked so much.

"So, you're siding with the Rebs now, are ye," growled Metcalf as he grabbed Langworth by the collar and pulled the smaller man up on his feet. "Feeling sorry for your own kind, are ye?"

"Wait a minute, Metcalf," Townsend said, holding his arm out. "Let him speak his mind. I asked. He's just answering my question."

"You got no cause to call me a Reb," Langworth cried out. "I'm wearin' a blue coat, ain't I? Cause of this uniform, I've paid a price. Those snake-faced, regulator critturs in my hometown would damn well string me up from a tree—"

Before Langworth could finish, a petty officer from Naval headquarters interrupted.

"Lieutenant Townsend! Commander Ransom wants you to report to the USS *Yucca* immediately."

Townsend shook his head as he plopped back in his seat. "Is that right? I'm afraid that won't be possible, Ensign. I'm busy." He took another drink, knowing full well that this would only irritate the junior officer even more.

"These orders came directly from the commander, Lieutenant."

"What's the occasion?" Townsend asked cheekily.

"He says you are not to delay. He wants you on board ship immediately. I'm to escort you there."

Metcalf and Langworth chuckled as Townsend made his way to his feet and followed the junior officer through the door of the grog house.

As he climbed the ship's rope ladder and surfaced on deck, Townsend could feel all the rum swirling in his head. It took him a moment to steady himself on the rail. A group of sailors were rubbing up the brass of the ship's thirty-pound Parrott rifle gun. Others were scrubbing the deck. The USS *Yucca* was small by steam gunboat standards at only 145 feet in length, but it was brand new, commissioned by the Navy shortly before the war's end.

A smiling Commander Ransom dressed in his formal blue coat greeted Townsend in a spacious saloon area with a dining room and a small library. He was standing next to a tall, thin, well-dressed man who had the look of a city dweller with smooth skin, well-oiled hair, and neatly trimmed sideburns. He was carrying a dispatch bag.

"Ah, Townsend, there you are. I have an important matter to discuss with you. I want you to meet Mr. William Rudd. Mr. Rudd works closely with Secretary of State Seward. He has come all the way from Washington."

Townsend not so much stepped but swayed forward to shake the man's hand. Commander Ransom approached him but then recoiled and turned his head away. The expression on his face made Townsend think of a saucer of curdled milk, or of someone who had just picked up some dirty socks.

"You been drinking, Townsend?"

"I had liberty, sir. I was just relaxin'," he slurred. "I may have downed a few glasses with a couple of my men. I'm alright—it's the boat that's rockin'."

Ransom turned to Rudd with pursed lips.

"As I told you, Mr. Rudd, Townsend may not be the most reliable man for the job. I have other officers . . ."

"That's quite alright, Commander Ransom. Townsend is who we want. We are quite aware of his past record—good and bad."

Ransom didn't say anything, but he glowered in Townsend's direction. Townsend blinked and focused his energy on standing up straight. He could feel Rudd's eyes on him. Commander Ransom escorted his guest along with Townsend to a small table in the saloon.

"As I was saying, Mr. Rudd, I believe some of the Southerners who've taken refuge in Mexico need to be watched, I fear they have dreams of a slave empire there. France's continued occupation of Mexico makes for a very unstable situation. It may be important to keep an active Naval station here."

Standing beside the table were two wild-eyed sailors with disheveled, matted hair, ready to serve the lunch. They looked like stray cats with their smudgy, forlorn faces. *Where did Ransom find these men?* Townsend guessed they were poor immigrants, crimped by the Navy from the New York docks for war duty.

"What will you be serving us today, sailor?" Ransom asked with a smug smile.

"Der cook dun prepared sum green tuttle soup, sir."

"And the main plate, steward?"

The man paused as he looked nervously over at the other seaman, who immediately chimed in.

"Sum fishy fish, sir."

Ransom stared at both men, his face turning beet red.

"Fishy-fish?" declared Ransom as he tugged at his long beard like a church bell ringer pulling on the bell rope. "Tarnation! What in blazes is a fishy-fish, man! You are a couple of worthless chowderheads with the brains of fruit flies!" He waved them off and cleared his throat, seeming to pretend not to hear Rudd's laugh.

"So, Lieutenant. I know you are wondering why you are here."

"Yes, sir."

"To be direct and to the point, you have a new assignment, Townsend. We are sending you to Cuba."

The blood drained from Townsend's face, and his back stiffened. The ship started to roll back and forth, or was it the rum? He closed his eyes, which only made his head swirl.

"Do you have a problem with that, Townsend?"

"No, sir."

Townsend blinked rapidly. He thought of his experiences on that island before joining the Navy—which included being thrown into the Spanish dungeon at El Presidio in Havana. He'd been forced to work for a Spanish merchant supplying arms to the Confederacy and had been lucky to escape from the island with his life when the man discovered he was spying for the

North. He had nightmares about that man—Don Pedro Alvarado Cardona. Last he'd heard, Don Pedro had been banished from Cuba by the Spanish government when word had reached England of his involvement in the murders of an English diplomat and an English detective. Townsend had helped uncover Don Pedro's ties to those crimes, and as a result the Spanish merchant had tried to kill him.

"The Spanish are holding an American-flagged merchant ship. It seems there's been a murder of an American sailor there that requires an investigation."

"Investigation, sir?"

"Holy good Jesus, man, are you deaf or just bamboozled with grog? Steward, bring this officer some coffee. Sober up, man. Mr. Rudd, are you quite certain I can't assign a more . . . serious officer to the case?"

Rudd's face betrayed no emotion. "I have the utmost confidence in Lieutenant Townsend's abilities."

Ransom pulled on his long beard and turned back to Townsend.

"Where was I? The murder took place in one of them sugar outports on the northern coast. Busy place with lots of American ships. The main town is called Sagua la Grande, but they call the port settlement Sagua. Ever heard of it?"

"I've heard mention of the town, Commander," Townsend said. He knew that Sagua was to the east of Cárdenas and Matanzas, but he didn't know much more than that.

"Good. We need to do our own investigation, but the Spanish police and Navy are not being cooperative. They are preventing our consular agent from having any access to the ship or any ability to interview the sailors on board. We haven't even been given the name of the man who was killed or if there are any suspects. The Spanish say our consul has no authority in such sensitive matters. They believe his only function is to deal with passports and shipping matters. We are in complete disagreement, but then that's a legal and diplomatic matter that won't be resolved quickly. At any rate, they finally have agreed to allow an American military official to come to the port of Sagua to conduct interviews. The Spanish seem to value men in uniform so that's where you come in, Townsend. We want to know the name of the man who was killed and who was responsible. If the murder suspect is an American, we need to know that."

"Aye, aye, sir."

One of the mop-haired stewards brought Townsend a cup of coffee, and he quickly drank it, nodding his appreciation to the man.

"From the port of Sagua you will go to Havana. I will let Mr. Rudd explain the full reason for your mission there. Here are your written orders, Lieutenant."

Ransom pushed a brown envelope across the table.

"Make sure your ship is ready for departure by tomorrow."

"Aye, aye, sir."

The commander excused himself, leaving Townsend alone with the man from Washington. Rudd took a cigar from one of the stewards and immediately began rolling it back and forth in his mouth before looking Townsend in the eye.

"How are you feeling now, Lieutenant? Head any clearer?"

Townsend nodded as he continued to sip his coffee. "Much better, sir."

Rudd pulled a letter from his dispatch bag and handed it to Townsend. It had florid writing and at the bottom of the page a waxed imprint and a signature from an official, who signed his name with the title, "Minister Plenipotentiary of her Catholic Majesty."

"This letter is from the Minister of the Spanish Legation in Washington, Gabriel Tassara. He has agreed to our sending a military man. It is nothing more than a courtesy letter asking for the local authorities in the port of Sagua to cooperate with you. I don't need to tell you, Townsend, this is no guarantee, but it may help you in certain situations."

"Aye, aye, sir," Townsend stammered, nodding his head even as he felt a measure of doubt sweep through him. "Excuse me for asking, Mr. Rudd. Why me? Like Commander Ransom said, I may not be the right choice."

"We've heard good things about you, Townsend."

"But . . . but you may not be aware—I've run into problems in Cuba before." Don Pedro's face again flashed into his mind. His finely chiseled features, the hair slicked back tight against his skull, his twisted smile. He could only hope that this dangerous man wouldn't be allowed back on the island. Don Pedro had a certain malignant charm and many powerful connections. Even Townsend's grandmother greatly admired him. She had tried to force his mother to marry Don Pedro, no small part of the reason his mother had fled to the United States.

"Not to worry, Lieutenant. Your service as an informant during the war in Havana before you joined the Navy did not go unnoticed. We know from talking with our Acting Consul General in Havana during the war, Thomas Savage, who is now on leave in the United States, that you are a good intelligence man. He said you supplied him with the details of Confederate agents and slaving interests in Havana, which led to the capture of a Confederate ship. Is that correct?"

"Yes, sir."

"And you speak Spanish?"

"Yes, sir."

"And, well, you also have been involved recently in a matter that interests the federal government," Rudd said. He gave Townsend a sharp look as he smoothed down his already slicked-back hair. "Nothing I'm about to tell you is written down in your official orders. Understood, Lieutenant? There is more here than just a dockside mugging. The murdered man came in to see the American consul agent in the port of Sagua a day before he was killed. Said he wanted to make a statement about what he called 'some foul dealin'' on board ship. Unfortunately, the consul didn't take him seriously, and of course the sailor never returned."

"What's the name of the ship?"

"*Southern Cross*. US flagged ship out of New Orleans. A brigantine schooner said to be a former Confederate blockade runner because of the lead gray color of the hull. Some of us think it's possible this ship has something to do with these kidnappings of freedmen that I know you've been investigating."

Townsend's eyebrow lifted. He felt the coffee taking its effect, clearing his head.

"The Secretary of State has demanded more information as soon as possible."

"Sir!" exclaimed Townsend. "The Secretary of State?"

"Secretary Seward and his entourage will arrive in Havana on January 20 on board the USS *De Soto*, his last stop on a swing through the Caribbean before returning to Washington. In Cuba, we expect this sensitive matter will be discussed with the Spanish Captain General Domingo Dulce, discreetly of course. This visit is an important one to reestablish our relations with Spain now that the Confederacy is in the dustbin of history. He will see you at his hotel after his arrival."

"What is Secretary Seward expecting to get from me?"

"Well, for one thing, his confidential personal correspondence over these past two weeks," Rudd replied as he handed him the dispatch bag. "You are to hand this bag with the letters and documents over to him, and no one else. Is that understood?"

"Yes, sir."

"Beyond your courier duties, Townsend, the Secretary will want a thorough briefing on your intelligence in a written report. You may also brief him on what you've found out over these past months patrolling the coasts of Florida."

Rudd now stood up and walked over to one of the portholes looking out at the harbor.

"Any new information you discover about that ship's so-called foul dealing, you are to report to Secretary Seward, and only to him. He will decide if he wants to involve you further, and no doubt will explain why this incident is so important to us."

"What am I to say to the American Consul General in Havana?"

Rudd rolled his eyes and sighed.

"You will have to go see him, of course. That is protocol for any visiting US Navy ship. I will say that William Minor is a good man. Appointed by President Lincoln. He was a former governor in his home state of Connecticut. You didn't meet him when you were in Cuba?"

"No, sir. I believe he arrived after I'd left Havana."

"Well, he has been in Cuba for the last two years, and served honorably. Let me just say he is anxious to get home. The Spanish have persuaded him that no American freedmen have been re-enslaved in Cuba. He believes them. I'm convinced that he's convinced—but I'm not certain he's right. As far as he is concerned, you should tell him that your report is for Secretary Seward only. That's all he needs to know."

"Aye, aye, sir."

"Lieutenant, remember you're there to get *information*, nothing more. I know about your . . . reputation. We don't need more diplomatic drama with the all-too-sensitive Spanish. Do you understand?"

Townsend took a deep breath and nodded. "Aye, aye, sir."

HAVANA, CUBA

Part Two

"The island is rich, production is large, commerce flourishes . . . and if a man does not concern himself with political or religious questions, he has nothing to fear."

—Richard Henry Dana,
To Cuba and Back, 1859

12

January 10, 1866

In the gray light before dawn, the sailors on board the USS *Rebecca* weighed anchor and headed for Cuba with only a whisper of wind to fill the sails. Their destination, the port of Sagua, was two hundred miles to the southeast, directly into the wind. The Naval supply yard had given them provisions for two weeks—everything from barreled meats and bags of flour to canned goods and potatoes. Little was said on board as the gunboat schooner silently slid through the calm, glassy water off Key West's Marine Hospital.

Townsend pulled out a cigar and lit it. He looked at the dark harbor, nearly empty of Navy vessels in so-called peacetime. The war had torn up the fabric of the country, ripping apart towns and families like some kind of giant threshing machine. His own brother had died at Antietam fighting for Lee's Army and the Confederacy. His brother's decision to join the rebel cause had broken their family, just like the war had broken the country. And now his immediate family was gone.

Townsend took a few more puffs on his cigar as a way to soothe the nagging unease seeping into his mind. He looked up at the dark parapets of Fort Taylor, where he could see the ghostly silhouette of a soldier on guard duty. He watched the armed sentry walk back and forth. *Nothing I'm about to tell you,* Rudd had said, *is written down in your official orders.* At the time it hadn't dawned on him fully what the State Department man was saying. But now it hit him. He was being sent on a secret intelligence gathering mission in a foreign country disguised to look like an approved diplomatic visit. That troubling insight lingered like the taste of the bitter fruit from one of old Sandy Cornish's tamarind trees.

The bosun emerged on deck, bringing the coffee pot and his mug. Red-eyed and pale-faced, Metcalf looked in worse shape than Townsend and Langworth after twenty-four hours of drinking. They'd had to retrieve him last night from the Navy grog house.

"Thought we might need some coffee before the serious sailing begins, Cap'n," the bosun muttered as he placed the coffee pot on the top of the wheelhouse. Townsend turned up his nose. He had already sampled Metcalf's early morning brew and had found it undrinkable.

"I already had some," he lied. "But from the looks of you, Metcalf, you'll be needing the extra mugfuls. Here, take the wheel. I need to inspect the ship."

Townsend walked forward to check that all the hatches were toggled down. The only noise in the harbor came from a few squawking seagulls following a small flotilla of Bahamian fishing smacks and sponge boats headed out to the reef. In the half gloom, Townsend could see the men were preparing to raise the heavy mainsail. De la Cruz and Langworth stood on the starboard side holding onto the peak halyard. Tollman was on the port side, ready to pull up the throat halyard. With the clicking of mast hoops and the creaking of blocks, the men began to heave away and the big sail slowly traveled up the tall mast.

Townsend told Metcalf to steer toward the Sand Key lighthouse some ten miles away to the southwest that was easy to spot with its fixed light and intermittent flashes. The Navy lieutenant puffed away on his cigar as his gaze lingered on the broad-shouldered bosun. He had grown fond of this Penobscot River man. He chuckled to himself at Metcalf's story about why people in Maine have a dark turn of mind. "Too many snow and ice storms in April," he'd said. "The pessimists Down East say the winter weather can't get any worse, but the optimists say, oh yes it can." Townsend had told him the Key West version. "The pessimists say you're gonna catch yellow jack. The optimists say, no you won't, you're jes' gonna catch a case of the French pox." Townsend remembered how hard they'd both laughed, guffawing like two schoolboys.

With a freshening early morning breeze, the schooner was soon heeling over on a southwesterly course toward the Sand Key lighthouse. Townsend continued checking the portholes and hatches amidships. He watched as the shadowy forms of the men tied down the mainsail halyard lines and then neatly coiled the excess rope on the deck in front of the pins as he'd ordered. He could hear the men talking about Havana.

"Ain' been to Havana since I was a boy, but *Dios mío, es un paraíso* for sailors—the women, the gambling, the taverns and bodegas. All the rum and cigars you could want. It's paradise compared to Key West," said de la Cruz.

"It's no paradise for Black sailors," Langworth said. He looked over at Tollman. "Foreign Negro sailors ain't welcome ashore in Cuba. If they catch you, they might sell you as a slave. That's what I heard."

"Stop ya stupidness," Tollman said angrily. "Ya talkin' nonsense. I deh a free man now. Same as you."

"Shut your pan, Langworth," Metcalf said. "Every time you open your mouth, cowchips fly out."

"I ain' lying, bosun," Langworth said. "What I'm saying is true. They treat a Negro like a gentleman in Florida compared to what they do in Cuba. Ain't it so, Cap'n?"

Townsend looked at the men as they waited for his answer. Cuba was a complex racial mix. Roughly half the population was white, half Black. There were free Blacks, but the vast majority of the Black population were slaves. Article 21 of the Captain of the Port regulations in Havana stated that all Colored sailors, slave or free, arriving from foreign countries were required to be sent to a holding cell if they came ashore, or pay a hefty security bond of one thousand dollars to be returned only when the Negro was removed from the island. Townsend had heard of Black sailors who disobeyed this rule and ended up disappearing from the Havana docks. Without the proper papers, they could indeed be taken to the plantations to work as field slaves. He gave Langworth a rueful look, but then nodded his head. He looked over at Tollman. "You'll need to stay aboard the *Rebecca*. I wish it were otherwise. It's for your safety."

Townsend watched as Stumpie Tollman turned, walked up toward the bow, and stood there alone, looking back forlornly toward Key West. Even in the dim light, he could see the wistful look on the man's face. Townsend thought about talking to him. He took one step toward the man, but the steely look from Tollman stopped him. He knew he should have warned him about these restrictions, but there hadn't been time. He realized he had little solace to offer.

The truth was, Townsend was nervous not just about his men's safety but also about his returning to Cuba. He was quite familiar with the dangers of Cuba's ports where floating bodies in the water were as common as pieces of driftwood. He was glad the darkness allowed him to conceal his furrowed brow. It wasn't just his own personal history. He knew the Spanish didn't like any interference in their affairs, particularly on the slavery issue. During the war, Spanish Cuba, while technically neutral, had been a center of Confederate activity. He'd seen that firsthand.

Townsend had heard that the Spanish authorities were more cooperative now with the US Navy, but he was certain they would not take kindly to a US Navy officer poking around a murder case or asking sensitive questions about stories of kidnapped American freedmen. That must be the reason why the Naval commander had left the cabin for Rudd's unofficial briefing. Ransom wanted no connection with this off-record mission in case the lieutenant ran into trouble.

As the schooner neared the Sand Key lighthouse tower, a sudden burst of morning sunlight revealed the jade and turquoise waters speckled with dangerous coral heads. With the tall tower directly ahead of them, Townsend signaled to the crew to pull in the sails and gestured with his other hand to Metcalf to tighten their heading and steer toward the Rock Key Channel.

"Close hauled to Cuba, Mr. Metcalf," Townsend called out.

"Aye, aye, sir."

As the schooner's heavy bow heeled sharply in response to the stiffening breeze, the men hauled in the sheets even more tightly. Townsend breathed in the tangy salt air, enjoying the sudden speed and the pitch and heave of the ship as they headed out the channel into the deeper blue of the Florida Straits. He closed his eyes, listening to the welcome hum of the rigging and the splashing of water against the hull.

For the moment, his worries were behind him, along with the memories of the war. He focused his mind on the voyage ahead. He knew it was going to be a wet, brutal ride. The southerly course he'd chosen would cut across the axis of the Florida Stream, so he hoped this would give them a slightly favorable push to the east. They would need it. It would take them a couple of days to get to Sagua.

With plenty of open water ahead of them, Townsend walked down the companionway stairs. He could hear the sputtering of eggs on the frying pan. The smell of smoke from the cabin mingling with the aroma of smoked pork drifted up to him. He found de la Cruz leaning over the wood-burning stove pulling out some johnnycake as a fresh pot of coffee was brewed.

"I hope this is better than the early batch of tar water Metcalf prepared?"

"Aye, Cap'n. This is strong coffee, *estilo Cubano*. It will give you a jolt and make your heart race."

"Sounds like having a brush with some of those barmaids in the grog house," Langworth said as he poked his head down the hatch.

"This is better," de la Cruz said.

"Better than making a stitch with a bar maid?" Langworth asked. "I better tell the bosun."

The young Cuban sailor laughed. "Well, maybe not, but it's the best you can get on a Navy ship."

Townsend helped de la Cruz put the food on platters, and then he pulled out a frayed Blunt chart of the Old Bahamas Channel from 1858. When they were getting the boat ready to sail, Townsend had been surprised to find out that de la Cruz was familiar with the northern coast. The Cuban-born sailor had spent his childhood fishing with his father near where they were going. He had grown up in a town not far away from the port of Sagua called Cai-barién, another shipping outport for sugar and tobacco.

With the chart spread out on the table, Townsend drew his finger along a chain of barrier islands and reefs off the Cuban coast stretching for nearly three hundred miles to the southeast, all the way from Icacos Point in the western province of Matanzas to the Bay of Nuevitas.

"What can you tell me about these waters, de la Cruz? They look as peril-ous as the Marquesas and the Tortugas."

"This was *la ruta antigua*, the old sea route for the Spanish treasure fleets, the way they returned to *España*," de la Cruz said, pausing to sip his coffee. "The *corsarios* would wait for them, hidden behind these barrier islands. Francis Drake, Henry Morgan, the Dutchman El Griffe—they all ambushed the treasure ships from here. The King's Gardens, *Jardínes del Rey*. That's what the Spanish explorer, Diego Velásquez named them in 1513. Named in honor of King Ferdinand II of Aragón."

"How is it that you know all of this, de la Cruz?" Townsend munched on a piece of johnnycake and smoked pork.

"*Mi madre*, my mother taught me. My father was a fisherman, but my mother was well-educated. She always told me we were descendants of the Cuban pirate Diego Grillo who sailed with Morgan."

"Descended from a pirate, you say? Maybe your ancestor and Henry Morgan were just tending the King's Gardens with their pistols and drawn cutlasses?" Townsend said with a half chuckle.

The young Cuban sailor laughed, almost choking on a mouthful of cof-fee. "*Sí, sí*, they were the King's gardeners, pruning and trimming, keeping it tidy." De la Cruz turned his attention back to the eggs on his plate. With his fork in his hand, he pointed to their destination on the chart. It was on a peninsula sheltered by several barrier islands.

"That's where we're headed, Cap'n. The port of Sagua is known for the river, the *Río Sagua la Grande*, one of the two biggest rivers in Cuba. The river has a colorful history. Full of legends about pirates and, yes, some treasure too. Runaway slaves live nearby in some caves. They are armed with machetes. People are afraid to go there."

Townsend cocked his head at the mention of slaves. "How far can you get up that river in a boat?" Townsend asked.

"Some fifteen miles. Are we going up the river, Cap'n? It's prime sugar growing land. Rich soil."

Townsend said nothing, still staring at the map. He finished eating his eggs, smoked pork, and johnnycake. He had told the men what their written orders were, but nothing more. He bit his lip as he thought of Levi Jacobs and his two sons. For all he knew, all three of them could be in Cuba now, brought there and sold by Ezekiel Hodge. It was only a few days' sail from the northern coast of Florida to this part of Cuba. Several hundred miles across the Old Bahamas Channel was all that separated freedom and enslavement for someone who was Black.

By nightfall, they were some fifteen miles off the Cuban coastline. Townsend could just make out the dark shape of the high mountain called Pan de Matanzas that told him they were still 120 miles west of their destination. He scanned the dark, shadowy coast. The reality of returning to Cuba now confronted him. He had been born and raised in Havre de Grace, a Maryland boy with Chesapeake mud in his toes. But his mother's family had deep roots in Spanish Cuba. He knew he was a stranger to this island, but he recognized he was connected to it nonetheless.

Townsend stared out into the blackness. Pinpricks of light were visible here and there, presumably the red fires shining from the furnaces at the sugar mills. They burned night and day. Somewhere in the dark interior to the south of Matanzas was the plantation where his mother had grown up and where his grandmother still lived. He shivered at his memory of the place. Mon Bijou, my jewel in French. He imagined hearing the clanging of the plantation bells over the sound of the wind blowing against his face. The Black figures crashing and crackling through the sugar cane fields, swinging their machetes all under the dominion of the whip. He'd come to know the harshness of slavery in Cuba, the brutality in the fields. He'd only spent a week there, but the memory had stayed with him like the bitter taste of lime juice.

He looked up at the deep gray-black sky. On his grandmother's plantation, the nine chimes of Vespers would now be sounding, signaling the end of the day. The field slaves would be herded into the padlocked barracks called the *barracón* until the predawn hours when the bells would toll again. He remembered at night listening to the African drum beating out the rhythm accompanied by the wild songs and shouts. He would wake up to the chimes of bells the next morning and hear the wailing of the slaves and the curses of the overseers. It was no wonder that his mother had fled the island, swearing she would never return.

Townsend hadn't responded to his grandmother's most recent letter from the month before, and he felt badly about that. She knew he was undecided about what he would do, but she was persistent. She wanted him to come see her as soon as he was discharged. She'd written how much he meant to her and how much she missed his mother, her beloved Esperanza. Every Sunday she lit a candle in the chapel on the family estate for his mother. She would prepare her mother's room for him as soon as he let her know he was coming.

Suddenly he saw an image of his mother, the dark black hair, her sharp Spanish features, the soulful eyes. He always had to be truthful to her. She was shaking her head warning him to stay away. He could never forget her words about his grandmother. She'd called her own mother a witch. *She'll have your soul if you let her*, she'd said.

Townsend closed his eyes and gave the order to tack away from the coast back across the Old Bahama Channel toward the Salt Key Bank. They would have to sail all night and part of the day tomorrow tacking back and forth along the coastline. He told Metcalf to take his bearings from the Piedras Key lighthouse off Icacos Point.

"Give it a wide berth, Metcalf."

"Aye, Cap'n."

13

January 12, 1866

The Marillanes channel looked like an immense garden, as vibrant as a painting with swaths and streaks of color. The blue-green water and the sugary white beaches on some of the barrier islands reminded Townsend of the Tortugas. He could see a fisherman's hut on one of the islands with the man's nets drying on a long pole. The shallow areas were marked by stakes, which reminded him of sailing into some of the rivers on Florida's Gulf Coast during the war. Confederate saboteurs were always switching the stakes to confuse the Navy ships and make them run aground. Townsend ordered Tollman to keep taking soundings with the lead as a precaution, as there were many shoaly areas.

With his telescope raised to his eye, Townsend could now see the clusters of tall palm trees and the red tile roofs of the small port settlement of Sagua in the distance. De la Cruz pointed to the afternoon sunlight on rolling hills fifteen miles inland.

"Cap'n, look—those are the Jumagua hills I spoke of—where the runaway slaves hide."

Townsend nodded, but he wasn't paying any attention. He was too busy scanning a forest of merchant ships flying American flags. There must have been forty ships there with so many fluttering stars and stripes it looked like an American port. He knew they were all there to pick up cargos of sugar.

Townsend spotted a Spanish navy gunboat called the *Neptuno* with the familiar red and gold flag of Spain. He could see an officer on the quarterdeck with his dark blue jacket and sword on his belt watching them with his own telescope. *Had they been notified about our arrival?* He was glad that Rudd had given him the authorization letter from the Spanish minister in Washington. He'd read it. Rudd had been right. It was just a courtesy letter asking the Navy commander to extend every courtesy to this American Navy lieutenant.

They dropped anchor not far from the sturdy two-story customs house built at the end of a pier. He could see a figure in the upstairs window with a telescope pointed in their direction. They'd only just arrived, and Townsend already felt he had many eyes watching him. *An uneasy position to be in*, he thought to himself.

From the bow, de la Cruz shouted that a Spanish Navy longboat was headed their way. Townsend spotted the thirty-foot harbor patrol launch with six oarsmen wearing the flat-brimmed straw hats of the Spanish Navy. Within minutes, they came alongside the schooner and a Spanish Navy officer stood up in the stern of the launch, notifying Townsend he must go to the customs house and present his papers there.

"*Cuál es el propósito de su visita?*" the officer shouted through his trumpet.

Townsend's Spanish was not eloquent Castilian, but he was able to communicate in near-perfect Spanish that he was an American Naval captain with an important letter to show the Spanish Navy commandant. The Spanish officer grew quiet as he visibly tensed up. His eyebrows raised. He looked dismissively at Townsend and told him he was in Spanish waters and must follow Spanish regulations.

"*Vaya a la aduana donde puede presentar sus documentos.*"

Townsend knew the rules for a Naval officer in Cuba. He was required to wear his uniform ashore. He quickly put on his blue officer's coat with the gold lace stripes on the sleeves and the gold bars on the shoulders to indicate his rank. Then after some thought he strapped on the leather belt with the holstered Colt Navy revolver. He had de la Cruz row him in to the customs house and told him to wait at the landing.

The customs house was a beehive of activity, filled with ship captains presenting their ship's papers, manifests, and bills of lading. The room was so filled with cigar smoke and body odor that even Townsend found it hard to breathe. He could hear the bureaucratic customs officers demanding invoices in quadruplicate with the value of each article and the weight, and then, as if on cue, a slew of cussing in English from frustrated American ship captains.

One of the officials called Townsend over.

"It is unusual to see an American Navy ship in this port. As you can see, we mostly deal with American merchant ships."

Townsend nodded and handed the man his ship's papers. The official had a strong smell of rum about him, and he decided to lecture Townsend on why the US government should be aware that Spanish rule in Cuba was necessary to keep commerce going to America.

"What is your business here?"

Townsend explained in Spanish that it was of vital importance for him to speak directly and immediately to the Naval commandant. The customs official stroked his well-trimmed moustache and then began speaking in a dismissive tone.

"*Hay poca probabilidad de que el comandante tenga tiempo para un teniente.*"

Ignoring the insult that the commander would not speak with such a junior officer, Townsend continued. "It is an urgent matter involving the American merchant schooner, the *Southern Cross.*"

At the mention of the ship, the customs officer excused himself and walked into a private office, leaving Townsend to wait. Fifteen minutes later, a junior Naval officer finally appeared.

"*Teniente, lamento informarle que no es conveniente,*" he said, and then repeated himself in heavily accented English. "I'm sorry. It's not convenient. Try again in a week's time." He handed Townsend the ship's papers.

"*¡No puede ser!*" Townsend blurted out. "That's not acceptable."

"You may consult with the American consul in town on all matters related to the incident with the *Southern Cross.*" The young Naval officer looked at him with a quietly hostile smile.

"*Que tenga un buen día, teniente.*"

Cursing all Spanish officials, Townsend left the customs building with his landing permit and a stamped passport and told de la Cruz to stay with the boat until he returned from the American Consulate. Once he was away from the pier, the breeze disappeared. Townsend took a deep breath and scrunched up his nose. The swampy air was pungent, a faint noxious odor coming from the stagnant water and refuse around the town's many stilt houses.

Soon Townsend was shoulder to shoulder with a swirling mix of disheveled sailors, donkey carts, and work gangs. A fishy smell hung in the air. He wanted to cover his ears against the clip clop of donkeys' hooves, the squeal of wheels, and the shouting in English and Spanish. He weaved his way through an army of shirtless Black stevedores who were rolling oak barrels of molasses onto the pier, their backs glistening with sweat. Their faces were tattooed around the eyes and cheekbones, which told Townsend that these were slaves who had been brought over from Africa. The Spanish called them *bozales*, the muzzled ones. The overseers stood by, their short limber whips in hand, their eyes flashing as they watched for any sign of trouble.

Townsend stopped to read some of the American-flagged ships' names, *Empire, Cornelia*, a British bark named *Sea Gem*. No sign of the *Southern Cross*. He jumped at the sudden crack of a whip. He wheeled around and spotted one of the thin white overseers in his white shirt cursing a shirtless Black dockworker for being slow and lazy. The Black man had dropped to his knees, his arms outstretched, and was plaintively crying out for his master to forgive him—"¡Amo! Amo. Perdóneme!" It was almost as if the slave welcomed the master's punishment and viewed him with awe and submission, but Townsend knew it was all a well-rehearsed act, a matter of desperate self-defense.

The Navy lieutenant grimaced as the overseer struck the dockworker on his bare back with his plaited whip, causing the man to moan. He could already see the blow had left a mark on the skin. When the overseer drew back his arm to strike the man again, Townsend reached for his pistol, but then he remembered his orders not to create an incident. The next lash and the man's cries were a dark reminder to Townsend that he was back on a slave island. He had fought in a war to end this hateful institution, but now he had returned to a world of human bondage and cruelty.

Townsend couldn't help but notice the heavy police presence. Some of the officers clearly had picked him out of the crowd as a person of interest. The hostile way they eyed him made him feel uncomfortable. He knew his American Navy uniform attracted attention. He was an intruder. With their dark blue coats and broad-brimmed felt hats, these officers were part of the *Guardia Civil*, the special branch of military police on watch for any threats to the Spanish colonial government in Cuba. He'd seen them on the docks of Havana making arrests. He pushed his way through a dizzy blur of Black and white faces, ducking in behind some stacked crates and barrels, and then following some street peddlers. He kept his head down and made a point of not looking in the officials' direction. He didn't want to give them an excuse to stop and question him.

Townsend quickened his step. The rhythmic work songs of the Negro dockworkers had now faded, giving way to the clomp of boots marching and the gruff commands from a platoon officer. Outside one of the American trading houses, he noticed a slender man in a rumpled linen suit with a bramble of black side whiskers and a fuzzy black beard. The man held himself like a military man, and it was hard for Townsend to ignore his piercing stare. *Another set of eyes*, he thought to himself, *in a place filled with sharp-eyed stares.*

Finally, he spotted the American flag. At the consulate, Townsend was greeted by the consul's assistant, a middle-aged man who explained that the consul, Mr. J.H. Homer, had been called away. He introduced himself as Horace Winthrop and again emphasized that he was just filling in for the consul. Townsend studied the man, as he poured Townsend a cup of coffee—round face with glasses, thinning hair, a droopy moustache. He was dressed in a generously cut suit that helped hide the fact that he was slightly overweight.

"Forgive me, Mr. Winthrop, do I detect a Boston accent?"

"I must say you have a fine-tuned ear, Lieutenant. Yes, I'm a Boston man. One of my wife's sisters is married to a Spanish plantation owner nearby." He patted his ample belly as he lit a large Cabañas cigar. "I'm afraid I've grown to enjoy the life of being a frequent guest at their lovely estate. Nothing better than a Cuban planter's lounging chaise where you can put your feet up and enjoy a few rum drinks and a good cigar." The man held up his cigar with a big smile. "Finest and oldest cigar brand in Cuba."

Townsend smiled politely and got right to the point.

"I'm here on orders to investigate the incident involving the *Southern Cross*, Mr. Winthrop. I trust you can give me the details of the incident and tell me where the ship is located."

The man looked away with discomfort written all over his pinched face and then finally spoke. "The Spanish authorities have released the men, and the ship was allowed to leave port, Lieutenant."

Townsend stood up so fast, his coffee spilling out of the cup onto the floor.

"That's impossible. My orders from Commander Ransom in Key West are to interview the sailors on board. Why did they release the ship?"

Winthrop fondled his cigar, then took a puff, watching the smoke waft over toward Townsend, who finally sat back down in the spartan desk chair.

"We were only informed yesterday. The initial report by the police which claimed the sailor was murdered was found to be incorrect. The ship was released by orders of the Supreme Marine Authority of Cuba. They have jurisdiction over such matters. It seems the man's death was due to an unfortunate accident. A particularly vicious plantation dog got free from its handler and mauled the man. As I said . . . a terrible accident."

"Where did this happen?"

"About a block from here. We think he was on his way here when the dog attacked him."

"And the dog killed him?"

"Yes. That's what the police have determined."

Townsend paused as he absorbed this information and studied Winthrop's nervous face and the poker smile.

"I was informed that this man met with you the day before his death, and he told you he wanted to make some kind of statement—something about foul dealing."

The man now squirmed in his chair, as if taken off guard by how well-informed this young Navy lieutenant appeared to be.

"Yes . . . yes, that's right. The seaman did mention his ship. The *Southern Cross*. Said he'd come back the next day with evidence. The truth is we didn't take him seriously."

"Why not?"

"For one thing, he wouldn't give us his name. He was very agitated. *Not* reliable. We thought he'd been drinking. Suffering from delirium tremens." He shrugged.

Townsend could tell the consul was being evasive. His unflinching stare now bore into the man's face.

"Why do you think the police changed their mind?"

He shrugged again. "Maybe they found an eyewitness? I can tell you the consul and I certainly can attest to the fact that the man suffered a violent death. He was torn to pieces."

"So, you saw him, the dead man on the street?" Townsend asked abruptly. He was surprised that this important piece of information hadn't been divulged earlier.

"Well, yes, the body was just a block away from the Consulate. There was blood on the stone pavement. His clothes shredded, gashes all over his body."

Townsend looked out the window of the office and took a deep breath.

"Mr. Winthrop, isn't it a little suspicious?"

"I don't catch your meaning," replied the assistant consul.

"The Spanish dropped all suggestions of murder charges, released the men, and allowed the schooner to leave port just a day before I arrived. They almost certainly knew I was being sent here. Perhaps they didn't want the American Navy poking their nose into the hold of that ship? Do you have any idea what cargo that vessel was carrying?"

"They had a cargo of cotton on deck. More than that I don't know."

"So, what was the foul dealin' the man came to talk to you about?"

"I have no idea. Probably pure poppycock."

"And who was the dog handler?"

"I'm afraid we don't know. The police have told us that the Consulate has no legal authority to get involved in this matter."

"Are you aware of the rumors that American schooners are leaving various Gulf ports for Cuba with cargoes of American Negroes, whom they plan to sell here as slaves?"

Winthrop's eyes widened. "Why . . . why would you ask such a question?"

"I'm just asking if you have heard those rumors."

"Well . . . yes," the man said. "I have heard something to that effect, but nothing credible. You're not suggesting—"

"Isn't it possible the *Southern Cross* could have been involved in kidnapping freedmen?"

"What! Certainly *not*, Lieutenant. I can assure you we would know about it. Besides, the Spanish officials here would never allow it. We have excellent relations with the port authorities, and they would inform us of anything illegal such as you are postulating."

"But—"

"Furthermore, that question shows how ill-informed you are, *Lieutenant* Townsend. The Navy must have been short-staffed to have sent a junior officer like you. You may have noticed in your brief time here in this port the very visible presence of police and the *Guardia Civil*."

"Indeed, I have," replied Townsend, trying to hide a cold anger sweeping over him.

"The war may be over in the States," Winthrop began quietly, "but Spanish authorities fear it may be about to start here. It's not just the danger of a slave uprising. It's the threat of a civil war between *los peninsulares*, the Spanish citizens here, and the Cuban-born white population, *los criollos*. The Spanish colonial government here worries that some of these rebellious Cubans have become emboldened by the end of slavery up north and are seeking help from sympathizers in the United States. That's why the authorities are searching American ships," he practically hissed.

"What are they looking for?"

"Arms, revolutionary leaflets, political exiles being smuggled back into Cuba from New Orleans or Key West. They are intent on eliminating anyone conspiring against Spain."

"So, who do you think killed that man?"

"Killed? No, I didn't say that," Winthrop said, shaking his head. "There was no murder. The police said they made a mistake. The man's death was an *accident*."

"The police haven't even given you his name, have they?"

"No, as I said they don't want us involved."

Townsend raised an eyebrow and then looked away. He had to press his lips together to control his rising anger.

"Our principal job here in Sagua is to make sure that the island's essential exports are loaded onto ships for the United States. We need excellent relations with the Spanish port authorities as well as all of the planters. I hope you understand. The sugar here is the cheapest in the Antilles thanks to the . . . low-cost labor available here, and the United States buys the vast majority of the island's exports."

"Rest assured, Mr. Winthrop, my report to Secretary of State Seward will reflect your thoughtful and insightful analysis of the importance of Cuban *slave sugar*," Townsend said with little effort to hide the heavy layer of sarcasm.

The assistant consul glared at Townsend, his eyes sparkling like chips of black mica.

"Lieutenant, I don't like your insinuations or your tone. I consider the incident closed. I hope you have a safe return voyage."

14

It was almost dusk when Townsend stormed out of the US Consulate onto the street. "Bootlicking lackey," he seethed. The meeting had left him with more questions than answers. All his instincts told him the Spanish police were hiding something. The assistant consul wasn't about to say anything against the Spanish. That much was clear. Townsend needed time to think about what his next step should be. He had thought this part of his mission would have been relatively routine. Talk to the sailors, get their testimony, find out more about that ship, and then write up a report. Lost in thought, the Navy lieutenant jumped when a figure stepped out from behind a long line of donkey carts leaving the docks for the day.

"Welcome to Satan's little corner in the tropics, Lieutenant," a voice said in perfect English. Standing in front of him was the man wearing a slouch hat he had seen before he walked into the Consulate. "Welcome to the port of Sagua—the last stop for the sugar trains coming from the interior. Nothing here but mud, mangroves, and mosquitos."

"Who are you?" Townsend demanded as he took quick measure of the man and reached for his holstered pistol. With his thin, stony face, black beard, and dark eyes, the man looked Spanish but strangely his accent was American.

"Don't be alarmed, Lieutenant. I'm an ex-Union man. Quiñones is the name." He held out his hand to Townsend. "Former Union Army officer, Captain William Quiñones, discharged a year ago. Fought with the 114th Pennsylvania Infantry in Gettysburg."

Townsend slowly took the man's hand while giving him a hard look. He spoke flawless English, with only a slight hint of a Spanish accent. He had a sad face that captured the ache of surviving the war. He looked like a man who had seen the elephant, as soldiers liked to say, but Townsend remained suspicious.

"How do I know you're telling the truth?" Townsend asked.

"Just ask my former commanding officer, Lieutenant Colonel Federico Fernández Cavada. He's back in Cuba now. He is the US Consul in the town of Trinidad on the island's southern coast. He'll vouch for me."

"So you're Cuban?"

"Cuban *criollo*. Raised here in Sagua la Grande. Spanish father. My father was a doctor. American mother. Thanks to her, I am completely bilingual. She took me back to Philadelphia just before the war after my father died. Federico recruited me there. Both of us were captured at Gettysburg and sent to Libby prison in Richmond. Lucky to have gotten out of that Confederate hellhole alive."

Townsend knew—there was no bleaker hell than Libby prison. The man's eyes had a certain pained, weary look, and he noticed for the first time that he favored one leg.

"What is it you want from me?"

"I have some information you may need," Quiñones replied in a whisper.

"I see," Townsend narrowed his eyes at the man. "How do you even know who I am?"

"The whole town knows who you are and why you're here," the man responded in a soft voice. He looked at Townsend's uniform. "There are few secrets in this place. I got your name from the customs officer. By the way, he was impressed with your Spanish."

Townsend ignored the compliment. "Is that what you wanted to tell me?"

"What I have to tell you, Lieutenant," Quiñones whispered, "is about that sailor on the *Southern Cross*, the dead American sailor. You should know his death was no accident."

Quiñones motioned for Townsend to follow him. They entered a building near the John Thompson trading house not too far from the Consulate. They walked into a room filled with crates and barrels and boxes of cigars and tobacco with stenciled labels indicating they were bound for Amsterdam. Townsend followed the man upstairs where there were several large desks and a view of some of the harbor. Quiñones offered Townsend a cigar and a seat in front of the window.

"Let me try to reassure you, Lieutenant. I'm one of the engineers working in cooperation with this trading house. Unlike many of the American machinists and engineers who come for only the sugar harvest, I'm here year-round. This company handles all the sugar purchases and shipping concerns for the New York–based banking company Moses & Taylor. Some big-name planters like Jose Baró, Tomás Terry, and the American William Hood work with Moses & Taylor, among many others. I help install and repair the expensive American steam machinery imported here."

Townsend nodded impatiently. "How very interesting, Captain Quiñones. You appear to have landed on your feet after the war. But tell me what you know about this man you think was murdered?"

"I saw it all happen," Quiñones said, pointing out to the street where the donkey carts were lined up. "Right out this window. It was dusk, just like it is now."

Quiñones paused and looked away from Townsend as he puffed on his cigar.

"By all rights, I should keep my mouth shut, Lieutenant. I'm sure you realize Cuba is a place where it's best to speak softly—if at all. The walls have ears. But I'm putting aside my better judgment cause my conscience won't let me do otherwise."

"Go on."

"This man had this big dog on a leash, one of those Cuban-bred slave hunting dogs. He was a big man. Black hair with a Panama hat and a linen suit. Walked with a hell devil step, like a soldier. He was tailing another fellow who looked like he was in a hurry, afraid. He kept looking back over his shoulder. I knew something was wrong."

"So, what happened?"

"I didn't expect it. I saw that fellow stoop down and let that animal smell something in his hand. Looked like a piece of clothing. And then he released the dog from his leash. There is no doubting his intentions. That hound dog took off—knocked the other man down from behind and went for his throat. I saw that clear as day. Tore that man apart. At first, I was too shaken to move. Then I ran down the stairs, but by the time I got to the street, the dog and its owner had disappeared."

"Could you identify the man with the dog?"

"No, I never saw his face. He had his back to me, and it was getting dark."

"What about the man who was attacked? He was apparently a sailor."

"He was just lying there in a pool of blood. He was still alive, moaning. I reached out to touch him. Then I shook him, but he didn't say anything. I ran to the police, and they eventually brought a doctor who pronounced him dead. When I left, they were going to check with the American Consulate."

Townsend paused to take measure of the man's face. His earlier suspicions had begun to wane, and he began to think Quiñones might be a good source of information.

"You know that dead man was on his way to report what he called foul dealing."

"No, I didn't know that," Quiñones replied. "But that's no surprise. There's plenty of hornswoggling and gulling going around this port. Squabbles among the sailors are fairly common."

"I believe this to be something else, something to do with his own ship. I'm under orders to speak to the crew members." Townsend shook his head. "I reckon they could have told me a great deal, but that ship is probably halfway to the Bahamas by now."

"The *Southern Cross*? Hell no, it went up the Sagua la Grande river yesterday and hasn't come back yet."

Townsend straightened up immediately.

"Are you sure?

"Yeah, she's a brigantine schooner with a square-rigged foremast. Easy to spot."

"Upriver, you say?" Townsend asked.

The man nodded and puffed on his cigar. "Probably trading directly with the plantation owners upriver. There are a couple of dozen sugar mills along the river—Santa Isabel, Santa Ana, and Delta, to name just a few of the estates, but there are well over a hundred in the larger area around Villa Clara. A lot of contraband goes up that river to escape Spanish duties on imports."

"What kind of contraband?"

"Could be everything from perfume to lumber to machine parts to flour—all pay enormously heavy duties to Spanish customs. So American ship captains just bribe the local customs officers and police to look the other way. *Es una cosa cubana*, as they say here. A Cuban tradition."

"That must have something to do with this foul dealing?"

"One thing for certain—whatever it was that man had on his mind, it got him killed. Again, it's not terribly surprising. This area has a colorful history of people operating outside the law. Foul dealings are as common here as mosquitos and fireflies, particularly on the topic of slavery."

"Give me some specifics."

"To start with, this whole northern coast is where the *negreros*, African slave traders, have come for years to drop their human cargo. They land them at night on one of those deserted islands off the coast, and then small luggers and schooners like yours carry them up the river or onto some mangrove peninsula leading to a plantation."

"Is that still happening?"

"I wouldn't know. What I can tell you is that what goes on up that river is under the dominion of those plantation owners, and right now many of them are looking for a new supply of Negroes. It doesn't matter whether these plantation owners are Spanish, Cuban-born, or foreign. Demand for new slave labor here in Cuba is strong. Business is booming, and the merchants are making plenty of money, too. Moses & Taylor sells whatever sugar they can get their hands on. I've heard they're making an annual return on their capital now of 50 percent."

Townsend now stood up and walked over to the window.

"What do you know about any American freedmen being kidnapped and brought here to be sold as slaves?" Townsend blurted out abruptly.

"What? Kidnapped? American freedmen? Now hold on there, Lieutenant." Quiñones sat forward in his chair. "I don't know anything about that, and I think I may have told you all I need to."

"Let's speak in vague terms then," Townsend said. "What if those planters up that river were to be offered American Negroes for sale? Would they buy them?"

Quiñones shrugged. "Some planters would. Some wouldn't. I don't think the Spanish government would do much about it. They prefer to look the other way on matters to do with the plantations. And you have to understand most of the planters here are not opposed to slavery."

"What would they sell for?"

"Hell if I know, but I'd guess any devils engaged in a kidnapping business like you're talking about could probably sell an American freedman here for one thousand dollars. So, if that's all gain, it would be a tidy profit for the kidnappers. As for the planters, they'd certainly have to pay more for *bozales*, direct from Africa, so they would see a purchase of American slave labor as a bargain."

"I would have thought any former American slave who was re-enslaved here would be a risk. He might cause trouble and then run away. Maybe too much trouble."

Quiñones snorted. "You clearly don't know much about plantations around here. Any American freedmen would disappear with no trace—given new identities, never allowed to leave the plantation, unable to speak the language. They'd be lost and forgotten. It's a cruel place, Lieutenant, if you're unfortunate to be enslaved."

"You don't sound like you are too fond of working in the sugar trade."

"I hate this business of slavery. That's why I agreed to fight with the Union in the American war. The only reason I'm working here in sugar country is my friend, Federico. He got me this job. I'm just biding my time until I can get involved in fighting for Cuba's future. As you may know, there's no love lost between the Cubans and the Spanish. Spain's Cuba is built on slavery, brutality, and corruption. My hope is that the American government decides to invade and get rid of the Spanish, bring in democracy, and free the slaves."

Townsend ignored that last remark. "How far up the river can a big schooner like that go?"

"The ocean tide will carry a sailboat some seven to eight miles up to where there's a horseshoe bend. My guess is that's where they would go. I've been there. Might you be heading up the river?"

"I don't know."

Quiñones picked up a notepad and tore a hand-drawn map out of it.

"Here, take this sketch. I drew it a few weeks ago when I took a steamer up river. You have navigable water all the way to the town of Sagua la Grande."

Townsend looked at the map. It was professionally done and showed the mangroves and tree-lined banks for the first section of the river, and then the vast sugar mills and cane fields on either side. Townsend felt like he was looking at an Army map of Confederate positions and movements. He raised an eyebrow at Quiñones and held it up.

"I was an engineer by training but with a talent as a sketch artist," Quiñones explained to him. "When the Union generals discovered I could draw, they put me in one of those hot air balloons and had me sketching enemy positions from the air."

"I'd like to have one of those balloons right now," Townsend said. "We might find out where that schooner is."

"Well, at least this map will show you the terrain, Lieutenant, as well as the twists and turns of the river."

Townsend nodded. He stared at the sketch. The distinctive turns of the river which doubled back on itself in loops reminded him of a rawhide whip swirling and circling in the air. Something was familiar about that distinctive shape. He traced his finger along the meandering path of the river that seemed to stretch all the way into the heart of Cuba. He was back on board that shipwreck off the Marquesas looking through that packet of navigation charts and sketch books of the Cuban coastline. One of those drawings was of a river that looked much like this one. *That's where he'd seen it.* His face hardened. "Hodge," Townsend whispered under his breath, clenching his teeth tightly. *He had a map of this same damn river.* Then he thought of the man with the plantation dog that had killed that sailor, and he wondered aloud to himself, "Could it be?"

"What was that, Lieutenant?"

He shook his head. "Nothing, just talking to myself."

"If you go upriver, tread carefully. The authorities in Cuba don't always wear a uniform, and justice in Cuba as you might know comes in many forms. Those plantation owners control the rural police and the soldiers, and as I told you there will be people spying on you. There are a lot of eyes on the vessels that go up and down that river."

15

January 13, 1866

By four the next morning, the USS *Rebecca* was headed up the Sagua la Grande river, riding the flood tide through the smudgy darkness. Townsend gripped the wheel tightly as he scanned the width of the river. He had just enough visibility of the shoreline on either side to keep the schooner on a course down the middle. The combination of an easterly breeze and the incoming tide kept them moving forward slowly against the current.

Townsend was more concerned with stealth than he was with speed. To avoid any notice from the port authorities, he had ordered the crew to raise only the small jib to keep the noise down. He took the same care with the anchor, choosing to have the men slowly pull up the anchor line by hand, and then allowing the forward motion of the boat to break the anchor free. With all lights doused on board, Townsend was pretty sure their departure had not been noticed.

The Navy lieutenant had told the men what he had learned from the assistant US Consul. He told them about running into Quiñones and what that former Union officer had said he'd seen.

"If the *Southern Cross* is up that river," he told the men, "we have little choice but to find it and investigate. Our orders are to get all the facts and interview all the sailors." He considered mentioning his suspicions about Hodge and what cargo that boat might be carrying, but he decided against it. If he were wrong, he would lose face.

Soon they were well inside the river, and the darkness seemed more intense. He heard the whistle of a bobwhite. The only other noise was the gentle splashing of water against the sides of the boat. Along the flat banks were the dark silhouettes of mangroves with tall palm trees scattered here and there.

"What's the plan, Cap'n?" Meltcalf asked, fidgeting with a small knot at the end of a sheeting line. "Not sure I like this river much."

"We have our orders," Townsend replied, pretending to be nonchalant. "I aim to locate that ship if it's up here and interview those sailors."

"What if we run into some hostilities?"

Townsend raised his eyebrow and looked at the bosun. He didn't reply, and the bosun didn't press him. The truth was, Townsend didn't know what he would do if they were confronted by ex-Confederates or if they were stopped by Spanish police or soldiers. His official orders were simply to investigate. He knew his motivations were more complicated than that. A part of him also wanted some sort of justice. He wanted to know what had happened to Jacobs. He wanted to confront Hodge and question him about the men he had locked inside his ship. Why had he abandoned those freedmen? His fury at what Hodge had done had not abated.

Once they cleared the first loop in the river, they raised the mainsail with a loud clatter, which caused some large birds in the mangroves to flap their wings and squawk in alarm. Townsend heard a splash in the water and a rustling bush on the bank.

"I saw some figures behind the trees," de la Cruz said in a hushed whisper. Townsend didn't say anything and instead turned to Tollman who was busy throwing the lead line.

"What's our depth?"

"Fifteen feet, Cap'n," replied the sailor as he threw the lead again. "Plenty water."

The *Rebecca* drew just over four feet with the centerboard up so Townsend felt relieved. The shoreline soon gave way to higher banks lined with a tangled mixture of large umbrella-like trees which created a partial canopy. It was still so dark it was hard to see too much of anything. They had left the open air of the sea, and Townsend could smell the damp richness of the forest. The river curved through the land like a lazy snake undulating through dark woods. De la Cruz had told him that this area had once been a dense tropical forest filled with cedar, mahogany, ebony, and granadillo, but had been heavily logged by the Spanish in decades past. Townsend began sniffing the air. There was another familiar odor, sweet and tangy. He looked over at de la Cruz for confirmation.

"*El perfume de Cuba*, Captain," de la Cruz said as he gestured with his hands. "The smell is boiling sugar cane juice from the mills. Steam, fire, and smoke."

Townsend handed off the wheel to Metcalf and climbed up the ratlines to the crosstrees. In the distance, he could see the sugar mills' towers which were sending thick, oily plumes of black smoke into the pre-dawn sky. On either side, through the claw-like branches of the trees he could see burning piles of cane husks and a vast dark sea of waving sugar cane fields. They were literally sailing between two fires.

It was then that he saw a sudden movement above him. A flock of small green parakeets bounded through the gray black sky, chirping and squawking, like playful children skipping through a field. Townsend stood transfixed, watching these tiny emerald birds flutter into the gloom until they were swallowed by the ghostly trees and the forest silence. He thought of his mother and father, and then his brother, and he felt an ache of longing.

He looked down at his feet on the crosstrees and realized he was standing on the same spot where Hendricks had been gunned down by Confederate bullets. He felt a lump of guilt in his throat. "I'm sorry, Hendricks," he whispered softly. There was no answer from his ghostly companion.

The Navy lieutenant climbed down to the deck just as the first blush of daylight pierced through the branches of trees. Some slow-moving white herons with their distinctive tufts of hair flew over the boat and landed on wharves ahead of them on the shoreline. A work gang of Negroes accompanied by an overseer was beginning to load barrels of molasses onto a heavy barge. Work stopped as the *Rebecca* pulled into view. Townsend felt the overseer's eyes on the American flag flying off the mainsail as they passed by, but he ignored him. He was sure they were being watched by more than one set of eyes.

It was near noon when Townsend gave the order to drop sails and for the men to man the sweeps. The tide was still pushing them along through the brackish water, but the river current was getting stronger. The rhythmic dip and pull was slow going, and after two hours of hard pulling the sixteen-foot oars, Townsend began to doubt that they could reach the horseshoe bend Quiñones had mentioned. As soon as he realized that the ocean tide was no longer flooding, he gave the order to halt and throw out an anchor near mid-stream.

"Barge coming down the river, Cap'n," de la Cruz yelled out.

Townsend pulled out his telescope and spotted a slow-moving barge heavily loaded with barrels and sacks. About four or five Negroes were poling down the river under the watchful eye of a white overseer.

"De la Cruz signal them to come over," Townsend said. "Ask them how far it is to the horseshoe bend."

The white man responded it was just a mile up the river. Townsend called out in Spanish asking if there was a schooner there. "*¿Hay alguna goleta allí?*" Seemingly taken off guard by Townsend's sudden use of Spanish, the man nodded, but then seemed to regret his quick response. He shouted to the slaves to pole harder. "*¡Arre! ¡Arre! ¡Más fuerte!*"

It was mid-afternoon when Townsend decided to take Langworth and de la Cruz in the jolly boat to row upriver, leaving Metcalf and Tollman behind to watch over the boat. He wanted to at least confirm the schooner was there. They had completely lost the ocean tide now so they had to bend their backs at the oars to make any forward progress against the river current. After rowing around a tight curve, they spotted some figures standing on the shore next to a large ceiba tree. Townsend caught the glint of a raised gun barrel in the afternoon sun.

"Soldiers, Cap'n," de la Cruz whispered.

Townsend reached for his Navy Colt, but the crack of a rifle tore through the forest, a spurt of water splashing just several feet away from them. The three of them dropped to the floorboards. Langworth poked his head over the gunwale and pointed out another area where several armed men with rifles held at their chest had formed a skirmish line. They were dressed in the blue and white seersucker uniforms of the Spanish army. A voice called out in Spanish. "*Preséntense aquí en tierra o les disparamos.*"

For a moment Townsend thought of fleeing back to the *Rebecca*, but the sound of another gunshot changed his mind. He knew no matter what they did, they were within easy rifle range from the shore, and between them they only had one gun, his Colt revolver.

"Keep your heads down," Townsend said to Langworth and de la Cruz, his jaw set as he glared fixedly at the soldiers on the shore. He lifted his hands in the air and signaled that they would be coming ashore. As soon as they beached the jolly boat, Townsend saw a half-dozen soldiers emerge from the forest with their rifles ready.

"Langworth, stay in the boat. De la Cruz and I will do the talking."

Townsend walked up to the soldiers with his right hand on his holstered pistol. He demanded in Spanish that they take him to see their commander and for an immediate explanation why they were being shot at.

"*No se mueva de ahí,*" one of the soldiers ordered. "Don't move from there." The sound of branches breaking in the underbrush told Townsend that the man in charge was coming. Soon enough, the commanding officer emerged from the forest with his sword drawn. He was a stout-chested Spaniard with his hair and beard cropped short. His blue seersucker uniform with shiny brass buttons looked neat and fresh, and his wide-brimmed palm leaf hat decorated with a flashy red cockade gave him the air of a man who paid attention to detail. *A brag and bluster man*, Townsend thought to himself.

"*Buenas tardes*," the Spanish officer said. "*Soy el Capitán Gabriel Ramos Portillo of the Regimiento de Infantería de Ultramar* now stationed in the Villa Clara district of Cuba's Central department. *¿Quiénes son ustedes y que hacen aquí?*"

Townsend immediately introduced himself in Spanish as the commanding officer of the US Navy schooner *Rebecca*. He held out his hand, but the Spaniard only looked at it dismissively.

"I repeat my question, Lieutenant," the Spanish officer said more emphatically. "Under what authority have you come here?"

The Spanish army captain raised his sword and pointed it at the Navy lieutenant's chest. Townsend's sense of diplomacy had evaporated, but he tried to ignore the sword and all the rifles pointed in their direction. He glared at the officer with unveiled anger.

"Why don't you first tell me why you fired on us? We are here on a *peaceful* mission," Townsend said in Spanish.

The officer stiffened. He narrowed his eyes at Townsend.

"I have orders to shoot any intruders caught with weapons in their hands," he said. "That includes foreign *filibusteros* working alongside Cuban *insurgentes* seeking to incite open rebellion against Spain." He glanced over at de la Cruz and let his accusatory gaze linger on the young sailor. "Cuban agitators against Spanish rule are using many different disguises now. You will have to follow us back to our base, where you will be questioned."

Townsend studied the man closely as he reached into his coat and pulled out the letter from the Minister of the Spanish Legation in Washington. With an exaggerated flourish, he presented it to the Spanish officer. "*Capitán*, you ask under what authority I have come here. A very reasonable question. This letter should explain and disabuse you of any misconceptions you might have. We are here as guests of Her Majesty's government."

Townsend took on the role of an indignant emissary sent with the full knowledge of the Spanish Crown. "As you can see from the letterhead, this dispatch comes from the *Legación de España en Washington*. It has a waxed royal seal with the signature of His Excellency, the Minister of the Spanish Legation, Gabriel Tassara, who I need not explain to you is the Minister Plenipotentiary of Her Catholic Majesty. He is Queen Isabella's most trusted representative in the United States."

The officer took the letter from Townsend and held it close to his face. Just from looking at the man's furrowed brow, Townsend guessed that, like so many junior officers in Cuba, Ramos Portillo had little formal education. As a result, he would find the formal written diplomatic Spanish almost impossible to decipher.

Townsend knew he had to remain calm so as not to offend the prickly Spaniard any more than he already had, but he also knew he needed to press his advantage. He smiled at the man and spoke politely.

"I am sure you would not want to be an obstacle to the wishes of officials at the highest level of Her Majesty's government. This letter grants me the right to interview American sailors on board an American-flagged schooner believed to be anchored a short distance from here. As you know, our country is now reunited, and we are eager to reach out to all *ex-Confederados* here in Cuba. It is imperative, *Capitán*, that you allow me and my men to proceed at once. Otherwise, I fear this might be considered an insult to my government."

The Spanish captain glowered at him with an intense stare that reminded Townsend of a bull pawing the ground, just before it was ready to charge. The officer let the hand with the letter drop to the side, and Townsend thought he was wavering, but then Ramos Portillo shook his head.

"I know of no such authorization. I have my orders. You are not allowed further up the river. *No está permitido.*"

"But the letter clearly gives me—"

"*Basta. Ya terminó esta conversación.* I will consult with my superiors about this letter and contact you tomorrow. You may return to your ship, but you are not to raise anchor. Until then, *Teniente.*"

The ebb tide and the current along with their rowing allowed them to make good speed back down the river. De la Cruz complimented Townsend on a superb bit of bluffing, but Townsend only grunted in reply. It was late afternoon, and the shadows were lengthening. The edge of the river already was wrapped in an ominous gloom. When they came around the last bend before the river straightened out, Townsend expected to see the *Rebecca*'s familiar masts, but instead there was just the empty river. He looked to the left and right, but there was no sign of his schooner.

"What in thunderation! The boat's not there."

De la Cruz and Langworth stopped rowing and turned around to look.

"I'll be hog-wallered!" Langworth said. "You're right, Cap'n. Must have slipped her anchor."

"Not like Metcalf to let that happen," Townsend replied. "But with this current there's only one direction the boat could have gone."

They rowed as quickly as they could and with the help of the tide, they sped along at three knots.

"Look over yonder, Cap'n!" Langworth shouted.

"¡Caray!" exclaimed de la Cruz. "It's the Rebecca."

Across the river, the ship's hull and masts were leaning up against some overhanging trees. It looked like she was stuck fast in the mud in about three feet of water. Fortunately, the hull had not canted over to one side so the decks remained level. A dark figure was waving at them. Now they could hear Metcalf shouting. As soon as they arrived, the bosun explained that some fishermen in a dugout canoe came by to sell them part of their catch.

"They were friendly, Cap'n. Too friendly, I reckon. One of 'em must have cut the anchor line. It didn't help that neither Tollman nor I could speak the lingo."

"Are you sure they cut it?" Townsend asked.

"Reckon so. While Tollman and I were paying them in gold coin and collecting the fish on deck, one of the other fishermen in another boat must have done it. We both went below to store the fish. I didn't realize the ship was adrift until I looked out the portholes and saw the trees going by. By then it was too late to stop us running with the current and the ebb tide. I guess we were lucky to snag up here on this bank."

"Don't fret, Metcalf," Townsend replied. "We faced our own misadventures." He sighed. "I think it's safe to say we're not welcome on this river. We need to move on as soon as we can. No sense waiting for Spanish guns. We'll try to kedge our way out of here."

In the dark shadows, he and the men tied a separate anchor to the halyard on the main mast and towed the anchor in the jolly boat about fifty yards away from the ship. They set the anchor in the soft river bottom and used a strong block and tackle to pull the boat away from the shore. It was no use. As hard as they tried, the boat remained motionless, stuck in the mud. They would have to wait for the flood tide to come back in, which would not be for another few hours.

A half-moon emerged above the tree line on the eastern horizon cutting through the gloom with a faint light. Townsend ordered all hands to eat and drink. De la Cruz volunteered to prepare some of the river fish Metcalf had just purchased and cook some white peas. All agreed that was more appetizing than the alternative—hardtack biscuit with salt pork.

After a quick meal, Townsend put de la Cruz and Langworth on watch, one at the bow and the other in the stern. Metcalf and Tollman tried to get some sleep. Townsend stayed next to the helm in case of any trouble. He tried to keep his eyes open, but he must have dropped off because he woke with a jolt when de la Cruz shouted, "Big ship sailing down the river, Cap'n."

Townsend jumped up. Then he heard Metcalf right next to him.

"Comin' fast, Cap'n. Full canvas. Should we clear for action?"

Townsend didn't respond. He was too surprised by the sight of a big cargo schooner barreling down the river under full sail. Whoever was at the helm knew their way by night because they were flying toward them at seven knots. The moonlight filled the ship's white sails with a pale light that made the brigantine schooner seem like a ghost ship. It reminded Townsend of running through the Union blockade from Mobile at night where there was little margin for error.

Metcalf and Langworth stood by the pivot gun.

"Cleared and ready, Cap'n," the bosun cried out. "She'll be in range soon. We can fire a warning shot across her bow—she'll get the message."

Townsend stood watching as the schooner's bow cut through the river water sending rolling waves toward the shore and the *Rebecca*. The schooner was now directly across the river from them, less than one hundred yards away. They were so close, Townsend could hear the captain giving orders, calling out to the helmsman for more starboard helm.

Another voice Townsend knew only too well whispered to him that this might be his last chance. Townsend felt the knot in his throat as he imagined Hendricks standing next to him. He wavered. He almost gave the order to clear for action, but then he remembered the hostile look on that Spanish captain's face. Firing the howitzer would just bring the Spanish soldiers, and he thought of Rudd warning him to not make trouble.

"No. No. Don't fire," he hissed. "Let them go. We don't know for sure if that ship is the *Southern Cross*."

Townsend watched as that big schooner raced by with her mainsail and foresail booms extended out over the port side of the boat. There was only a faint pinprick of light from the lantern on the bowsprit. He brought the telescope up to his eye and focused in on the ship's transom. In the dark, it was hard to see any of the lettering, but the faint light from the moon revealed the carving of a large cross. "Damn it to hell," he swore to himself. "It is the *Southern Cross*." He thought of that dirt wag Hodge. There was no proof that he was the captain of that boat, but all his instincts told him he was.

Townsend immediately told the crew that the schooner was the one they were pursuing. The Navy sailors immediately renewed their efforts to kedge the boat off the mud. With the help of the flood tide, they were able to pull the schooner into deeper water two hours later. In the dead of night, they sailed down the river without any lights. No one said a word. They looked around every curve and bend for any sign of the schooner, but they saw nothing. The only sound was the rustle of the wind in the trees and the chirping of tree frogs. Townsend felt a shiver in the tropical night.

As they left the port and headed out the dark channel to the open water, neither Townsend nor Metcalf spoke as the trade winds filled the sails. The two veteran sailors swayed back and forth on the rolling deck, eyes on the horizon.

"What was that ship doing up that river, Cap'n?" Metcalf asked, not breaking his gaze ahead as if he were addressing the wind as much as Townsend.

The Navy lieutenant looked at Metcalf and decided it was time to tell the bosun about the unwritten orders he'd received from William Rudd, the man from Washington, and Townsend's suspicion that the *Southern Cross* was under the command of Ezekiel Hodge. Townsend knew that in Havana, he would need the bosun's help.

16

January 16, 1866

Havana

The early morning sun shone directly in Townsend's face as he steered the USS *Rebecca* past the crashing surf into the narrow entrance of Havana harbor. It had taken them a little over twenty hours to make the nearly 150-mile-journey from Sagua. At his order, Langworth fired the gun salute required of all visiting military ships, and seconds later, they received a symbolic cannon blast in return. Townsend shielded his eyes with his hands and looked up with trepidation at the black silhouette of El Morro fortress. It had been more than two years since he'd last stared up at those stone walls. He felt an odd sensation of traveling back in time.

His mind flooded with vivid memories of running through the Union blockade sailing under the Spanish flag. So much had happened to him then. He wasn't sure if he was even the same person. Dark thoughts and fears now crowded together. He glanced over at the Presidio building near the Punta Fort where he had been imprisoned—where he'd been stripped naked, brutally interrogated, and otherwise held in solitary confinement—and then to the high walls of *La Cabaña* fortress. He thought of his narrow escape from Havana harbor in the dead of night with all those ships ablaze—his own doing. Amazingly, he and his crew along with Emma had gotten away from Havana on a slow scow schooner to Key West, undetected. That now seemed to him like another lifetime, but the fear he had felt then remained—a dull ache in his bones.

The noise of guns firing, church bells clanging, and bugles blaring traveled across the water as they sailed past the walled fortresses and cannons that straddled the harbor entrance. Swarms of small boatmen with their straw hats accompanied them into the three-mile-wide harbor crowded with shipping from all over the world. Townsend's eyes darted in all directions. Ahead of them was the centuries-old city of Havana crowned with church spires, towers, and belfries. He searched for any sign of the *Southern Cross* as he remembered the assistant consul in Sagua had told him the ship had a cargo of cotton piled up on its decks. His best guess was that they might have wanted to sell that cotton in Havana. He noticed with interest that some of the fast, sleek Confederate and English steamships that once spent the war running through the Union blockade were now abandoned like broken down racehorses. A *fitting resting place*, he thought, as Havana was the last foreign port to supply weapons to the South on the Galveston run.

He looked over toward the northern edge of the city with its colorful tapestry of houses. He scanned the rooftop terraces until he found the one he was looking for—Emma's mother's boarding house. His eyes lingered there. This is where she would come to paint. He blinked as if to conjure her slim figure, but there was no sign of Emma.

Townsend breathed in deeply as he spotted the twin towers of the city's ancient cathedral where Columbus was buried.

"Quite some harbor," Metcalf said.

"Spain's crown jewel in the Caribbean," Townsend replied with a sardonic smile. "But all that glitters is not gold, Metcalf. Beautiful walls outside, but inside those Spanish forts, it's dark and moldy."

"Wa'al, it might have its shambles, Cap'n," Meltcalf snorted, "but speakin' as a first-time visitor, it's sure an improvement over lil' Key West."

Townsend laughed at the comparison. He handed over the wheel to Metcalf and instructed him to anchor the boat several hundred yards off the central wharf area, which was a lively forest of masts pierced with the shouts and curses of sailors and dock workers. As familiar as it all seemed, Townsend knew something was different. It took him a moment to realize what it was. Gone were the quivering Confederate Navy jacks flying from the mastheads and the crates of weapons waiting to be shipped to Mobile or Galveston. The easy money to be made in Spanish Cuba by merchants and ship owners supplying the Confederacy was no more.

While the crew dropped the sails and set the anchor, Townsend stood amidships soaking in the sights and sounds he knew so well. Nearby, he could hear the twang of the guitar and the squeak of fiddles. The landing was full of heavy horse-drawn wagons stacked high with barrels filled with molasses and muscovado sugar waiting to be loaded onto ships. In the distance, he picked out the clattering of the city's carriage wheels and the cries of the candy street vendors.

Townsend had Langworth row him ashore to the customs house to submit the ship's papers. Knowing the harbor regulations as he did, he then went to the offices of the Captain of the Port to pay the various shipping dues and harbor entrance fees. Once inside the smoke-filled building, Townsend's dark blue Navy uniform and distinctive cap immediately drew attention. A cluster of military police officers were standing imperiously against the wall. Townsend guessed that these were *Guardia Civil* assigned to patrol the docks. He quickly spotted the man in charge. The officer's wide-brimmed felt hat and his rooster-like posture made him stand out. On a whim, Townsend decided he would walk over and speak with him.

The Navy lieutenant loomed over the short, thick-set muscular man. He looked down at him and immediately sensed that this officer had an insecure and suspicious nature. Townsend sought to win him over by introducing himself in Spanish.

"*Es un honor conocerle, Capitán,*" Townsend said, giving his name, rank, and the name of his ship.

The Spanish police captain remained silent, looking Townsend over, then finally nodding in acknowledgment and giving his name, *el Capitán Humberto López Villanueva*. Townsend knew he needed to embellish his importance for this man to even speak with him.

"I am here in Havana to assist in the upcoming visit of the American Secretary of State, William Seward, with His Illustrious Excellency, Captain General Domingo Dulce. An extremely important event, wouldn't you agree, *Capitán?*"

Townsend noticed with satisfaction that these grandiose words to describe the Spanish Captain General had the desired effect. The officer's gamy eyes gleamed with self-importance even as he assumed a more rigid military posture.

"I am charged with maintaining order here on the docks. The US Navy can be assured that my squadron of men with the *Guardia Civil* will guarantee the security in the harbor."

"I am gratified to hear that," Townsend replied as he nodded respectfully.

"We will be increasing our patrols in advance of the Secretary's visit," the captain continued as he straightened his shoulders and adjusted his broad-brimmed felt hat. "You should have no doubts that we will silence any protests that might surface."

"I hope you will let me know if I can be of assistance to you should there be any threat," Townsend said, making a courtly bow.

During his time in Havana, the Navy lieutenant had learned the value of puffery with the Spanish authorities, but he didn't want to overdo it.

"Oh, and *Capitán*—the American Navy is looking for a brigantine schooner called the *Southern Cross*. I'd be grateful if you could notify me if that ship comes into the harbor. My orders are to interview the men on board. A *sensitive matter*," he added quietly, as if sharing a confidence.

"*Desde luego, Teniente,*" replied the Spanish officer, praising Townsend for his good Spanish. "I hope you will also keep an eye out for anything unusual in the harbor. I am confident this visit by your Secretary of State will be an historic event."

The US Consulate was only a short distance away from the main landing area. When Townsend reached Obispo Street, he could hear the rattling of drums and the blaring of bugles from the nearby Captain General's palace at the Plaza de Armas. He spotted the well-known Cabarga ship chandlery and just beyond it, the American flag over the Consulate. Given his instructions from Mr. Rudd, there was little for him to discuss with the Consul General, but it was expected protocol that he would visit the Consulate.

The Navy lieutenant climbed the stairs into the large office space with its high ceilings where there were a mixture of clerks, deputies, and translators. When he walked into the Consul General's office, William Minor stood up and greeted him with a politician's firm handshake. He was a large man, dressed formally in a dark suit with a black cravat. Townsend guessed he was about fifty years old, sporting a bushy white walrus moustache and a whiskery neck, but a strangely hairless chin with no hint of any stubble.

"I saw you come into the harbor, Lieutenant, with your gunboat schooner. First time here in Cuba?" the consul asked as he adjusted his wire-rimmed glasses.

"No sir, I've been here before," Townsend replied as his eyes scanned the familiar office with its large bookcases, mahogany chairs with caned seats, and a brass telescope mounted by the window. The consul waited—curious to hear more, but Townsend didn't say anything, and Minor didn't press him. Clearly the man was unaware of Townsend's past as both a captain of a blockade running schooner and later as a Union informant in Havana.

The diplomat signaled to a young Cuban who walked into the office carrying some coffee.

"Do you take sugar?" Minor asked.

"Yes, one spoonful, please," Townsend replied.

Minor motioned for Townsend to take a seat and then looked at him with a penetrating gaze. "Lieutenant, I believe you are carrying the dispatch bag for the Secretary of State?"

"That's correct, Mr. Minor. I'm under orders to deliver it to Secretary Seward upon his arrival here."

"Yes, of course—I quite understand why the State Department would want a military courier to deliver those important documents. Such an important task. But tell me, I understand you have just returned from the port of Sagua where there was a murder of an American sailor? Difficult situation, certainly for our Consulate. Were you able to conduct any interview with the sailors?"

"No, sir, I was not. The Spanish police determined it wasn't a murder. They released the men and allowed the ship to leave port."

"Well, I'll be dad-blasted," Minor blurted out. "Sometimes there's no rhyme nor reason here on this God-forsaken island."

"Sir?"

The Consul General coughed and spilled some coffee. "Don't know why I said that," he quickly stammered. "Forgive me, it's the enervating influence of this heat. Makes me say things I don't mean. I've been here at this posting for two years now."

He leaned forward and whispered to Townsend. "My hope is that my replacement, Mr. Savage, will return soon, allowing me to leave the island before the coming season of yellow fever. My health is not what it used to be."

Townsend nodded politely. Feeling awkward, he decided it was best to change the topic "So, are there many ex-Confederates here in Cuba, Mr. Minor? I had heard there were quite a few?"

"Oh, yes, since the end of the war they've come through here like dairy cows headed for the milking parlor. The Cubans call them *Sureños*, and they're well-liked. Scattered about the island from Cárdenas to Cienfuegos to Havana. Seeking the good life, you know." Minor paused for a moment to puff on his cigar. "In fact, some have just arrived here—a rather bedraggled group. Have you heard about their shipwreck?"

"No, sir. I don't believe I have."

"Forty-two Southerners, mostly from Alabama. Their ship went up on the rocks west of here. Miraculously, all were saved. They were headed for Brazil. Their captain claims the ship was sabotaged by Yankee agents. Seems unlikely, but the Army has sent an intelligence officer here from New Orleans to investigate."

"Army officer? What's the man's name?" Townsend asked.

"Name of Hutchinson. Major Hutchinson. Bureau of Military Information, I believe. He was just in here speaking to me yesterday."

Townsend almost fell out of his chair. He hadn't heard a word about Hutchinson since he'd seen him in Key West after the hurricane. The last thing he'd expected was to find him here in Cuba. *Perhaps he is still investigating the kidnappings?*

"Is he a friend of yours?"

"Not exactly. I met him briefly in Key West."

"Most charming and most agreeable fellow," Minor said. "Impressive war record operating behind enemy lines. I told him he would make an excellent politician. If you want to see him, he's taken on a secret identity. He's posing as an ex-Confederate. I wasn't given the details, but I believe he's rooming at the same place many of the Southerners are staying, the Hotel Cubano owned by that Mrs. Bremer. I think his real purpose here is to uncover any secret plots or conspiracies that may be going on."

The Consul General stood up and shook Townsend's hand.

"Enjoy Havana and its many amusements, Lieutenant. My biggest task is to write yet another dispatch to persuade our government to stop sending me more unsubstantiated foolishness about American freedmen being kidnapped and then sold into slavery here. I've repeatedly asked the Spanish Captain General, His Excellency Domingo Dulce, about these allegations, and he has told me there is nothing to them."

"I see," Townsend replied. "We have heard rumors on the Florida coast. Does the Captain General deny these reports outright?"

"Yes, indeed. In fact, he's deeply offended as you might imagine. You have to understand he has been of enormous help in resolving this ongoing case of the three young American slave children from New Orleans who were brought here during the war. It looks like they'll be freed and returned to their mother soon."

"That's good news," Townsend said.

"Captain General Dulce is an honorable man, and he has given me his word that nothing like these nefarious reports of kidnapping could be happening in Cuba, and I believe him."

Townsend started to say something but then bit his lip.

✦

At first, Townsend thought he would try to locate Hutchinson at the Hotel Cubano, but as soon as he left the US Consulate, he changed his mind. If the Army major was in disguise, he presumed he wouldn't want to be seen talking with a Navy lieutenant. Instead, Townsend walked out onto the crowded Plaza de San Francisco and absorbed the noise and sights surrounding him. One of the strange looking Cuban carriages called *volantas* with their six-foot-high wheels and the sixteen-foot-long shafts almost ran him over. The postilion shouted at him to get out of the way.

More clattering silver-trimmed carriages passed by with smartly dressed gentlemen and elegant ladies flirting behind their fans. It was as if no time had passed, and his thoughts were drawn to Emma and their time together in Havana. He took notice of the bright pastel colors of some of the buildings, contrasting colors of salmon pink and lilac purple, and remembered riding by there with Emma in a *volanta*. He was headed toward the northern end of old Havana, where Mrs. Carpenter's boarding house was located. Townsend was so familiar with these streets he could almost have gotten there blindfolded.

The first glimpse of the three-story boarding house caused Townsend to stop and stare. He looked up at the flat-roof terrace with the high stone parapets where they had gone to escape her mother's notice, and a wave of self-doubt overcame him. He felt a tightening in his chest, but he still forced himself forward. Townsend stepped inside and immediately felt the relief of the soft breeze blowing through the airy interior. He listened to the hum of voices and the rustle of bustling petticoats and silk. But then he heard Mrs. Carpenter's loud voice upstairs yelling at one of the Irish maids. He knew he might not be welcome, but he didn't care. He walked toward the broad marble stairway. No one stopped him, but no one greeted him either.

He walked into an inner parlor room where some ladies with flowers in their hair sailed by in long trailing dresses with their husbands in top hats following close behind. He moved to one side to let them pass and found himself standing on the other side of an arcade from a sad little group of women dressed in stiff-collared black dresses. They had their children with them and seemed to be watched over by an older man with a red, bulbous nose. Just from the shaken expressions, he guessed they were some of the shipwreck survivors. He could see the pride, the humiliation, and the fear in their faces. He heard a little girl tell her rag doll, "Why no, Missie, we can't go back to Alabama—it will never be the same. Mama says we're going to some place even better where there won't be any bluebellies."

Mrs. Carpenter suddenly appeared and asked them if she could be of any assistance. Her dark wavy hair was more heavily streaked with gray, but otherwise she was like he remembered. As soon as she spotted Townsend, she excused herself from her guests and approached him like a freight train, skirts in hand. Her eyes narrowed as they lingered on him, seemingly taking in everything about him.

"My, my, Everett Townsend. You've returned. I do declare. I almost didn't see you behind the arcade. I never thought I'd lay eyes on *you* again, certainly not as a Navy officer. I suppose only a war could make an officer of a young man once dismissed from the Naval Academy. Whatever brings you to Havana?" Her left eyebrow was arched halfway up her forehead.

Townsend felt the unpleasant sting of that reference to his dismissal from the Naval Academy, but he tried to ignore it. He could feel her disapproval in her stony stare, and he wanted to say how sorry he was. He knew she thought he had simply taken advantage of Emma. He shuffled his feet.

"I'm here in Havana to deliver dispatches to Secretary Seward when his ship arrives, but I . . . well, I thought I would just stop to say hello to Emma. Is she here?"

"I would have thought a young wandering man like you would have other *distractions*." She pursed her lips. A prolonged silence hung in the air like a dense wet fog. Townsend felt trapped and didn't know what to say.

"She's in the courtyard," Mrs. Carpenter finally said. "She and a few of her musician friends are entertaining some of our guests. Don't linger, Mr. Townsend. As you can see, we are very busy with all these poor, desperate people from the shipwreck."

Townsend could hear a cello and violin playing in harmony and the sprinkling of notes from a piano. He followed the music to the open courtyard he remembered so well. He stopped when he saw Emma. The graceful line of her thin neck. The fluid movement of the bow as she moved in tandem with the cello player. It sounded like one of Bach's concertos, which Townsend had always loved listening to when his mother played them on their piano at home in Maryland.

When they finished with a flourish, the small audience stood up and applauded. Emma was quickly surrounded by admirers, most of them young men seemingly eager to make her acquaintance. She was beaming. Her face radiated self-confidence. He tried to catch her eye, but she didn't notice him. He just stood there. He suddenly felt adrift, like a nomad with no home. *Maybe we're just another casualty of war*, she had said. He turned away and began retracing his steps through the salon. He looked back one last time at the marble stairway that led to the rooftop terrace, and then walked out, nodding to the doorman.

17

January 17, 1866

At daybreak the next day, the signal gun from the guard-ship awoke Townsend along with the shrill trumpets of soldiers at drill and the clanging of church bells from every part of town. He surfaced on deck to a blast of sunshine and immediately crinkled his nose. The black smoke billowing from a passing steamship now covered the harbor and the ships with a sooty residue. Townsend scanned the docks with his telescope. There were lots of fruit boats that traveled weekly between Key West and Havana, and some trading schooners, but no sign of the *Southern Cross*.

What he did see was a visible presence of police. He thought he could pick out the stout figure of the captain of the *Guardia Civil* overseeing the search of crates and boxes on the landing. No doubt he and his men were looking for everything from banned publications and anti-government pamphlets to ammunition and guns—anything that might be perceived as a threat or an embarrassment to the Spanish colonial government.

Metcalf alerted him to an approaching bungo boat coming from the ferry landing. Townsend picked out the passenger boat with its tiny sails. It had one passenger—a man seated under the awning whose face was hidden by a Panama hat. At first, Townsend thought it must be someone from one of the hotels trying to see if he could drum up some new business. He held up his telescope to his eye to have a closer look and was surprised to see a familiar face.

"Who is it, Cap'n?" Metcalf asked.

"Believe it or not, it's that Army major from New Orleans I met in Key West."

A few moments later the small sailboat circled around their schooner until the bungo boat captain brought it into the wind and coasted up next to the schooner. Hutchinson clambered up the ship's ladder with his signature smile.

"The Consul General told me you were in Havana Bay, Lieutenant," the Army major said as he shook Townsend's hand and nodded to Metcalf and the crew. "I'll be leaving tomorrow morning for New Orleans on the steamer that just came in, so I thought I'd take the opportunity to see you."

"I appreciate the gesture," Townsend replied, noticing the man's probing eyes wandering around the ship. He wondered what the man wanted.

"Mr. Minor said you'll be talking with Secretary Seward?"

"That's correct," Townsend replied. "Delivering his correspondence."

"A weighty responsibility for such a junior Naval officer," Hutchinson said, finally letting his eyes rest on Townsend.

"I suppose so," the Navy lieutenant replied. "But then again, there aren't many of us Navy officers left in Key West."

Hutchinson laughed. "Indeed, Key West will soon be nothing but a coal depot with a bunch of sponge fishermen and some salvage boats. Care for a cigar? *Partagás*, one of Cuba's best. I recommend one."

Townsend shook his head. As Hutchinson lit a *Partagás* for himself, the Navy lieutenant took more notice of what his visitor was wearing. He was dressed like a stylish Spaniard in a high shirt collar and a white linen suit. If it weren't for his blue eyes, he'd almost look Cuban or Spanish.

"You look right at home here in Cuba, Major."

"Why, thank you, Lieutenant. As you can tell, I'm posing as an ex-Confederate officer by the name of Hawley, Major Joshua Hawley. Same as I did in New Orleans. I'm sure the Consul General told you, I've been interviewing some of those Southern emigrants who were shipwrecked off the coast here. The Army wants to find out what these people's intentions are."

"And what have you learned, if I may be so bold to ask? Can you share anything?"

"But of course, Lieutenant," Hutchinson said with a broad smile. "The ship that sank, the *Neptune*, was chartered by an ex-Confederate named Major Lansford Hastings. He's the one who's been recruiting these Southerners to emigrate to Brazil. Poor sods. Secretary Seward might find the interviews I've done interesting. The war may be over, Townsend, but I'm tellin' you, the bitterness runs deep. These people believe the country is ruined and without slavery it will become a howling wilderness. They all are determined to take the next ship bound for Brazil. Pure madness, as far as I can see." The Army officer scanned the bustling harbor and then abruptly turned toward Townsend. "The Consul General told me that the Spanish authorities released the ship you were looking for, the *Southern Cross?* I was informed there was a murder on board, one of their sailors?"

Townsend raised his eyebrows. "You knew of that investigation?"

"Well, Consul General Minor mentioned it in passing," Hutchinson replied. "I just thought it was interesting. A murder of an American sailor that the Spanish police now claim was an accident. A bit odd, don't you think? I may keep an eye out for that ship when I get back to New Orleans. Do you think it might be involved in cotton stealing?"

For a brief moment, Townsend considered sharing what he knew about the man's death and his suspicions, ask for the Army officer's insight. But then he remembered Rudd's words—"deliver the report to Secretary Seward *and only to him.*"

"Yes, I was very disappointed to find that the Spanish had released the *Southern Cross* and crew," Townsend said. "Not much I could do about it."

"Do you think the Spanish were hiding something?"

"Don't know. Many unanswered questions remain. Seems complicated— like so many things here in Cuba." Townsend decided to change the topic. "By the way, Major, I never did hear what happened to that man Hodge. Are you still investigating him?"

"Hodge. Oh yes. We continue to look for him in New Orleans, but he and his men just disappeared."

"What about the reports of kidnapping? Have you come across any new leads?"

"That remains a matter of concern. We are keeping our ears to the ground. I imagine Secretary Seward will raise that troublesome topic with the Spanish Captain General. Have you heard anything new?"

Townsend simply shook his head. Hutchinson puffed away on his cigar and then reached out to shake Townsend's hand. "I wish you a safe journey back to Key West, my good man."

The Navy lieutenant watched as the Cuban boat captain expertly sheeted in the sails and headed back toward the ferry landing with his passenger.

"What did that smilin' crittur want?" Metcalf asked.

"Not too sure. He seemed quite interested in our voyage to Sagua. It had a whiff of bulking up his report to impress his superiors. He's looking for a promotion, I would say."

"Did you tell him what we saw up the Sagua la Grande river?" the bosun asked.

"No, I didn't, Metcalf."

"Probably a wise decision."

That same afternoon, Townsend spotted Emilio Hernández's cargo schooner the *Paloma* as the ship sailed toward the main landing. With his telescope, he watched as the men on board, most of whom he recognized from Key West, dropped the sails and let the schooner coast into the docks. He told the crew he would be going ashore to get some fresh food supplies and speak with Emilio Hernández to get the latest news from Key West. He left Metcalf in charge of handing out the ship duties, everything from holystoning the decks to checking the rigging and the sails. He promised them that they would get liberty soon.

Townsend rowed up to the *Paloma* and called up from the jolly boat. One of the sailors spotted him and notified Captain Emilio Hernández that they had a visitor from the Navy.

"Everett! *Bienvenido*. Come aboard! What brings you to Havana Bay? I thought you would be in the Tortugas."

"Greetings, Emilio. No, I'm here on official business—delivering Secretary Seward's correspondence and dispatches. The Secretary of State will be here in Havana in a few days—his last stop on a swing through the Caribbean."

"*No me digas*. I didn't know that. Will you meet with him?"

"I'm not sure. I suppose so."

Townsend had clambered aboard, and he reached out to shake Emilio Hernández's hand.

"My orders are to deliver those letters personally to Mr. Seward as soon as he arrives at his hotel."

"You should inform him what's going on in Cuba."

"Meaning what?"

"He needs to know that Cubans want freedom of speech and equal rights, not to mention a way to participate in the government. Change is coming here." He waved his arm at some troops marching in the Plaza de San Francisco. "Tell him about Spanish repression. He should know that the colonial government is sitting on a powder keg. There could be a popular revolt here soon."

Townsend glanced around to see if anyone was listening.

"Speak softly, Emilio."

The man laughed at Townsend. "I'm not concerned on my own ship." He looked at Townsend with a sparkle in his eye. "So . . . have you gone to see Emma yet?" Townsend smiled weakly and looked at him.

"I think you know we're no longer together."

The Key West merchant nodded. "Indeed. But if you want my advice, I wouldn't give up. It may not seem apparent to you, Everett, but I think Emma still cares for you."

Townsend scoffed.

"*Hay que tener paciencia, mi querido amigo.* When I took her back to Havana the other month, I asked her what she would miss about Key West. She said she would miss *what might have been.*"

Townsend lowered his eyes. "That doesn't sound too encouraging."

Hernández looked back at him with a bright gleam in his eye. "On the contrary, I think it means that she's still thinking of you. Take some advice from an older man—don't give up at the gate." He laughed and patted Townsend on the back. "Persistence pays off, *mi amigo*. Trust me, I'm her brother-in-law. I know Emma. You've got to show her you mean it."

Hubbub suddenly broke out on the wharf. A squad of *Guardia Civil* officers had arrested a sailor and had begun parading him along the wharf with chains on his hands and feet in a show of force.

"What's going on, Vásquez?" Emilio asked his first mate.

"The *Guardia Civil*, Captain—they're now searching all cargo and making arrests for any type of offense," the young sailor replied.

Townsend could see a long line of officers charging up gangplanks onto American cargo schooners. They were ordering the ship captains to open everything. He noticed that Emilio had now become quite agitated, repeatedly wiping the perspiration from his forehead.

"What's wrong, man?"

Emilio shook his head and motioned for him to follow him down below.

"Take a seat, Everett." He paced back and forth in the small cabin at the stern of the boat.

"I have a problem, my friend. Normally the harbor police don't pay much attention to us."

"What are you worried about?" Townsend asked. "I thought you were in the food trade. What do you have on board—salted codfish, beans, potatoes, and salted pork? Those items are in high demand in Havana. They won't bother you."

Hernández shook his head back and forth slowly. "I'm in trouble, Everett. If they search my boat now, I will be put in jail. I think the Spanish Consul

General back in Key West has been spying on me. He may have tipped off the authorities here."

"Tipped off the authorities about what? It's not as if you have guns on board." Townsend chuckled, but one look at Hernández's panicked face made him realize the man was serious.

"I am working with the Cuban Independence Movement."

"Good God, man!"

"Opposition to Spanish rule is spreading like sparks flying out from a bonfire. I am carrying several boxes of pamphlets, *pro-independence* pamphlets that were printed in New York and delivered to me in Key West. If they find them, I will be charged with sedition."

Townsend blinked at his friend. "You should get rid of them now."

"I think it's too late. Besides, Emma is expecting them. I need to get them to her."

"Emma! What has this got to do with Emma?"

"She gives them out to the university students, and they spread them around the city."

Townsend was speechless.

"I thought you knew. Emma has been part of the movement for some time now. She's working with the Cuban exiles in New York—Juan Manuel Macías, Cirilo Villaverde and his wife, Emilia Casanova de Villaverde. Their publication is called *Voz de América*. Emma is starting to gather information and write reports for them."

"Voice of America," Townsend whispered. "Bugger me blind. Does Emma's mother know?"

"I'd think not. At least, not the full extent."

"How long has this been going on?"

"When Emma came back here from Key West, she was lonely. She learned that some of her old friends were now volunteers in the movement and that some of them had been arrested for no good reason. She saw that hostilities between the Cuban *criollos* and the Spanish were growing. Then when my brother Raúl was picked up by the police for nothing more than reading political articles to tobacco workers, she and I both decided to join the movement."

Townsend was silent.

"It's a just cause, Everett."

"*Ya vienen, Capitán,*" one of the sailors shouted. "*La Guardia.* The *Guardia Civil,* they're coming."

Townsend's mind worked quickly.

"Emilio, put all the pamphlets in canvas bags to make them look like sails and rope."

Hernández starting yanking the bags out of the lockers, and he and Townsend began stuffing them in with the sails. He couldn't help but read some of the articles about Cuba. They were calling for nothing less than an end to Spanish rule.

Townsend climbed up the stairs and scanned the docks. Somehow, they had to get these papers off the ship. He looked around the crowded wharf area in desperation. He didn't know what he was looking for, but he knew he had to think of something quickly. Sweaty dockworkers pushing drays filled with barrels of sugar. Mulatta street vendors sauntered and swayed by him with their baskets of bread rolls and guava sweets balanced on their heads. A Chinese crockery peddler with a bamboo yoke on his shoulders was tossing plates in the air, catching them before they broke into pieces.

"Where are they now? I'm just about done," Emilio cried from below. "What are we going to do with these bags?"

"They're about one hundred yards away," Townsend cried out.

The Navy lieutenant's eyes darted from left to right. He spotted a man with a small umbrella style hat perched on top of a small donkey. He was a poultry dealer from the country, *un guajiro*. What caught Townsend's eye were the two large baskets filled with live chickens attached to the saddle. There must have been three dozen chickens in those two baskets, clucking and clacking, flapping their wings against the sides as they tried to escape. The man also had another two dozen chickens tied up by their feet and strung from the horse's neck.

"I've got my eye on a few dozen chickens. Are you hungry? *¿Tienes hambre?*" He looked down into the cabin at Emilio Hernández and winked at him. "I'll need some empty bags along with those full ones."

"Vásquez, take all these bags and follow Lieutenant Townsend."

When Townsend walked up to the poultry dealer and told him he would like to buy all his chickens, the man looked at the uniform and immediately started haggling over the price. Townsend stopped any quibbling by handing him a handful of eighth-ounce gold coins worth two dollars each. The man nodded and gestured that he should go ahead and inspect the chickens. Townsend picked up the string of chickens hanging upside down and transferred them from the horse's neck to his own. He then opened the baskets, allowing the noisy birds inside to poke their heads out, and get a look at their surroundings.

Townsend motioned for Vásquez to bring the empty bags over to him.

"*Pongamos los pollos en estas bolsas,*" he told the poultry vendor, gesturing with his hands at the bags and the chickens to make sure the man understood. The man nodded his approval. But instead of transferring the chickens into the sail bags as he'd said, Townsend stepped to one side of the donkey's rear and yanked and twisted the animal's tail. The donkey let out an ear-splitting bray and jumped and kicked with both hind legs, throwing the poultry dealer onto the stone landing. Townsend could see he was conscious but stunned. The baskets came loose from the saddle and all three dozen chickens were launched into the air in a symphony of mad clucking and frantic flapping. In that noisy commotion, Townsend freed the other chickens hanging from his neck with a knife and soon there was an even greater explosion of feathers.

With all the sudden confusion, the panicked donkey continued to kick and buck to free itself of one of the remaining baskets. A litany of curses and shrieks echoed up and down the docks as the airborne chickens flew over people's heads. Fruit vendors dropped their baskets. The Chinese crockery peddler watched in horror as all his plates and saucers fell and shattered in a resounding clash and clatter. Barrels of molasses rolled off the drays, spilling their sticky contents out onto the landing, causing people to slip and fall.

Townsend took advantage of all of this yelling and motioned to Vásquez and one of Hernández's other crewmembers to help him with all the sail bags. He pointed to his small rowboat tied up right next to the schooner.

"In there!"

The two sailors just stood there, dumfounded by all the noise and chaos around them. Emilio yelled at them to do as the Navy lieutenant had instructed. Townsend hopped into the jolly boat.

"I'm off, old friend. I already paid the man for the chickens so you can keep any of the birds you might catch."

Once in the rowboat, Townsend pushed the sail bags under the seats where they couldn't be seen, and then calmly rowed out to his ship. The yelling and the cursing continued even after the chickens had found safety on the warehouse roofs. A few fights had broken out. As he stepped on board the *Rebecca*, Townsend could see the *Guardia Civil* officers finally arriving next to the *Paloma*. Metcalf wanted to know what had happened.

"Seems like those birds didn't like your dinner plans, Cap'n," the bosun said with a chuckle.

"You might say that, bosun."

"What's in the bags?" he then asked, staring at the cargo.

"Just some old sails Captain Hernández didn't want. I thought we could use them for any patching we need to do with our own."

"I see," Metcalf said skeptically.

As Townsend carried the canvas bags down into his cabin, a sobering thought struck him—he suddenly realized he was now in possession of anti-government pamphlets. If he were caught with these, he would be accused of being involved in sedition against Spain. He had just placed himself directly in danger's way.

18

Townsend tried to swallow down a rising sense of unease as he closed the door of his small cabin and threw the three sail bags onto the side of the bunk. He pulled out some of the newspapers. They were four- to six-page pamphlets, all written in Spanish and published in New York. There must have been several hundred copies. A swath of afternoon sunlight from the large skylight overhead provided the light he needed to scan the columns of small print. One newspaper headline caused his neck muscles to tense up. "*A las armas, cubanos!* Cubans, take up arms!" Hernández had told him these were anti-government newspapers, but he hadn't mentioned they were actually calling for an armed insurrection.

Townsend cursed Emilio under his breath as he continued reading. In Cuba, the censorship of the press was absolute. One paper called for freeing and arming the island's slaves to rise up against the Spanish government and the *esclavócratas*, the aristocratic slaveholders. Another described the growing discontent with Spanish rule and how the colonial government on the island would soon be "bathed in blood."

This is open sedition. He couldn't believe Emma was involved with these exiles. If these papers were discovered by the Spanish authorities, they would show no mercy. Anyone found printing or distributing anti-government material in Cuba would be hauled in front of a military tribunal. Even possessing revolutionary pamphlets like these would bring a long jail sentence or possibly death by the firing squad or by the *garrote* where a prisoner is choked to death by an iron collar around his neck. He knew he needed to get rid of these bags and newspapers as quickly as possible.

A sudden banging on the door made him jump.

"We got visitors, Cap'n," the bosun shouted. "Might need to come up on deck."

"What's so urgent, Metcalf?" Townsend replied, trying to catch his breath.

"Spanish longboat coming in our direction."

"Damn it to hell," Townsend whispered to himself. He told the bosun to put out the ship's ladder and muster the men for review. He quickly stuffed the newspapers back in the bags and hid them in the locker inside the back of his closet, underneath some heavy rope.

The sound of cannon fire startled him. He quickly grabbed his holstered revolver and clambered up the companionway stairs to the deck. Townsend's eyes darted around the harbor. The light was strong, blades of sun slicing through the clouds of gun smoke in the harbor. Metcalf pointed toward several Spanish warships nearby where the gunners were practicing firing their signal guns into the hot afternoon sun. Through the gauzy smoke, a thirty-foot rowing launch with the red and yellow Spanish flag fluttering from the stern slipped into view.

Townsend pulled out his telescope and held it to his eye. There were six men heaving on the oars, all Spanish Navy seamen with their blue shirts and flat-brimmed straw hats. Two Marines armed with rifles were seated in the bow. In the stern next to the coxswain was a stocky, uniformed officer wearing the signature wide-brimmed felt hat of the *Guardia Civil*. Townsend recognized him immediately.

"Friends of yours, Cap'n?" Metcalf asked sarcastically.

"Not exactly," Townsend replied drily. "But I have made the acquaintance of the officer in the stern. Captain Humberto López Villanueva. I met him when I went to pay the fees to the Captain of the Port. He's in charge of security on the docks."

"You expectin' trouble?"

"Not sure."

"Maybe he's coming to collect one more harbor fee," Metcalf snorted with a half laugh.

This was too much of a coincidence. He glanced over at the docks, and he could see the *Paloma* was still tied up there. He couldn't see any sign of police. That was good news, but he knew he needed to gird himself for the possibility that Emilio was under arrest and had implicated Townsend. *Keep calm and deny everything*, he told himself. He was glad he'd hidden the pamphlets well. The Spanish would have to conduct quite a thorough search to find them underneath all those ropes.

The Spanish longboat came alongside the starboard side of the *Rebecca* with a heavy thud and the thick-set *Guardia Civil* captain clambered up the rope ladder. Townsend could feel the beads of sweat gathering on his forehead and dripping down his face like warm raindrops. He imagined the Spanish captain accusing him of sedition and then ordering the two Marines to arrest him, throwing him into the launch boat. He looked at the crew. He had put them all in danger.

Townsend and Metcalf stood to one side as the Spanish captain stepped on deck with his heavy black boots, the two Marines following close behind. Townsend chose his next words carefully. He knew he needed to find the right balance so as not to overdo it.

"*Capitán López Villanueva, Bienvenido,* welcome. Please come aboard," Townsend said, doing his best to relax his shoulders and smile naturally. He knew full well he had to continue to feign respect for the Spanish officer and be tactful.

"As the sole representative of the US Navy in Havana harbor, I want you to know we are being more vigilant than ever. With Secretary Seward's arrival just a few days from now, I know matters of security are of the utmost importance. Is there some assistance you need?"

The Spanish captain pulled the Navy lieutenant aside and said quietly that he needed to speak with him in private. Townsend felt a cold shiver run down his spine as he tried to imagine why that was necessary. He escorted the captain down the companionway steps into the hot, musty cabin.

López Villanueva looked dismissively around the bare whitewashed cabin with its wood burning stove, gimbaled lamps, and the small raw-board table. The mens' hammocks were lashed up in tight round bundles, but some of the tableware and cooking utensils had not been put away in the mess chest. The captain took a few steps toward one of the chairs and then got right to the point, this time surprising Townsend by speaking mostly in English.

"I wanted to speak to you privately to inform you we have arrested several American sailors at the commercial docks. I'm sure you will be pleased to know that these potential troublemakers have been put behind bars."

Townsend paused, his heart beating rapidly. "Indeed, I am," Townsend wanted to know the names of the ships and more about the sailors, but he pressed his lips together. *Best not to be too inquisitive.*

"We suspect these men have ties with traitorous Cuban exile communities in Key West and New Orleans. They will be questioned extensively regarding their activities. We want to make sure there is no secret plot to disrupt the upcoming meeting between the Captain General and Secretary Seward."

"I am heartened to hear of these developments," Townsend replied. "I am confident Secretary Seward will be pleased to hear of your efforts to ensure the success of the upcoming meetings with His Excellency, the Captain General."

The Spanish official's eyes now hardened, and the smile faded.

"Una cosa más, Teniente."

Townsend braced himself for the bad news. "Yes, what would that be?" he replied, wiping the sweat off his brow with a bandana.

"You should know our informants in Key West and New Orleans believe there is a sizable shipment of revolutionary pamphlets on board one of these American schooners here in Havana harbor. We have not yet found this seditious material, but I can assure you we will. We intend to uproot these traitors like tree stumps in a field, but we will need your help."

"I am most impressed by your thoroughness," Townsend said awkwardly. If Emilio had been arrested, there was nothing he could do for him now. "You can be assured—"

López Villanueva surprised him by interrupting him.

"Lieutenant, I thought I would suggest something that should be of mutual satisfaction for both of us."

Townsend raised his eyebrows ever so slightly and cocked his head at López Villanueva.

"The schooner you asked me to look out for. The *Southern Cross*. Wasn't that the name?"

"Yes, that's correct."

"That ship came into Havana harbor early this morning. Dropped anchor over on the northeastern side of Havana Bay near the town of Casa Blanca, just past the fishing fleet and the commercial piers."

Townsend's eyes lit up. He knew that part of the harbor well. A small town filled with warehouses and ship-repairing establishments. It was where many of the cargo schooners went for repairs before they unloaded or loaded cargo at the Havana docks. Shipping supplies could be found there, but so could men for hire, and floating bodies.

"We would naturally board and search this ship ourselves given our current security concerns, but I know you have orders to question the sailors. A sensitive matter, you said? *¿Verdad que sí?*"

Townsend nodded.

"May I ask why you are so interested in the sailors on that ship?"

"They are men who are suspected of criminal activity," Townsend blurted out quickly.

"*¿Conspiradores?*"

"I am not at liberty to reveal anything else."

"I see . . . I thoroughly understand, *Teniente*. As the officer of the *Guardia Civil* charged with police security on the waterfront and the liaison with the Captain of the Port, I will not do anything to deter you from carrying out your orders. Naturally, I hope you will share any pertinent information you might uncover."

"But, of course," Townsend replied quickly. "A matter of courtesy. I thank you for this timely notification. It is greatly appreciated. Is there anything else?"

Captain López Villanueva thanked Townsend for his hospitality and marched up the companionway stairs into the bright late afternoon sun, his heavy boots echoing inside the small cabin. At the top of the stairs, he turned and looked back at Townsend, his face now a black silhouette.

"One more thing, Lieutenant. *Hay un dicho aquí*. There's a saying here that Havana's black water tends to run through Casa Blanca on the way out to the ocean. *Tenga cuidado*. Be careful in that town across the bay."

Townsend took a few minutes down below to digest what had just happened. Mostly, he felt a huge relief that he wasn't under arrest. He breathed out slowly as he heard the splash of the oars in the water and the sound of the coxswain's commands to the oarsmen.

Once he'd recovered his composure, he called the men together and told them the news that the schooner that had eluded them on the Sagua la Grande river was now in Havana harbor. Townsend knew he had been given a second chance, and he intended not to squander it. The pamphlets would have to wait.

Shortly afterward, they raised the anchor and under light sail coasted in the direction of Casa Blanca. Townsend could see the red-tiled roofs and the whitewashed houses that wound their way along the shoreline and up the hillside. The Navy lieutenant wiped his nose with displeasure. The breeze had disappeared, and the smell of the harbor's refuse and sewage wafted over the schooner.

With the help of the late afternoon sun, de la Cruz, perched in the cross-trees, spotted the large schooner anchored away from the shipping lane on the far side of a shoal area. It was near some old steamships, probably some abandoned Confederate blockade runners. In the light air, Townsend sailed the *Rebecca* close in to shore and then dropped anchor behind a row of schooners. In the distance, he could hear the sound of marching and drilling from the nearby Cabaña fortress.

As the sun disappeared, Townsend could see activity on the schooner. Three of the sailors on the *Southern Cross* had begun rowing to the wharf area in one of the ship's yawl boats.

"Get out of those Navy duds, de la Cruz," Townsend ordered the young sailor. 'We don't want to lose sight of these critturs."

Townsend threw on some old clothes as well. Going ashore in a foreign port without his uniform was against Navy regulations, but he felt they had no choice if they wanted to avoid trouble.

By the time Townsend and de la Cruz reached the waterfront landing at Casa Blanca in the small jolly boat, the light was fading quickly. The leftover glow in the sky hung over the steeples and domes of old Havana across the bay like a basket of pink and yellow rose petals. The sound of the splash of their oars was drowned out by a cannon blast from the fortress signaling the end of the day. As they reached the landing, they could just barely see the three men walking along the main street called Calle de la Marina. Townsend and de la Cruz pulled their slouch hats over their heads and followed at a safe distance, so as not to be seen.

The three figures ducked into an alley between some old stone warehouse buildings. Townsend and de la Cruz began walking faster. They turned at the same alleyway but found themselves staring at a cross-section of small roads and cart paths. Townsend looked around in dismay at the layers of dark rooftops that wound up the hill and the odd mixture of woodworking shops, bodegas, and private homes around them. He could see no sign of the men.

With the light now mostly gone, the two men passed some drunken sailors coughing and spitting outside a one-story building and walked inside. A Spanish guitarist was strumming a melancholy tune in the corner. The room was dark and moldy, the walls chipped and yellowed with layers of grease and dirt. Townsend quickly surveyed the tavern. Dim lanterns lit up corners of the room revealing tables of rough-looking men, but none looked like the three men they'd been following.

They walked up to the bar and ordered two tankards of rum.

"Let's settle in," Townsend said. "Like most sailors coming ashore, sooner or later, they'll show up here."

In addition to the bartender, he could see they were now being watched by two of the barmaids. The young women, dressed in revealing low-necked chiffon dresses, came over and attempted to strike up a conversation in broken English.

"*¿Americanos?* Sailors?"

"Yes, we are."

"You like . . . something?"

One of the girls dressed in green smiled with her powdered face and arched eyebrows as she sidled up to Townsend.

"Where you from? *¿Nueva York? ¿Nueva Orleans?*"

Townsend purposely said they were off a merchant ship from Boston, thinking that would not interest her. But the mention of Boston, a destination known for its shipping wealth, only seemed to encourage her more.

"*Boston, ¡Ay, qué maravilla!*" she exclaimed, as her smile broadened. She brushed her body up against him. "I love Boston. So does my friend, Marisol."

Townsend looked over at the other girl. Her brown hair cascaded down her back in waves of corkscrew curls. She smiled at him as she began tugging at de la Cruz to go into another room. Townsend wondered how they were going to extricate themselves from this situation. He was about to warn de la Cruz he might regret any hasty decision when he saw a familiar figure walk into the bar. It was Pancho Menéndez dressed up in a white linen suit, a black cravat, and a flat-brimmed hat. He'd grown a moustache, but otherwise the long thin nose and the curly black hair were unmistakable.

Townsend immediately turned away and pulled the slouch hat over his head even as he tapped de la Cruz and told him to do the same. Menéndez approached the bar not six feet away from where they were standing and ordered a drink. In a panic, Townsend pulled the girl dressed in green next to him even closer and buried his face in her heavily perfumed black hair, which caused her to respond in kind, giggling as she did. Menéndez laughed at this sight of the two men and told the bartender in Spanish that most men are all the same, like drought-stricken cattle in need of water.

"*Lo único que necesitan es un abrevadero.* The only thing they need is a watering trough. *¿Verdad que sí?*"

The bar man and Menéndez laughed. Townsend slowly lifted his head out of the girl's hair and watched the former Confederate leave the bar with a tankard of rum and walk through a door into a brightly lit room. Inside he saw a man with sandy-colored hair and a scraggly beard. Townsend instantly recognized him. It was Ezekiel Hodge. He was talking with a stocky, bald-headed man with a large nose who looked like a Spaniard, well-dressed with a top hat and a brightly colored vest.

Townsend grabbed de la Cruz and pulled him away from the curly haired girl who was now wrapped around him like a windblown flag around a pole. He didn't think Menéndez had seen their faces.

"Sorry ladies—we're no longer in the mood," Townsend said in Spanish.

"*¡Qué cosa!*" the black-haired girl in green exclaimed, clearly taken by surprise by this rejection and Townsend's ability to speak Spanish. The two women stood there, at first with pouts, then with cold, hard faces. To prevent a scene, Townsend gave each of the women a quarter-ounce gold coin.

"You know any of them men in the back room?" he asked in Spanish.

"The only one we know is the bald-headed one," volunteered the girl named Marisol.

"What does he do?" Townsend asked.

"*Es un comerciante.* He is a merchant from Havana. A Spaniard. They call him *El Gallego.* He buys and sells from the American ship captains. He used to work with *los Confederados* during the American war."

Townsend gave each of the two women another coin.

"I need a favor. Spend some time in there and report back to us what he and his companions are talking about."

This was easy money, and the two barmaids readily agreed. Townsend and de la Cruz settled down at a table in one of the bar's shadowy corners. Townsend was feeling the effects of the rum. His eyes gleamed as he thought of catching up with this man who had eluded capture all these months. He told himself he would make Hodge confess to murdering those freedmen in the ship. Then he thought of Jacobs, and he just shook his head as he tried not to imagine the nightmares the man may have faced at the hands of Hodge. He didn't want to think what could have happened to him.

"Are we going to arrest Hodge, Cap'n?"

"No. We can't do that unfortunately."

"I'm not sure I like this place, Cap'n. There aren't too many friendly faces here."

Moments later, they spotted Hodge, Menéndez, and two other sailors walk by their table, laughing and joking. They pulled down their hats until they'd gone by. The two barmaids arrived at their table and settled right onto their laps, only this time the one with the corkscrew curls named Marisol picked Townsend. The other girl dressed in green arched her eyebrows and laughed as she stroked de la Cruz's hair. She told him that her name was Isabela, "*como la reina de España,* like the queen," she said, chuckling.

Townsend could see that young de la Cruz was an easy mark for this woman and might soon be quite willingly led away to a back room. He decided to direct his questions to her as she did seem to have a more intelligent look to her face.

"What were they talking about in there?" Townsend asked.

"The men . . . they were haggling over a price," Isabela replied. "The man with the flat-brimmed hat—the one they called Pancho—translated *El Gallego*'s Spanish for his three friends."

"What were they selling?" Townsend asked.

"*Quién sabe*," she said. "They just talked about the postmaster and packages. They told *El Gallego* that they'd just delivered a big shipment of packages down the coast. This was their bonus, an extra package. Their last bit of business before sailing for New Orleans"

"How much were they charging for this package?"

"We couldn't hear," she replied. "They lowered their voices. We did hear that the Americans wanted payment in gold. *El Gallego* said he could have the money by tomorrow night. They agreed to meet down at the fishermen's dock here after the firing of the evening cannon at the fortress."

Townsend was now fighting to maintain his concentration. The girl on his lap was unbuttoning his shirt. He breathed in her strong perfume.

"Let's go, de la Cruz. We need to return to the boat."

The two women looked at each other with puzzled expressions, but Townsend was already standing up. He reached in his pocket and gave Marisol and Isabela a few more gold coins. "One last favor, ladies," he said. "Tell *El Gallego* that the men he just spoke with have come back. They are waiting for him outside the bar. Tell him those men need to talk with him to go over some details."

Townsend and de la Cruz watched the two barmaids disappear into the back room and then got up to leave. Outside, they found a dark spot up against the building under some bougainvillea vines. Soon enough the man called *El Gallego* came outside and began looking around.

Townsend called out the man's name from the darkness.

"*¿Quién está allí?* Who's there?" the Spaniard asked nervously, taking off his hat and peering into the shadowy light.

Townsend and de la Cruz stepped forward where they could be seen.

"We're associates of Pancho Menéndez and Captain Hodge. They've sent us back here to tell you the price you negotiated for the package is not enough."

The Spaniard looked them up and down before saying anything.

"Look, I don't know who you two *pendejos* are, but I know you're not who you pretend to be."

The bald-headed man gestured with a twist of his head. Townsend was suddenly grabbed from behind. Someone with a foul-smelling hand covered his mouth and then he felt a sharp blow to the head followed by intense pain. He felt himself falling as everything now became a shadowy blur before turning to blackness.

19

January 18, 1866

Townsend was jolted awake by a man kicking him and then hurling a bucket of seawater on him. "*¡Borrachos sinverguenzas!* Shameless, deadbeat drunks," the man shouted. The briny water was oily and stank of rotting fish. Townsend tried to sit up. It was dark but a kerosene lamp allowed him to see de la Cruz lying next to him on the deck of a boat. Another bucket of seawater was thrown in his face and this time something fleshy landed on his lips. He spit and coughed. He fought back a wave of nausea when he realized that the man was using a draw bucket filled with bits of bait fish.

The shadowy, grizzled face of his tormentor peered down at him. He had a red bandana wrapped around his head and was chomping on a cigar. The man stuck his boozy smelling face next to Townsend, almost burning him with the tip of his cigar.

"*¡A la puta calle, imbéciles!*"

Another Cuban kicked both Townsend and de la Cruz several times in the ribs, and then picked them up and threw them onto the wharf. Still disoriented and in pain, they stumbled down the pier. In the distance, Townsend recognized the lights where they'd tied up their rowboat. He shook his aching head and rib cage and tried to remember what had happened. They were set up. That much was clear. The two barmaids must have told *El Gallego* that a couple of American sailors were asking a lot of questions. *Those two backstabbing floozies*, he thought to himself.

It would be no problem for a man like *El Gallego* to have some of the muscle men at the bar knock them out and dump them on the fishing boat. They were lucky to be alive.

Townsend knew they had no time to waste. If *El Gallego* sent word to Hodge about what had happened, he would probably pull up anchor and leave Havana.

"Hurry, de la Cruz," he said as the young sailor groaned behind him.

They jumped in the jolly boat and rowed out to the *Rebecca*. He guessed it was about 3 a.m. It was still dark, but fortunately, Metcalf had lit two kerosene lamps together by the bowsprit as was customary, so it was easy to locate the boat among the others.

Even before they arrived, Townsend was calling out for all hands. When he climbed the ship's ladder, Metcalf met him on deck.

"Damnation to hell! What in blazes?" the bosun cried out as he took one look at Townsend and de la Cruz. "You two smell like you been swimming in a fishmonger's swill hole!"

"Get the anchor up, Metcalf," Townsend said. "No time to explain. We're going to board that ship. Clear the howitzer for action."

"Aye, Cap'n."

Townsend went below to put on his Navy uniform. His orders were only to interrogate these sailors about the incident in Sagua. He knew he had to be careful. He was a Navy lieutenant and needed to carry out his orders legitimately. But he also wanted Hodge to pay for what he'd done. He felt the simmering rage inside him. *Control that anger.* If he went too far, he would be no better than some of these ex-Confederate soldiers who were taking the law into their own hands.

By the time he finished buttoning his coat and tightening his gun holster, Townsend knew what he was going to do. They would board the *Southern Cross*, but without creating a ruckus in the harbor. He didn't want any close-action fighting inside or on deck. Nor did he want any loud protests questioning their authority in a foreign port. They needed to use surprise to their advantage. He told himself his orders required him to not just question these sailors, but also to thoroughly search the ship. The best way he could think of doing that was to smoke them out.

Townsend had seen yellow fever ships being fumigated in Key West with buckets of pine tar and hot irons. The pine tar smoke would disinfect the insides of a ship, but the putrid smell would also drive anything alive out of the cabin to escape the smoke. He yelled for Tollman to come down to the galley.

"Heat up some irons in last night's stove embers, Stumpie, and fill two buckets with pine tar. Get those irons scalding hot."

"Aye, Cap'n."

Townsend climbed up on deck. Slowly at first and then more quickly, the schooner was gathering headway. He felt a light sea breeze brush his face. The smell of wood smoke mixed with coal told him that the fire in the iron stove must already be getting hot. His head throbbed, but he felt the excitement of the moment, and realized that part of him still thirsted for the intensity of war. He wanted to board that ship. Maybe Emma was right. The war was over, but he hadn't stopped fighting it.

As the night began to give way ever so slightly to the dark gray of early morning, Townsend could just make out the shape of the *Southern Cross*. With his telescope he scanned the deck of the large cargo schooner for any sign of activity. He was worried that they might have placed a sailor on watch, but fortunately they all must have passed out from too much drinking. There were no lights. There was no sign of anyone. He was particularly relieved not to see any sign of Menéndez's dog.

Slowly, Townsend nudged the *Rebecca* into the wind as they came along-side the bigger schooner. Langworth stood at the ready with the deck gun set to fire in case they were surprised by any hostile action. At a wave of Townsend's hand, de la Cruz dropped the jib. Within seconds they'd hurled the grappling hooks into the ratlines and shrouds of the *Southern Cross* and pulled the two ships together like they'd practiced in their Navy drills. He could see the gleam of his men's drawn cutlasses. Combined with the Colt re-volvers the bosun and Townsend routinely carried, they were well-equipped.

To try to make as little noise as possible, all the men had wrapped their shoes with old rags. Townsend boarded the vessel first and signaled to Tol-man and Metcalf to follow him with the buckets of tar and the hot irons. The Navy lieutenant felt a tightening in his gut as he grabbed a hot iron from the metal drum. He picked up one of the buckets of pine tar and then crept down the companionway stairs, careful to keep the scalding hot iron away from his face. It was still dark, but he knew the layout of these merchant schooners. The sleeping quarters for the captain and the first mate were in the stern. He was going to place the bucket right outside the captain's cabin.

Suddenly out of the blackness he heard the pad of a boot. Then footsteps coming toward him. He heard someone breathing nearby. He still couldn't see anything. He started to reach for his gun, but instead he raised the red-hot iron and plunged it into the bucket of pine tar. A plume of acrid black smoke rose up into the cabin with a snake-like hiss.

"God damn it to hell," a voice cried out.

Townsend jumped in surprise. Whoever it was, they were right next to him. He ducked to one side and yelled out, "Fire in the hold. Fire in the ship." He heard a frantic banging on the door and lots of cursing. A cry for the captain. He then ran up the stairs to the deck and pulled out his Colt revolver. Metcalf and Tolman had now surfaced on deck from the crew's quarters up forward, and Townsend could see a curl of black smoke coming out of that cabin's portholes. He signaled to all the sailors to wait with their cutlasses drawn.

Almost immediately, Hodge and another man came stumbling out on deck, their shirts and pants unbuttoned. They were coughing and spitting, taking deep breaths. The two men came to a sudden halt when they spotted Townsend and de la Cruz with a pistol and a cutlass pointed at them. Townsend could see that this wily ex-Confederate had already noticed the deck gun on the *Rebecca*, pointed at his ship. Hodge looked around in desperation. The other sailors in the forward bunkhouse came crawling out on their hands and knees, gasping for air.

"Stay at your station, Langworth," Townsend cried out. "If they try anything, fire that deck gun into the rigging."

"What right have you got to board my ship? You high-tone Yankee bluecoats can never stop, can ye?" Hodge yelled at Townsend. "The blockade's over. As far as I know so is the War of Northern Aggression."

"The war is over, Hodge." Townsend snapped back. "Seems like you Southerners are the ones that need to accept that reality."

"You're in a foreign port. This is outside the law."

With his gun out, Townsend personally began directing the coughing man back to the Navy ship. He was going to interview him in his cabin. With such a shorthanded crew, he was taking no chances. He instructed de la Cruz to remove the pine tar buckets from the *Southern Cross* and air out the ship. "Get rid of that smoke and then search the ship thoroughly. I want to find out what this package is they were selling."

Townsend then turned to the bosun. "Metcalf, take these sailors to the fore cabin of the *Rebecca*. Keep a gun pointed at them at all times, and start questioning them. Get their names and where they're from. The Navy will want all the details. I want to hear from each of them about what took place in Sagua, and who that dead man was."

Then he turned to Hodge and introduced himself, giving the man his name and rank.

"We haven't actually met, Captain Hodge, but I feel like I've known you for a good spell of time."

"That so?" the thin-faced man said as he cocked his head to one side. "I'm willin' to bet my salvation I never laid eyes on ye before."

"Shut your face and walk."

January 19

Townsend took Hodge down below into his cabin and sat him down on the chair by his small chart desk. He put his gun down on the desktop, within easy reach. The early morning sun shone through the portholes onto the man's face. This was the first time Townsend had observed Hodge up close. He had a thin and tense face with a bramble of side whiskers and a fuzzy beard. He could see the man was no dirt floor redneck, but his cold, light blue eyes suggested he had no hint of a heavy conscience about anything.

Hodge had now collected himself enough to start demanding his rights.

"You got no right to board my ship. I'm a cotton man, I am. Legal and fair cotton merchant. Just look at my manifest. Go inspect the cargo hold."

"Shut your fart catchin' bone-box, Hodge. I have my orders from Navy headquarters in Key West to question you and your crew so you keep your filthy gullywash to yourself."

"This is a foreign port, damn ye. Yankee law don't apply here."

"It does in your case, Hodge."

This was intentionally vague, and not quite accurate, but Townsend had never been bothered with exaggerating when it suited his purposes.

"Why don't you start by telling me what you were selling to that Spaniard in Casa Blanca?"

"Don't know what yur talkin' about," he said defiantly, his eyes gleaming with resentment. Hodge took out a plug of tobacco and put it in his mouth. Townsend could see that the man's teeth were yellow with tobacco stains.

"Last night . . . What were you selling? What was the package, damn you?"

Hodge didn't say anything.

Just then de la Cruz appeared in the doorway. "You need to see this, Cap'n."

"What?"

De la Cruz pointed toward the bosun's cabin, which was adjacent to the captain's quarters.

"He's in there. We found him in the anchor chain locker on top of some piles of chain and rope."

Townsend holstered his gun and walked over to the other cabin. He saw a man he knew, but hardly recognized. Levi Jacobs was lying prone on his side. Townsend gasped at the sight of Jacobs's face. His eyes were hollow and haunted, his body bony and gaunt. From the swollen eyelids, Townsend could see he'd been beaten. There was no sign of his spectacles.

"Is he alive?" he asked de la Cruz.

"Aye, sir. He's breathing, but not speaking."

"Jacobs, can you hear me?" Townsend cried out. He shook the man's shoulders gently. Jacobs moaned and rolled to his other side, but it was clear that he was only semi-conscious. Townsend felt a sinking sensation come over him as he realized that Jacobs must have been the reason why Hodge was in Casa Blanca.

"See if you can get liquids into him, de la Cruz, and tell Metcalf to bring that medical book we have up forward in the chest."

Townsend stormed back into his cabin and pounded his fist on the desk.

"What have you done?" Townsend asked. "You were trying to sell an American Navy veteran, a freedman as a slave! You will pay for that. What did you do to him? I know you drugged him."

Hodge didn't even flinch. He responded without hesitating, his badger eyes gleaming unpleasantly.

"That insolent Negro caused me too much trouble. Not fetched up properly, he ain't. He had the devil in him right bad. He attacked me, yellin' about his two sons. Then he grabbed the wheel and tried to run us onto the riverbanks. That was up in Appalachicola. He was a madman."

Townsend pulled out his knife and held it up to Hodge's face. "I'll scrape that scruffy beard right off your face. Now start talking."

"Gave him a glimpse of hell, that's all. Some jimsonweed. Made him holler and twitch a bit, but when he got too bad we calmed him down with some valerian. I guess the jimsonweed worked. He stopped accusing me of kidnapping his sons. Never gave us any more trouble."

"Did you kidnap his sons?"

"Why would I do that? I told you I'm a Southun cotton man. I transport cotton from the Gulf to Cuba."

"So you say, but in this case you were a slave trader."

"How do you figure that? I hired him in Key West for fifteen dollars a month. Good money for a wash bucket boy. More than he'd get on any plantation."

"You were selling a human being, damn it! Here in Cuba!"

"Not so. I was just getting rid of a bad sailor. No different than what any other ship captain would have done. He crossed me one too many times. I could have flogged him with a rope's end and thrown him overboard. Probably should have. I thought it would be more *humane* to leave him in Cuba. All I was doin' was jes' turning him to good advantage."

Townsend looked at that pinched face and had to struggle to restrain himself.

"Rest assured, Hodge, as soon as I can get this man's testimony, I intend to take you back to Key West for trial."

"Go ahead and try, Lieutenant," Hodge snorted. "That boy won't tell you much. I put him in irons and gave him a regular dose of that devil potion so the only thing he saw was his own inner demons. He doesn't know anything. Besides, who's going to believe a crazy Black man when it's just his word against mine?"

"Damn your stinkin' hide, I saw those dead bodies out in the Marquesas in the cargo hold of the *Hard Times*. I talked with a survivor. You *murdered* them all."

Hodge's eyes narrowed as he glowered at Townsend.

"The *Hard Times*. Yes, she was a right smart, pretty boat. Sorry to lose her. We had no choice but to put those Negros in the hold. Ain't no kindness to be given those former slaves. They tried to take over the ship. Wouldn't have done to set em free, not in that hell-fire storm. Pity they all died."

"Where were you taking them?"

"Up the coast to some yellow pine forests near New Smyrna. A turpentine work crew. Clairin' land."

"So you deny you were taking them to Cuba?"

"Why would I take them here?"

Townsend knew the man was lying, but he had no way of proving it.

"What were you doing up the Sagua la Grande River? Did you have another load of kidnapped freedmen? More hidden cargo? You should know we followed you."

"We have our customers up that river. They pay well. Planters who request special items, machinery to perfume. We pay off the Dagos at customs. Standard practice in Cuba."

"Standard procedure as well to kill one of your own sailors?"

"What? What are you talking about?"

The silence hung in the air. Hodge shifted in the chair. For the first time, Townsend thought the man was rattled.

"That dead American sailor in the port of Sagua . . . he was on your ship."

"Oh, you mean Hogg. James Hogg. Bad drinker, that one. Got mauled by a runaway dog. Very unfortunate. The Spanish police finally determined it was an accident. I don't know how they got so confused."

Townsend didn't let on that he hadn't known the man's name. "Was that dog owned by your war buddy, Pancho Menéndez, by chance?"

Hodge didn't answer, and Townsend pressed ahead.

"I saw Menéndez with you last night in the back room at that bar in Casa Blanca. Looked like you and he were doing some dealin'. I'm told it was with a Spaniard by the name of El Gallego. That should jog your memory? Where is that bugger Menéndez now?"

"You continue to surprise me, Lieutenant. A regular high-tone gentleman, you are. Mr. Menéndez went back to Havana last night. He's the owner of this ship, you know. Had to see some business associates. Line up some future shipments, you understand."

"More cotton customers?" Townsend said sarcastically.

"You might call it that."

Townsend sneered at the man. Part of him wanted to attack him and force him to confess, but he knew that would never hold up in any court. He had to acknowledge that Hodge's denials were more convincing than he expected, and he despaired that he might have to set this man free.

The Navy lieutenant left Hodge with de la Cruz and walked into the galley area where Metcalf was trying to interview the crew members. He spotted the man with the bald head and cloven lip who had yelled at him along with Menéndez when he came ashore after the hurricane. The man clearly didn't recognize him.

Townsend looked the others up and down. He'd seen their type hanging out in Havana's bars before he'd left to join the Navy in 1863. Grim faces, sullen and resentful. Blockade runners or Confederate operatives under orders back then to capture passenger ships for the Confederate Navy. He pulled the bosun aside and signaled to him to go up on deck.

"What have they told you?"

"They're refusing to talk, Cap'n. They won't say anything about what happened to that sailor in Sagua. They're afraid to speak. Maybe if we had some information from Hodge, we could get them to talk?"

"He's told me nothing. He's a slippery customer," Townsend replied. "Lying through his teeth. He doesn't even seem worried about Levi Jacobs' possible testimony. I think he believes he's untouchable."

Even as he said that, an idea was formulating in Townsend's mind. It would solve two problems at once. He told the bosun he was going to search the Southern Cross himself and see what he could find. He went back into his cabin, pulled out the three canvas sail bags, and pushed them up through the hatch onto the deck. Langworth was still at the deck gun. Townsend told him to go help Metcalf watch the sailors. He didn't want anyone to see him with the bags.

As the man disappeared into the fore cabin, Townsend stepped on board the *Southern Cross* and quickly hid the bags in Hodge's cabin. When he came back on board the *Rebecca*, he told Metcalf he'd come across something important onboard ship, and he would need to inform the Spanish authorities about this matter.

"What did you find?"

"Something our Spanish friend will find of value."

Metcalf accepted this without asking any more questions, and Townsend didn't offer any more explanations.

"What 'bout Hodge and these critturs?"

"Give 'em coffee and biscuits. In another hour or so, if this breeze keeps up, their cabins should be aired out. Then you can let 'em return to their ship."

"So, we just goin' to let 'em go?"

"'Fraid so, Metcalf. No way around it. I'd like to arrest them, but we don't have the authority. Not much more we can do in a foreign port. Even if we could, I think that snake Hodge would wiggle out of any prosecution. We followed our orders, Metcalf. I'll deliver my report to Secretary Seward and brief the commander when we get back to Key West."

It was early afternoon when Townsend returned to the *Rebecca*. He was met by an agitated Metcalf who told him that a Spanish Naval boat full of Marines had come steaming by the *Rebecca* and then boarded and seized the *Southern Cross*.

"I thought they were coming for us, but they went right by us. Those Spanish Marines boarded that schooner and began searching the ship, tearing it apart."

Townsend pretended to look surprised.

"Heard anything about that ashore?"

"I heard some sailors had been arrested, but nothing more."

"They tied up Hodge and his men like they were taking a bunch of hogs to market. They were plenty rough with them with their bayonets. Landed them at the docks and then marched them toward the Naval dockyard. Maybe these Spanish officials changed their minds about that incident in Sagua?"

"I admit, as a matter of courtesy, I told Captain López Villanueva about some printed pamphlets I saw on board the schooner. One of them called *La Voz de América* was of particular interest to him. He was grateful for this timely assistance."

"What is that newspaper?"

"*La Voz de América*, The Voice of America. Printed in New York by Cuban exiles. That's all I know."

"Critical of Spain, is it?"

"That might be an understatement."

"Wouldn't have thought that a former Confederate would dip his toes into that swillhole. I mean why would Hodge dabble in any business against the Spanish after all the Spanish colonial government did for the Southerners during the war? Makes no sense. Could he have been taking money from some of the revolutionary groups here?"

Townsend didn't answer and shook his head. His mind was swirling with rationalizations.

"How long do you think they'll hold him in jail?"

"I don't know, Metcalf. I would say he may be in some trouble."

A smile slowly emerged on the bosun's face as he began to understand that Hodge and his men were probably headed for a long stay behind bars.

"Well, the hand of Providence works in unusual ways, don't it Cap'n? That varmint is getting the rough justice he deserves. You did the right thing by tellin' that Spanish captain about those revolutionary pamphlets."

The Navy lieutenant nodded, but Metcalf's praise didn't relieve the uneasy feelings running through him. In his gut, Townsend knew he was in the wrong. He'd planted evidence to falsely incriminate someone. If the Spanish authorities found out about this deception, they'd all be thrown into prison. As a Navy officer, the consequences of his actions were also serious. During the war, a ruse like this one might have been considered acceptable, a clever way to trick the enemy—but now it would be considered a crime. Still, he knew deep down he didn't feel that much remorse. He'd gotten his revenge on Hodge. His only regret was that he hadn't been able to get Menéndez arrested as well.

Townsend knew that no one could know the full truth about what he'd done. Any investigation of where those pamphlets came from might end up leading back to Emma and Emilio. For that matter, if the truth were known, he might end up as a prisoner in the Dry Tortugas along with that fellow Samuel Mudd and his cohorts.

20

January 20, 1866

The booming of the cannons from the gray stone walls of El Morro fortress announced the arrival of Secretary of State Seward on board the USS *De Soto*. From the deck of the USS *Rebecca*, Townsend watched the big American sidewheel gunship fire off a return salute and then pick up its pilot. He pulled out his watch. It was shortly after noon. The smell of wood smoke and fried fish, mingled with the aroma of salt biscuit, made him realize he was hungry. It was de la Cruz's turn to prepare the meals, and the young seaman was down below preparing lunch. The entire crew was on board to witness the arrival of the Navy ship.

Townsend knew he was expected the next morning at the Hotel de Almy where the Secretary would be staying. He was nervous about having to hand over his report about the *Southern Cross*. He'd been working on it over the last few days while the crew alternated, taking liberty ashore. He still was struggling with what he should include, and what he should say about Hodge.

He turned to Metcalf and asked him how Levi Jacobs was faring.

"Has he said anything more?"

"Not much, but he responded well this morning to the sound of eggs sputtering and cow beef popping in the frying pan. In between mouthfuls, he wanted to know where that crittur Hodge was. I told him he was locked up in a Spanish prison. He just smiled when he heard that. I think those small doses of valerian have helped."

Townsend had also spent the last two days tending to Jacobs. He and Metcalf had studied the medical books on board, particularly one by two medical doctors from Philadelphia. They found plenty of information about jimsonweed. It was also called thorn apple or devil's trumpet, but the proper medical name was *Datura stramonium*. It was a powerful narcotic sometimes used for epilepsy that caused hallucinations, and in poisonous doses could cause blindness, heart problems, and death. The medical manual called for laudanum or valerian to help him recover, both of which they fortunately had on board the *Rebecca*.

Metcalf had closely followed the instructions, at first giving Jacobs a small dose of the sedatives every hour and then gradually lengthening the time between doses. Jacobs' speech and vision were now better, but he remained confused about what had happened to him. He'd had some memory loss and was still suffering hallucinations. Townsend hoped the man could provide more information about what Hodge was doing in Sagua, but despite their best efforts, the man's recollections had been sketchy at best.

The booming of the cannons continued as the USS *De Soto* steamed into the bay, its single funnel billowing out clouds of black smoke. Townsend watched as the big ship's paddlewheels thumped to a halt, and the crew dropped anchor in between a group of French military supply vessels and the Spanish Navy fleet. The last time he'd seen this big ship in Havana harbor was in 1863 when he was the captain of a blockade-running schooner. The warship with its array of Parrott thirty-two-pounder rifles and its eleven-inch Dahlgren was much feared by those attempting to run guns through the Naval blockade.

In the distance, through a gauntlet of smoking funnels and masts with fluttering flags, Townsend could see the *Southern Cross* anchored near the Spanish Naval dockyard. The schooner's decks were still swarming with *Guardia Civil* and armed Marines. The ship was now clearly the property of the Spanish government.

Townsend wondered what hellhole dungeon Hodge and his men had been taken to. They would be interrogated, possibly tortured, and then brought before a military tribunal that would decide their fate. He knew Hodge would be hard-pressed to talk his way out of this situation. He watched as the boat carrying the American Consul General chugged its way out into the harbor to greet the Secretary, passing the neglected hulks of a few former Confederate blockade runners. He thought of the war that had just ended. Fighting against slavery had been justified. *Justice comes in many forms, and travels in many directions*, he told himself. *In the case of Ezekiel Hodge that man is facing the reckoning he deserves.*

Townsend could no longer resist the welcome aroma of fried fish. He went below to see how lunch was coming along. De la Cruz was sprinkling generous heapings of garlic and onion into the spattering pan, which made Townsend's eyes tear up. He was surprised to see Levi Jacobs sitting up in his bunk, drinking his coffee.

"Jacobs! I'm glad to see you're up. Feeling any better?"

"Yes, suh. My memory comin' back with all dis good food you givin' me. Ah' preciate what you dun for me."

"I'll bet you wish you were back in Key West."

"Sho nuff. I could do wid sum soothin' words from Preacher Cornish. I feel like I bin to hell and back."

"I understand. That fellow, Hodge, poisoned you with some bad drugs, Jacobs. He gave you overdoses of jimsonweed. That will take you to hell. If we hadn't come upon you, you might be property of a Spanish agent now."

"What did Old Sandy say? De Lawd will provide. De bosun tells me de Spanish arrested Hodge?"

"Yes, they did. I believe he was found with printed material on his ship that is strictly forbidden in Cuba. I think he and his men are facing some serious prison time."

"Praise de Lawd," Jacobs said. "His heavenly hand works in mysterious ways. Dat man, Hodge is de devil's own."

"I know you have memory problems. Anything you can recall about your time on that ship?" Townsend asked. "Anything at all? We suspect he had a ship full of freedmen when he arrived here in Cuba. *Kidnapped* freedmen. Did you see them?"

"He took sum fifteen men."

"Where?"

Jacobs described sailing to Appalachicola from New Orleans. A work gang was waiting at a plantation landing upriver from the town. Hodge and his men were all dressed up in Yankee uniforms to meet them.

"Blue uniforms?" Townsend blurted out. "Like Union soldiers?"

"Das' right. Dem buckra boys all dressed up like federals, make dem freedmen tink dey gon' protect dem. I believe dey picked up de uniforms in New Orleans. Easy to find now dat the war deh over."

Townsend shook his head in astonishment. "So these men weren't forced aboard. They were tricked."

"Like settin' cheese for mice. Hodge told dem dey gon' work clearin' land and makin' turpentine at twenty-four dollars a month. Das twice what dey would make workin' on sum plantation. When dose freedmen step on board, dey lifted dar hats and start shoutin' dey be free now. Free from de plantation. Free from slave work."

"But you suspected something?"

"I remember dat story you tol' me about dem freedmen you found who drowned in de storm. Locked in de cargo hold and trapped down der. I watched Hodge and dem put dat work gang down below. Dey threw donkey straw down dar for de bedding. Buckets of corn mush for food and den dey lock down de hatch from de outside. Das' when I began to suspect something bad. I aks'd one of de crew why dey lock de men up, and he told me it was for de men's own safety. I knew dat was a lie."

Townsend scribbled down notes. He now had firsthand information how this kidnapping was taking place. It made sense. Hodge was offering opportunity—a job and a salary to people who were desperate. Most freedmen would have trusted anyone wearing a blue uniform.

Jacobs described how later in the voyage he finally decided to confront Hodge. With his draw bucket, he pretended to be scooping up seawater from overside to scrub the decks, eventually approaching the quarterdeck where Hodge was standing.

"I aks him, I say, Cap'n Hodge whar we headed? He said dat was not for me to know. But den I aks him 'bout dem people he pick up at a plantation up de Mississippi called Fannie Place. I could see he was surprised. Up until den he jus' saw me as anudah former slave, singin' and shufflin', but now he look at me different. He said what business did I have aksin' questions about his commercial dealings. Das' when I could no longer pretend anymore."

Townsend wrote frantically, even as de la Cruz placed a plate of fried fish in front of him.

"I took de mop and shook it at him. Tell me, I said. I want to know whar you take dem people you pick up at Fannie Place plantation. Tell me now. *Hell, if I know*, he replied. *Why do you care?* I tol' him I cared 'cause my two sons were part of dat work gang and I want to find dem. Whar deh be? He look at me real funny and said he wa' gon' tell me later, and I should get back to scrubbin' de decks. He walk away from me. Das when I knew dis man had something to hide."

"So did he ever tell you where he took your sons?"

"He ain' say nuttin."

Townsend looked up from his notepad at Jacobs' face. He could see just talking about his two sons had caused him distress in his weakened condition. His hands trembled. Despair was written all over the man's face, criss-crossing lines of worry converging on his furrowed brow.

"If you're strong enough, I'd just like to ask a couple more questions."

Jacobs nodded.

"When did you first know you were bound for Cuba?"

Jacobs described how he began listening to conversations between the crewmembers. He heard some of them talking about selling mules in Cuba, and where they were going. Up some river.

"Das when I realize I mus' be on a slave boat, runnin' freedmen to Cuba back into slavery. Worse still, I knew dat man Hodge had mos' likely dun de same with me two sons. I was livin' my worst nightmare."

Jacobs then described how angry he became at this sudden realization. It was like his mind disappeared down a black hole. He lost all control. He told Townsend he flew into an uncontrollable rage as he imagined his two sons once again enslaved. He walked back toward the stern of the boat where Hodge was standing by the helmsman. He shouted at him, pushing him away, and then tried to grab the wheel and run the boat ashore.

"At dat moment, I ain' care if dey kill me. I wanted revenge. Retribution, I'm tellin' you. I could see de fear in der eyes, and I want dem all to suffah. I was goin' to sink dat ship."

Jacobs described that he was hit from behind and the next thing he remembered was waking up in a dark hole. There was no light. No air. He was lying on an anchor chain and soggy rope. They'd taken his spectacles. His head throbbed. He began yelling and someone came and forced some bitter tea down his throat. He told Townsend that each morning they would give him more of that devil medicine. It caused him to have fever and the sweats, terrible shaking and trembling.

"I kept havin' dese visions, but I tol' me'self deh ain' real. Voices too . . . terrible voices. Das all I remembah. All I wanted to do was sleep. I tellin' you. I'ain remembah anything else. Just dem voices."

Townsend realized that Hodge had been right. Jacobs had been so drugged no one would have believed his story.

"One of the sailors on board was killed in that port town. Do you know anything about that?"

Jacobs just shook his head.

"I jus' heard dem voices. When I slept, I kept fallin' into de same dream. I was in some kind of cave or black hole. I think I saw me wife, Lena dere, beckonin' me. She tellin' me it was a passage out of de darkness. Come wid me, she said. I ain' want to follow her. I hear bats flyin' around me. Der were plantation dogs snarlin' nearby. I wa' scared. Den I wake up, sweatin' and shiverin'. Am I goin' mad, Lieutenant?"

"No, you're not going mad, Jacobs. Those drugs would make any man question his sanity. You're lucky to have survived." Townsend sighed.

"Listen I have been tasked with delivering a confidential report to the Secretary of State who is visiting Havana. It's very important. I need any relevant information you can remember about Hodge and his business connections. Maybe something when you arrived in New Orleans from Key West?"

Jacobs looked at the table. Then sipped his coffee. "When we fus arrived at de docks in New Orleans, it was dusk. Dey had me load cotton bales off de dock onto anudah ship. It was the *Southern Cross*. I saw Hodge and Menéndez approach a man, who stepped out of a carriage, well-dressed like a dandy man."

Jacobs described hiding behind some cotton bales. The stranger on the dock handed Hodge a big envelope and told him that should be enough for provisions and operational expenses until he made the delivery and returned to New Orleans. He assured him there would be no Navy ships looking for them.

"Did you get that stranger's name?"

"No, but I remember one of dem joked dat he was like a postmaster. Sortin' and deliverin' de mail. Dey all laughed."

Townsend didn't say anything. He sipped his coffee while he finished writing his notes. It took him a moment to remember where he'd heard mention of the postmaster. It was those bar girls in Casa Blanca. They'd said Hodge and Menéndez had mentioned the postmaster. It was a nickname. *Whoever that man is,* Townsend thought to himself, *he is probably the one running things from New Orleans.*

Jacobs leaned over to try to see what he was writing. "So, Lieutenant, you gon' have a meetin' with de Secretary of State? Mr. Lincoln's friend, Mr. Seward? Das important, right? He deh a powerful man, right?"

Townsend nodded. "Yes. Tomorrow morning. I will pass on everything you have told me. I think it is valuable information."

"Das good. Maybe he can aks dem Spanish to help find me two sons. I know dey on dis island somewhere."

Townsend looked at Jacobs' still swollen face, so filled with grief and fatigue. The man's eyes kept twitching. Townsend felt a wave of sympathy sweep over him. "Do you still have those little wooden horses, the ones your sons carved?"

"Yeh, I do," Jacobs said as he pulled them out of his pocket. "Dey took my spectacles, but lucky dey nevah take dese carvings from me. When I was hearin' dem voices, I held close dese little hosses."

"I know you told me the names of your boys. Tell me their names again? How old are they now?"

"When dey sold all of us, Caiphus was ten and Henry was eight, so they would be seven years older now."

"Almost young men then."

"Yes, indeed. You right 'bout dat. Too much time gon' by."

Townsend wanted to tell him not to get his hopes up, but he didn't say anything. Jacobs had been through too much of an ordeal. "I'm sure the Secretary will do his best, Jacobs. I promise I will mention your two sons to him."

"Even if he can't help me, you know, I gon' stay here. I ain' leavin' Cuba without me two sons."

"That might not be wise, Jacobs. These Spanish will lock you up and sell you as a slave."

"Dem Spanish can do whatever dey want. I need to find me sons. I ain' care if I get kill'd."

"I can't leave you here. As soon as this meeting with the Secretary is over, I'm due back at Naval headquarters in Key West. I have to take you with us."

Jacobs just started shaking his head back and forth. He began humming that spiritual, "Wade in the Water," and Townsend strangely felt the presence of his old friend Clyde Hendricks as he listened. He knew Hendricks would have wanted him to help this man as much as he could.

Jacob stopped singing and began writing slowly on a piece of paper. Townsend watched the determined look on the man's face as he wrote slowly and carefully in block letters.

Missing in Cuba
Caiphus Jacobs, age seventeen.
Henry Jacobs, age fifteen.
Sold in Georgia at the Butler Plantation. March 2, 1859. Last seen at Fannie's Plantation in Plaquemines Parish, Louisiana. Send what you know to the boys' father.
US Navy veteran, Levi Jacobs.

He gave Townsend the piece of paper and asked him to deliver it to Secretary Seward. Townsend promised he would.

January 21

The next morning, the Navy lieutenant walked through the crowded Plaza de San Francisco with its clattering carriage wheels and bobbing black top hats to the Hotel de Almy. During the war, this small hotel that overlooked the harbor was known as the favorite boarding house for Havana's Yankee visitors. Townsend checked his cutlass dangling down below his belt to make sure it was hanging correctly. He straightened his Navy cap and his long blue coat. He passed by noisy street vendors and mingled cheek by jowl with a mix of brown-robed priests and country farmers riding donkeys.

The Navy lieutenant looked down at the report he was clutching in his hands. He'd treated it like the many dispatches he'd been required to write to Naval headquarters during the war. Over the past two years, he'd become adept at writing these accounts of military engagements and sea chases. It was just six pages long. It covered a complete account of their time in Sagua, the trip up the river, and the discovery and boarding of the *Southern Cross* in Havana harbor with a synopsis of the interviews he'd done.

He pulled aside to a quiet corner off the central square and read his concluding paragraphs again.

In summary, with regard to my investigation of the American merchant schooner the *Southern Cross*, it is my belief that the seaman, who has been tentatively identified as James Hogg, was murdered by someone who wanted to silence him. A reliable eyewitness says the dog was intentionally set loose and directed by its owner to attack the man. The decision by the Spanish police to declare this incident an accident and then release the ship and the crew remains highly suspicious.

As I have explained in detail in this report, it is my humble opinion that the *Southern Cross* and the men onboard were involved on this trip in luring American freedmen in Appalachicola onto their ship under false promises, and then selling them in Sagua la Grande, Cuba, to work as slaves. It is also likely that the captain of this ship, Ezekiel Hodge and a close associate of his, Francisco Menéndez—both ex-Confederates—had accomplices in New Orleans and among uniformed Spanish officials in Cuba. All of this was denied by Hodge. His men refused to make any comments.

Finally, it should be emphasized that it remains unknown exactly why the *Southern Cross* was seized and the crew arrested by Spanish authorities in Havana a few days ago. It is believed that this action is not connected to the beforementioned suspected kidnappings and re-enslavement of American freedmen, but rather is related to some form of seditious activity against the Spanish colonial government on the part of Hodge and his men.

I have the honor to be respectfully yours,
Lt. E. J. Townsend, USN
USS *Rebecca*

Townsend put the report under his arm and walked through a large door-way into a courtyard lined with restaurants, then up some stone steps to an open plaza where the hotel was located. A Spanish porter came out of his vestibule and escorted the Navy lieutenant upstairs to the suite where Secre-tary Seward was staying. As he walked through the hallway, Townsend had a tightening in his chest. *It was for the larger good*, he told himself. A guilty man was now going to jail for some time. What Townsend had done was justified.

21

January 21, 1866

Townsend walked into the room and was taken aback by the man in front of him. Small in stature with a pinched face and a long beaky nose, Secretary Seward reminded Townsend of one of Audubon's spoonbills or flamingos. His rumpled clothes and shaggy silver hair and eyebrows gave him a disheveled appearance—not what Townsend expected in a statesman who dined with diplomats and politicians, and who unquestionably had been one of Lincoln's closest advisors.

Seward's attentive eyes never left Townsend's face as he stood up and shook the Navy lieutenant's hand. Townsend noticed the redness on the older man's cheek and neck, the still visible scars from the knife attack he had suffered at the hands of a Confederate assassin.

"Lieutenant, this is my son, Frederick Seward, the Assistant Secretary of State. Please have a seat—join us for breakfast."

Awestruck, Townsend dutifully handed off the diplomatic satchel filled with the Secretary's private correspondence and sat down. He couldn't believe he would be sharing breakfast with the Secretary of State. As the Sewards began sorting their mail, Townsend told them he had prepared a written report for them on the incident at the port of Sagua as he'd been instructed to do by Mr. William Rudd. Seward nodded and reached out to take the written report.

"Thank you, Lieutenant. I'll take a look at it over breakfast, and most certainly will have a few questions for you."

Seward's own butler brought in coffee and a full American breakfast of porridge, fried eggs, sausage, and toast. Seward asked him to bring more butter and then turned his full attention to Townsend. "You know, Lieutenant, I originally received your name from Mr. Thomas Savage—he was our Vice Consul General here in Cuba earlier in the war, Frederick. Mr. Savage had only the highest praise for your detective work here in Havana harbor in that important year of the war in 1863."

Townsend nodded as he sipped his coffee. Instead of eating, Seward quickly leafed through the six-page report, a cigar never leaving his hand. As Seward studied the report, Frederick, in between mouthfuls and sips of coffee, spoke to Townsend about their trip through the Caribbean. They had left the Potomac River on December 29 in the middle of a snowstorm. He commented on the excellent harbor on the Danish island of St. Thomas— "the Gibraltar of the West Indies." He was just recounting the dramatic rescue of the highly overweight US Consul in Santo Domingo, who had fallen overboard while trying to board the ship, when Seward abruptly interrupted his son. He looked Townsend squarely in the eye.

"This man Hodge is an unreconstructed rebel, I presume?" Seward asked, lifting up his grizzly eyebrows.

"Yes, sir."

"You have suspicions, but still no concrete proof that he's selling American freedmen into slavery here. Is that correct?"

"Yes, sir, but . . ."

"You have not actually witnessed them being sold?"

"No, sir."

"And you feel that the sailor in the Cuban port of Sagua was killed. The dog mauling was not an accident?"

"Yes, sir. A reliable witness—"

"I know, I read that in your report, Lieutenant. Let me be forthright with you. The death of the man in the port of Sagua you were sent to investigate is of particular importance to us. Sensitive matter. I don't want you to mention this again, but that man, Hogg, was working undercover. He was one of the new federal agents with the newly formed Secret Service attached to the Treasury department. He was investigating cotton stealing. This foul dealing he uncovered, unfortunately we don't know what that was, but it must have been important for him to take the risks he did with the urgency he did. We think he was betrayed somehow—not sure by whom—maybe someone in the Treasury Department, the State Department, or even the Department of War."

Townsend raised his eyebrows in surprise but said nothing as the Secretary now quickly went through his pile of correspondence, clearly picking out the more important letters marked urgent. After a few quick minutes of intense reading and shuffling of papers, a somber-faced Seward now began puffing more quickly on his cigar. He picked up a document and turned to address his son, seemingly forgetting that Townsend was even there.

"Listen to this," Seward said waving the paper at Frederick. "Testimony from Senator Sumner on the floor of the Capitol. That old Republican Radical says he has received reports from every state in the Gulf that a system of kidnapping freedmen and sending them to Cuba has commenced."

Seward took a sip of his coffee.

"If this dirty business is going on, Frederick, it will cause a political furor in Washington."

"I certainly agree it must be stopped," Frederick replied. "But how? We can't blockade the South all over again, or search *all* merchant vessels going to Cuba."

"It's complicated. The war is over, the Union saved. In my mind, we need to stop interfering so much with the affairs of the South. It's time for peace. But this kidnapping business is a worry. We can't ignore it. The problem is, if we crack down and expose these Southerners who are involved, the publicity will just rub salt in the nation's wounds."

Seward now put down his cigar and took a moment with fork and knife in hand to eat several mouthfuls of sausage and eggs. He was buttering his toast when he surprised Townsend by suddenly turning to him.

"Lieutenant, are we looking at the beginning of a new slave trade?"

Townsend swallowed his last bite of egg and looked back and forth between the two Sewards, wondering why these two statesmen would want his advice.

"I have no specific information except to say that Cuba's sugar plantations are highly dependent on slave labor. With Louisiana's sugar industry virtually destroyed by the war, demand for Cuban sugar is up in the United States. If this is a new slave trade, it might be hard to stop. Smuggling contraband of any kind into Cuba is as common as a tropical rain squall."

Seward paused, then leaned in toward Townsend.

"The Spanish representatives in New Orleans and Washington naturally have steadfastly denied that anything like this is happening. So has the Spanish Captain General here in Cuba. I'm curious, Townsend—in your report you say the *Southern Cross* was seized here in Havana, and the men arrested, probably for carrying seditious pamphlets. Given how accommodating the Spanish authorities were to Hodge and his men in the port of Sagua, why did the military police decide to search the *Southern Cross* here."

Townsend blinked. He knew he had to be careful what he said.

"Sir, the Spanish authorities were conducting searches of American ships throughout Havana harbor. Looking for weapons, ammunition, and any seditious written material. They are quite concerned about the growing signs of rebellion here on the island. When I informed the Spanish captain charged with maintaining port security that we were looking for this ship, the *Southern Cross*, he informed us when it had arrived in harbor. He said he would not prevent us from questioning the sailors. Thanks to this officer, we were able to interview Hodge and we freed that Black sailor, who gave us the valuable information mentioned in the report. In return, I thought it appropriate to notify the Spanish captain that I'd seen certain newspapers and pamphlets on board that he might want to look at."

Seward fondled his cigar as he motioned to his butler to refill his coffee cup. A broad smile had spread across his face.

"My, my, Lieutenant, it appears you have been engaged in some sensitive diplomacy of your own. Some might say you were acting as an agent of the Spanish government? Informing on an American citizen—albeit one of questionable virtue."

"No, sir. That was not my intention."

Townsend knew what he'd done was much worse than that. He braced himself for more difficult questions, but instead the Secretary surprised him.

"I like your initiative, Townsend. We need more men like you in government. Tell me something, I believe you have family here in Cuba?"

"Yes, sir, I have a grandmother here, my mother's mother."

"And she owns a plantation? That's what Vice Consul General Thomas Savage told me."

Townsend nods. "Yes, sir. In the province of Matanzas."

Seward blew out a large cloud of smoke.

"The answer to this puzzle, Townsend, lies here in Cuba. We need someone within the Cuban plantation system who is not viewed as a threat. An insider. Someone who has the freedom to move around, someone who speaks Spanish. Can ask questions and listen to what people are saying. Visit other plantations. We want to find out more about the slave traders and the sugar planters and their connection to this new slave trade." The Secretary pointed at him with his cigar. "We think that person is you, Lieutenant. You are a member. They will confide in you."

Townsend sat speechless at the table. Every bone in his body told him this was not a good idea. He knew he was being pulled into a tidal hell hole he might not get out of.

Seward looked him straight in the eye. Frederick also fixed his eyes on Townsend.

"You would be an informant, just for several months. You would retain your position as a Navy lieutenant, of course. We would pay you a decent wage above and beyond what you receive from the Navy. You will have a cover job of completing a report for the US government on Cuba's plantation economy, emphasizing the growing economic ties between the United States and Cuba. It would be a look at how to improve trade—make it more efficient and less costly. Needless to say, that report is for appearances only. In reality, you will be preparing reports about this kidnapping business for my eyes only, which you will send to Mr. Rudd in Key West."

"I'm not sure I'll be effective, sir. As you know, foreigners, particularly Americans, are not fully trusted here."

"I have complete confidence in you, Townsend. I can't tell you the number of informants of varied trustworthiness I dealt with during the war, everyone from dockside thugs to unemployed sailors. I know you are the man for the job. You think about it while I finish my breakfast."

Townsend sipped his coffee as he continued to weigh the offer. He did need to see his grandmother, and this was one way to do it. *Maybe staying in Cuba will help me see Emma again.* He thought of the dying man on the *Hard Times*, Thaddeus Burrell and the corpses in the hold—their watery grave. He thought of the mauled sailor, who he now knew was an informant. He could meet the same fate as that man if he took this assignment.

After five minutes of eating and chatting with his son, Seward wiped his mouth with his handkerchief and complimented the butler on the excellent breakfast.

"What do you say, Lieutenant?" Seward asked.

"I'm not certain, sir . . ."

"What can I do to persuade you? We are truly afraid of these kidnappings. If they indeed are real, they could spiral out of control."

"Yes, sir. I understand the importance." Townsend thought of Jacobs, and the danger the man would be in if he stayed in Cuba. He tried to imagine what would happen to him. This American freedman, a veteran of the war for his own independence, would be jailed and then enslaved on some plantation where he could not speak the language. He would be lost and forgotten, as Quiñones had said, and probably die on the floor of a barracoon.

"I'll do it, but I do have one condition."

Seward raised one bushy eyebrow.

Townsend reached into his pocket, then handed Seward the piece of paper Jacobs had given him with the names of his children. Seward looked perplexed. "This note came from the freedman we rescued on board the *Southern Cross*, the man I mentioned in the report. You can see his name, Navy veteran by the name of Levi Jacobs. He wrote this and asked me to give it to you. Those are his two sons. He believes they were sold into slavery here in Cuba."

Seward looked at the names. "Kidnapped by Hodge?"

"That's what we believe. Yes, sir."

"Are you saying you want this man to go with you to your grandmother's plantation?"

"Yes, sir. Jacobs could be useful in gathering information, sir. The problem is, people of color—free or slave—who arrive in Cuba are not allowed ashore unless a security deposit of one thousand dollars is paid."

"You want the US government to pay for the bond? Is that it, Lieutenant?"

"Yes, sir."

Seward looked over at his son. "Frederick, I know your dear mother, my beloved Frances, if she were still alive, would not hesitate on this question. What do you think, son?"

"I believe she would want to begin the search right away."

"There you have your answer, Lieutenant. We'll take care of the details. Any American freedman willing to take the risk of traveling in Cuba to find his two kidnapped sons must be an extremely brave man—although some might say a foolish one as well."

January 23

Two days later, Townsend watched from the edge of the fish market next to the Cortina de Valdés promenade as the USS *De Soto* made its way out of the harbor. He held up the telescope to his eye. He could see Secretary Seward on the deck in a lounge chair with a shawl around his shoulders. Church bells were ringing, and Townsend reached into his pocket to look at his watch. It was eleven o'clock. A cold north wind was blowing in from the Gulf, pushing wispy black smoke back over the ships at the docks.

Cannons blasted from the stone walls as the USS *De Soto* approached El Morro castle, and the guns of the American ship responded. The Spanish were giving the American Secretary of State a warm sendoff, a clear indication they wished to maintain good relations with Cuba's neighbor to the north. Townsend had run into the US Consul General earlier that morning, and the beaming official had told him the meeting had been a great success. "Nothing had happened to mar the good feelings called into existence by this important visit," Minor had said. Townsend realized then how worried the diplomat must have been that something would go awry.

A steam whistle blew right next to him, and Townsend whirled around to see a chartered ferry boat pass by the docks. The decks were filled with enthusiastic young Cubans waving their hats and handkerchiefs, some holding American flags. He thought he could hear some of them shouting. "¡Viva la democracia!" Probably university students, he thought to himself. Townsend couldn't hear much else over the cannon blasts. He held the telescope to his eye and began scanning the decks, worried that he might find Emma there. To his relief, he didn't see her amid the earnest faces.

Townsend felt a twinge of regret for these students. Seward was leaving and with his departure went any immediate hopes for democratic change in Cuba. He wondered if these young Cubans understood the danger they were now in. What they were doing would not go unnoticed. In most countries, this support for democracy would not be considered a threat, but for the Spanish it was a serious demonstration of defiance. As if on cue, Townsend spotted a Spanish Navy vessel with steam up begin to pull away from the Naval landing. On the deck of the Spanish Navy boat was a small contingent of Spanish Marines and a familiar figure standing in the stern. It was Captain López Villanueva.

Townsend turned away, not wanting to seem too interested in what he knew would happen next. He felt in his pocket for the paperwork he'd been given and took it out to review it. Seward had handed him documentation for Levi Jacobs including a passport and a receipt for the required one-thousand-dollar bond, as well as an authorization letter from the Captain General. The letter granted Jacobs and Townsend permission to travel into the interior. Townsend knew this was a special letter of recommendation.

He thought of Seward's words last night at the hotel. A military band had been playing outside. It was late and Seward had just returned from the opera, irritable and tired after a day of discussions with the Spanish Captain General. He warned Townsend that there would be no official record of any report he filed. If he were arrested and charged with spying, the federal government would deny any knowledge of that. Seward had handed him his papers and explained to him with a smile that the Captain General wanted to make sure that el Señor Townsend had everything he might need.

"Ironic isn't it, Townsend," Seward had said. "The Spanish Captain General aimed to help your mission with this introductory letter. He thinks you will be doing a positive report on Cuba's shipping ports. My guess is he won't like your reporting at all."

Seward's eyes twinkled, and an elfish smile came across his face.

"Remember, the Spanish may not like us, but they fear and respect us and they need our trade. If we can confirm that American freedmen are being re-enslaved here, I believe we can force the hand of the Spanish government to end it—even if they never *admit* to it."

Those words swirled about in Townsend's mind as the USS *De Soto* slipped out of sight behind the land on a northerly course toward the east coast of Florida. The Spanish Navy Marines had boarded the ferryboat and were arresting the students. He turned and started walking up past the Old Cathedral to Tejadillo Street into the upper section of Old Havana. Mrs. Carpenter's boarding house was just four or five blocks away. He was intent on warning Emma about the *Guardia Civil*'s crackdown as well as telling her his news that he would be going to stay with his grandmother in Matanzas. He had already sent his grandmother a telegraph, and she had sent a quick reply that he was welcome to stay at Mon Bijou as long as he wanted. His grandmother's townhouse where she lived during the hot summer months was just on the other side of the Santa Catalina church, a few blocks closer to the remnants of the ancient city wall.

As soon as he reached Madame Tregent's boarding house on Havana Street, Townsend could see nearby the small sign for Mrs. Carpenter's inn. He walked through the iron gate into the courtyard and was surprised by the amount of commotion. It was a noisy scene of excitement and confusion filled with the jingling of harnesses and the clanking of silver spurs. A coachman stood by a Victoria carriage with two horses stomping their hooves on the cobblestones. Servants bustled by with luggage. Mrs. Carpenter appeared at the doorway with a frenzied look on her face as she directed two of her maids and a butler to load up a valise and two trunks onto the top of the carriage. She noticed Townsend but barely acknowledged him.

"Is there something wrong, Mrs. Carpenter?" Townsend asked. "Can I help?"

"No, I'm afraid you can't," she snapped back. "We're quite busy now as you can see."

"I came by to see Emma."

Before she could answer, he heard Emma's voice. He walked through the door into the familiar hallway where he saw Emma coming down the marble staircase. She was formally dressed in a long frock with a bustle draped at the back. She had a worried look on her face

"What is it, Emma?" he asked.

"I'm leaving," she said simply.

"Leaving? What? Where to?"

"My mother and I, we're taking the train to Cárdenas. My mother says it's too dangerous here in Havana," she said quietly.

"What do you mean?"

"The military police have come here. They did a search, ransacked our rooms. Emptied every cupboard and interrogated the maids. They are demanding to know what our connection is to some anti-government agitators. Specifically, they seem interested in me because of the young university students who have come here to see me."

"Friends . . ."

"Yes, of course. My mother thinks they may already have been arrested, and they are trying to get more names. The police used Secretary Seward's visit as an excuse to crack down and make arrests."

"How did they know to come here to the boarding house?"

"Informants. As you and I know, even these walls have ears. We're going to stay with an old friend of my mothers, Julia Thornton de González. A widow. She lives alone in a townhouse in Cárdenas."

Townsend pulled her aside and whispered to her.

"You know the *Guardia Civil* almost got Emilio several days ago, don't you?"

"No, I didn't. Where?"

"Down at the commercial docks. They were searching the schooners from Key West and New Orleans."

Emma's face turned ashen white. "What did they find?" she hissed. "Is Emilio—"

"He's fine," he replied. "They found nothing."

"That's a relief." Emma looked at him for a long time, her eyes probing. He knew what she was thinking, but he didn't say anything.

"I believe Emilio has left the harbor now. I didn't see his schooner today."

"Did you know I was leaving?" she asked. "Is that why you came at this critical moment?"

"No. My timing is pure serendipity. I wanted to tell you that I'll be staying in Cuba for a while. The government wants me to do a report on the northern ports on the island, the growing trade between United States and Cuba. I'm staying in Matanzas at my grandmother's plantation."

He thought he could detect the hint of a smile.

"That's not far from Cárdenas," she said.

"Perhaps I could pay a visit," Townsend asked hopefully, tilting his head toward her. "I should be coming to Cárdenas for my work at some point."

"I read your letter—"

Before Emma could say anything else, her mother showed up.

"Come, Emma. The coachman is waiting. We'll miss the train."

Emma quickly wrote down an address and handed him a piece of paper.

"I have to go, Everett. . . . Goodbye."

Emma's upturned face caught the late afternoon light revealing a faint smile. Townsend helped her to get in the carriage and watched it as it clattered out of the courtyard onto the street. He stayed there for several moments as he listened to the fading clip-clop of the horses' hooves. When he turned around, he was all alone. He looked up at the upstairs windows and saw the face of one of the maids. He could tell she was scanning the area—looking for anything unusual.

SUGARCANE PLANTATION

Part Three

"We have heard of horrible places in the interior of the Island where the crack of the whip pauses only during four hours in the twenty-four, where, so to speak, the sugar smells of the blood of the slaves."

— Julia Ward Howe,
"*A Trip to Cuba*"

22

January 28, 1866

The morning sun was peeking out of the clouds as Townsend and Jacobs left Matanzas on horseback heading south. The two horses they'd hired from a livery stable were small, but like most Cuban horses, they trotted with a rapid but easy pace. As they crossed the stone bridge over the San Juán River on the outskirts of Matanzas, they passed a line of pack horses and huge one-ton ox carts lumbering into the city with produce. The drivers were complaining about the bad conditions on the road ahead. Townsend's grandmother's plantation was about eighteen miles away near the Valley of Magdalena. Even with the rutted roads, Townsend thought they'd arrive by early afternoon.

The crew had left them off in Matanzas harbor yesterday afternoon, and Townsend had watched the USS *Rebecca* sail out of the harbor with a sense of melancholy. He knew it might be the last time he saw that schooner. The Navy would probably soon auction it off. His men would be discharged and might also be gone like dust to the wind by the time he returned to Key West. He felt awkward without his Navy uniform. He was now more spy than seaman. Seward had said that Townsend should consider this to be a three- to four-month-long assignment with additional pay of three hundred dollars a month above his military pay—a generous amount for an informant. A young diplomat wouldn't even make that much. Townsend had offered Jacobs nearly half of that amount, which he could tell was greatly appreciated.

He once again tried to engage his companion. "Those men were like family to me. I will miss them."

Jacobs nodded but didn't say anything.

Townsend looked over at his riding companion. He was now wearing brand new wire-rimmed spectacles that they'd bought at an optical shop in Havana. As far as he could tell, Jacobs had mostly recovered from the jimsonweed poisoning, but he seemed strangely silent. Townsend thought he must be preoccupied, thinking about his two sons—*or maybe he is worried about traveling back into a world of plantation slavery.* With little to say, Townsend fixed his gaze on his surroundings. To the right were the wooded hillsides gradually rising till they reached the Pan de Matanzas, a towering landmark for any sailor. Ahead of them were waving fields of sugar cane dotted with the tall, whitewashed chimneys of the sugar mills. Pastureland mixed with scrubby savannah and palm trees weaved in between the smoking sugar chimneys. Behind them, he could see the city of Matanzas and the masts of the ships at anchor in the harbor.

Townsend breathed in deeply and felt the hot air fill his lungs. They were now in the heart of the older section of the Matanzas sugar belt, which extended from the outer Yumurí Valley across the mountains to the town of Santa Ana and the rolling plains of Limonar. The smell of boiling sugar juice was in the air, and the pungent aroma brought back memories of his visit to Mon Bijou nearly three years ago. He remembered how awkward he'd felt meeting his grandmother for the first time. His mother had always called her a witch, but Townsend had a more complicated view of her.

He thought about land and family. He remembered his grandmother's story about her grandfather, José Miguel Quintana, his great-great-grandfather. She said Don José had always loved the nearby Yumurí Valley with its sharp peaks, the winding river, and the fertile, undulating land. It reminded him of the pilgrimages he'd taken as a boy walking on the *Camino de Santiago* through Asturias in northern Spain. But the Yumurí valley was too small an area for his large ambitions, so he moved eastward across the mountains where he purchased the land he later called Mon Bijou, my jewel in French.

As he grew older, the elderly man became forgetful and easily confused. He was convinced their plantation was in his beloved Yumurí Valley. Everyone knew he was losing touch with reality, and the family decided to let him have that fantasy. *"La vida es un sueño,"* Townsend's grandmother had told him. "Life is but a dream," she'd said, like the Spanish bard Calderón de la Barca wrote long ago. "The Yumurí Valley was my grandfather's dream, and over time it became a reality for all of us. We all became accustomed to saying that Mon Bijou was located somewhere it wasn't. It was our family's fantasy."

Townsend hadn't found the courage yet to tell Jacobs much about his grandmother, Doña Cecilia Carbonell de Vargas, or even the fact that she was the owner of a large sugar plantation. He had simply said they would be staying with his family while they conducted their investigation. The fact was he dreaded the thought of introducing his imposing grandmother to Jacobs. He knew that even though the Black American was a freedman, or what they called in Cuba un liberto, she would not let him stay in the main house.

The two men were silent as they passed a small army of some two hundred Negroes cutting the cane and piling the fifteen-foot stalks on enormous ox carts. A mayoral or overseer stood by on horseback, a rawhide whip coiled and ready. Townsend looked over at Jacobs to see what his reaction was, but the man seemed lost in a trance. He was looking at one of the slaves whose bare back was scarred with raised welts. The pitiful faces of the workers caked with dust and sweat made Townsend grimace.

From behind them they heard the sound of clattering carriages and a drum beat of hooves. Townsend whirled around and put his hand on his gun. He'd been warned at the livery stable about highway robbers. Clouds of dust swept over them as several tall horsemen armed with long swords in silver-tipped scabbards galloped by, followed by three volantas filled with ladies wrapped in flowing silk and lace. Winter was the time for cutting the sugar cane and grinding the stalks, but it was also the social season on the plantations, when the wealthy owners left their townhouses in Matanzas and Havana to come socialize in the countryside.

The whirling dust from the passing carriages caused Townsend and Jacobs to shield their faces with their arms. The two men rode in silence for the next five or six miles, passing groups of slaves filling in potholes with stone and rock. Townsend realized this was the man's first look at Cuban slavery. He must be worried about his sons.

"No disrespect intended, Lieutenant, but dis place deh plenty worse den de rice fields of Georgia or de cotton land on de Mississippi. I ain' need dese spectacles to see dat."

"It's a hotbed of slavery," Townsend replied without any further elaboration. He decided not to mention that during the sugar season, the enslaved were required to work day and night and were only allowed four hours of sleep.

"How many sugar plantations dis island have?"

"Maybe fifteen hundred. Hundreds of tobacco and coffee plantations as well, all with slave labor."

"How many slaves on de island?"

"They say half a million. No one really knows for sure. Some of the African laborers are called *emancipados*. They are the Africans who were freed from captured slave ships. They supposedly only serve five-year terms, but in actual fact their work contracts are usually extended until they die."

Jacobs said nothing, and all Townsend could hear were the clip-clop of the horses' hooves as he looked out at the rolling expanse of green all around them. Off to the right, he could see the undulating hills with tall palms and large umbrella trees. Dark green patches of coffee, coconut, and banana trees were scattered up the slopes.

"Your grandmuddah, she deh a slave owner?" Jacobs asked abruptly.

Townsend felt a sudden lump in his throat. He'd been expecting this question, but not quite so soon. He didn't say anything at first, pretending he was adjusting his stirrups.

"Yes, yes . . . she is," he finally answered.

Jacobs pulled on the reins of his horse.

"What—What de hell!" Jacobs shouted, his face grimacing. "Lieutenant, you fought to end slavery. And you tellin' me, *only now*, your family own slaves here?" He glared at Townsend. "All de time I tinkin' I knew you, but I guess I nevah did. You evah tell Ol' Sandy dat you own slaves?"

Townsend shook his head. "It's not me. I'm not the slave owner. It's my grandmother. But no, I never did tell Old Sandy."

"Preacher Cornish told me you were a good man, you know. I should trust you, he said. You weren't like some of dem white people in Florida. I believed him. Now I ain' so sure."

A cloud of uncomfortable silence once again fell over the two men as their horses trotted on through a small village of thatched houses surrounded by a grove of coconut trees. Townsend felt the sting of those words, but he was glad that Jacobs now knew.

As they were escorted out of the small village by a chorus of barking dogs, Townsend noticed that Jacobs rode with a firm seat and a straight back. He remembered back in Key West when the man had told him about his time at the Butler Plantation. He was the stable manager, and his expertise was horses. Townsend knew then what he would tell his grandmother. Jacobs would be his personal assistant, someone who could help with the horses at the estate and take care of the horses on the trips they would be making into the interior.

"So how many slaves ya granmuddah own? Fifty of dem?"

Townsend looked away, but Jacobs persisted.

"One hundred. Two hundred?"

"More like four hundred," Townsend muttered uncomfortably. "She owns three thousand acres of land. It's one of the bigger sugar estates in this area of Matanzas."

"Lawdy. Lawdy. Das a big piece of land. As big as all of Key West. And she got plenty slaves too. Your family must be *royalty*, Lieutenant. What made you decide to fight for de Union? Seems like de Confederate flag should have been more to your likin'."

Townsend didn't answer even as he detected the barbed tone in Jacobs's voice. He tried to explain his complicated family background the best he could. He told Jacobs about how his mother had fled Cuba because of slavery and that he had only seen the Cuban plantation once. His grandmother was the only family he had left so he had gone to see her before, and he felt an obligation to see her now.

Jacobs didn't reply.

"I'm sorry, Jacobs. I meant to explain it better," Townsend said, the words stumbling out of him. "This is not easy for me. We have to work together. We have an important mission for the government, and hopefully we'll find your two sons."

Jacobs sucked on his teeth in an expression of disgust. His face was pained, and Townsend recognized the look of someone who felt betrayed.

"What you gon' do wid me, Lieutenant? Gon' make me work as a slave now? Wha' you gon' tell you granmuddah 'bout me?"

He looked away and shook his head.

By the time they reached Mon Bijou, the two horses had worked up a lathery sweat. The sun was now baking hot, and there was little to no breeze. It had taken them three hours of slow trotting and walking to reach the plantation over the rutted, stony roads. Townsend had a sinking feeling in his stomach as they trotted up the long driveway lined with one-hundred-foot-high royal palms. His companion kept shooting him suspicious glances and muttering under his breath.

As they wound their way up the narrow road of red earth, Townsend felt an ache of sadness. He looked out at the miles of sugar cane fields all around them with the plantation's towering chimney smoking away off to one side in the midst of a cluster of buildings. The stone manor house was visible in the distance, only one story but more than one hundred feet wide. It was as stately and elegant as he remembered. This is where his mother had grown up. Her childhood home that she had left, never to return.

Off to one side he could barely make out the estate's small church with its white cross. The burial ground there contained the graves of many family members including his great-grandparents and his grandfather. For his grandmother, this was sacred family ground, but for him, these were ancestors he knew nothing about.

A half dozen Black children, barefoot and shirtless, now came running down the long driveway. "*El Amo, el Amo.* The Master, the Master," they cried out, interrupting Townsend's thoughts. He wanted to tell them to stop calling him that, but instead he kicked his horse to speed up. As they arrived at the stone house, all the household servants were lined up at the circle. His grandmother had fifteen servants in the house, including five maids, two butlers, four laundresses, two cooks, and two kitchen helpers. "*Bienvenido Amo.* Welcome Master," they called out in unison, crossing their arms over their chests and bowing. It was clear his grandmother had staged this to be a homecoming. Townsend felt awkward and confused, a sense of being pulled into another world he didn't want to enter.

A few of the staff he recognized from his brief visit to the estate three years earlier. One of them was a woman in a calico dress who had a yellow turban wrapped around her head. It was Mercedes, his grandmother's principal servant. She was a woman in her late forties with a light mahogany-colored skin. He remembered his grandmother had told him she was Jamaican, and that's how she came to speak English. She smiled at him, and he nodded to her. *She has a proud and self-confident look to her face*, he thought to himself.

Once he reached the edge of the veranda, his grandmother stood by the large front door with her arms outstretched. She was wearing a long white ruffled dress with a black lace shawl over her shoulders. Here was the woman he had heard his mother curse all of his life. He and his younger brother had been told never to speak of her. He walked up the stone steps to the veranda to greet her. She grabbed each of his shoulders with her hands and looked him over, probing him with her eyes like a farmer examining livestock.

"Everett, *querido*, it has been so long. Nearly three years. *No lo puedo creer.* Look at you with your beard. *So handsome.* You look just like my poor late husband, Rafael, your grandfather. May he rest in peace."

She led him into the house, never pausing to take a breath.

"I can't believe you are here. Now you are back in Cuba. *Me da tanta alegría.* How was the trip?"

"Dusty, but we had two good horses."

"You must be starving. As soon as you get cleaned up, we can have something to eat in the courtyard."

Townsend nodded. Her thin voice was just as he remembered. Soft and disarming. Her manners gracious and alluring. He thought she looked older. There was more white in her hair. He guessed she was well into her late sixties now, but she still carried herself like someone younger.

"I have someone who is traveling with me," Townsend quickly interjected as he looked back through the door at Jacobs still standing in the circle with the two horses.

Her eyes darted from him back to the Black man in the circle.

"Who do you mean? *Ese negro?*"

"My personal attendant. An American. He's not a slave. He's a freedman. *Un liberto.* Levi Jacobs is his name."

She looked at him strangely, her inquiring eyes probing.

"I thought while I'm here at Mon Bijou, he could help out at the stables. He's excellent with horses. He'll be traveling with me on some of the trips I have to make. I didn't tell you much in the telegrams, but I will have to travel to some of the northern ports to complete a report I'm doing for the American government."

"I see," Doña Cecilia replied. "But of course. Your man can stay in one of the stone cottages for some of the other free Black workers on the estate. Julio will show him the stables."

She shouted to a young man through the grated window and told him to help Jacobs take the horses to the stables where they can be washed and fed.

"Do you remember Julio?"

Townsend could barely see a young man with a bushy head of hair and a big toothy smile.

"Mercedes' son?"

"That's him. Yes. He's grown up since you were here. Almost a young man now. He's sixteen. Mercedes purchased his freedom finally last year. He's my postilion, but he's also acting as the assistant stable manager. But then that's another topic. First, let's get you settled. I want to hear everything about your plans."

Townsend offered his grandmother his arm as they walked from the veranda into the house, which was now filled with servants scurrying soundlessly on their bare feet.

"You remember where the rooms are."

Townsend nodded as he looked around at the high ceilings with the immense beams of solid cedar, open-air grated windows, and the faded white marble floors. It was much as he remembered: the dark old Spanish furniture, a mixture of large bureaus and cabinets, planters' chairs, and cane sofas. The portrait on the wall of his mother dressed in lace and satin when she was a young girl was in the same place. So was the Erard piano she used to play, now gathering dust, the silk flutings slightly frayed. Townsend ran his fingers along the keys and some cockroaches sprang out.

Nothing had really changed from his brief visit three years ago. It was a big house for an older woman alone. He noticed some reading glasses on a table near his mother's portrait. There was a book by the sixteenth-century Spanish playwright, Calderón de la Barca, and a copy of the newspaper *Diario de la Marina* and the local business paper in Cárdenas, the *Boletín Mercantil*. He picked up one of the papers. Next to an editorial praising Spanish rule in Cuba were some headlines about the execution of one Cuban insurrectionist and the capture of two others. His mind suddenly shifted to worrying about Emma. He wondered if she knew these people. He felt the card she'd given to him in his pocket with her address in Cárdenas and told himself he would go there as soon as he could.

"I've put you in your mother's old bedroom, *cariño*. I thought you'd like to see some of her old things. It's silly of me, but you know I haven't moved a thing from your mother's room since she left all those many years ago."

She now touched his arm and pulled him closer to her. He noticed the wrinkles on her forehead, her swollen fingers.

"I'm so glad you have come during the social season. I want to show you off to some of the finer people here in Matanzas—and some of the available young ladies."

She laughed and told him the meal would be served in an hour in the courtyard. She'd asked the cooks to prepare some *pastelitos de guayaba*, guava jam tarts because she remembered how much he liked that dessert during his last visit.

Townsend walked into the bedroom that once upon a time had been his mother's. Mercedes was still there doing some dusting. "*Está todo listo, Don Everett*," she said. "*Igualito como en los tiempos de su madre.*" She then repeated herself in Jamaican English. "Jus' like yo mudda left it long ago."

The bed had been made with crisp white linen. The chipped gilded mirror stared back at him, a flickering candle dancing back and forth as if it were trying to conjure up ghosts. He looked around at his mother's old linen dolls with their painted faces on various shelves, imagining his mother playing with them as a young girl. He picked up the collection of carved wooden horses and sat down on the mahogany bed. They reminded him of the carved horses that Jacobs had, his only keepsakes of his two sons. It was clear the man was on edge. Townsend began to wonder if he'd made the right decision to bring him along.

A half hour later Townsend heard the clang of a bell, and he guessed that this was the signal for the meal. He walked out to the veranda in the courtyard where his grandmother and the estate's Scottish overseer, William McKintyre, were standing. They were clearly caught up in a serious conversation. His grandmother spotted him and called him over. Her thin face was now changed, somehow sharper, giving her a dark and foreboding appearance.

"You remember Mr. McKintyre, don't you, Everett?"

"Of course," Townsend said as he nodded at the burly Scottish overseer whose gray beard was even longer than it was when he'd seen him last. He despised the man for his cruelty to the slaves and she knew it, but he summoned up his Naval disciplinary skills and shook the man's hand.

"Welcome home, laddie," the overseer said in a loud voice. "Ah heard yoo've hud a good war up north? Nothing like a proper war for a young man."

"Let's sit. *Vamos a comer.* We will have to eat quickly I'm afraid. Mr. McKintyre has an urgent matter to attend to. Some of the Blacks in the field are refusing to work. A few of them are demanding *wages* now."

"What will you do?" Townsend asked,

"Whit has tae be done, ay course," McKintyre replied in his thick Scottish brogue. "Twintie-five lashes athwart th' back of each ay these trooblemakers."

"It's the only way to deal with the Blacks," his grandmother said, her eyes narrowing. "A certain amount of whipping is necessary. That's what teaches them respect. It's for their own good. I know you don't like to hear that, Everett. Your mother was the same way, but it's the only thing they understand. They need to fear us. *Así es la realidad.* That's the way it is."

As they walked toward the table on the veranda, Doña Cecilia clapped her hands for her two serving maids, who both were named María. She explained to Townsend that she had to come up with different names for the two servants to avoid confusion. She called one of them *María Gorda* and the other *María Vieja*, Fat Mary and Old Mary.

"I didn't know what else to do! I suppose I could have sold one of them, but I decided not to. They don't seem to mind the nicknames I've given them." She chuckled quietly. "Why even the other servants now call them by those names as well."

The two Marías were just bringing in the platters of food as Doña Cecilia tried to steer the conversation back to what was happening on the social scene. She said that one of her neighbors was the Marquis Ignacio Calderón de Molina, and that he was currently in residence in *el campo* and entertaining in a most lavish and hospitable manner.

"The Marquis has several sugar estates around the island. We are lucky to have him here this season. He has told one of our neighbors the most extraordinary story. Apparently, he was inquiring with some of his contacts in Cárdenas about purchasing some new *bozales* from Africa or acquiring more Chinese coolies, and he was told that there might be an alternative. Some American boats are starting to bring in *negros* from the American South!"

Townsend almost choked. "Really," he replied. "Who is doing this?"

"I'm told they are *Confederados*. They have many contacts in Cárdenas. Mr. McKintyre, we should make some inquiries there, don't you think?"

"We'll dae 'at, mem."

Townsend felt like a wave was crashing over him, swallowing him, devouring him. A righteous anger followed. He wanted to yell at her that those Black Americans had fought a war for their freedom and won't live in chains, but he bit his lip. *This is what I came to learn.* And he kept silent.

23

January 29, 1866

The next morning Townsend woke up at dawn to the clang of the plantation bell signaling the slaves to form up outside the barracoons. It was still
dark outside. He could hear the shouts of the slave drivers and the crack of
the whip. He hadn't slept well because all night long he'd heard the inces-
sant grinding of wheels and clanking from the sugar house. The slaves who
were keeping the furnace fires going kept calling for more fire, chanting,
échale candela. He had laid there in the bed, eyes wide open, his troubled
mind mulling over his grandmother's words. His own grandmother had said
she would be interested in buying and re-enslaving American freedmen.
He wanted to scream out and beat the walls. She was no different than the
Confederate firebrands he'd been fighting.

After a morning coffee with daylight now spreading itself over the cane
fields, Townsend walked toward the sugar mill. He watched as a long line of
scantily clothed Black men marched outside the brick slave barracoon. Then
he saw another line of men, all Chinese in baggy pants, beardless with shortly
cropped hair. They were being loaded onto a row of empty ox carts under
the watchful eye of the slave drivers. Townsend watched the heavy ox carts
lumber off, the mournful creak of the wheels still hanging in the air long after
they disappeared into the cane fields.

Townsend turned and walked to the stables to see Jacobs. Not surprisingly, he found the man restless and unsettled. McKintyre had him mucking
out the horse stalls and polishing the silver on the carriages.

When they were alone, Jacobs whispered to him that he heard those slaves last night. They'd been put in the stocks, and they were moaning in pain all night long from the whipping they got from the overseer. Townsend felt a knot form in his stomach. Jacobs pulled him over and pointed at a door.

"Go in and see for yourself. You can't hide from dis cruelty."

Townsend did as he asked. He opened the door slowly. One look inside made him step back in horror and disgust. The eight-by-eight-foot room was filled with leg irons, whips, woven rawhide crops, and thick whips of manatee hide called the *mandinga*, which Jacobs said was the heftiest of the whips.

Townsend averted his eyes. He felt the heat of shame and guilt rush up his body—this was his own family's plantation. "I will speak to the overseer, Jacobs." He didn't know what else to say. It was a hollow promise. He knew not much could be done to change the way things were managed at Mon Bijou. McKintyre had the full support of his grandmother.

Jacobs eyed Townsend with a baleful glance. "When we gon' leave here, Lieutenant?" Jacobs asked. "What's your plan?"

"I need to get more information before we leave here. My grandmother mentioned a nearby planter whose contacts offered kidnapped freedmen from the American South. Have patience."

"Patience," Jacobs scoffed, his eyes blazing. "Easy for you to say, Lieutenant. You nevah bin whipped. You ain' know what dat fear be like. You ain' know slavery. How you gon' know anyting about de life for slaves."

"Don't tar all white people with the same brush, Jacobs," the Navy lieutenant retorted. He almost said something about the war, but instead he left the stables, biting his tongue. Jacobs was right—but Townsend's task as an informant required him to seem unaffected to the dreadful cruelty, not the opposite.

Townsend spent the next few days with his grandmother, who wouldn't stop making a fuss over him. She was overly indulgent, which embarrassed him. She made sure that her staff treated him like a prince, showering him with one plate of food after another. Eggs, rice, fish, poultry, vegetables, and fried plantains. The special attention wasn't just at meals. Everywhere he went in the house, several white-gloved servants followed close behind, walking ever so softly on their bare feet.

Doña Cecilia made sure he familiarized himself with all the rooms in the house, the paintings and cane chairs and sofas that had been passed down in the family. She guided him to her lavish quarters with the bedstead of gilded iron brought over from Spain surrounded by elaborate mosquito netting that fell from the ceiling to the floor. Mercedes was carefully dusting the furniture, and Townsend saw that she took special care with a small painting of a bearded man.

Doña Cecilia suddenly yelled, demanding that Mercedes stop what she was doing. *"¡Mercedes, deja de hacer eso!"* Townsend caught the flash of her eye and could just barely make out a lightning bolt glare Mercedes hurled back at Doña Cecilia before she nodded respectfully. Townsend was reminded how mercurial his grandmother was. Her tenderness turned to cruelty with little warning. There was an awkward silence in the room, and then his grandmother smiled at him.

"Mercedes tends to dust with a heavy hand. That's a delicate painting. A portrait of my late husband when he was a young man. Your grandfather, Don Rafael Espinoza Vargas. Now that you have grown a full beard, you remind me of him."

She then pointed to a small mahogany table and a silver embossed oil portrait of a pretty young woman hanging above it. The woman was dressed in silk attire, with flowing black lace covering her bare shoulders, her black hair crowned with flowers.

"That's your great-grandmother," she said. "My mother, Maria Luisa Quintana de Carbonell. *La bella*, they called her. Prettiest girl in all of Matanzas." She nodded at an adjacent portrait of a man. "And that's her husband, your great-grandfather. Pierre Carbonell." Townsend looked at the man's thin face with a well-waxed upturned moustache and the prominent nose. He was dressed in a black suit with a black umbrella.

"Are they not the perfect couple? The portraits were done when they were in Paris," she said with a smile. "I was a baby then. My mother gave birth to me in Spain. Such a life my father had. Imagine, he arrived in Cuba as a young man, alone with nothing. He fled Haiti at the time of the slave revolt and the massacres there. Came across the Windward Passage in a small boat with only a carpet bag. He was the only one in his family who survived." Her face hardened and turned sour. "His parents and his two sisters were all killed when the plantation was burned down by the slaves. *¡Madre mía! ¡Que horror!* Those slaves killed them all with machetes."

Townsend studied the faces of the two portraits. He knew nothing about his great-grandparents. His mother had never mentioned anything about them.

"She was a beauty, don't you think? Thank goodness your mother didn't inherit your great-grandfather's nose."

They both laughed.

"Your mother was such a beauty as well. My Esperanza. She could have been the Queen of Matanzas." She sighed heavily. "Did she not tell you about your great-grandfather, my father?" Without waiting for his reply, Doña Cecilia continued on. "My father was a talented man of business. After arriving here from Haiti, he borrowed money and bought sickly *negros* off the slave ships, and then, after nursing them back to health, he would sell them several months later to plantations for double the price. Clever, don't you think? Planters like Tomás Terry did the same thing and made sizable fortunes. My grandfather recognized my father's talents for making money and hired him, eventually making him a partner. That's how my father met my mother. Love at first sight, I was told. It was my father who suggested to my grandfather that he give his estate the French name Mon Bijou. To honor the French planters who were killed in Haiti. Such a shame that your mother never taught you French."

Townsend nodded, pretending to be accommodating, but in actuality he felt more tense. His mother had not just run away from a forced marriage arranged by his grandmother. It was deeper than that. She had run away from her family's heritage.

As they continued the house tour, Doña Cecilia announced to him that a clothing merchant from Matanzas would soon be arriving at the plantation with a newly tailored linen suit for him.

"It's the winter social season," Doña Cecilia said, "and my grandson must be properly attired." She smiled at him. "In the next couple of days, we'll go on a carriage ride through the valley. You must look your best." She looked over at Mercedes and asked in English, "Don't you agree, Mercedes? Wouldn't Esperanza want to see him properly attired?"

The Black woman looked up in surprise and nodded her head. *"Si, Ama."*

January 31

A few days later after breakfast, Doña Cecilia called for her *volanta* to be brought around. The air was soft from an unexpected early morning rain. The birds were twittering and the clouds moving swiftly across the sky. The postilion riding one of the two prancing white horses was Julio, who was dressed colorfully in a dark blue jacket with red trim, white pants, black boots, and a wide-brimmed straw hat. He had replaced his whip with two holstered pistols attached on either side of the pommel of the saddle. Townsend was learning that in the Cuban countryside, no one rides without being armed. For the first time, Townsend noticed that Julio wore a gold earring in his left ear, and he wondered if this was the way he showed that he was now *un liberto.*

Walking next to the carriage leading the other horse was Levi Jacobs. Townsend eyed Jacobs uncomfortably without saying a word as he helped his grandmother step into the *volanta*'s posh interior of crimson morocco leather. Dressed in his new white linen suit, Townsend felt like a stranger to himself. He knew he looked like a dandy. The cold stare from Jacobs made it quite clear what his companion was thinking. The guilt settled uncomfortably in Townsend's throat like an unripe piece of fruit as he remembered Jacobs' words.

In her soft high voice, Doña Cecilia directed Julio to take them on a tour of the valley. The *volanta* lurched ahead, clattering down the long driveway lined with tall palm trees. Townsend heard the clip-clop of horse's hooves behind the carriage, and he wheeled around to see who was following them. The rider was Jacobs. He was on a packhorse carrying a large bundle on the back of his saddle. He was staring up at the sky with an expressionless face.

Townsend turned back to Doña Cecilia.

"I didn't know that Jacobs was coming with us."

"But of course, *querido*. No one of the finer class travels here without a Negro attendant. I thought that's why you brought that Black man here to Mon Bijou? As you said, he seems to know horses well."

Townsend turned his attention back to the dusty road ahead. His grandmother was clearly accustomed to directing her postilion. At every turn in the road, she called out her orders to Julio, "*Dobla a la izquierda, Julio*. Turn to the left." "*Derecho! Derecho!* Straight ahead." She talked to him about the plantations in the area like Santa Inés, Jesús María, Los Ángeles, and San Cayetano, and the names of important families in the larger area of Matanzas—Alfonso, Aldama, Baró, Ibañez, Argudín. Names that meant nothing to him. He knew she was trying to be gracious and caring, but it grated on him that she never stopped talking about the importance of Spanish bloodlines and the land, *la tierra*.

"If only Don Pedro were here. I know he would help me with the estate. You know how fond I was of him." Don Pedro Alvarado Cardona—the Spanish merchant he'd been forced to work for as a ship captain running Confederate supplies through the blockade. She'd been so attached to that man, and so dependent on him. "All those years after your grandfather died of yellow fever, I would never have managed without Don Pedro. If only your mother had agreed to the marriage. Don Pedro had money and power and the privileges that come with being Spanish born here in Cuba which your mother did not have. *¡Que pena!* What a shame!"

It was this that caused Townsend's mother to run away, never to return to Cuba.

She looked at him with a weighty, prolonged stare. "You know after you left Havana, Don Pedro was exiled to Fernando Po, that dreadful island off the coast of Africa. Rumor was that he and his men killed someone in Havana harbor, an Englishman? They also said that Don Pedro was somehow connected with the unsolved murder of that English diplomat, George Backhouse years ago? ¡Dios mío! The British government found out, and the Royal Navy demanded that Don Pedro be turned over to them. It could have become a serious diplomatic incident! I was told the Spanish government had no choice but to make Don Pedro disappear. It was the only way to make the problem go away."

Her gaze rested on Townsend as if he could provide an explanation. He simply offered a breezy "what a shame" and looked away. He could have told her many things about Don Pedro, none of them favorable. He certainly hoped he would never see that man again. Not only was he guilty of cold-blooded murder, but he'd tried to kill both him and Emma because of the secrets they'd uncovered about him. He wanted to tell her these things, but he knew she wouldn't believe him.

After an hour-long tour, Doña Cecilia directed Julio to turn to the right onto a small road that was really nothing more than a dry riverbed. The *volanta* began springing over rocks with its enormous wheels until they arrived at a large umbrella-shaped ceiba tree at the top of a small grassy hilltop. Townsend could see a broad plain of waving cane down below, a carpet of green dotted with clusters of white and yellow red-roofed buildings and tiny church spires. His grandmother looked out over the vast ocean of sugar cane and pointed out the names of a dozen plantations. She knew them all.

Townsend thought he could detect a bitter aroma in the air. He asked his grandmother if she could smell it. She picked up the riding crop on the seat beside her and pointed out a cloud of black smoke in the distance to the left, thick and oily, rising up into the sky.

"Cane fire," Doña Cecilia said, twitching her nose with distaste. "It's my biggest fear. The end of the winter season is when it's most dangerous. Everything is so dry. Just a cigar can set off a blaze." She sighed. "As a twelve-year-old child, I saw our cane fields ignite. The flames were so hot, roaring like a storm. My grandfather died fighting the fire that day."

She paused as if she were paying her respects to his memory.

"Poor soul. He was so confused. He grabbed a machete like a crazed man and ran out of the house yelling that he would save the crop. Supposedly he ran directly into the flames, swinging his machete. *Una tragedia.*"

She looked up at the sky and then pointed to the pathways through some nearby cane fields made by the small army of slaves and the ox carts. The green fields shimmered and glistened like sparkling sun glitter on the surface of the water. Townsend recognized the manor house of Mon Bijou nearby. He could see the white cross of the small chapel off to one side.

She put her hand gently on his arm.

"These are *our* fields, fields of *gold*," she said, looking up at him. "The crop this year has been a good one. We grow enough cane to make eight thousand boxes of sugar each year. Twenty dollars a box. One hundred and sixty thousand dollars. Twenty to 25 percent of that is our profit at the end of the year."

"I see," Townsend said, surprised at his grandmother's knowledge of the estate's accounting records. Part of him felt pleased that she was entrusting him with this private business information, but another part of him understood how she was trying to manipulate him. He knew she was trying to spark his ambitions. Tempt him with a challenge.

"The Americans now need our sugar more than ever," Doña Cecilia said proudly. "With the collapse of the Louisiana sugar plantations due to the war, they have no domestic sugar industry anymore."

Doña Cecilia pointed to another area where he could see cattle grazing.

"If we turned that pastureland into sugar cane," she said, "we might match the production of the well-known Flor de Cuba estate in Cárdenas owned by the Arrieta family. One hundred more slaves would mean we could increase our sugar production by at least 20 percent. Wouldn't you like to see that, Everett? Maybe that could be your special project?"

Townsend took a long hard look at his grandmother, but he didn't say anything. He momentarily felt the attraction of managing such a vast business enterprise—the prestige it might give him—but one look over at Jacobs, and he dismissed that thought. He felt the presence of his mother, warning him to be careful.

Sensing that flicker of interest, Doña Cecilia became more emphatic.

"We need to invest in new machinery, but the major problem we have now is the lack of new African slaves. The abolition of slavery in the States has been *como una maldición*, like a curse. We used to get new slaves whenever we needed them! Every year since I was a young girl, there were always new shipments of African *bozales*."

"Why not consider paying the slaves, *Abuela*? Wouldn't that help increase production?" Townsend asked.

"Madness, absolute madness. We could never turn an acceptable profit without slavery. But now some people opposed to Spanish rule are actually talking about *ending* slavery. Even his Excellency, Cuba's Captain General, Domingo Dulce, instead of helping us, has been trying to stop the slave trade to appease the Americans and the British. He even banished the man trying to help us get more laborers, Don Julián Zulueta. Sent him back to Spain several months ago. *¡Imaginate!* And now Cuba's slave ships can't sail."

Townsend knew she was referring to the top shareholder of the African Expeditionary Company, which the planters called *la Compañía*. It was a slave import company which some said had a fleet of twenty ships, both sail and steam. Don Julián Zulueta was sometimes referred to as the ruler of Cuba's dirty kingdom. Together with Don Francisco Marty y Torréns, another key plantation owner involved in the slave trade, they had brought in thousands of new Africans over the past five years, distributing them to the so-called sleeping partners in *la Compañía* who were all plantation owners. All of this was technically illegal, but the Spanish authorities always looked the other way.

His grandmother pointed in another direction at the smoke from at least five different sugar mill towers. "Over there is the land owned by the Marquis Calderón de Molina. A personal friend, Don Ignacio. *Un caballero refinado.* A refined gentleman. Do you know anything about him?"

Townsend shook his head.

"He came to Cuba from Spain only about fifteen years ago. He was a captain of the royal guard before he came here. He was given the land and the title for his loyalty to the Crown. That's the official version, anyway," she said with a twinkle in her eye.

"And unofficially?"

"It's rumored that the Crown banished him to Cuba to avoid a scandal because he was one of the queen's secret lovers. She has had many, you know."

"I see," Townsend said.

"Well, the Marquis has sent word that he will be having a small luncheon affair this weekend at his estate, Flor de la Magdalena, and we've been invited. I thought you might like to come. Didn't you say you wanted to meet some of the neighboring property owners?"

"Yes," Townsend replied. "I would like that."

She reached over and grabbed his hand, causing Townsend to tense up from her cold touch. She squeezed more tightly, and he felt her hand tremble. Townsend looked at her, sensing her frailty at the moment. Her back was now slightly stooped, like she was carrying her sorrows there. It was almost as if he could see the sadness sifting through her.

"You know I am not as strong as you might think, Everett. That's why your coming here has been so important. I feel reborn. It's given me hope. I'm so happy you are showing an interest in Mon Bijou, *querido. Me encanta que estés interesado.* Remember, this is your land, Everett. Your family's land. *La familia,* my dear. That's what matters."

24

February 3, 1866

When they entered the gates of the Marquis' estate, guests from the surrounding plantations were already arriving in their silver-trimmed *volantas*
and on horseback, galloping up the driveway to show off their horsemanship.
Prancing white horses, ladies in colorful flowing robes riding sidesaddle,
gentlemen in Panama hats and spotless linen jackets sporting long cigars, all
swirling around one another like swarms of glittery fish. *So much opulence,*
Townsend thought to himself. It reminded him of a more flamboyant version
of the American South before the war.

Some of the men came up to Doña Cecilia and tipped their hats, exchanging greetings and formal pleasantries. There was so much banter and laughter
that Townsend found it hard to hear what was being said. His grandmother,
whose silvery hair was crowned with flowers, clearly enjoyed the deferential
treatment she was receiving. He watched as she fingered her string of pearls
with a diamond clasp and tilted her head just so. He could sense her pride
and how pleased she was as she met his eyes and nodded. Townsend looked
around for Jacobs, finally spotting him mingling with the other Negro atten-
dants, all dressed in black knee boots with silver buckles.

After a short wait, the Marquis strode purposefully out onto the veranda.
He wasn't hard to pick out with his suit of blue-striped linen, an embroidered
shirt, and a scarlet silk scarf wrapped around his waist. A young slave boy
followed behind him carrying a palm frond to keep the sun off his face. With
his head held high and all the airs of a grand *hidalgo* on display, the Marquis

announced to his guests that the food would be brought to them on the front lawn and that everyone should refresh themselves with coconut water, pineapple rum drinks, and orange peel.

"It will be *una comida campestre real*, a royal picnic," he said with a flourish.

With the advent of Lent approaching, he encouraged everyone to have a good time and he jokingly gave permission for the ladies and gentlemen to misbehave as much as they wanted to. He smiled and then held up a carnival mask to his face. *"He invitado a dos curas."* To the laughter of his guests, he said he had invited two priests to come along to say prayers at dusk to ask for forgiveness.

At his signal, a team of servants brought out platters of food, including several roast suckling pigs that had been decorated with pineapples and flowers. There were mixed dishes of meat and vegetables as well as a variety of local preserves, guava, soursop, and mamey.

As soon as the guests began eating, the Marquis rushed over to welcome Doña Cecilia, bowing to kiss her hand. Townsend noticed the heavy gold chain across his broad chest and his long fingers that sparkled with half a dozen jeweled rings.

"Doña Cecilia, I am deeply honored. My house, myself, and all I own is at your disposal." Then with a bow and a wave becoming a polished gentleman, the Marquis said in formal Spanish. "May I say that your beauty grows each day like the sparkle of a freshly cut rose."

His grandmother blushed like a young girl.

"Don Ignacio, I'm pleased to introduce my grandson, Everett Townsend. He is visiting. He fought in the war up north, unfortunately for the wrong side, but now he's here with me and I hope he will decide to stay in my beloved Cuba."

The Marquis eyed Townsend from top to bottom before he said, "I will do what I can to make sure he remains in Cuba for you, Doña Cecilia. He must escape the horrific fate of returning to the dreariness and tedium of Yankeedom." He looked at Townsend with a prolonged stare and smiled. "You will find that those who spend some time here become devoted to the island ways."

Townsend nodded and smiled. "It's an honor to be invited to your estate."

"Now that the two Americas have ended their disagreements and become one family again," the Marquis said with a slightly twisted, mordacious smile, "you might want to meet some of your Southern cousins who have moved here. Such gracious people, *los Sureños*. They seem to enjoy the languor of plantation life, and other distractions of course."

"I'm certain I would like to meet your Southern friends, *Marqués*." Townsend lied, trying to keep a straight face.

"Call me Don Ignacio, please. You are Doña Cecilia's grandson, and she has been a loyal friend, a true Spanish patriot. Almost like family."

Townsend saw that his grandmother turned to speak to another guest, and he decided to take advantage of his time with the Marquis.

"I wanted to ask your advice, Don Ignacio. A somewhat sensitive matter. My grandmother is very concerned. We have a pressing need for more field slaves, and she doesn't know who to turn to. I thought maybe . . ."

The Marquis raised one eyebrow, but then moved closer and placed a hand on Townsend's shoulder. Townsend couldn't help but notice that the man had a smell of tobacco and vanilla about him.

"We in the business of sugar all share this dilemma. Not enough slave labor. We can't exist without it. As you say, a sensitive topic. There's a policeman, a captain down at the docks in Cárdenas. He works directly with the *jefe de policía*, the chief of police. This man keeps me well informed. It seems some Americans, former *Confederados*, may be trying to sell us some of their Blacks, the former American slaves. They're bringing small numbers over in schooners to avoid any unwanted attention."

"I see," Townsend said. "Isn't that illegal? Won't those freedmen claim that they have been illegally enslaved and make trouble?"

"*Pura tontería*. Nonsense. Slavery may be illegal in Yankeedom but here in Cuba, the rules are a little murkier."

He laughed and winked at Townsend. "Once the slaves are physically on the plantation, no authorities are allowed to do a search, and it's hard for the slaves to make an appeal. Why, my Southern friend General Tombs confided in me—he recently came across his old man servant from Georgia here in Cuba. Seems his old slave was kidnapped from the streets of Jacksonville and then sold for thirteen hundred dollars. The man is demanding to be freed right now, but I don't believe much will happen."

Stunned by this story of miscarried justice, Townsend was about to ask another question when frantic shouts erupted from the crowd. He heard a deep throaty squeal from one of the horses. Two of the stallions were fighting. A quick glance told him that a young woman with a black hat riding sidesaddle was in trouble. Before he could react, the horse bolted down the estate's driveway with the woman clutching the pommel as if her life depended on it—which it probably did.

The Marquis ordered two of his men to grab two horses and follow her, but they were slow in getting started. Townsend could see that Jacobs had already jumped on the horse nearest him and galloped after her, disappearing into a cloud of dust.

Some fifteen minutes passed, and there was nothing to be seen or heard. People whispered and shook their heads. Then someone spotted two riders coming from a different direction across one of the estate's fields. It was Jacobs and the young woman. He was riding the runaway horse. She was slumped over the saddle of the other horse, her hat gone, her hair all askew.

When they got back to the front of the manor house, a dozen pairs of hands helped the young woman off the horse, and she was carried into the Marquis' house. Jacobs got off his sweaty mount as Townsend arrived at his side. "De young lady lucky," Jacobs said. "De hoss spook and she fall off on a pile of sugar cane cuttings." Townsend translated these details to a small group who had gathered there just as a burly Englishman pushed his way through the crowd. He looked at Jacobs and then the horse before finally turning to address Townsend.

"Name is Lawton, Edward Lawton. Bloody hell, that was some outstanding horsemanship," the man said, sniffing in sudden bursts. "Saw it all with my spyglass. How much do you want for that Negro? I'll pay you above the going rate. Fifteen hundred dollars."

"My attendant is a free man, and therefore not for sale."

"Crikey! That's a pity. I could use him. I'm the overseer of a plantation east of here. We need someone with those skills. I had a wild horse like that. A stallion. Well-bred from Spain. Excellent blood line. Reared up and struck the groom, breaking his shoulder. Had to sell that crazy animal, but now I regret it. The new owners invited me over last week. Two of their recently acquired slaves had quieted that devil horse down. I offered to buy one of them, but the stable manager said they work as a team—they're brothers, apparently, and—"

Jacobs interrupted the man. "How old deh be? De two slaves?"

The Englishman's mouth dropped open and he blinked rapidly at Jacobs.

"How old deh be?" Jacobs repeated. "Wha' deh look like?"

Lawton looked over at Townsend with a furrowed brow as if waiting for him to reprimand his attendant, but Townsend repeated the question.

"How old were they?"

The man sniffed and replied only to Townsend. "They were young. Under twenty I'd say. Actually, your boy here speaks a bit like they did—some kind of pidgin English, a patois with a bit of a lilt. Where is your Negro from anyway?"

Townsend ignored that question, but quickly responded. "Can you tell me the plantation they are on? I might like to go there. We'd be interested in observing some of the techniques of these two slaves working with that horse."

"Glad to help a young Yankee like yourself starting out here in Cuba. It's a big estate called El Capricho, Whimsy in English, east of Cárdenas. I'll write a letter to the owner on your behalf so they'll be expecting you. I'm sure he will be pleased to host one of the Marquis' guests, and the heir to a Matanzas plantation."

February 7

It wasn't until several days later that Townsend and Jacobs were able to leave Mon Bijou. Doña Cecilia had insisted that he meet several friends and neighbors. She also wanted McKintyre to introduce him to some of the sugar masters in the area. With all this delay, Townsend had to avoid Jacobs. He finally told his grandmother he could not wait any longer. He had to leave to begin work on the trade report he had been assigned to complete by the federal government. He promised her he'd be back as soon as he could.

The two men left early in the morning to escape the heat, bringing with them several coconuts and several flasks of tamarind water. They rode eastward toward Cárdenas, a thirty-eight-mile journey through prime sugar land. From there they would have to travel along the north coast toward Sagua la Grande. Still angry that they hadn't left sooner, Jacobs had wanted to go directly to the plantation, riding day and night. Townsend told him for the sake of the horses they needed to spend the night in Cárdenas which was roughly halfway.

Resting the horses made good sense, but Townsend still felt conflicted. He'd made Jacobs wait nearly a week. He knew that finding his sons was the man's only purpose, but he told himself he really had no choice. He'd received a short letter from Emma just before their departure. She'd written that she had some important information to share with him. He worried it was something to do with Emilio or her sister back in Key West. Worse still, something to do with the police. A stopover in Cárdenas would allow him to check on her. He'd never mentioned Emma to Jacobs, and given the man's anxious mood he decided to say nothing about her.

Townsend and Jacobs were sweaty and hot as they got closer to Cárdenas. They'd taken the main road to Limonar, fording the upper section of the Canímar River. Townsend marveled at the richness of the land and the miles and miles of open savannah with pockets of old growth forest. They passed through endless sugar cane fields interrupted by long alleyways of royal palms marking the entrances to big estates.

As they entered the town, there was a swampy smell in the air that reminded Townsend of parts of the Florida coast. In the distance he could see dozens of US flags fluttering from the masts of about forty cargo ships. He'd learned Cárdenas was known as Cuba's American city. It had been designed by Southern engineers to look like Charleston. Five thousand people lived there, and a goodly percentage were Americans working in the sugar trade.

His eyes darted from the waterfront and the stacks of hogsheads of sugar to the wide streets in the town. The main intersection was filled with stores and warehouses with American names like Safford and Company and Churchill, Brown & Manson from Portland, Maine. Men clearly dressed like Americans in canvas trousers, cotton shirts, and slouch hats were playing a game of New York baseball in a vacant lot. Others lounged about in rocking chairs on some of the porches of the stores and taverns, smoking cigars, chewing tobacco, and drinking tankards of rum.

"Looks like Key West. Hard to believe we're in Cuba, don't you think Jacobs?"

Jacobs grunted an acknowledgment but made no comment. They ate a quick meal of rice, eggs, and yam cakes at the new local market, and then went on to the boarding house. When they arrived at Mrs. Woodbury's inn, a place recommended for being clean and comfortable, Townsend quickly realized that most everyone there was speaking English.

"Lots of Yankees and Southerners in town now," the clerk said. "Which are you? Yank or rebel?"

"Neither. I'm an American," Townsend quipped.

"What brings you to Cuba, if I may ask?"

Townsend told the clerk his family owned a plantation near Santa Ana and he and his attendant were now on their way east toward Sagua la Grande. They would be staying in town for just one night to rest the horses.

"Wa'al keep your eyes wide open. The police and the *Guardia Civil* are on the hunt for some clandestine groups who are trying to stir up trouble."

"What kind of trouble?"

"Political trouble. Talk of insurrection against the Spanish. The Spanish blame the Yankees for giving the Cuban *criollos* and the Blacks too many ideas about freedom. And they're looking for excuses to put some Americans behind bars. You know they're still sore about López and those American filibustering mercenaries trying to launch an invasion of Cuba from here back in 1850."

Townsend thanked the man for his information and said he would be sure to be careful. He and Jacobs walked the sweaty horses to the livery stable where they made sure the animals were washed down properly and given plenty of guinea grass and water. Townsend left Jacobs there, telling him he had to meet an old friend. Jacobs looked at him suspiciously but didn't say anything. The Navy lieutenant reassured him that they would leave first thing in the morning, before dawn.

Townsend thought about what Emma had written in her letter. Her mother had returned to Havana. Her hostess, Julia Thornton de González, had asked her to continue giving violin lessons to her granddaughter. He again wondered what information Emma wanted to tell him. He hoped she was not in trouble. At the end of the letter, she'd signed it, "*con cariño,* Emma." His heart had leapt at the sight of those two words, "with affection."

The directions took Townsend past the Plaza Mayor with its cathedral and the bronze statue of Columbus, and up into the higher elevations of the town where the finer residences were. He finally arrived at a large townhouse. He was greeted in the hallway by a tall older woman with an athletic build and a piercing stare. She was wearing a thin green silk dress with a lace veil, and she carried an elaborate fan, which she wielded like an expert.

"Good afternoon, Mr. Townsend," she said curtly.

"Good afternoon, ma'am," Townsend replied as he took off his hat. He already knew something about this woman from Emma's letter. She was an American, originally from Boston, who had married into a wealthy, plantation-owning Spanish family. Her husband had died several months earlier so she was living alone as a widow.

"Please call me Doña Julia. Everyone does. I've heard so much about you from Emma and her mother. It seems you've known each other for some time. *Quite some time*, in fact."

The underlying tone of her voice made her meaning clear. Townsend nodded even as he felt the subtle sting of that remark.

"We are good friends."

"I'll bet you are," Doña Julia replied, pursing her lips.

Her probing eyes lingered on his face as she rapidly flicked the fan with the wrist of her hand. He was taken into a parlor room where Emma was teaching the violin to a young girl about ten years old. She was showing her how to use the bow and let her shoulders move with the flow of the music. He stood there watching Emma for several seconds. She was as beautiful as ever. He noticed the firmness in her jaw and her mouth as she concentrated on the girl's troubled efforts to play. When Emma looked up, Doña Julia interrupted the lesson and said it was time for a break.

The little girl got up from the bench and looked at Townsend with an impish grin.

"*¿Eres el novio, verdad?* You're Emma's boyfriend, aren't you?"

Townsend turned beet red. He didn't know what to say even as the little girl's face broke out into a wider, mischievous smile. She giggled and whispered in his ear.

"Emma says you are very handsome, but unreliable. But I think she likes you very much."

"I . . . I . . . see," Townsend said, smiling at this unexpected report. "I'm glad you told me."

Flustered, Doña Julia grabbed her granddaughter's hand and turned to Townsend.

"I apologize for my granddaughter's rudeness, Mr. Townsend. Come, Patricia, I'm going to show you something in the garden. Emma needs to talk to her friend."

Emma smiled awkwardly and offered Townsend a seat in a cane chair that faced a wall of books. Townsend again took a long look at her. Her face, all softness, her hair falling down to her shoulders in wavy curls. Her sandy brown eyes, alert and visibly intelligent.

"How have you been, Emma?"

"I am fine, Everett. My mother's friend Doña Julia has been so nice, like an aunt really."

"I've been worried about you. Ever since I got your letter, I thought maybe the police—"

"No, no problems like that. Not yet anyway. Doña Julia believes the military police will soon lose interest in me."

"What is it then?" he asked, leaning forward. "I'm always worried about you."

"Really?" she replied, cocking her head. "I think I rather like hearing that."

Townsend wasn't sure, but he thought she was flirting with him.

"Yes, well it's true. I do care about you, Emma. You know that. What was it you wanted to tell me? In your letter, it sounded important."

"Before I go into that, I wanted you to know that Emilio told me what you did for him. He came here and told me all about it. The police. The searches on the boats by the *Guardia Civil*. The arrests on the dock. It was a close call. Your quick thinking may have saved his life and protected me as well. I truly want to thank you."

She reached out and touched his hand. Townsend looked around the empty room.

"Can we talk here safely?"

Emma nodded.

"I'm glad Emilio is safe. You know the Spanish police are cracking down on all and any protests," he whispered. "It's getting more serious. I just read in the newspaper not too long ago that they executed one insurrectionist and jailed two others. You could be in danger."

"I know that," she said abruptly changing the tone of her voice. "But I need to be involved. For the freedom of Cuba. I'm sure Emilio told you about his brother who's still in prison. Some of my friends in Havana are now in jail. They are being charged with attempting to disrupt the visit of Secretary Seward. All they did was hand out handbills at the cigar factories where Seward was visiting and then waving American flags when his ship was leaving the harbor."

"But some of those pamphlets called for *insurrection*," Townsend whispered. "What did you expect from the Spanish? If you're caught, do you know—"

"Yes, I know the risks. This was not something I set out to do. It just stares you in the face. I don't feel I have a choice. It's about standing up for justice. The government here is a bigoted tyranny. We native-born Cubans are treated like second-class citizens, and the enslaved have no rights at all. I've been helping to gather information from some of the Americans who work as engineers on the plantations about the conditions in the countryside. That's where I heard the information I thought you should know about."

"Why come to me?"

"I didn't know who else to tell. We don't trust the American consuls in Cárdenas or Matanzas. They are too friendly with the plantation owners and the Spanish authorities."

"What is it you have heard?"

"A few of the American engineers who travel from plantation to plantation to repair the steam engines say they have heard English spoken among a few of the field slaves. A kind of an American patois with a few French words thrown in here and there."

"Patois," Townsend whispered to himself.

"One engineer asked the overseer and was told to shut up and not ask questions. Our informants think they might be kidnapped American freedmen newly enslaved on Cuban plantations, maybe from Louisiana."

"What plantations?"

"The engineers don't want to say. They don't want any trouble."

Townsend nodded and took a deep breath. After glancing around to check once again that they were alone, he began.

"Emma, this is just the type of information I need. You see, I am here at the behest of Secretary Seward, not to do a trade report as I told you before, but to investigate reports of such kidnappings. Seward believes my family connection will help position me among the planters as someone they can trust. He is right, and I've already heard that these abductions are indeed happening. The shipwreck I discovered after the hurricane in October—I believe it was involved. The captain, a man named Hodge, was at it again. I stopped him thanks to your pamphlets."

"My pamphlets—What do you mean?"

"I planted those pamphlets onto that man's ship in Havana harbor. Then I informed the Spanish authorities. The *Guardia* seized Hodge's ship and put him and his crew in prison."

"Land sakes, Everett. You are never quite who you seem to be. You've become a spy not just for the American government but an informant for the Spanish as well?"

"That's not the way I look at it," Townsend said uncomfortably. He hadn't expected to blurt out a confession about what he'd done. "I'm just doing what I think is right."

"Becoming a spy?"

"No," Townsend said. "Righting a wrong."

"You know they'll charge that man Hodge and his crew with sedition?"

"I know it seems wrong, but if I hadn't done it, Emma, Hodge would have gotten away, scot-free. He's a murderer, and he's trying to start a new slave trade. I believe Hodge may have dropped off another shipment of kidnapped freedmen up the Sagua la Grande River. If he hadn't been arrested, he was going back to the Gulf to pick up more. He had to be stopped."

He then told her about Jacobs and how they rescued him from Hodge's ship before he could be sold to a Spanish agent. He and Jacobs were now searching for his two sons who Hodge had kidnapped on an earlier trip. They had found promising information about two English-speaking slaves on a plantation between Cárdenas and Sagua, and they were on their way there now.

Emma's eyes now sparkled as she listened to what he was doing.

"Well, Everett Townsend. You're full of surprises. Maybe that's what I find so intriguing about you. I rather like the idea that you're on a mission to help this man find his sons. Justice in Cuba comes in many different ways."

They smiled at each other. For the first time, Townsend allowed himself to think that things between them might have changed. Certainly, the tension between them had gone.

"What is the name of the plantation you're going to, Everett?"

"El Capricho."

Emma pulled out a map of the area with the names of the towns and the scores of plantations in the area. She pointed to a sugar estate about thirty miles east of Cárdenas, past Hato Nuevo on the road to Sierra Morena.

"There it is," she said. "El Capricho. Whimsy."

Townsend didn't say anything. He grabbed the detailed map to look at it more closely. It was a bird's eye view of the entire area drawn with great precision, clearly the work of a professional cartographer. He could see the winding Sagua la Grande River off to the east and the port of Sagua.

"Who did this map?" he asked abruptly. His eye was drawn to the detail in each of the palm trees. It was so familiar.

"A new volunteer. A Cuban who fought on the Union side during the war. He grew up in Sagua la Grande and trained as an engineer in the States. He's been secretly doing these maps of the area."

"Does he work as an engineer for one of the merchant houses in Sagua port?"

"Maybe. I don't know his name."

"Quiñones," Townsend whispered. "His name is Captain Guillermo Quiñones. I know him."

25

February 8, 1866

As they reached a slight rise in the land, Townsend could just spot the Southern Cross shining faintly low on the horizon above the sugar cane stalks. This small constellation of stars which pointed south was invaluable to sailors, and now it helped him get his bearings. They had gotten up early and left the livery stable before daylight because Jacobs wanted to waste no time. He told Townsend he was more convinced than ever they would find his sons. It was almost pitch black, and they were soon swallowed by a dark sea of sugar cane fields on either side of the road.

The early dawn revealed the shape of ox carts rumbling into the fields like prehistoric dinosaurs, slaves already cutting cane and loading wagons, all under the watchful eye of a soldier-like man on horseback with a coiled whip in his hand. Townsend glanced over at his companion who looked straight ahead into the gray light. The man had been right. Even though Townsend might see slavery right in front of him, he knew he would never know it. He thought of Jacobs's ordeal and realized he could not begin to comprehend the fear, the grief, and the pain Jacobs had endured.

Townsend wondered what they would do if they found his sons. He knew enough now about the laws in Cuba to know that it would not be easy to free them. Each plantation was its own fortress. In the Cuban countryside, the planters and the rural police captains were in control, their power almost absolute.

"Tell me about your two sons, Jacobs. You've hardly told me anything."

Jacobs cast a cautious eye in Townsend's direction. He took his spectacles off and started cleaning them with his shirt. Slowly and steadily, he began talking about the life he once had with his two boys at the Butler Plantation. The words spilled out of him like water from a spigot. He said he taught the two boys how to ride when they were just five years old.

"I tol' dem to be firm but gentle with hosses. Nevah show fear. De hoss needs to trust and respect you."

"Which one was the most talented with the horses?"

"De oldah boy, Caiphus. He ain' deh too good with readin' and numbers, but he understood hosses and how to speak to dem. He made ridin' look easy. He could ride dem in his barefeet, no saddle, no bridle. Jus' a rope and a halter."

"And the younger one?"

"Henry, he was me wife's favorite." A big smile came across his face. "She spoil him too much. He was good at learnin'. Always wanted to read books. Nevah got riled up. I always knew of de two of dem he would be de one who gon' succeed. He could ride hosses too. He had a light gentle touch with de reins. I used to tink dey both would make good jockeys. Ride at de Savannah racetrack. But fate was cruel to us. Dat track was whey deh sold us all, you know."

Townsend nodded somberly. He knew what a trauma that had been for this man. "I remember, Jacobs. The weeping time."

"Das it. De weepin' time." Jacobs' brow became furrowed. "If we find me two sons, what we gon' do, Lieutenant? How we gon' free dem?"

Townsend paused before speaking. "Can't say as I know, Jacobs. We can offer to buy them?"

"Buy? What you talkin' bout," Jacobs responded with a glower. "Dey free men. The people who took dem should go to jail, not get paid. Lock dem up. What about de federal government? You know Mr. Seward. Can't he make dem Spanish free dem?"

"I don't know, Jacobs. Let's see if we can find them first."

"Dis island cursed with tears and blood, you know. Ain' no salvation for a place like dis."

Just then the rising sun emerged like a cannon blast and both men were temporarily blinded. Townsend pulled down his hat to protect his eyes and nudged his horse's sides. The road had veered off to the east, so they were now trotting directly into the bright light.

By mid-morning, they had passed the small town of Hato Nuevo and had crossed over the River of Palms, coming out onto a wide vista of open savannah covered with palm trees and coconut groves. They trotted through clusters of small houses with packs of barking dogs, and then headed up a trail into a range of heavily timbered hills.

The air was filled with the sweet aroma of mangos and wild oleander. They stopped for a rest in an open clearing where they picked and ate guavas, washing the sweet fruit down with some coconut water before continuing on. He looked down into the mix of savannah and palm trees in the valley below them and thought about the island. He remembered someone had once told him that Cuba in the Taíno language meant the "place where fertile land is abundant." *It definitely was a beautiful island,* he thought to himself. *So much natural beauty but so much human cruelty as well.* Cuba was a contradiction, he decided. It was as if God had determined he would place a human hell in a wild Garden of Eden.

By midday, they caught a distant view of the ocean through the trees, and Townsend told Jacobs they were almost there. He realized they were heading back toward the Sagua la Grande River along the same coastline that they'd traveled by sea on board the *Rebecca*. His thoughts wandered to the men in his crew, his countless months with the Navy at sea. All that now seemed like a dream from another world.

When they reached the gates to El Capricho, they trotted down a long drive-way lined with royal palms and then crossed a stone bridge built over a small stream. The house was situated on a slight rise in the land about a quarter of a mile from the sugar house and the smoking chimney. It was a one-story stone manor house like Mon Bijou, but slightly wider. A pretty garden of hibiscus flowers and bougainvillea surrounded the veranda in front. Townsend had been told that the owners were descendants of French refugees, who, like his great-grandfather, had fled Haiti after the revolution. Their last name was Rousseau but after a couple of generations in Cuba, the family was now more Spanish than French.

They were met by the burly, curly haired overseer who was dressed in a coarse linen shirt hanging outside his pants. He was riding a large black mule with a shaved tail and a cropped mane. Townsend noticed that on each side of the pommel of his russet leather saddle were two large pistols. Hanging from his belt was a long knife in an ornamental scabbard.

The man introduced himself as Ramón Ortiz Urrutia, a Basque from the mountains above San Sebastian on the border with France. He could speak no English, so he and Townsend spoke in Spanish.

"Señor Rousseau sends his most humble apologies that he could not be here to receive you, Señor Townsend," said the overseer, making no effort to hide the hollowness behind his tobacco-stained smile. "Unfortunately, he had to travel to Havana on business to acquire more Chinese laborers, and I am the only one here to receive you."

Townsend noticed how lined the man's face was with thready wrinkles and deep furrows from the constant exposure to the sun.

"I understand," said Townsend. "At Mon Bijou we are also desperate for new laborers."

"Señor Rousseau says he hopes he can entertain you and your family on another occasion. He sends his warm regards to the Marquis. He also says he knew your grandfather, Don Rafael Vargas. They were part of a slave-hunting militia in central Cuba many years ago. I've been instructed to offer you the hospitality of the estate. You can tell your attendant that he may get water at the stable when he gives the horses water."

Townsend nodded, grateful that Jacobs, who was standing next to him, couldn't understand Spanish, particularly the information about his grandfather. He glanced over at the veranda where there were hammocks and rocking chairs, together with guns and swords, all within sight of the sugar mill and the barracoons. Townsend explained that they hoped to take a look at the wild horse Edward Lawton had told them about. The overseer clearly had been expecting this request as he led him over to the stable and had one of the slaves bring out a white stallion. The horse stomped and pranced inside the stable, its eyes darting back and forth. The overseer yanked at the rope and raised his cane to hit the horse.

Instinctively, Jacobs held his hand up to stop the man from striking the animal. The frightened horse snorted, reared up with a squeal, and shook its head back and forth. Jacobs showed no fear. He calmly picked up the rope and then slowly walked toward the agitated animal, all the time speaking in a soothing voice. He held out his hand, palms open, and he told Townsend to tell the overseer to bring him a bucket of molasses.

The sound of Jacobs' quiet voice seemed to calm the animal. He slowly and carefully reached out to the horse's muzzle with his open hand and then touched and stroked its neck, all the time speaking in a sing-song way. Once the horse had been given some molasses, it began to quiet down until it relaxed enough to start eating some guinea grass.

"*Caray!*" the overseer exclaimed. "*¡Ave Maria Santísima!* Your Negro has the same gift as those two young slaves we had here."

"Mr. Lawton told me about those two," Townsend said, trying not to show too much interest. "That's one of the reasons I came here." Out of the corner of his eye, he could see Jacobs straining to understand. "Can I meet them?"

"They're gone. Ran away into the bush. *Cimarrones*."

"*Qué!* When was this?"

"Just a week ago. They disappeared along with two others. Ran off at dusk when the plantation bell was ringing. We sent our *rancheadores* with the dogs after them."

The man pointed to some dogs chained to a tree. Townsend recognized the distinct breed of bloodhound bred by Cuban planters to track runaways. Longer nose and legs but with the stocky build of a mastiff. Just like Menéndez's animal. Fierce and dangerous, trained to run for miles through fields and forest, and then attack.

"The dogs caught those two," the overseer said as he nodded his head over in the direction of two shackled Black men with their feet and hands sticking out of the stocks. "They've been in the stocks ever since."

"And the other two?"

"All the men found was their shirts they'd thrown down next to a stream. They ran in the water to fool the dogs. Smart move. They must be miles from here now."

"No hope of finding them, or them returning? Won't they come back as soon as they get hungry?"

"If they do, they know a proper lashing is waiting for them, one so bad that the skin on their backs will be stripped off. Señor Rousseau is quite upset about losing these two *bozales*. He just purchased them eight months ago. Paid in advance. One thousand dollars for each of them."

"Where did he get them?"

"Brought them here from the Sagua la Grande River. An American *negrero* schooner captain dropped off a boatload of them. It was just like the old days before the American war when Yankee ship captains brought in the African *bozales*."

"Where did they get their horse training?"

"Why do you ask?"

"I just wondered. Maybe there are others with the same training to be found?"

"I don't know whether those two were Congos or Lucumi. When they got here, like all the new slaves, we christened them with Spanish names, Javier and Pablo. They were . . . different. At first, they yelled a lot, making demands we couldn't understand, but we quieted them down with a few whippings. Señor Rousseau somehow figured out they knew how to work with horses. Then we used them at the stables."

Townsend could see that Jacobs was listening intently, but he didn't want to translate any of this to his companion just yet.

"Señor Lawton told me he thought they spoke some kind of English?"

"I wouldn't know," the overseer replied with a sneer. "I don't speak English. Why are you asking so many questions about those two runaways?"

"As I told you, we need more slaves at our family plantation. We might have bought those troublemakers from you—my man could have used them—maybe even tamed them like he did your horse." Townsend winked.

The overseer laughed. "The best guess is they've gone east toward a place called the *Lomas de la Jumagua* or as some are now calling it, the *Mogotes de Jumagua*. About eight rounded limestone cliffs filled with underground caves about twenty miles from here near the Sagua la Grande River. There's a settlement of runaways there. Living in the underground caves. Slaves know it as a place to hide on the way to the mountains in the far eastern end of the island."

Townsend dimly remembered that de la Cruz had made mention of these hills, but details escaped him.

"Will you send the slave hunters and the dogs after them?"

"It's difficult in those hills. They're like medieval castles. The local people are afraid to go there."

"How so?"

"Superstitions. There's a legend about a large serpent that lives in caves where there's water. They call this monster *Magüi*, or the Mother of Waters—and the local farmers are terrified of it."

The overseer pulled a piece of paper from his pocket. "Found this map on one of the runaways we caught." The man then spit on the ground. "You can see someone circled the hills there."

"Who drew this," Townsend asked. "It's quite impressive."

"No clue. But I will find out," the man said emphatically, tilting his head toward the two slaves in the stocks. "Those two *bozales* will eventually tell me."

Townsend glanced at the map of the area and the surrounding plantations.

He could see that those hills were nearby, not far from the town of Quemado de Güines just off the main road to Sagua la Grande. He squinted at the map for a closer look. He knew who had done it.

"So, what will you do?"

"The local military authorities are raising a slave-hunting militia. I hear some twenty to thirty men so far with Spanish military officers in charge.

They're gathering in the town of Quemado de Güines and will be marching soon to root out those runaways from their cave dwellings. Hunt them down."

It was nightfall when they arrived at the outskirts of the small farm town, which was only two hours away by horseback. The bar man at the local tavern told them where they could get lodging. It was a rooming house that offered nothing more than two wooden platforms with threadbare sacking and a fly-infested swillhole outside. Neither Townsend nor Jacobs slept much, but they got up at dawn and made inquiries about the slave-hunting militia. They found the men gathering in the central square.

Townsend immediately saw that these were irregular troops. There were no showy swords. Just men on horseback armed with rifles and machetes. A few of them were dressed as soldiers in seersucker cotton jackets and broad-brimmed straw hats, but most wore coarse linen trousers and shirts. Townsend noticed they had ornamented handles of knives peeking out from their belts—the Cuban version of Southern vigilantes in Florida.

Jacobs pulled his horse up. "What's your plan, Lieutenant?"

Townsend didn't have a plan, so he didn't reply. They dismounted at the opposite end of the square from the militia. They tied up their horses outside a bodega and Townsend went inside, leaving Jacobs with the horses. A bearded man with a wide-brimmed slouch hat sat at a table in the corner. Townsend bought some jerked beef from the storekeeper. He asked him about the armed expedition outside.

"The men across the square—what business are they undertaking?"

"Hunting for runaways. They'll be up beating the bush for several days. It's rugged terrain there in the *Mogotes de Jumagua*, but they're going to go from cave to cave. Capture any Negro they find. We can't allow these slaves to escape. They might start a revolt."

Townsend didn't say anything at first. The man in the corner had raised his face to look at them. He was now watching him intently.

"Looks like they're prepared for resistance."

"*Sí, por supuesto.* Yes, of course—they'll shoot to kill if they are attacked."

"Are there many runaways hiding there?"

"Why do you ask?"

"I've come from my family's plantation near Matanzas. We've had some slaves run off. We've been traveling east looking for them."

"You might want to join the slave hunters. Could be they'll find a good number of runaways. The *cimarrones* hide in the caves during the day. At night, I sometimes see small fires."

Townsend was about to thank the man and leave when he heard a voice behind him in English.

"You've come pretty far ashore, haven't you, Lieutenant. Have you lost your way? Where's your ship?"

Townsend whirled around to see who was speaking. It was the bearded man in the slouch hat. "And you are?" Townsend asked in English, his hand slipping down to his holstered Colt revolver.

"Guillermo Quiñones *a su disposición*. William Quiñones, at your service. You may remember, we met in the port of Sagua."

"Ah yes, Quiñones. I didn't recognize you with all that hair on your face. Your beard looks quite different now. What might you be doing here?" Townsend walked over and shook the man's hand.

"I myself am here on business, taking orders for machinery imports. But what about you? Did I overhear correctly—you've come from your family's plantation in Matanzas? Tell me how an American Navy lieutenant has come to be a Cuban landowner? That sounds like an interesting tale."

Townsend sat down at the table. He stared at Quiñones for several seconds, who waited for his reply with a small smile. Emma had said he was a new volunteer. Townsend weighed the risk of trusting him.

"My mother's family is Spanish and owns a plantation in Matanzas. I am visiting my grandmother."

"So, you're no longer with the Navy?"

"I didn't say that." Townsend paused as he looked nervously over at the shopkeeper. Quiñones told him not to worry about that man as he didn't speak any English.

"I'm still with the Navy. I have been assigned to write a report on the growing trade between the United States and Cuba, focusing on improving that trade in the northern ports."

"And that would bring you to the dusty farm town of Quemado de Güines? Hunting slaves? I'm not sure I understand, Lieutenant. What are you really up to?"

Townsend almost told him, but then decided it was too risky.

"I'm just a Naval officer tasked with writing a report about trade relations, Captain Quiñones. But the man I'm with—he wouldn't mind any information that would help him find his two sons. You see, I'm traveling with an American freedman, a Navy veteran who's looking for his two sons. They were abducted and sold into slavery here by some kidnappers. The US government is aware of what I'm doing, and any information I learn about these kidnappings . . . the government would be glad to know of that. Does that answer your question?"

"Indeed, it does." Quiñones sat back in his chair. "What can you tell me about this man's sons?"

"We don't know for sure where they are. We went to El Capricho looking for two young English-speaking slaves we heard were good with horses."

"The Rousseau plantation?"

"Yes, that's right."

"And did you find them?"

Townsend shook his head. "They escaped. We think they may be hiding out in the *Mogotes de Jumagua*. Do you know those hills?"

"I heard the shopkeeper tell you that. Anything else that makes you think they could be in those hills?"

Townsend pulled out the piece of paper with the detailed map of the area. "One of the runaways who was captured had this bird's eye view map on him. Looks to be professionally done."

"I see," said Quiñones.

"The overseer didn't know where he got it, but I think I do."

"How so, Lieutenant?" Quiñones snapped back.

"Doesn't this look familiar to you? It's the palm trees. Each frond has been meticulously drawn with such care. Just like that pencil drawing you gave me of the Sagua la Grande River." Townsend leaned forward. "I'm guessing from the topographic details, the artist must know this area well. Maybe just as well as those slave hunters out there?"

"Lieutenant, what are you up to? You seem more like some kind of detective or government informant to me. What are you? A federal spy?"

Townsend was silent. This man could get him arrested. The two men stared at each other until Townsend finally broke the silence.

"I believe we are more or less on the same side, Captain. I know you're working secretly with some local groups in the area fighting to end Spanish rule. I know you're helping slaves to run off. What do you say? Can you help us?"

26

February 9, 1866

The air was still and heavy with the heat of Cuba's dry season as the three men left Quemado de Güines on horseback that same afternoon. The sun was low on the horizon, sending a blaze of light and shadows down the street. Townsend hadn't expected Quiñones to offer to take them to the *mogotes*, but he had decided he trusted the man, and he was glad that they had someone knowledgeable as their guide. Townsend wiped his brow with the back of his hand as he scanned the barred windows on either side of the road, wondering what hidden faces might be looking out at them. They passed a small tavern with blistered walls where a team of ox carts was waiting for their drivers to return. They could hear voices and laughter inside.

"The fewer people who see us leave the better," Quiñones whispered. He kicked the sides of his horse and clucked at it. "¡Arre! ¡Arre! We need to be gone before these mule-assed slave hunters get underway. They'll probably be a few hours behind us."

Townsend tried to reassure himself that the risks he and Jacobs were taking were worth it, but he could not rid himself of the worry swirling in his head. If the Spanish caught them with the supplies they had for the runaway slaves, they would all be charged with sedition. Anyone helping a slave escape in Cuba could be executed. He had no idea what they would actually do if they found Jacobs' sons. The laws in Cuba would make it difficult to get them out legally. He doubted whether the US government would get involved, not in the case of only two men. There were few easy answers, and Townsend wondered if it was possible to find any justice on this island.

On the outskirts of town, Quiñones took them off the main road, doubling back through the surrounding sugar cane fields on narrow cart paths so that they were now heading east toward the *mogotes*. Townsend looked over at the slim figure of the former Army captain, who was pulling along a pack horse loaded up with supplies. The man was sitting straight up on his horse like he was straddling a knife's edge, the muscles on his neck taut as a bowstring. With his full beard and slouch hat he looked like he was a California gold prospector heading for the hills to stake a claim. Instead, he was a clandestine supporter of Cuban independence carrying provisions to some runaway slaves.

Before they left the bodega, Quiñones had said he had heard about the formation of this slave-hunting militia a few days earlier from one of the planters who'd come into the trading house in the port of Sagua. He'd immediately sent word to one of his contacts who had a small farm near the *mogotes*. The message to the runaway slaves was to ready themselves to flee. He would be coming as soon as possible with maps and supplies as well as information about the whereabouts of the slave chasers.

Townsend now leaned over in the direction of Quiñones' horse. "You didn't say how we contact these people."

"They're sending someone. We're meeting at dusk under a ceiba tree at the edge of the forest."

"Have you been there before?"

Quiñones nodded. "Always at night and with a guide. Alone you would probably be knifed or hacked to pieces with a machete."

"What about us, Jacobs and me? Won't they be suspicious to see more riders?"

"I'm hopeful it won't be a problem. They need the maps and the supplies I'm bringing them."

When they reached the open savannah, Townsend looked out at the soft, hazy landscape. He could see these strange hills called *mogotes* in the distance ahead of them, rising up from the surrounding plains abruptly like some gigantic ant hills. They looked to be about three hundred feet high with white limestone cliffs peeking out from dense underbrush. It was a smaller area than he expected, some two miles of bushy, forested hills surrounded by a mixture of flat savannah grasslands, palm groves, and sugar cane fields.

Quiñones pointed to a thick forest of tall palm trees that they were approaching. "That's where the militia will be camping tonight. The commanding officer told me they'll arrive at nightfall to avoid being seen. My guess is that in the early morning, they will send their scouts and trackers into the hills looking for footprints, and then plan their hunting strategy based on the information they find."

Townsend grimaced. Men hunting other men. Slavery revealed the human capacity for cruelty. Townsend was about to say so when Jacobs abruptly spoke up.

"Cap'n Quiñones, I want to know your honest opinion. You tink me sons deh in dese hills?"

"I don't know," replied the man. "If your sons ran away a week ago, they could still be there."

"And if deh ain' dere?"

"People say these African *cimarrones* travel to the east, looking for the land of their ancestors. It's a little like the Underground Railroad back in the States. They go from one hideout to another. They end up in the big mountain ranges in Baracoa and in the Sierra Maestra. That terrain is so rugged there in their *palenques* that the Spanish can't find them or they don't dare to."

Jacobs cocked a suspicious eyebrow as he looked at Quiñones. "Why you helpin' dese people? A white man like you."

"Cause I'm a Cuban and I want a free Cuba," Quiñones said simply.

"But you workin' for de sugar companies now. Deh be blood in dat money."

Quiñones didn't answer immediately, looking straight ahead. Finally, he turned to Jacobs.

"Look, what you see here in Cuba is not always what it seems. I fought in the American war against slavery just like you did, and I intend to fight in the war that's coming to Cuba. Freeing the enslaved here is the only way to free all Cubans, and helping these people escape the plantations is a way to cause change. I can do that with the job I now have. No one suspects me. My employer at the trading house keeps his mouth shut, but he wants change to come to Cuba as well."

Townsend looked at Jacobs, who grew silent. There was a sadness in the man's eyes, a weariness. He had seen that expression before in soldiers' faces during the war. It was the look of someone who was afraid to show any hope for fear that it would soon be crushed. He remembered Jacobs confiding in him in a moment of candor on the *Rebecca*. "My life deh caught up between a tiny shred of faith and an entire shroud of grief," he'd said. "De only ting dat keeps me goin' is de memory of me wife, Lena. I will fulfill my promise to her or die tryin'."

Rustling noises interrupted Townsend's thoughts. He could hear the rasping of guinea fowls in the tall grass. The light was fading to a dark gray over the savannah. He looked over at Quiñones, who pointed in a northerly direction toward a large tree with its giant arms extending outward. Once they arrived at the ceiba tree, they pulled off to one side under one of the large branches. The gloom of night had now settled in on the surrounding forest and the broad dark savannah. Townsend leaned on his horse's neck, listening. After an hour passed, they heard footsteps approaching. Townsend reached for his revolver. A moment later they heard a branch crack. Quiñones uttered the sentry's challenge.

"*Quién va?*"

The answer came back.

"*Cuba Libre.*"

Shadowy figures suddenly appeared at his side and grabbed the reins of his horse. Quiñones whispered back to Townsend that they would dismount here and would walk the rest of the way because of the rough terrain.

The horses were left in a well-hidden glade with a dense canopy of branches and trees. Townsend and Jacobs were each given some bags of provisions from the pack horse to carry on their backs. Not a word was spoken. Not even a whisper, just their labored breathing as they walked straight up a steep hillside, sometimes pulling themselves forward by grabbing onto tree roots so as not to fall backwards. Occasionally he heard the whack of a machete, and the crashing of branches falling to the ground.

After a half hour of walking straight up, dipping down into a ravine and then climbing again, they emerged into a cleared area where there was a small fire near the entrance to a large cave. The mouth of the cavern was filled with two dozen people, all Black. Most had no shirts. All of them had machetes hanging from their baggy pants.

A deadly silence hung in the air as all eyes focused on them. The guide called out something he couldn't understand, and they were beckoned over to the fire. The bags of provisions they'd brought were quickly distributed. Townsend stood back and watched as these men grabbed handfuls of rice and dried beef and threw the food in their hats, ravenously eating with their hands. Soon more people arrived out of the gloom, ghostly dark figures who also began eating. He could see the silhouette of Quiñones with his slouch hat going over the maps with a small group of the men. He gestured to Townsend and Jacobs to join him.

Townsend found himself coming face to face with two figures whose features he could not see well in the dark. Quiñones introduced Townsend and Jacobs as his *compatriotas*. The two men spoke in a Spanish patois Townsend found hard to understand, but he quickly realized that they were telling him about two young runaways who were now staying at a different cave. Townsend turned to Quiñones, speaking in English.

"Are they saying what I think they are?"

Quiñones nodded.

"What? Wat deh saying?" Jacobs asked, eyes wide.

"Another cave. They say they can't understand what language these two spoke, but it could be English. The cave they're talking about is not far from here. Unfortunately, it's closer to where the Spanish militia are camped."

They left immediately because they knew the trackers would be on the move soon, and they would need to get back to their horses before daylight. Townsend followed close behind Quiñones, listening to his heavy breathing and the whine of mosquitoes circling his face. He could hear Jacobs' footsteps directly behind him. In the blackness above him, he could see tiny red eyes staring down at them from the tree branches. The eyes didn't blink. Whatever animal it was, it didn't move either.

The moon eventually revealed itself, coming out from behind a curtain of dark clouds. After climbing for another thirty minutes, their guide made a bird call and then waited. They heard one in reply. The guide nodded to them, and they continued following a winding path. When they arrived at a clearing, the guide explained that this is where the two men were last seen, near the entrance to a hidden cave. He would take them no further.

"Why not?" Quiñones asked.

"That's where the serpent lives," the man replied. "The Mother of the Waters. Magüi. She drowns her prey there. Light disappears into darkness there."

No one responded, and the three men continued walking up the trail without the guide. The moonlight allowed them to see about ten feet ahead. The cave entrance was hidden behind some bushes, but they eventually found it. Slowly and cautiously, the three men walked inside. It was cooler inside the cave. Dark and quiet. The ground was strangely soft, like a thick cushion of moss in a forest. Townsend couldn't even hear his own footsteps.

"What are we stepping on?" he whispered to Quiñones.

No one answered. The cave was getting darker. They could barely see anything ahead of them. Townsend could feel Jacobs touch his arm.

"Lieutenant, I've bin here before."

"What?"

"In my dream . . . Lena brought me. She wanted me to come to dis place."

Before Townsend could answer, he jumped. He'd touched something cold and wet. A dark form loomed over him. He stepped back and reached for his gun, but then he noticed other giant human shapes on either side of him. He quickly pulled out his gun even as he noticed more dark objects.

"¡Manos arriba!" he shouted. "Hands up."

Quiñones grabbed his arm. "Don't shoot, Lieutenant."

"What the hell!"

"Just part of the cave. Stalagmites. Rock formations. The guide told me about them."

Townsend stared at these giant shadowy shapes in disbelief. He touched one with the palm of his hand and felt the cool uneven surface. They continued on, groping with their hands extended in front of them. He kept thinking about that serpent called the Magüi. *What if it was real?* Townsend heard a faint whirring presence above him like a sudden breeze, something making squeaking and chirping noises.

"What in tarnation?" he exclaimed.

"Bats," Quiñones whispered. "Lots of them. Don't pay any attention to them."

The pungent smell reminded Townsend of cleaning out a rabbit pen when he was a boy back in Maryland. He then guessed that the soft cushion they were stepping on must be bat dung, and he grimaced at the thought.

"¿Hay alguien? Anyone there?" Quiñones cried out.

There was no response, just a hollow echo and the chirping of bats above them. *Chwee chweee.* Townsend looked up and felt the cooler air on his face. They were now in almost total darkness, and there was no way to go much further without a light. Jacobs's voice suddenly broke the silence, startling Townsend.

"Caiphus, Henry! It's me, your Fadah! You mus' be here. I know you mus' be here. I've seen your muddah in me dreams, and she told me to come here."

Jacobs began singing. Softly at first then more loudly. "Wade in de water, God was going to trouble de water." The man's rich vibrant voice pierced the air, bouncing off the cavern's rock walls, and then lingering in the air like the sound of ocean waves rolling ashore. Jacobs kept raising his voice louder and louder, and Townsend guessed that they must be in a large amphitheater of some kind. He remembered the church service back in Key West. He felt the strength of the man's voice drift upwards in the darkness. It was like he was calling his two sons back from the dead.

Suddenly they heard some small rocks rolling against each other. The splash of water. Quiñones told Jacobs to be quiet. The three men ducked behind one of the rock formations and listened. Another stone rolled. They could hear footsteps.

Quiñones pulled out his gun. "*¡Quién vive!*" he called out in Spanish, then repeating himself in English. "Who's there? *Salgan y muéstrense.* Come out and show yourselves."

Jacobs pushed past him. "I know it's dem," he said. "I know it."

Townsend grabbed Jacobs, but he wrenched himself free and started walking toward the sound into total blackness. Townsend braced himself for a grunt of anger and the thud of a machete's blade striking bone. Instead, out of the darkness came a wrenching moan of anguish. For a brief moment, Townsend wondered if the Magüi serpent actually existed. Then he heard a clear voice in English.

"Fadah, it's Caiphus! Henry deh here too!"

"Boys! Me boys! I comin'! I comin'!"

Townsend could only see a blur of shadowy forms in the darkness stumble toward each other. He heard a deep sobbing. The crying and shouting then filled the cave like some thundering waterfall. Townsend couldn't see anything, but what he heard brought tears to his eyes, and made chills run down his spine as he listened to these cries of joy and disbelief.

"It's a miracle," Townsend declared in a hushed voice.

"A miracle indeed," replied Quiñones softly. "A miracle indeed. Sometimes things happen that defy all logic and renew our hope."

Townsend and Quiñones left the three sobbing men alone inside the cave and stepped outside where they could see something in the moonlight. The guide was there, and he signaled with his head that they needed to get going.

Quiñones nodded back.

"We have to get them off this island," Townsend blurted out. "It's the only chance they'll have. Can you get them on a boat?"

"I know a fisherman who goes to the *Cayo Sal* in the Bahamas to fish. He might take them. If we leave now and go through the swamps north of here, they won't be able to track us. God's gonna trouble the water, right?"

Townsend smiled.

February 10

It was barely daylight when they reached their destination, a small palm thatched hut in a clearing by a lagoon surrounded by mangroves. Townsend got off his sweaty horse and looked around at his muddy surroundings. Small armies of land crabs scurried from one small hole to the next. A formation of pelicans swooped low over the water toward a small fishing boat tied up nearby. Quiñones said he suspected the fisherman was hunting for crabs to use as bait, and he left to go looking for him.

With the sudden blast of morning light, Townsend thought of how close an escape they'd all had. They'd heard the dogs and the trackers coming up the hillside when they left the mouth of the cave. They'd had to abandon trying to return to their horses. Their guide had taken them on a different path to the palm grove forest where the militia had its main camp. They'd scared off the two sentries and taken five of the militia's horses before chasing the other horses away. They had ridden all night long, holding onto the horses' manes, never daring to stop for fear they might run into Spanish soldiers.

Townsend now looked over at Jacobs and then at his two sons who were all still on horseback. It was the first real look he'd had of these two young men in the daylight. The older one, Caiphus, looked exactly like his father with the high forehead and deep-set eyes. Henry had a different, thinner face with more delicate features, and Townsend imagined he probably resembled his mother.

Jacobs looked at Townsend staring at his sons and smiled.

"Lieutenant, dese are me two sons—Caiphus and Henry. Boys, dis man help me find you. He saved me from de same devil man who took you both. I owe me life to him. Everett Townsend."

"Mistah Townsend, Henry and I, we tank you for helpin' our faddah," Caiphus said shaking his hand. Henry also shook Townsend's hand and expressed his gratitude.

"Please tell me, Caiphus and Henry—tell me about how you came to be on Cuban soil."

The story of their kidnapping was similar to what Jacobs had described. There were fifteen of them who were lured on board a ship by men wearing Yankee blue coats. They promised them honest work and a good wage. At sea they were forced into the cargo hold. It took four days and four nights from the mouth of the Mississippi. Their captors never let them out on deck. Then on the fourth night they were brought out of the ship's cargo hold. They were on some river, shackled together and forced to march with a chain gang of slaves. They had no idea what was happening as they couldn't speak or understand the language.

"What about the others who were in the hold with you?"

"We ain' know," Caiphus answered. "It was dark when dey landed us. Deh split us up. We nevah saw dem again."

"And the people who kidnapped you?"

"Same. Nevah saw dem again. De last one we seen was a big man wid a huntin' dog on a leash. All night we marched through the bush until we arrive at a plantation. Dey lock us up. A man came to see us. A Frenchman. Or at least he spoke in French. From our time in Louisiana, we could speak a few words. Henry knows more French than me."

Townsend turned to Henry. "Did the man know you'd been kidnapped or where you'd come from?"

"He told us we were in Spanish Cuba now. I kept telling him. *Américains, nous sommes Américains.* I yelled out de word for freedom in French. *Liberté, Nous sommes libres.* Freedmen, I said. He just shook his head and said we were subject to Spanish law. We had been legally obtained as laborers and sold to him. Das when we knew what had happened to us. A priest came dat same day and touched our foreheads, speaking some language and then changed our names to Javier and Pablo. Dey had us sign those names in der registry book. The Frenchman came back and warned us never to speak to anyone. He said there would be trouble if we did. We nevah thought we could regain our freedom. Das why we ran away."

"What was your plan?"

"We were going east toward de mountains where der are settlements of runaway slaves. We heard we would be safe der."

The fisherman arrived with about forty land crabs in a hemp bag. He threw the sack on board his fishing boat and immediately started making preparations to leave. Quiñones walked up to them.

"I worked out an arrangement with the fisherman—he will take you as far as New Providence. You will be able to get a ship from there going north to New York, Boston, or Halifax. I wish you a safe journey wherever they take you."

When the fisherman was ready, Jacobs gestured for his sons to board first. He looked at Townsend. "I feel bad—I ain' got nuttin' to give you to tank you."

Townsend shook his head. "I should thank you. I've learned a great deal from you, Jacobs."

Then the Navy veteran smiled and reached into his pocket. He handed him the two carved horses as a memory. "I guess you could say we never would have found dem if not for a hoss."

"I reckon that's right," Townsend said as he rubbed the two little carvings in his hand. "Good luck to you. Where will you go?"

"Not too sure. Maybe we gon' stay in de Bahamas for a time? If you remembah, my muddah was from deh. She bawn and raised in New Providence. I want to see whar she lived. Maybe I gon' find sum family."

"When I get back to Key West, I will tell Old Sandy that God stirred up the waters for you and you made it back to freedom."

Jacobs smiled and embraced Townsend and then stepped on board.

"One other ting, Lieutenant. I should have told you before," Jacobs said as the fishermen pushed the boat into deeper water "Dat Black woman on your family's estate, de one who speaks English."

"You mean Mercedes?"

"Yes. She came out to de stables one day. She tell me she knew your muddah when dey were young. She want to speak wid you. Says she has sum tings to tell you, but your grandmuddah must never know."

27

February 10, 1866

Townsend stood with Quiñones and watched the small fishing sloop sail out of the lagoon and disappear into the open water of the Sagua channel. For Townsend, it was another sad farewell. Like his old crew from the *Rebecca*, he doubted he'd ever see Levi Jacobs again. He'd asked the man if he would be willing to sign an affidavit about what had happened to him and his two sons. Jacobs had paused, finally saying said he'd think about it. He'd decide when they got to the Bahamas. The painful expression on his face told Townsend that Jacobs would probably stay silent. He wanted to forget the past, not relive it.

The two men freed three of the horses they'd taken from the Spanish militia, and then went their separate directions. Quiñones promised he would stay in touch. Townsend was exhausted after the all-night ride, but he kept himself awake by chewing wads of tobacco. Later that afternoon after eight hours on horseback, he arrived in Cárdenas to the blare of trumpets and the banging of drums as a military band marched down the central street of Calle Real toward the waterfront. The Plaza de Armas was crowded with people of all classes cheering and dancing, and the streets surrounding the new market echoed with the clattering of *volantas* and carriages.

Townsend saw a few young men jumping into carriages with some masked ladies adorned with ribbons in their hair. He asked them what was going on. "*Carnaval!*" they shouted in unison. "*Ven con nosotros a bailar.* Come with us to dance." He realized then it was the weekend before Ash Wednesday, and all over many parts of Cuba, people would be attending masked balls.

With some difficulty he fought his way through the *Plaza de Armas* with his horse, finally arriving at Mrs. Woodbury's boarding house and securing a simple room—the last available. Once he got his horse stabled, he freshened up and wrote a short report for Secretary Seward explaining what had happened to Jacobs and his two sons, giving him some details about their kidnapping and what had happened to them. Without mentioning his grandmother, he wrote that the demand here in Cuba among some of the planters for kidnapped American freedmen is an undeniable reality. He mentioned what the overseer at El Capricho had said about the pressing need for more labor. Townsend dropped the dispatch off at the American Consulate in town, addressing the envelope to Mr. William Rudd, Naval Squadron Headquarters, Key West, as he'd been instructed.

There was one person he wanted so badly to tell about the events of the last few days and the extraordinary reunion he'd witnessed—Emma. He was worn out and covered with saddle sores, but Townsend was determined to see Emma. He hired a *volanta* cab, and on the way to her house he conjured up the image of her playing the violin. With the clatter of the horses' hooves beating in his ears, he started humming the high playful notes of Mozart's Concerto No. 5 allegro aperto, one of her favorites. He pictured them joining the celebrations in town, Emma in an enchanting mask, twirling ever closer into his arms.

When he got to the house in the upper part of the town it was dusk. Townsend noticed a man leaning up against a building across the street. Just from the way he was standing and looking at him without moving, Townsend guessed he was a plain clothes policeman or police informant. His breath caught in his throat. He knocked on the door. A maid opened it, and Townsend could tell from the woman's frightened face that something was wrong. He was escorted into the parlor room where Doña Julia paced back and forth in front of the large window overlooking the courtyard. Townsend braced himself for bad news.

"Where's Emma?" he asked.

Doña Julia whirled around to face him, her wide, worried eyes telling him what he didn't want to hear.

"They came last night and took her away."

"Who? Who did?"

"The *Guardia Civil*. They said she was wanted for questioning. A matter of national security. I tried to stop them. I told them I'd have their jobs. I demanded she be released. I mentioned my late husband's name. Nothing worked."

"Where is she now?"

"I went to the *cuartel* this morning. The officer I spoke with knows my husband's family. He was apologetic, but he said there was nothing he could do."

"*Where is she?*" Townsend demanded.

"The policeman told me that the *Guardia Civil* agents put her on the morning train to Havana. They were taking her to the *Casa de Recogidas*. In English, they call that place the asylum for abandoned women. It's where they hold the street prostitutes and the mentally ill. The female convicts too. It's where they put the women who dare break society's rules." She began to sob. "The only reason they've taken her is to threaten her and humiliate her. They want to break her so she'll confess."

Townsend didn't say anything. He just stood there, his chest heaving. His mind blank. He was in a state of shock.

As the train lumbered and clanked along at its maximum speed of fifteen miles an hour, Townsend settled into the wooden seat and leaned up against the open window to breathe. Somehow, he'd caught the last train from Cárdenas that could get him to Havana. He'd been lucky the train was running late. The departure schedules had all been changed because of the celebrations. He'd pushed his way by street vendors and porters and managed to jump on the train just as the engineer gave a blast with the horn.

He let the noisy clattering of the wheels distract him from his troubled thoughts and looked out at the shadowy sugar fields and the dark hills covered with palms and banana trees. All he could think about was Emma. To soothe his mind, he began humming the same Mozart concerto. It was music that now filled his inner silence with longing and helped to stave off his mounting worry. After one stop where he had to change trains, he leaned back on the cane seat, resting his head against the window. The next thing he remembered was waking up to the screeching of the train's wheels and the conductor shouting that they had reached the train depot on the outskirts of Havana.

Townsend's first inclination was to go to Mrs. Carpenter's boarding house to inform her about Emma, but he decided it was too late. She would be asleep, and he didn't want to alarm her. Instead, he hailed a *volanta* cab to take him to the asylum. To get there they had to enter the old city through the remnants of the fortified walls, passing into a rough section of Havana.

A few gas streetlamps cut through the gloom, revealing drunken sailors stumbling along, waiting for some mugger to end their misery or some prostitute to take their money. Townsend's mind was as dark as the street shadows. *What could he do to get her out?* He thought about notifying the American Consul General, but he knew enough to realize this would be a hopeless effort. The Spanish would ignore any entreaties the diplomat might make.

"*¡So! ¡So!*" the postilion cried out as he reined in the lead horse. The *volanta* came to an abrupt stop on Fundición Street as the man pointed to a large brown stone building, black with age, dotted with barred windows. "*Casa de Recogidas,*" he said simply.

Townsend got out and looked up at the asylum's thick walls. He tried not to imagine Emma inside such a place.

February 11

For several hours, the Navy lieutenant paraded back and forth in this shadowy corner of the old city near the Roncalí harbor promenade, trying to think of how he would get her out of there. At first light, Townsend approached the guard outside the asylum and told him he needed to see the warden. It was urgent. He had an important letter from His Excellency, the Captain General, Domingo Dulce. The guard remained stone-faced. Townsend pulled out the letter and handed it to him. He'd carried this letter with him ever since Secretary Seward gave it to him. He knew it was no guarantee of anything. All the letter did was to ask military authorities to cooperate with the American Navy lieutenant. But it had the Captain General's signature, and that was worth its weight in gold in the hierarchical colonial system in Spanish Cuba.

After an hour wait outside the walls, much to his surprise, the guard passed the word to Townsend that the warden would receive him. Townsend's hopes lifted as a soldier escorted him down some dark hallways. But he felt himself getting the chills when he heard some women yelling and the clanging and banging of metal bars. There were no windows and no light. He turned a corner and found himself paraded by crowded cells. Women's hands reached out through the bars. Some were jeering, others pleading for help. The cacophony was overwhelming. He turned away in horror at the sight of one young woman curled up in a corner of the cell, her arms wrapped tightly around her body, a vacant stare in her eyes. He felt a wave of nausea hit him. "What piece of hell is this?" he whispered to himself.

He took a deep breath of the foul, stale air as he was ushered into the warden's office, where he was greeted by a well-dressed man with a curly silver beard and hair, and coal black eyebrows. He introduced himself as Doctor Javier Alfonso Castellanos.

"What is it I can do for you, *Teniente?*" he asked. "I understand you have a letter from the Captain General?"

Just looking at the man Townsend knew he was in trouble. He felt his hope for justice sink like a granite stone. He was looking at the quintessential Spanish bureaucrat dressed in linen and silk, intent on exerting his power. He handed the warden the letter.

"I have been tasked by Secretary of State William Seward to complete an extremely important report on how to improve the shipping trade between the United States and the northern coast of Cuba. This enterprise has the full support of the Spanish Captain General."

"Most impressive, *Teniente*, but tell me . . ." He paused as he stroked his beard and eyed the letter in his hand. "Tell me, what does this report you are doing on trade have to do with *this* establishment? Why are you here?"

"I'm here to request the release of a young Cuban American woman you are holding," Townsend replied. "She has done nothing wrong, and she is certainly not mentally ill."

The warden's eyes hardened. "What is her name?"

"Emma Carpenter Lozada. The *Guardia Civil* in Cárdenas arrested her and brought her here."

Townsend used her full legal name even though he knew Emma went by her mother's name Carpenter. Her Spanish father had abandoned the family when Emma was just a little girl, but Townsend saw no reason to mention that.

The warden called over one of his assistants and began conferring with the man in a soft voice. He finally turned toward Townsend.

"I'm wondering why you are so interested in this woman," the warden asked suspiciously. "She has been brought here to be questioned on some serious charges. What does this have to do with your report on trade?"

"La Srta. Carpenter Lozada has been helpful in the writing of my report. I would like to speak with her," Townsend demanded with a sudden air of authority. "I'm certain the Captain General would want to be kept appraised of any obstacles I'm encountering."

This was a dangerous moment for Townsend. He was bluffing. The warden clearly wanted to say no, but the mention of the Captain General had its desired effect. He nodded at the assistant.

"Bring the woman to me."

Five minutes passed by without a word being spoken. Townsend thought he could hear prison guards insulting someone in the hallway. The door opened, and a woman was pushed inside. It was Emma. Her hair was disheveled, her dress torn, and her wrists manacled together.

Emma glared at the warden as she stepped further into the office. Townsend could see the leer on the man's face. She looked around the room, her eyes flashing until she spotted Townsend.

"Everett, thank God. You must get me out of this hell hole."

"I'm afraid that won't be possible," the warden said in English, unfurling a cruel smile as he made it clear he understood what she had just said. "Only the military official in charge of questioning the prisoners here, Major Humberto López Villanueva, can authorize that, *Señorita*," he said, pointedly using his mastery of English.

"Wait!" Townsend said. "Did you say López Villanueva? The captain involved with harbor security?"

"I did," the warden replied with surprise. "However, he is no longer a captain. He was recently promoted. Major López Villanueva is now a highly ranked officer charged with heading up a special military unit gathering intelligence on the growing threat from anti-Spanish insurgents."

"I'd like to speak to the Major. We worked together on matters of security in the harbor. Just mention my name. He will know me."

The warden stared at Townsend, his expression flat. Townsend could see Emma eyeing him as he held the warden's gaze. "Very well. Excuse me. I will speak with him."

Townsend and Emma waited silently, any hope of communication dashed by a guard who watched them intently. Finally, a door banged and a familiar short, stocky figure wearing a dark blue coat trimmed with red and gold and a grey felt hat marched into the room, followed by the warden.

Major Humberto López Villanueva looked over at Emma, allowing his eyes to linger. When he turned and spotted Townsend, the military officer broke out into a warm smile.

"Ah, my good friend, *Teniente* Townsend. I'm glad to see you are still here in Cuba." He turned back to the warden. "This young man helped me apprehend some important American smugglers who were in league with the Cuban revolutionaries during Secretary Seward's visit. Quite a successful collaboration and an important arrest in the fight to safeguard Spain's most faithful island. Thanks to Lieutenant Townsend's assistance, nothing happened to harm the good relations between the two countries fostered by this important meeting between the Captain General and the American Secretary of State."

He patted Townsend on the back. "This is indeed a pleasant surprise. I see you're out of uniform now, Lieutenant?"

"I'm still in the Navy, Major, but I am currently on special assignment to complete a report on American shipping and trade to Cuba's northern ports."

"So I'm told by the warden. Quite an important assignment. I also understand His Excellency, the Captain General has shown a special interest?"

Townsend now took a deep breath and stood up straighter.

"Indeed. We are looking at the accessibility of the Cuban ports to American ships, the expenses and charges in the ports, and how to improve the general efficiency of imports and exports flowing between the United States and Cuba. Naturally we will be looking at how the efforts of smugglers undermine both the economic interests of our two countries and the authority of those who police the harbor. We believe this report will be of interest to both governments as well as the merchant houses and the planters."

"Impressive. And how can I help you? Something to do with this woman, I believe?"

"I think we can help each other, Major, as we did with the *Southern Cross*."

"Really," declared López Villanueva, eyebrows raised.

"This woman is completely innocent."

"Our informants tell us otherwise. They say she is in league with student revolutionaries. A serious charge. I am here today to begin questioning her."

"There must be a logical explanation, Major. Miss Carpenter Lozada is important to me for several reasons, and she might be of use to you as well."

"I'm sure she could be," replied the Major salaciously as he once again allowed his eyes to wander over Emma, scanning down her body. As if on cue the warden and the soldiers laughed.

Townsend didn't flinch at this crude remark, although he could see Emma press her lips together in an effort to keep her mouth shut. He knew if she were close enough, she probably would have kicked the Spanish military officer.

"I'm just joking, Lieutenant. *Un chiste de caballeros.* Tell me why is this beautiful young woman so important to you?"

"She knows people I don't know. Merchants and ship captains, people in the shipping business she met through working at her mother's boarding house. They can tell her which American ships are smuggling goods into Cuba."

"What kind of smuggling?"

"Guns and other weapons," Townsend blurted out without thinking. "To be used by Cuban revolutionaries against the Spanish authorities."

"You know of instances of this? Do you have names?"

"Nothing reliable yet. But we are making progress."

Townsend had no idea where his fabrications came from. When he spoke Spanish, the balderdash just seemed to flow freely through him without much thought involved—probably because he saw it more like theater than anything else.

The major frowned and glanced over at the warden, who also looked very concerned. Townsend was quite aware that he'd made promises he couldn't deliver on, and that he'd just volunteered Emma and himself as government informants. The report he spoke about was pure fiction, and so was Emma's role. He didn't know a thing about gun smugglers. He kept his face expressionless, and silently willed Emma to do the same.

"*Tal vez*, la Srta. Carpenter Lozada could work directly for us as an informant?" Major López Villanueva said, "assuming she indeed has these contacts." The Spanish officer now smiled and once again looked over at Emma. "We would release her, of course, but she would still be under our control now that we know her usefulness, reporting *directly* to me, naturally."

Townsend felt a sudden wave of panic. He realized his plan had just backfired. The Major clearly expected more from Emma than just information. Suddenly a thought struck him—he would appeal not only to the officer's self-interest, but also to his sense of Spanish honor and chivalry.

Townsend took a deep breath before plunging ahead.

"There is another reason I would like you to release this woman. It's highly personal information I had not planned to reveal, but in light of these circumstances I believe it is necessary."

The two officials leaned in closer. He could see how he now had captured their attention.

"La Señorita Carpenter Lozada and I have not made this public yet, but you should know we are engaged, engaged to be married."

Townsend could see the look of astonishment on their faces. He glanced at Emma whose face had fallen to the floor. *No turning back now*, he thought to himself and decided to further embellish the story.

"I'm looking forward to having my fiancée meet my grandmother, Doña Cecilia Carbonell de Vargas who owns Mon Bijou plantation in Matanzas and is a close friend of the Marquis Ignacio Calderón de Molina. We are of course planning our wedding here in Cuba and hope that the Marquis will host an event for us. I know that Vice Consul General Thomas Savage, who is returning to Cuba, will want to attend the wedding as I know him personally, and I'm hoping to extend an invitation to the Captain General as well—although I am sure His Excellency will be too busy."

Townsend had played all his cards—his government connections, including to Secretary Seward and the Captain General, his family's land holdings, and his close ties with Spanish royalty. He looked at López Villanueva, who, like any good military man seemed to know when it was time to retreat.

"Release the woman," López Villanueva snapped at the guards. "Immediately! Take off her manacles."

He now turned to Emma and bowed to her.

"Señorita, I want to apologize to you personally and extend the most fervent good wishes to you and Lieutenant Townsend. May your union be blessed by the Holy Spirit."

He then bowed again to Emma and turned toward Townsend, extending his hand.

"*Felicidades, Teniente.* Congratulations, Lieutenant. I'm sorry for any misunderstandings. I didn't realize how many mutual interests we have. I look forward to our future collaborations."

Townsend led Emma out of the building as fast as he could. Neither one said a word as they passed by some of the screaming women in the cells. As soon as they got out of the asylum and were walking toward the Roncalí promenade along the harbor, Emma turned to him.

"What have you just done, Everett Townsend! You've sold me to the devil! How could you have said those things?"

"Well, you're free, Emma. . . . You have to admit you're free. We're lucky that my bluffing and bluster worked."

"And for that I will forever be grateful. But look what you've done. Whatever were you thinking? You've turned us into government informants? Spies for the Spanish? For a moment there I thought you would give them Emilio's name as one of my so-called smuggler *acquaintances.*"

Townsend shrugged. "I do admit there are some challenges ahead, and perhaps it is an unsettling collaboration. I did stretch the truth here and there."

"You just make up stories like some kind of carnival man! Honestly, Everett—what happens when they find out you were lying?"

"Getting you out was no simple task, you must agree. We can worry about the other problems later. Besides, they weren't all lies. There were elements of truth."

"Really! Tell me. I know you're not doing this fictitious report on trade you talked about."

"But I am investigating smuggling."

"Smuggling of kidnapped American freedmen, not guns. You don't know anyone smuggling arms, do you? I certainly don't, despite what you told them."

"It was all to get you free."

Emma sighed. "But none of it was true. You said we were engaged. We're not engaged."

"I know, but we could be." Townsend smiled at her.

"Could be? What in God's mercy do you mean by that? Imagine hearing you're already engaged with your hands in manacles and those repulsive men eyeing you like a cow in a stockade. Frankly, if I could have slapped you, I would have."

"I admit it was bit of wishful thinking on my part," Townsend said with a sparkle in is eye.

Emma shot him a sideways glance.

"What exactly do you mean by *wishful thinking?*"

Townsend stopped walking and took her hand, turning her to face him. "Shouldn't we be engaged, Emma? I mean I am completely serious. I love you. I think you know that. I made mistakes, I'm not perfect. I'll stay here in Cuba if that's what you desire. Once I'm free from the Navy, we can make our own lives wherever we want. Say you'll marry me Emma."

"You don't give in, do you, Everett?" she said with a smirk.

"Not easily." He winked at her.

"Stubborn mule of a man," she said, shaking her head with only a hint of a smile. "Maybe that's your best attribute, Everett. You are relentless. Never take no for an answer."

"Well, you would make me more of an honest person."

"How's that? By agreeing to marry you?"

"There are worse things."

She shook her head back and forth. "You've already announced our engagement. When were you going to consult with me?"

"I'm sorry, Emma. I hated the way that they all were eyeing you, and I blurted it out. Even so, I assure you I had been thinking about it. In fact, I've thought about it a great deal."

"Will you be sending an invitation to the Captain General?"

"I gave quite less thought to the invitation list, I confess."

She slipped her hand into the crook of his arm.

"I'll give your proposal some thought. How's that for an answer? By the way, Lieutenant Townsend, this is a pretty bad neighborhood you've taken me to. Do you have a plan on how we safely get out of this part of Havana?"

28

February 16, 1866

The silence hung in the air like the calm before a storm when Townsend arrived at Mon Bijou. He stepped out of the *volanta* and breathed in the sun-baked air of the countryside, brushing off the red dust from his clothes. There was no one there to greet him, and that seemed strange. His mind was still swirling over the last five days he'd spent in Havana when Emma had told her mother about her arrest and imprisonment. A frightened Mrs. Carpenter had asked him to stay at the boarding house for several days, just in case the *Guardia Civil* returned. It was the end of Carnival, and the streets of Havana teemed with music and dance. Townsend had been only too glad to spend more time with Emma.

He and Emma had celebrated her freedom by going to the masquerade ball at the Tacón theater the next night along with hundreds of others. The slow, inviting melody of the *danza criolla* with the wail of violins and the rhythmic scraping of the *güiro* echoed in his ears. He could still feel the sway of her light body amid the gentle twirling, round and round across the floor. His senses were heightened by her lavender scent and her brown hair falling down her back. All night long her almond-shaped eyes and her full lips had bewitched him through her mask. It was as if every nerve in their bodies tingled after their brush with danger at the *Casa de Recogidas*.

These musings occupied his mind as he walked into the house and looked around the familiar white stucco walls. A few small green lizards and a procession of ants were scurrying over the chipped terracotta tile floors, but there was no sign of the servants. The only sound was the faint rustling of the wooden jalousies from the wind. Townsend found his grandmother eating alone in the dining room. Doña Cecilia looked up to greet him with a half-hearted smile, adjusting the black lace mantilla falling down her shoulders. Her thin face was pale, and she was picking at her food. At that moment, she seemed older, her back stooped. He asked her what was wrong. She just shook her head and mumbled an apology for not meeting him at the veranda. He could see that she'd been reading a letter and asked her if he could help in any way.

Doña Cecilia looked up at him. Her dark eyes were circled with red from crying. She wiped her face.

"It's terrible news, Everett. It's Don Pedro."

Townsend felt the back of his neck tense up at the mere mention of Don Pedro Alvarado Cardona. Even though the man had been banished from Cuba by the government, in the back of his mind Townsend had never stopped worrying about his return. The prospect of ever running into the corrupt Spanish merchant again had kept him on edge. He knew the man would try to kill him if he could.

"What is it?" Townsend asked, trying to calm his breathing. He heard a noise from the kitchen, and he whirled around in that direction. He could see a yellow turban. It was Mercedes. She was standing within earshot in the shadows, her arms folded together.

"He's dead," his grandmother cried out. "I received this letter today informing me of his death in Fernando Po. Some kind of fever disease, they said. They treated him with leeches and bleeding, some borage tea, and mustard on his feet. The poor man. The doctors over there probably *killed* him."

"I'm, sorry to hear that," Townsend said flatly. The truth was, he was immensely relieved. He stood there silently, awkwardly, as she slowly wiped away her tears and collected herself. He knew he should try to comfort her, but he didn't. He couldn't bring himself to. He'd always found it strange that a man so cruel and so lacking of any morals had been so beloved by his grandmother. *May the devil stoke the fires in hell for Don Pedro,* he thought to himself.

"Sometimes I feel as if I've had more than my share of misfortune," she said softly. She sighed with tightly compressed lips. "My two little girls, your mother's sisters, Blanca and Pilar, my husband Rafael—all dead from that yellow fever outbreak. Then came the slave revolts in the early 1840s. Those were bad times here in Cuba. Your mother abandoned me. I was so distraught. I don't know what I would have done if not for Pedro. He saved me. I kept hoping your mother would come to her senses and return, but she never did. *Gracias a Dios por Pedro*, Thank the Lord for Pedro. He continued to help me run the estate even as he tended to his own business affairs."

Townsend put his hand on her shoulder. He realized that she was frightened and worried about the future. He felt sorry for her. She looked up and smiled and forced herself to sit up straight.

"But enough of that," she said. "Enough of an old woman's tears. Suffering and loss are part of life, and we must all learn to cope with our sorrows. Now tell me, where have you been? Do you have some good news? Tell me something to cheer me up."

Townsend told her where he'd been but refrained from giving too many details. He was also vague about what he'd done in Havana. He explained how his attendant had run away, probably sneaking on board an outbound US merchant ship.

"Maybe that was for the better, *querido*. I never much liked that attendant of yours. Too surly and unpleasant. I didn't trust him. McKintyre felt he would have created trouble."

Townsend thought about defending Jacobs, but quickly decided to say nothing. Instead, he plunged ahead and told her about Emma, and how wonderful she was.

Just the mention of a young woman caused Doña Cecilia's face to freeze ever so slightly, but she quickly recovered her composure and smiled broadly.

"I see. . . . This is excellent news, Everett. Tell me more about this delightful young woman. I'm sure she's beautiful. What's her full name?"

"Emma Carpenter Lozada."

"A Spanish girl?"

"No, she's Cuban American. Born here. Her father is Spanish."

"Lozada, Lozada . . . I don't know of any Lozada," she said with a slight disdainful twitch of her nose.

She asked Mercedes to bring Don Everett some *café con leche* and his favorite guava pastries, and then began to quietly coax more details out of him. Just his lighthearted tone of voice must have told her this was more than just a casual encounter. When Townsend told her that Emma's mother ran a medium-sized boarding house in Havana, Doña Cecilia seemed to stiffen.

"Tell me about her father—this—Señor Lozada."

"I don't know that much. His name is Enrique Lozada. He was a merchant in Havana. I believe he returned to Spain. Emma doesn't remember much about him. She was just a young girl then. I have the impression that they haven't heard from him, at least not for quite some time."

"Is he coming back?"

"I don't know."

His grandmother pursed her lips and remained silent. Townsend avoided mentioning that it was rumored Don Enrique Lozada had another separate family in Spain. Doña Cecilia changed the topic and wanted to know how he and Emma had come to know each other. Townsend told her he first met Emma at her mother's boarding house three years ago and they had later seen each other in Key West where she was staying with her sister, but the war had separated them.

"All this time . . . my, my. However, did you find each other again in Cárdenas?" she asked with a wry chuckle. "Or did *she* find *you?* It sounds like Emma is quite a determined young woman."

Townsend could sense her probing stare.

"We'd stayed in touch. She wrote me a letter. She has been staying at the house of Doña Julia Thornton de Gonzalez, tutoring her granddaughter in the violin."

"Ay *sí*, Doña Julia, the recent widow. A wealthy woman. I don't know her, but I'm told she is one of those Americans who came to Cuba hunting for a rich husband, and she found one. I'm told she's now developed some unfortunate ideas about freeing the slaves."

"I've been to see Emma in Havana. We went to the masquerade ball at the Tacón theater."

"So, you are serious about this girl?" Doña Cecilia asked, eyes wide.

"Yes, I am."

"Tell me more about her mother's family."

"They're from Philadelphia. I believe the Carpenters are well known in social circles there."

"Carpenter? I don't know that name. Are you thinking of marrying her?"

Townsend thought it best to be circumspect. "It is . . . um . . . a possibility."

"Well, then this is important. I must meet her. We must invite Emma and her mother to Mon Bijou. This is the height of the social season. There will be lots of activity, and McKintyre will be training a batch of new Chinese laborers we've just acquired. What's her mother's name? I will write a letter immediately to be sent out on the afternoon train to Havana."

February 19

A few days later, Townsend went to pick up Emma and her mother at the Matanzas train station. Plantation owners with wives and children along with country merchants had arrived on horseback and in their *volantas*, all headed for the wide shed at the depot. Amid shrill calls and tinkling bells from street vendors, teams of shirtless slaves pushed bags and luggage in drays. It was mayhem, and Townsend had to push his way forward on the platform.

The train trundled into the station with a mournful blast from the horn. He finally spotted Emma and her mother and waved so that they would see him. That's when he noticed two men behind them. They looked like plain-clothes military men with their coarse linen suits. They stopped and stared at them, and then quickly turned away. Townsend narrowed his eyes. Emma was likely being followed by some of López Villanueva's men. He decided to refrain from telling her anything before he was certain.

When they arrived at Mon Bijou, his grandmother had all fifteen servants out on the veranda to greet them. Dressed in a formal white cotton dress with colored silk and her pearl necklace, she came down the stone stairs like a Spanish Royal to personally greet Mrs. Carpenter and Emma, who both called her Señora Carbonell de Vargas.

"Oh, please don't call me that. Call me Doña Cecilia," she said with a big smile. "You'll make me feel like an old lady if you don't. I hope you don't mind if we speak in Spanish."

Townsend could see that his grandmother was using all her considerable charms and social skills that she normally reserved for people she wanted to impress. She directed Julio to take the ladies' bags to the spare bedroom on the far side of the house and have the maids put their clothes away. She then personally led the two women into the house, talking nonstop about the social season in the countryside, mentioning the names of the wealthiest families who lived nearby.

Townsend followed, walking alongside Emma. She seemed so confident and proud. He smiled at her discretely and rolled his eyes as Doña Cecilia took her guests on a tour through the house. She told Mrs. Carpenter all about the history of Mon Bijou and how her grandfather had given the estate a French name in honor of all the white planters who were killed in Haiti. She then focused her attention on Emma.

"Tell me, how was Havana? Did you have a good time at the masquerade ball at the Tacón theater?"

"Yes, we did," Emma replied.

"I used to love *los bailes de máscaras* at the Tacón theater when I was a bit younger. Such a marvelous theater and such an elegant ball, isn't it, my dear?"

"It is a lovely theater indeed," was all Emma said.

"Did you go to the Louvre restaurant afterward for a drink? That's what all the finer people do in Havana. When I attend the opera at the Tacón, I always go there. To be seen, of course."

Doña Cecilia offered a tight smile and looked about to continue her grilling when the barefoot butler named Alejandro shuffled in wearing a white coat and white gloves and whispered to Doña Cecilia that the food was prepared. She led her three guests to the dining room.

"I hope you stayed out of the moonlight in Havana, my dear," she said to Emma with a faint smile that barely reached her cheeks. Townsend wondered if Emma could see how fake it was. "You know what they say here in Cuba. If the moonlight shines on your head, it can be dangerous to your health."

"I'm well aware of that superstition, Doña Cecilia," Emma politely replied. "Fortunately, Everett and I stayed mostly inside. Didn't we, Everett?"

Townsend nodded as he suppressed a chuckle. He glanced at Emma, who smiled back at him mischievously. His gaze lingered on her as he thought about their adventures that night and how much this spirited woman bewitched him. After the ball, they had walked outside into the gardens of the Paseo de Isabel Segunda and joined the street festivities. People were running wild in the streets, singing and dancing. Once they got back to her mother's boarding house, Emma had taken him up to the rooftop terrace where they looked out at the ships in the harbor. The air was so cool and balmy. There alone above the noisy city below them, they had kissed and enjoyed the moonlight shining over Havana Bay, wrapped in each other's arms.

Townsend's reverie was interrupted by the two Marías and one of the cooks bringing out the platters of steaming hot food. Roast chicken garnished with olives and raisins, okra and tomatoes, yellow rice, and a whole roast pig decorated with tropical vegetables. The aroma of olive oil, garlic, and roasted meats filled the dining room.

Doña Cecilia proudly announced that her roast pork was the best in the region because her pigs were fed on guinea grass and palm berries. She then made a big production out of seating everyone. "Everett, do sit here, *querido*, next to me." She tapped the chair where Townsend was to sit and then extended her arm. "Mrs. Carpenter, as my guest of honor, I welcome you to sit at the other head of the table, with Emma by your side."

Townsend looked at Emma apologetically. He could see that she and her mother had felt the subtle sting of Doña Cecilia's hospitality as the empty chairs stretched between them.

Later that afternoon with the sun dipping down below the towering chimney of the sugar mill, Doña Cecilia insisted on taking the two ladies for a ride in her four-wheeled *barouche* with two horses. She wanted to show them the scenery and take them to see the small family church. Townsend helped the three women get into the carriage and stood to one side as the carriage lurched forward and then headed down one of the small farm roads.

As the three women swayed back and forth on the seat, Townsend could see his grandmother pointing to an ox cart in the distance where a small Black boy was running alongside poking the ox in the ribs with a long stick. He felt a sudden sense of dread about bringing Emma here—and leaving her and her mother alone with his grandmother.

Townsend was on his way back to the house when he noticed that Mercedes was eyeing him. He remembered what Jacobs had said and he approached her. She immediately asked him about Levi Jacobs.

"Did he find his two sons?" she asked in Spanish.

Townsend couldn't help but grin. "I'm pleased to say he did. It was quite extraordinary. We found them hiding in a cave—they had run away from a plantation. All three escaped on a boat to the Bahamas. It was nothing short of a miracle. I still can't believe it. The impossible somehow became possible. I can't explain it."

"*Un verdadero milagro,*" she replied with an expression of wonder. "It was the power of love." Her face broke out into a broad smile. "I am so happy for him. He and I, we talked, you know. I came to the stables to see him. He is a good man who has suffered too much."

Townsend nodded. "Before he left, Jacobs said you wanted to tell me something about my mother? Is that right?"

She nodded and led him to an area in the garden outside the plantation house where there was a well. She slowly cranked the wheel, which made a mournful creak as a bucket of water slowly emerged from inside the well. She told him to follow her and then carried the bucket of water on her head onto a path flanked by arbors draped with vines. All around were fruit trees—zapotes, guavas, bananas, lemons, and oranges. She pointed to a wooden bench.

"They won't see us here."

"Who are you afraid of?" Townsend asked.

She didn't answer and then again spoke in Spanish. "I hope you don't mind my speaking to you in Spanish. I prefer it, particularly with matters that are difficult to explain." She pulled out a packet of envelopes from under her calico dress.

"These are for you—the letters your mother sent me from Maryland all those years she was away."

Townsend was speechless as he took the bundle of letters. There must have been twenty letters.

"Your mother and I wrote each other once or twice a year."

"But how . . . ?"

"We grew up together here at Mon Bijou. I'm older but just by two years. When we were young, we had the same tutor, read the same books, and rode horses together. We shared our thoughts and secrets. We were aware that we were different, but unaware that our different colored skins would define our lives."

"But you're my grandmother's maid," Townsend said, perplexed.

"Yes, but when I was young, I was your mother's best friend."

Townsend nodded and looked at Mercedes, then looked at the letters in his hands. She paused a moment before speaking again, this time in a subdued tone of voice.

"I just wanted you to have these letters. She did miss Cuba."

"But she never wanted to come back."

"She had her reasons."

"I know some of those reasons, I think. The forced marriage to Don Pedro? Allowing my father to be falsely accused and imprisoned? I can imagine that these problems would have caused quite a battle of wills."

"Yes, but it was more than that. I know you worked for Don Pedro when you last were here. I wanted to tell you then, but there never was an opportunity." She paused and then took a deep breath. "I probably shouldn't tell you this, but I will now that we know Don Pedro is dead."

Townsend looked at her expectantly.

"When your grandfather died in 1840, your grandmother was overwhelmed. She was grieving for her husband, as well as for her two younger daughters. She turned to Don Pedro to help her with the management of the plantation. He was like her financial advisor, helping pay off debts with 20 percent interest. But then it became more than just that."

"What do you mean?"

"She became attached to him. When your grandfather died, she was lonely."

"What do you mean? She was older . . ."

"But only by about ten years. She was in her forties then, and she was an attractive woman. She'd known Don Pedro since he was a boy. I suppose she was flattered by his attentions."

"He seduced her?" Townsend stared at Mercedes, who only nodded.

"Why did she want Don Pedro to marry her daughter?"

"He was going to leave her. She was desperate to keep him. She couldn't give him children, so she offered him your mother. She told Don Pedro he could inherit Mon Bijou. Esperanza could be his wife and give him children, but he would stay with her as her lover."

"However do you know this . . . ?"

"I had become your grandmother's maid by then. There are very few intimate secrets a lady can keep from her maid."

"Did my mother know any of this?"

"I told her. She was secretly seeing your father then. I felt your mother needed to know. She was eighteen and had her life ahead of her. She confronted your grandmother. Doña Cecilia was angry and told her that marriage was no different than business and she needed to think of her future and the future of Mon Bijou. Your mother flew into a rage and called her horrible names. She left the next day on your father's ship, never to speak to her mother again. To this day, I don't know if I did the right thing."

Townsend got up and paced around, confused and uncomfortable from what he had just heard. He thought of his mother's face, her anger when a letter from his grandmother would arrive at their home in Havre de Grace. She'd had every right to flee. This was a betrayal beyond most people's imaginations. Her own mother had been willing to sabotage her daughter's life and her future. Her own mother wanted to share a marital bed with a man she detested. It was no wonder his mother never wanted to see Doña Cecilia ever again. It was no wonder she cut off all ties.

Townsend turned to face Mercedes. His eyes were moist.

"How could you stay here? You're enslaved, I know, but couldn't you have run away? How could you remain here, knowing what you know?"

"It may be hard for you to imagine, but I had no option. I couldn't run away. My mother was sick and in need of care, living as a slave woman in the barracoons. She needed my help. I don't know if you know she was bought as a slave by your grandfather, Don Rafael Vargas, when he visited Jamaica. That was in the early 1820s when slavery was still legal there. I was born the next year here at Mon Bijou."

Townsend gave her a quizzical look.

"Do you mean . . . ?"

"Yes, I was your grandfather's first child, an illegitimate child from an enslaved woman. I was your mother's half-sister. Your grandmother didn't like me, but your grandfather felt differently. He never openly admitted that I was his child, but he told my mother that he would free me. Then, he died unexpectedly, and—"

"You're my aunt?" Townsend blurted out. "My grandmother told me a different story. She said you were sold to her and that you were born in Jamaica."

"That's not true. Doña Cecilia has never liked revealing the truth about me. No, I was born here, and I spent my childhood in the plantation house where my mother was one of the cooks. When we were little, your mother and I used to run around the kitchen barefoot. We played together like most sisters do."

"So, you are my Aunt Mercedes?"

"Yes," she replied and then laughed nervously. "I'm not sure your grandmother accepts that. If she knew I told you any of this, she would have me beaten. She may be my stepmother, but she is also my mistress and I am her slave. She never lets me forget that."

The plantation bell sounded marking the end of the day, and Mercedes told him she had to go. She reached into her dress again and handed Townsend a silver diamond-encrusted band with a gold star on it.

"This was your mother's, given to her on her fifteenth birthday by Don Rafael. Before she left Cuba, she gave it to me and said I should have it because Don Rafael was my father too. I've never forgotten that kindness. I want you to have it now and give it to that pretty girl who's here with you. I can tell by the way she looks at you that she adores you."

Townsend hugged Mercedes and whispered his thanks. He wasn't certain what had just happened to him. He walked out of the fruit orchard as if in a daze, clutching the ring and his mother's letters. He turned back to say something, but Mercedes had already gone. A clattering of wheels and a horse whinnying told him that the ladies must be returning from their excursion, and he rushed back to the house to hide his treasures from his grandmother's sharp eyes.

29

February 20, 1866

Townsend felt a tingling emptiness inside him as he tried to digest all that Mercedes had told him. The notion that she was his aunt but also a slave to his grandmother was hard for him to comprehend. He had gotten up early to sit out on the veranda in the gray light before dawn. He watched a fluttering leaf fall to the ground, twirling and spinning, lifeless but still in motion. Some said falling leaves were a sign that a ghost was walking in the branches. He felt his mother's spirit there next to him. She wore a muslin scarf over her head and was looking at him. He could hear her voice calling out to him—*mi hijo, comprendes ahora,* now do you understand, my son? *Now do you understand why I would cry and swear every time your grandmother's name was mentioned?*

The heavy clang of the morning plantation bell announced the beginning of the workday in the cane fields. It was six o'clock. Townsend could see the blurred shadows of the enslaved trudging out from the barracoons for another long day of misery in the suffocating heat. The *contramayorales* were yelling and cursing at them to walk faster.

A mournful groan from a wagon wheel heralded the arrival of the daily morning delivery of vegetables from the mountains—yams, malangas, and plantains. These vegetables would be weighed and apportioned out to the cooks. Alejandro shuffled onto the veranda in his bare feet and handed him his *café con leche* along with a letter. He said it had been dropped off the night before by a *montero* on horseback who came from the east.

Townsend looked at the letter with a puzzled expression. The small brown envelope was addressed simply with his name and underneath that, Ingenio Mon Bijou.

"Was there any message, Alejandro?"

"*Ningún mensaje, Amo,*" the man said shaking his head.

The letter was written on small notepaper-size stationery, the kind used in counting rooms. The handwriting was neat and tidy. It was from Quiñones. He wrote in English that he had changed jobs and had moved from Sagua to Cárdenas. He was now working out of the counting room offices of a Portland, Maine, company called Churchill, Brown & Manson as one of the engineers available to install imported machinery on the plantations. The note said Townsend needed to come to see him in Cárdenas as soon as possible. He turned the page over, but nothing else was there.

Townsend had no idea what Quiñones was writing about. It was a cryptic note, perhaps intended to be intentionally vague in case it had been intercepted by the authorities. As he pondered that troubling thought, a name struck him—Jacobs. The Spanish Navy could have intercepted the fishing boat off the Cuban coast. If they suspected he and his sons were runaway slaves, they would have arrested them and thrown them in prison. The fisherman could even face a death sentence by the *garrote* for helping slaves to escape.

Townsend heard his grandmother's voice call for one of the serving maids, and he tucked the letter into his pocket. Just the sound of her voice made him tense. He had avoided her probing eyes at dinner the evening before. He wasn't certain he could look into her face without revealing how troubled he felt. He braced himself as footsteps drew closer, but then breathed a sigh of relief when Emma emerged on the veranda. Alone on the veranda, they kissed in the shadowy light. He'd arranged with Julio at the stables to saddle up two of the horses so that they both could take a ride around the property.

The morning sunlight was just emerging over the hills when he and Emma mounted up and headed out into the fields of waving cane. Townsend waited until they were well away from the house and were riding on an empty cart path through some pastureland before he told her about his conversation with Mercedes. Emma kept shaking her head in amazement. She had only met Don Pedro once, when he had held a knife to her throat. Like Townsend, she had been delighted to learn that the Spaniard was no longer alive.

"The image of a younger Doña Cecilia dancing cheek to cheek with that hateful Lothario, it's hard to believe," Emma said, grimacing. "She must have felt alone and vulnerable, and needed a strong man in her life."

"Well, she certainly picked a man of a brutal mind," Townsend growled. "He was a ruthless snake."

"Maybe that's what she wanted?" Emma said. "Someone who she felt would take care of her problems and deal with any threats from her slaves. But how unforgivable, to be willing to give up her own daughter's happiness."

"Yes, with my grandmother it's always been about money and supporting the plantation. The world revolves around her and this land."

Townsend looked down at the horses' hooves and sighed, lost in his thoughts. He could hear the rustling of the long slender cane leaves.

"Do you have any sympathy for your grandmother?" Emma asked.

Townsend didn't respond.

Emma persisted.

"It's not just what she did to your mother—think about Mercedes, your grandfather's illegitimate daughter. Your aunt! Your grandmother has kept her as her own personal servant all these years! Like a prisoner. Here in Cuba, many families would have freed a mixed-race slave fathered by someone in their family. That's not unusual. After all, they're family. What your grandmother has done to her is cruel beyond words."

"I don't know what I feel, Emma. I'm a ship at sea. It's like a hurricane has hit me."

Emma paused for a few moments.

"Everett, I hope you won't take offense. Just from spending the afternoon with her yesterday, I can see that your grandmother is a stubborn, proud woman who doesn't like to admit she's wrong. Part of her might have regrets, but she'll never tell you. After all this time, she will have convinced herself that she was just trying to help your mother. She will excuse every choice she made. She probably would say she did Mercedes a kindness, keeping her on in the house."

"You sound like you've gotten to know her in quite a short time."

Emma's brow furrowed. One look at her face told Townsend that all had not gone well during yesterday's excursion.

"Tell me what happened."

Emma explained that while her mother was in the chapel, his grandmother had shown her the family cemetery nearby. Doña Cecilia talked about her Spanish roots and the importance of Spanish rule on the island.

"She took me to see the gravestones of your mother's two younger sisters. I have to say, I was touched. The poor things died from yellow fever days apart. They were so young, not even twelve years old. Your grandmother pointed out what was written on their stones. '*Encantadoras en la vida y cercanas en la muerte.*' Lovely in life and not long separated in death. She said that losing those two girls made her lose faith and hope in life, but then she said she put aside her sorrows. She talked about the importance of Mon Bijou. This land was where she had spent her childhood, the happy years she had spent with her parents before she was sent off to finishing school in Paris. She said slavery is essential to the welfare of the plantations and therefore the continuing prosperity for all Cubans and Spaniards on the island. 'It's how we keep our traditions alive,' she told me. She asked me what I thought."

"And what did you say?" Townsend braced himself for Emma's words to his grandmother.

"I didn't say anything, but my face must have betrayed me. She asked me why I made such a face. I said I had serious doubts about slavery. It was morally indefensible and a hateful institution. I told her I thought Cuba's slaves should be freed immediately."

"Oh, no," Townsend rubbed his face. "I should have come with you. What happened then?"

"She said that freeing the slaves would bring utter ruin to Cuba. She said Spanish rule here has never been more important. I told her I didn't agree. Her face soured and darkened. She said how disappointed she was in me. She said my views were threatening a way of life, and that I reminded her of her daughter Esperanza."

"She said that you were like my mother?"

"Yes—she said Esperanza was pigheaded, unrealistic, and always found fault with everything. On the trip back in the carriage she spoke to my mother but never to me. She never even looked at me."

Townsend quietly groaned. That explained the many long silences at the dinner the evening before. "I am glad you stood up for your beliefs, Emma. Honestly."

"I'm not sure we'll ever get along, your grandmother and I," Emma said. "I'm sorry. I think she may have decided to dislike me even before we met."

"Why do you say that?"

"I think she sees me as a threat."

"A threat? What do you mean?"

"She doesn't want to lose you."

When they got back to the stables, William McKintyre was standing with a whip in one hand and a leash with two big dogs in the other. He was observing the unloading of fifty newly arrived Chinese laborers from a large wagon.

The men tumbled out of the wagon, pigtails dangling from underneath large cone-shaped straw hats. It was a sad sight. They were skin and bones, dressed in loose baggy trousers and shirts that accentuated how razor thin they were. Clearly, they'd just arrived from the months-long journey across the ocean. Some of them were carrying nothing but a wooden pillow they'd brought from China. Holding a stout whip in his hand, the burly overseer was already busy examining his new laborers, touching them and poking them, walking up and down like a military officer in front of new recruits.

Townsend knew his grandmother had signed a contract for Chinese workers. She already had about fifty on the estate. She'd told him that she'd had to secure a loan from a Havana merchant to pay for them. Three hundred dollars for each one, she'd said and explained that it was a labor contract for eight years. She would have bought more African slaves, which she far preferred, but there had been no new landings of African slaves.

McKintyre stopped to speak with one of the plantation's old Chinese workers. Spotting Townsend, the overseer waved. Townsend and Emma dismounted and handed the horses' reins to one of the stable boys. The Scotsman tipped his hat to Emma, whom he'd met the day before, and then addressed Townsend.

"Ah know they're a miserable sight," he said. "Still showin' th' horrors ay th' Middle Passage, Ahm afraid. Fed only rice and tea, and packed into that ship like rats in a cage. Within a week, Ah can assure ye we'll hae these coolies working in the fields."

Without commenting, Townsend looked at the bedraggled Chinese lined up in double rows. He felt their misery even as he felt his own discomfort standing there next to Emma. The sullen faces reminded him of the prisoners at Fort Jefferson in the Tortugas, that same look of total despair and hopelessness. He'd heard that these laborers were sold into servitude by their own government. Some of them may have been felons, but others had been kidnapped or crimped, and then lied to about where they were going.

With the help of the old Chinese man as translator, McKintyre began to explain to the new arrivals that under their contract they would be paid four dollars a month. And for that money, they were expected to work sixteen hours a day, six days a week whether in the fields, the sugar factory, or the carpenter shop. Townsend looked at the movement of the gnarly, twisted hands of the translator as he interpreted McKintyre's pronouncements. He watched these men's downcast faces darken as they heard the words in their language. The overseer pointed to the garrison-like brick building nearby and said they would be living there. Inside they would find a wooden cot for each of them, and they would be given food. It would be padlocked at night.

"Is 'at understood? Dae ye hae onie questions?"

The men were restless, shifting their weight from one foot to the next and exchanging furtive glances with one another. Townsend had the distinct impression that these men were learning for the first time what misery lay ahead of them, and it was clear that they didn't like what they heard.

McKintyre beckoned to several of the Negro slave drivers who were standing by to come over. He told the Chinese men to line up next to an overturned molasses barrel. One by one, the Scotsman grabbed each one of these walking skeletons and with his sword sliced off their long pigtails on the top of the barrel. This triggered a torrent of protest.

The Chinese workers began yelling. One man, who had a tattoo of a golden dragon coiled around his neck, tried to grab McKintyre's sword, but he was beaten by some of the *contramayorales* and kicked into submission. The slave drivers then began cracking their whips in the air as they circled around the men, penning them in like cattle. McKintyre began whipping the man with the tattoo and cursing at him.

Townsend was horrified. "By God, man leave these people some dignity. Look at them. They're like walking dead men."

"That's nat th' way it works, son," McKintyre snarled. "In th' beginning these Chinese need tae be severely disciplined. They're rebellious by nature, unmanageable. Once they submit, the treatment gits better."

Emma had been glowering at the Scotsman and now spoke up forcefully.

"Mr. McKintyre, I implore you to stop this denigration. These people are starving. Let them eat. Where's your humanity?"

"This is none of yer business," the Scotsman snapped back with a growl, but then seemed to have second thoughts. "Alrigh' Miss Carpenter," he seethed, "if 'at weeill make ye an' Mr. Townsend happy, ah will give them some funchee and some dried beef. We'll see hoo they loch African slave food and hoo they behave. Min' ye, Doña Cecilia wouldn't loch tae see me daein' this. Ah can teel ye 'at."

The Scotsman ordered the slave drivers to release the Chinese and dole out the food from wooden pails. Townsend and Emma walked back to the plantation house without looking back. When they got to the veranda, Doña Cecilia was just coming out of the house.

"Is that mob of coolies causing a ruckus? Tell Mr. McKintyre to show them the lash."

Townsend was about to explain what had happened when they heard a rapid pealing and ringing of the plantation bell followed by a rumble of shouts and yells. Townsend swung around and looked back toward the sugar mill. He could see the silhouette of one of the slave drivers standing by the high wooden frame where the plantation bell was mounted on top. The man was frantically pulling on the rope, making the huge nine-hundred-pound bell clang in rapid succession. One look at his grandmother's terror-stricken face put Townsend on high alert.

"*Dios mio!*" Doña Cecilia cried out.

"Close all the windows and the doors," she shouted to the maids inside. "Those Chinese coolies have attacked the men. Alejandro, get my shotgun." Townsend could now see that the Chinese men, freed from their shackles, had begun picking up rocks and hurling them at McKintyre and the slave drivers.

The Scotsman stumbled in retreat toward the estate house, blood running down his face. One of the stones had found its mark. His pursuers jumped over the low stone walls that surrounded the cluster of buildings around the plantation house. A few had grabbed hoes and shovels from outside the barracoon and were now headed toward the plantation house.

Doña Cecilia yelled at Townsend to do something.

"Everett, stop these demons! They're going to attack us!"

She handed Townsend the shotgun and told him to fire. Townsend suddenly felt himself back in the war in the middle of a Confederate ambush. He took the shotgun and aimed it at one of the men who was about to catch McKintyre. The Scotsman was limping and looked like he was about to fall. His pursuer was in range. Townsend's finger circled over the trigger, but at the last second he fired upwards.

Startled by the gunshot, the Chinese man stopped running, giving the bleeding McKintyre time to reach the safety of the veranda. The yelling intensified. Townsend pushed his grandmother and Emma into the house and remained on the veranda with the butler and the wounded McKintyre at his side. The angry mob continued coming, dozens of them, throwing stones as they ran toward the house. The alarm bell kept clanging its warning. He looked at the sea of violent faces. He heard his grandmother from inside the house shouting at him.

"Shoot them, Everett! Protect us!"

This time he fired into the onrushing crowd and one man fell down, screaming, holding onto his leg. Another reached for his shoulder. Julio and some of the slave drivers then emerged on horseback from the stables, galloping toward the house to head off the attack. They lashed and whipped the ringleaders, stopping the momentum of the mob even as the yelling in Chinese continued.

Townsend looked up at the sound of thundering hooves and the shouts of men. Scores of armed riders from the neighboring plantations who had heard the alarm bell were galloping at full speed down the long driveway, kicking up clouds of red dust. These *monteros* were followed closely by the rural police who were well-armed with swords and pistols. The arrival of these reinforcements brought the short rebellion to an abrupt halt.

The police rounded up the disgruntled Chinese men, shackled them, and marched them off to the stocks. The wounded were taken to the plantation infirmary. The district police captain took down Townsend's statement about the attack and assured him he had done the right thing.

Badly shaken, Townsend sat down on one of the rattan chairs on the veranda. Emma remained with her mother inside. He thought about the moment he decided to fire into the crowd. He told himself he had no choice. He could hear his grandmother's voice telling him to shoot. He realized he'd fired because it was what he'd been trained to do in war.

Out of the corner of his eye, Townsend recognized two plainclothes men walking by. The same men he'd seen at the train station. López Villanueva was still keeping his eye on both of them.

A familiar voice called out to him. He looked up and saw the friendly, concerned face of Don Ignacio, the Marquis Calderón de Molina. He had just arrived with a contingent of twelve of his men, all prepared with swords and pistols strapped to their belts. He asked about Doña Cecilia and if there had been any injuries. Townsend described what happened and the Marquis stood there, shaking his head.

"Cuba has been importing these *colonos asiáticos* for at least the past ten years. I have always said, with no good results. The Chinese coolies are affordable, but unpredictable. All too often there is violence."

Townsend didn't say anything. The Marquis patted him on the shoulder and congratulated him on defending the house the way he did. He told Townsend that he had some good news for him.

"Those Americans I told you about, the *Sureños*, the Southerners bringing in Negro labor from the Gulf. They are now in Cárdenas with their Spanish partners. My police friend contacted me, and it seems the timing couldn't be better. From the looks of things, your grandmother needs new laborers."

The Marquis went on to explain that these American suppliers have acquired some new ships, steamships, and they have more ambitious plans. He said he thought they were cooperating with Don Julián Zulueta's network of police contacts.

"They're talking about bringing in several hundred with each shipload, landing them on the deserted cays on the north coast. I have asked my friend to invite them to my townhouse in Cárdenas in a few days to explain their proposition. You ought to come. As I understand it, they are looking to sign up interested buyers. It's a private sale, no public auction. I heard twelve hundred dollars per Negro. A good price."

At that moment, Emma came outside, and Townsend introduced her to the Marquis. The man immediately bowed to Emma and told her how lovely she looked.

"I hope you will join Everett for the gathering at my townhouse. It won't be all business." He winked at Townsend. "We will have music and food. No doubt you would like to meet some of the high society ladies from this area. We must never forget, Everett, one must always obey the will of the dear ladies."

30

February 21, 1866

At sunrise the next morning, Townsend left for Cárdenas, riding alongside the *volanta* carrying Emma and her mother. The heavy rumble of the carriage's huge wheels and the clattering of the horses' hooves prevented any opportunity for conversation. Townsend wasn't certain what he would say anyway, after their abrupt departure. He felt embarrassed and angry at the way Emma and her mother had been treated. He looked over at the sullen faces of the two women. They were looking straight ahead as the horses trotted down the estate's long driveway lined with palm trees. "¡Arre! ¡Arre!" shouted the postilion as he kicked the lead horse he was riding to get him moving faster.

Townsend steered his horse into the long shadows of the trees as he tried to make sense of his grandmother's erratic behavior. At dinner the night before, Doña Cecilia had made no effort to hide her contempt toward Emma, whom she blamed for the Chinese revolt. When Eleanor Carpenter had thanked her for her hospitality, Doña Cecilia had snorted, grudgingly nodded, and then turned away. Tellingly, she had not invited them to come again, as is customary in polite social circles in Cuba's plantation society. Afterward she had pulled him aside and told him she didn't like Emma.

"It is a minor miracle all of us weren't killed by those *diablos asiáticos*," she'd declared, "all because of your friend Emma's ignorant notions."

"It wasn't just her. I told him to stop as well," Townsend said. "McKintyre needed to be controlled. Those Chinese workers rebelled because of his cruelty."

His grandmother's eyes gleamed angrily, shining like black river stones.

"That girl is not for you, Everett. Don't waste your life by choosing the wrong woman."

"I've asked her to marry me, *Abuela*."

His grandmother's face had sagged in astonishment. She cast her eyes down to the ground before speaking, and then abruptly raised her head and spoke more softly.

"I can see why you would be attracted to Emma. She's pretty. But I fear she has some dangerous ideas. She will bring you trouble—political trouble. Let them go to Cárdenas alone. You're needed here. I am your family."

Townsend had just shaken his head. "I must accompany them. The roads are not safe."

"But what if there is more trouble here with these Chinese? You must remain here at Mon Bijou."

"The rural police are on alert, *Abuela*. Some of them are still here, monitoring the Chinese. They will protect you."

She continued arguing with him about his family obligations until he told her what the Marquis had said about American Negro workers being brought to Cuba.

Just the mention of the Marquis had caused the older woman to stop and listen. He told her there was to be an important meeting in Cárdenas tomorrow at the Marquis' townhouse and he would attend and represent Mon Bijou. He had put on his best acting face and told her he would find out the details of what these American smugglers were planning. He would give her a full report when he returned.

Only then did she relent, her voice softening. "I'm so glad you are thinking of the estate, Everett. You're finally shouldering your responsibility. I'm proud of you." She had put her hand to his cheek and smiled.

Townsend had thought this was the end of their arguing, but then she had surprised him in the stables as he'd prepared to mount his horse. As usual she wanted the last word.

"You must tell this girl it's finished. She is not one of us."

"What in blazes do you mean by that?" he'd angrily replied.

"She's too selfish. She cannot be trusted," she hissed, her clenched teeth revealing her hidden anger. "Stubborn like your mother."

The mention of his mother hit him in the gut, after what he'd learned from Mercedes. Townsend wasn't even thinking clearly as the words spilled out of his mouth.

"My mother left you because you gave her no choice, *Abuela. You* drove her away. The honest truth is you wanted to control her destiny and now you are trying to control mine. Enough."

A dark cloud seemed to envelop Doña Cecilia, causing her thin face to get tighter and more pinched, her eyes twitching.

"It should have been your mother who died from yellow fever all those years ago," she said, glowering at him.

Townsend gasped. "How could you say such a thing?"

"It should have been Esperanza, not my darling Blanca and little Pilar. They didn't deserve to die so young. They would never have done what your mother did to me. They were my little angels. Your mother was a devil child."

"You can't mean that!"

A pregnant silence greeted Townsend like the calm before a hurricane. His grandmother's black eyes remained fixed on him. He wasn't certain what to say. He didn't even recognize this woman. She was fierce, but suddenly she looked very small and very alone, her hateful words made powerless by her delusion. Emma had been right. Doña Cecilia would never admit she was wrong.

"It's a shame, *Abuela,* you didn't have the daughter you had hoped for, someone who shared your dreams. I'm sorry you didn't get that wish. I'm sorry you and my mother were estranged. I also feel great sympathy for the tragedies you've endured. Even so, you must accept that I have to live my own life. Emma is the woman I want to marry."

He remembered the expression of hurt in his grandmother's upturned face as he pulled himself up into the saddle and gathered the reins. The deep furrows in her forehead revealed her sad memories and her worries. He looked back as he trotted out of the estate. She hadn't moved. It was like she was a block of stone. He had thought about turning back to reassure her that he would help her with the plantation, but then the *volanta* carrying Emma and her mother had pulled away, and he followed them down the driveway.

Along the way, his thoughts tormented him. His grandmother was living a life he hated, one she was desperate to share with him. Yet she was all he had left of his family, and he knew she needed his help. A gnawing dread began to consume him, and he realized that, like his mother, he was facing a crossroads. In the back of his mind, he knew that his life would come apart if he stayed at Mon Bijou, but he also knew she saw him as her last hope.

By mid-morning the road was hot and dusty, and Townsend began to look for some place to rest the horses and give them water. He noticed some of the *mayorales* on horseback scanning the cane fields with a telescope. He wondered what they were doing. That's when he noticed how the vegetation along the road had begun to dry and curl. He remembered what his grandmother had told him about the dangers of fire season. All it took was a half-extinguished cigar to set off an inferno in the dry cane fields.

As they sped along the hard-packed road, Townsend looked over at Emma, her strands of wavy curls loose in the wind. Her face caught the light, which made her eyes glow like honey. Her posture implied toughness and determination. He felt the ring in his pocket which Mercedes had given him, and he suddenly knew what he needed to do. They had just crossed over the upper section of the Canímar River, and the miles of savannah opened up before them like a sea of green.

Townsend motioned to the postilion to pull over to an arching canopy of shade trees where there was a stand of some old growth mahogany trees on the banks of a stream. He hopped off his horse and approached the front of the *volanta*. Emma and her mother asked him if something was wrong. He shook his head.

"I want to tell you something important. I'm sorry for my grandmother's behavior—but that's not what I want to say." He took a deep breath. "Mrs. Carpenter, I know you've had your doubts about me for some time, and I can understand why. I know this is not the perfect location, but I feel I must say this now. I'd like to officially ask for your daughter's hand in marriage."

Townsend paused as he looked at the faces of the two stunned women.

"I've already asked Emma, but with your consent I would like to make a more formal proposal to her."

Emma looked like a startled deer. A flustered Mrs. Carpenter managed to only stutter a reply.

"Oh, my. Oh, my . . . I . . . I don't know. It's up to Emma."

Townsend then looked directly at Emma and pulled out the ring from his pocket. With both women seated in the *volanta* firmly clutching the sides as they looked at the diamond encrusted silver ring with the small golden star, he explained that this had been his mother's, a gift from her father when she had turned fifteen.

"For now, it's all I have. Will you marry me, Emma?"

Emma looked at her mother and then, her eyes aglow with intensity, she shouted a resounding "*Yes!*" and jumped out of the *volanta* chaise, throwing her arms around Townsend. The two of them twirled around in each other's arms before Emma's feet landed on the ground and they finally kissed.

Townsend smelled the sweet smell of lavender in her hair, and he breathed in deeply as he wrapped his arms around her.

For the rest of the journey, Emma and Townsend couldn't keep their eyes off each other or stop smiling. Townsend had never felt happier. The plan was for Emma to continue her stay with Doña Julia while her mother would return to Havana. She'd already agreed to come with him to the Marquis' house for the luncheon with the planters. She wanted to see who these American kidnappers were. They both thought that this might also be a good time to reveal their engagement to some of the prominent families in the area. They would stay in Cárdenas for a few days, and then they both would return to Mon Bijou to formally tell Doña Cecilia about their wedding plans.

As they approached the street where Doña Julia lived, Townsend noticed the two men he'd seen at the train station and at Mon Bijou after the Chinese incident. They were standing under a *mamoncillo* tree. He trotted by them and asked them if the fruit was ripe yet even though he knew it wasn't. They shook their heads awkwardly.

Once safely inside the house, Townsend warned Emma that she was being watched by what he suspected were two plainclothes officers with the *Guardia Civil*, and that it would be best if she kept a low profile. He told her he would be staying at Mrs. Woodbury's boarding house and would come to see her the next day.

Townsend wasted no time in going to the wharf area where the counting houses were located. He walked into the building with the sign for Churchill, Brown & Manson and asked for Guillermo Quiñones. The clerk said he could probably find him at the bar where all the American sailors in town gathered at the end of the day. Townsend could hear the music from a block away. A fiddler and a banjo were competing with two Spanish guitarists while a drunken chorus sang the lyrics of the sea shanty called "Running Down to Cuba."

Townsend walked into the crowded bar. A group of sailors were now stomping their feet with the music as one man led the singing.

> "Give me a gal can dance Fandango
> Weigh, me boys, to Cuba!
> Round as a melon and sweet as a mango.
> Running down to Cuba."

A quick glance around the room revealed Americans of all types, a mixture of wharf rats, speculators, sailors, and ship's engineers mixed in with counting room clerks and plantation machinists. It was a portrait of Americans living and working in the sugar trade in Cuba. Townsend could pick out the Southerners. It was something about the stubborn set of their eyes. They sat on one side with their chairs tipped back, chewing and spitting out gobs of brown tobacco juice. They looked like some of the men he'd seen in Havana's bars during the war who'd been sent from Galveston and Matamoros to spy on Navy steamships and man blockade runners. Clearly some of these *desperados* had stayed behind on the island, preferring Cuban hospitality to an uncertain welcome back home.

On the other side of the tavern, he could see Quiñones playing cards with a group of men who from their dress and manners looked to be a mixture of counting room clerks and cheap hacks. He waved at Quiñones who immediately excused himself from the card game and pulled Townsend outside.

"I'm glad you came."

"What was so urgent? Is it Jacobs?"

"Jacobs? No, why?"

"You wrote you had important news. I was worried."

"No, not Jacobs."

They walked back to the counting house where Quiñones said he felt they could have a quiet conversation, unobserved and unnoticed. He took Townsend in a back room where they sat on a pair of stools.

"So, what is it?" Townsend asked.

"Remember that fellow with that big bloodhound mastiff?"

"The one in Sagua?"

Quiñones nodded.

"Menéndez. Ex-Confederate," Townsend said. "He and Hodge tried to sell Jacobs in that Casa Blanca bar. Menéndez never went back to the ship, so he disappeared."

"Wa'al, he's here now. He's been hiring lowlife loafers in the bar and telling everyone that his business associates in New Orleans have purchased an old blockade-running steamship. It's coming into Cárdenas tomorrow. One of the top people from New Orleans is on board. Someone he calls the postmaster."

Townsend's ears pricked up at that name. It wasn't the first time he'd heard mention of the postmaster.

"Any idea who that might be?"

"Some say a former Confederate officer living in New Orleans. Someone mentioned the name of Greenleaf Andrews, who was involved in developing explosives for the Confederate Secret Service, but the truth is I don't know. Menéndez is hiring a full crew—three engineers, four coal heavers, and three sailors. Word is that they're headed for the Gulf Coast of Florida and Louisiana to get themselves a fresh load of mules and bring them back to Cuba. Land them on some of the islands off the north coast."

"Mules?"

That's what they say. It's pretty clear what they mean. Menéndez is talking like someone in the African coal trade, Townsend. That's why I wanted to get you down here."

"Why is he bringing the ship here to Cárdenas?"

"Less scrutiny. He can pick up a crew of ex-Confederates here who won't ask questions, and he seems to have valuable cargo stored here. They'll be loading tomorrow. Menéndez has a Spanish friend handling the business affairs. Around here they call him the *mayorista*, the wholesaler. He seems to be well known as someone with ties to the Spanish slavers, Julián Zulueta and Francisco Marty y Torréns. I believe he was here during the war, working with Confederate agents to ship arms into the Gulf."

A shiver went down Townsend's spine as he thought of Don Pedro. That description fit him like a glove. He could only hope that his grandmother was right, and the man was dead.

"No doubt this Spaniard has good relations with the local authorities?"

"Yes, indeed. The local police hover around him like flies on garbage. The stench of bribery here is pretty apparent. He's been hiring coolies who have completed their work term on the plantations, turning them into his personal work gangs. I followed him to a warehouse the other day. I don't know what's inside that building, but I'm betting it's not just rum and cigars. Word is that it's where sailors go to enjoy the dream stick."

"Dream stick?"

"Opium pipe."

Townsend and Quiñones waited until dark to walk toward the warehouse. They soon arrived at a shabby, blistered building with large wooden doors. A group of Chinese workers were unloading a wagon filled with unpainted wooden boxes and crates. They stayed in the shadows and watched the activities, and soon noticed a side door to an adjoining building guarded by a large Chinese man wearing wide cotton pants and sporting a long pigtail. He was letting a steady stream of people into the building who had the slouch and shuffle of drunken sailors. Townsend and Quiñones pretended to be drunk and told the doorman they were looking for one of their crew. The man waved them inside. They walked into a smoke-filled room, dimly lit with two candles where a collection of women were draped around half-clothed, dopey-eyed sailors.

In the corner over a small flame a Chinese man was mixing together a black sticky substance. Townsend peered through the haze at the people lying on the bed. Blank, glassy eyes stared back at him. Another man held up a bamboo pipe and offered it to him. Townsend shook his head, not realizing he didn't have a choice. The man pulled out a club and reached for Townsend, but Quiñones put a knife in the man's back and whispered in his ear that he must take them to where they keep all the valuable goods.

The man led them through another door, down some stairs, and into a large storage area filled with crates and barrels. They quickly tied the man's hands and feet and then put a bandana in his mouth. They knew they didn't have much time. Townsend started opening up one of the barrels. Inside he found containers of pig lard, but then he realized there was a false bottom. His hands reached further inside and pulled out wooden cases. Inside were British-made Kerry single-action revolvers and Enfield rifles. Quiñones dug through another barrel and found boxes filled with American-made pistols, Remingtons and Spencer repeating rifles.

"Holy Moses," said Quiñones. "There's a whole darned arsenal here. What the hell are these?"

They rummaged through some of the other boxes and barrels and found crates filled with gunpowder and shells, and hundreds of rifles. Some of the wooden cases had faded black stenciling with the initials CSA—Confederate States of America—and underneath that, Galveston. Down below in darker black ink were new labels and a crest with a regal crown at the top, an eagle in the center and two flying griffons on either side. Underneath was written Imperio Mexicano.

"There's your answer," Townsend declared. "The Imperio Mexicano, the so-called cactus throne. Weapons originally intended for the Confederate armies in Texas. The Confederate agent in Havana, Charles Helm, fled Cuba in a hurry. No doubt he left behind warehouses filled with supplies. *El Gallego* must have bought these abandoned weapons for cheap and with his new American partners expects to sell them to Emperor Maximilian and the French armies in Mexico. Wouldn't be surprising if ex-Confederate military men like Shelby and Magruder had something to do with this. They fled across the border. They'd like nothing better than to take another swipe at the Yankees."

Townsend's eyes fell on several burlap bags that looked like they were filled with coffee beans. He opened one up and pulled out a heavy black lump about four inches wide.

"What in tarnation is this? It's like a rock."

Quiñones took it from him, wiping the coal dust on his hands. He scratched the surface, his eyes lighting up as he showed Townsend the thin layer of beeswax mixed with coal dust that covered the heavy rock.

"It's a coal torpedo, an explosive invented and used by the Confederate Secret Service to blow up Union ships. It looks like a lump of coal, but it's made of cast iron. Hollow inside and filled with gunpowder."

Townsend's eyes opened wide as he reached down to pick up another one. He could feel the metal, which had been shaped to look like an uneven piece of coal.

"When I was locked up at Libby prison in Richmond, I heard about this contraption. These coal bombs were manufactured right near the prison on the James River at the Tredegar Iron Works. Some of the guards bragged about them. Confederate agents just had to drop them in a coal bin. They looked just like a lump of coal, perfectly disguised. Once they were shoveled into the boiler firebox along with the coal, they would explode. Blow up the ship's steam boiler."

"Sink the ship?"

"Possibly. The best part is they left no trace."

Just then they heard a noise. A door opened with a bang. A dog started to growl. A man shouted in Spanish. "*Hay alguien?*" The Chinese man next to them began squirming. It was time to go. Townsend grabbed a bag of these coal bombs. He could see that Quiñones had the same thought and took another bag. They shouted out to attract the guard and then ran in another direction toward the back of the warehouse. They could hear the screams of the man they'd tied up and the growls of the dog. They broke through a window and crawled out the back of the warehouse into an alley. They could still hear the shouting inside the warehouse as they ran back toward the center of town.

31

February 22, 1866

Early the next morning, Townsend watched as the rising sun spread itself across the wide expanse of Cárdenas Bay. The docks were quiet. The only noise was the gentle flapping of American ensigns on the merchant ships' masts. He and Quiñones stood by the counting offices of Churchill, Brown & Manson near the warehouses and the railroad tracks, waiting for any sign of the steam ship. Townsend spotted the black smoke first.

"There it is. Dead ahead. About two miles out."

Quiñones took out his telescope, nodding his head as he handed the glass over to Townsend. Even from this distance, Townsend could tell it was a medium-sized steamship, about 150 feet long, a sidewheeler with big paddle boxes. He could just barely make out the name of the ship in gilded letters on the paddle boxes. The *Suwannee*. Just seeing that name made him shiver. So many months had passed. As much as he tried to forget the war and that river, the memories were still with him.

Townsend could see the ship was headed for the central wharf that extended about a mile into the harbor. A loud prolonged steam whistle from the incoming steamship jolted the waiting stevedores awake. An overseer barked out commands and scores of shirtless Black and Chinese stevedores tumbled out of the warehouses pushing creaking drays loaded with crates and barrels. Clouds of black smoke now filled the air, causing the acrid smell of burning coal to blend in with the swampy air of the town.

As the small army of stevedores pushed past him, he recognized the cargo as what they'd seen in the warehouse last night, but all the CSA markings had been rubbed out. In their place were newly painted black and white sten-ciled labels, identifying the contents. Muscovado sugar, honey, Yara tobacco leaf, and Caracolillo coffee beans. Familiar exports from central Cuba. It all looked legitimate. But Townsend could see the bulky lumps in the burlap coffee bean sacks which he was certain were the coal torpedoes.

"A total whitewash." Quiñones snorted with disgust. "I'm no lawyer but with the Confederacy now in the sack heap of history, these weapons are spoils of war, property of the US government. But look at these Spanish customs officials and police. I'm sure they know what's inside, and they just look the other way. They're all in on it. It's hard to find an honest man in uniform here in Spanish Cuba."

Townsend looked up at the customs officials who stood nearby with a bill of lading. They were counting the numbers of barrels, kegs, sacks, and bales and checking them off, but not one of them made little more than a thin gesture to inspect what was inside. It occurred to him that this cache of weapons falling into the hands of groups unfriendly to Spain was just what the Spanish were now worried about.

"What about the officers in the *Guardia Civil?*"

Quiñones flinched at the mention of the *Guardia*. "Military police. Ha! I try not to think of those vermin. They can detain you whenever they please and charge you with whatever crime they choose. What about them?"

"Wouldn't they want to know that there are Confederate weapons being smuggled on board an American ship right under their noses?"

Quiñones shot a confused glance in Townsend's direction. Townsend raised his eyebrows in response. They'd had a good laugh when Townsend had told him how he'd gotten Emma released from the *Casa de Recogidas* by proposing marriage to her in front of her jailers. But now Quiñones turned deadly serious.

"Exactly what are you suggesting, Townsend?"

The Navy lieutenant shrugged. "I'm not sure, Quiñones, but the fact is, we can't let this ship leave port."

"What's that supposed to mean? Are you planning to blow up the ship?"

Townsend didn't say anything.

"So . . . what then? We're not in wartime anymore, Lieutenant. I thought your job was just to gather intelligence. You're blundering in the wrong di-rection. You don't want to become a person of interest for the *Guardia Civil.*"

"Too late for that, I'm afraid. I'm already in their sights. Plainclothes policemen have been following Emma, even to Mon Bijou. I am certain they are under orders to be in regular contact with Major López Villanueva."

"Why would they follow Emma?"

"Wa'al . . . I gained her freedom by promising to help track down American smugglers supplying Cuban rebels. A total lie, but it worked."

"You did what? What are you now, a Spanish spy? Are you turning me in next?"

"Of course not, Quiñones. I had to do something to get Emma free. It was all I could think of."

"What happens when they find out you're a paid federal informant?"

"I'll cross that bridge when the time comes."

Quiñones' eyebrows lifted but then he shook his head. "If you go to the Guardia Civil, I want no part of it."

"Why is that?"

"Too risky," Quiñones said emphatically as he took his hat off and ran his hands through his hair. "The Guardia does not give a whit about smuggling unless it's a threat to the government. Their priority is to silence any kind of dissent. Protect public order. With these smugglers, they'll probably seize the cargo and fine them, but then let the ship go. You have nothing to tie those weapons to Cuban rebels."

Townsend was silent. He knew Quiñones was right. It would be risky to go to the Guardia Civil. For all he knew, they'd also been bribed. He stared out toward the harbor, which was now filling up with rowboats and small sailing boats. The grinding of wheels and the clanking of chain alerted him to the fact that the Suwannee was dropping its anchor as close to the shore as it could get.

Townsend followed Quiñones' gaze to a Spanish Naval patrol gunboat called the Júpiter that was getting resupplied with coal from a Naval barge. The gunship had its steam up, a wisp of black smoke coming out of the funnel.

"That gunboat will be leaving to go back on coastal patrol as soon as they recoal their bunkers."

"So, what of it?" Townsend asked.

"There's no guard on the barge. See how it sits low on the water."

Townsend nodded, paying little attention. He was more interested in a large dory leaving the dock that was headed toward the newly arrived steamship. He held up his telescope to get a closer look and then pointed to the two men rowing and the two passengers in the stern. The rowboat was far away, but he could pick out Menéndez with his dog by his side. The other passenger in the dory was wearing a linen suit and a Panama hat. When the man took off his hat to reveal a shiny bald dome, Townsend immediately recognized him. It was the Spanish merchant who had tried to purchase Levi Jacobs from Menéndez and Hodge in that bar in Casa Blanca.

He turned to Quiñones.

"That's the man I met in Casa Blanca. *El Gallego*, they called him."

Quiñones took the telescope from him and took a look. He shook his head and said he hadn't seen him before. "Maybe he's the one they call the *mayorista*, the wholesaler?" He handed back the telescope.

Townsend turned his attention to the captain on top of the large paddle box along with a small man who looked like he was the harbor pilot. They were waving at the two men in the rowboat. A tall lanky figure suddenly appeared on top of the paddle box.

"Who's that?" Quiñones asked. "Do you recognize him?"

Through the telescope, Townsend could see the well-dressed man who was now standing next to the captain. He had a familiar stance like a military man, but Townsend couldn't make out his face.

Townsend shook his head. "I feel like I've seen him before, but I can't place him."

"Maybe that's your mystery man, the one they call the postmaster?"

"Maybe," Townsend muttered with a sudden feeling of foreboding as he wondered again if Don Pedro could be alive and somehow involved in this conspiracy. He hoped his grandmother was right and the man was well and truly gone from this world.

Hours later, Townsend and Emma, dressed in their finest, walked into the Marquis' lavish villa located in the elegant upper part of town. Inside the house, a busy mix of white-jacketed Negro servants shuffled across the shiny marble floors, handing out drinks to the guests. A piano player and a violinist were playing some languid Havana contradanzas, and a few of the younger couples had already started to dance.

Townsend took a moment to look around at his surroundings. The main room was large with high ceilings. The newly frescoed walls, the beautifully inlaid mahogany cabinets from Spain, all spoke of new wealth. Adjacent was a door to a library that he noticed was slightly askew. Townsend could see a small group of men in formal suits standing inside smoking cigars. He wondered if that was where the business part of this social function would take place.

The food was being served in a separate room leading out to a veranda, and most of the guests were moving in that direction. Townsend could see that the Marquis was corralling a select few of the men to come with him into the library. He was dressed flamboyantly in one of his signature striped linen suits with a gold silk scarf wrapped around his waist when he spotted them. He came over and made the proper introductions, bowing and kissing Emma's hand as he lavished praise on her. Townsend took the opportunity to tell the Marquis that he and Emma were now engaged. The Marquis seemed genuinely surprised as he looked back and forth between them.

"¡*Felicidades!* I am so pleased to hear this and offer you my heartfelt congratulations. Does your grandmother know the wonderful news?"

"Yes, she knows," Townsend said softly.

"I would have thought she would have mentioned it. I spoke with her just before coming here to Cárdenas."

"We haven't picked the date yet. We'll be returning to Mon Bijou shortly to go over the details with her."

"I see," the Marquis said as he turned his head to Emma with a gleam in his eye. "I dare say you are the prettiest of all the women here, Señorita Carpenter. So pretty that the moon envies you when it appears in the sky. *Eres una joya brillante.* You are a shining jewel. I hope you will allow me to host a gala in your honor at my estate."

Emma smiled and nodded her appreciation.

The Marquis waved at several of his older lady guests who were chatting in a group together as they fluttered their silk fans. He told Townsend and Emma to come meet some of the high-society women of Cárdenas and Matanzas. The Marquis made a fuss over the ladies, who were all smiles, silk, and diamonds, and then with a theatrical flourish introduced Townsend and Emma as newly engaged. This announcement caused a flurry of excitement with the pearl-powdered ladies, and the Marquis used the moment to excuse himself, whispering to Townsend to follow him into the library.

As he and the Marquis entered the smoke-filled room with its inlaid cedar floors and mahogany bookcases, Townsend spotted Menéndez facing a group of ten to twelve Spanish planters. The Marquis introduced Townsend to a few of the planters as the American grandson of Doña Cecilia Carbonell de Vargas, the owner of Mon Bijou plantation. Her name was clearly known—the men nodded with respect as they shook his hand. Menéndez came over to greet the Marquis. The thin-faced man blinked at Townsend, giving him a long look.

"Haven't we met before?" he asked. "I feel like I know you."

Townsend felt a knot forming in his stomach. He straightened up, trying to appear confident, and shook his head. "I don't believe so."

"Maybe during the war?" Menéndez asked.

"I was a blockade runner," Townsend said. "Traveled from Havana to the Gulf." Menéndez was silent for a moment, then shrugged. "Must be my mistake."

They shook hands, and Townsend breathed a sigh of relief. He guessed his full beard disguised his features enough so that the man couldn't place him.

An unmistakable voice from behind him caught Townsend by surprise. He knew that voice. He whirled around, coming face to face with a man he hadn't expected to ever see again.

"Major Joshua Hawley, businessman and investor," the man said as he held out his hand, a broad smile splashed across his face. "So pleased to make your acquaintance. Mr. Townsend, is it?"

The man hadn't changed. The same large moustache, stubbly beard, and thin nose. It was Major J. K. Hutchinson, without the uniform and with a different name. Joshua Hawley was the alias Hutchinson had been using when he'd last seen him in Havana harbor. *What is the man doing here?* Townsend thought to himself.

"There you are, Major Hawley," the Marquis exclaimed. "Just the man I was looking for. I see you have already met my good friend, Don Everett. He is a war veteran like yourself. His family is deeply rooted in the island's plantation society. His grandmother is a true patriot of Spain and a close friend. She owns an exceptional sugar estate called Mon Bijou. And might I add, I know from speaking with her that the plantation is in great need of field laborers."

He smiled at Townsend, who remained speechless, and winked at the man he called Hawley.

"Indeed," Hutchinson replied, even as his eyes never left Townsend's face. "How interesting. I'm always pleasantly surprised when I come across my countrymen here. How is it that you came to have family ties in Cuba, Mr. Townsend, if I may ask?"

Townsend cleared his throat, trying to regain his composure. He didn't want to blow the man's cover. "My mother's family is from here," he replied. "My great-great-grandfather was a Quintana. I'm only just now becoming more familiar with the estate."

"Learning the sugar business, are you? I see. With the war over, it's important to have new beginnings. Which side did you fight for?"

"I joined the Navy in Key West after doing a bit of blockade running here in Cuba. So, I guess you could say I experienced the war from both sides."

"How fascinating. An adventurous young man with an open mind. I like that. Well, there's plenty of money and adventure to be had here in Cuba. Isn't that right, Don Ignacio?"

The Marquis nodded his head and told Hutchinson to come meet more of his guests.

"I hope we can talk after I make my brief presentation," Hutchinson whispered to Townsend even as he flashed him his broad, toothy smile. Townsend smiled back, amazed by Hutchinson's guile at having infiltrated and ingratiated himself among such a dangerous mix of people.

White-jacketed servants made the rounds with glasses of the finest Manzanilla dry sherry and boxes of the large *Imperiales* and *Regalías* cigars favored by many of the planters. In the smoky haze from all the cigar smoke, the Marquis presented Major Joshua Hawley to the other planters as a war hero and said that he had come to talk about a new venture to help the Cuban sugar industry. Hutchinson stepped up on the library steps and introduced himself as an American military man who had cast his lot with the Southern states. *He is playing the role well,* Townsend thought to himself.

Menéndez translated as Hutchinson spoke with a tone of authority about the state of affairs in the American South.

"Slavery is over in the United States, and conditions are desperate there. Tens of thousands of former slaves are looking for work, but there is no work to give them. These former slaves should to be sent to where they are needed, and Cuba is that perfect place."

Hutchinson spoke like a born salesman. No hint of principles or any attachment to his duties with the US Army. He was so deeply undercover that he seemed to be a mastermind of this smuggling ring. Hutchinson coldly went on to describe the syndicate he represented as well-financed with important investors not only from New Orleans but also from across the country, including New York. He told the planters that they were going to expand quickly with several steamships capable of carrying hundreds of former American slaves from the Gulf ports to the north shores of Cuba. He said they had an extensive organization in place in the states of Louisiana, Alabama, and Florida, and a network of local contacts and partners in Cuba.

Townsend could see by the nodding of heads that Hutchinson's pitch was effective. He was telling them what they wanted to hear.

"You planters here in Cuba don't need to go to Africa to get new slaves, not when there is such a convenient labor supply so close to home. We can get new laborers to you in a matter of days, not months. We guarantee that they are fit to work in the fields as soon as they arrive."

One of the planters asked about the American government's attitude. Hutchinson was prepared for that question with a carefully crafted response.

"With the US Navy decommissioning most of the vessels in its war fleet, the American government has very little capability to search ships." Hutchinson then shifted his gaze and looked directly at Townsend. His eyes remain fixed on the Navy lieutenant. "I can also tell you from very reliable sources that the US government has disbanded the Army's Bureau of Military Information. With fewer agents in New Orleans and elsewhere, the federal government will find it difficult to stop our trade."

Townsend stared back at the man. These last remarks left him with the sinking feeling that this might not be an act. Hutchinson had just admitted he no longer had a job with the US Army. *Maybe he isn't playing a role. Maybe he has become the man he once pretended to be.* Townsend shook his head in astonishment. He hoped that wasn't true.

When his presentation was finished, several planters surrounded Major Hawley. Menéndez was there by his side to translate, jotting down names of those interested and the numbers of laborers each of them wanted. When the last of the smiling planters left the room to rejoin the ladies, Townsend and Hutchinson went off to a far corner of the library where there were two red leather chairs close together. Hutchinson spoke first.

"I must admit I wasn't expecting to see you here, Townsend. I had no idea you had family in Cuba. What made you decide to come?"

"The war is over," Townsend replied. "I needed a job and a new direction, and my grandmother needed me. I have a new life here."

"You're a lucky man. So, you've left the Navy?"

"Oh, yes," Townsend lied.

"I wasn't sure I could trust you, but the Marquis has assured me you are what you say."

"I could say the same thing about you, Major Hawley. Are you now who you pretend to be?"

Hutchinson's grin escalated into a chortle. "If you mean am I still working with the Army. The answer is no. The Army closed down the Bureau of Military Information, as I mentioned in my presentation. I was discharged. Major Hutchinson is now a figure of the past. At first, I was uncertain what to do, but then I was offered an opportunity I couldn't refuse, and I decided to become my alias, Major Joshua Hawley, a Confederate war hero."

Townsend tried hard to show no reaction. The man had just confirmed his worst fear. He was a double agent. It was hard for him to comprehend the level of the man's treachery against his own government. Hutchinson was no different than Hodge.

"Any regrets?"

"No, can't say there are. These are uncertain times, and there are no easy answers. To be quite honest, I feel relieved."

"Relieved?"

"No more reason to pretend."

"You know this trade can't last. The American government won't allow it."

"We shall see, Townsend. I have decided these kidnappings aren't such a bad thing. Perhaps they're even good for the country. The federals are giving the freedmen the vote, and you and I both know that won't sit well in the South. Ex-Confederates are going to start lynching and killing, demanding retribution. At least here in Cuba, these Blacks will be housed and fed. Maybe that's as good as it gets. I fought in the war to preserve the Union. I never fought for equal rights for Blacks. Did you?"

Townsend didn't say anything. All he could do was to try to contain what felt like a tidal wave of despair. He pictured the lifeless eyes of Thaddeus Burrell. He thought of the desperation of Caiphus and Henry Jacobs, and of their father—his friend—who had risked everything to find his two sons.

Hutchinson paused and looked at Townsend's somber face. "It's just a business, Townsend. Not unlike any other transportation business. Deliver and pick up cargo. It's somewhat like the post office, collecting and delivering packages."

Townsend looked at him. "So, are you the one they call the postmaster?"

"That's correct. I send the mailmen out, and they pick up the packages and deliver them."

"And the *mayorista*. I've heard his name mentioned. Who is that?"

"The wholesaler. Menéndez picked that man. An old acquaintance of his. He's a Spaniard. Some people call him *El Gallego*."

"I see," Townsend said as he breathed a sigh of relief. No mention of Don Pedro, his old nemesis.

"You seem pleased?"

"No, just intrigued."

"Menéndez gave me the nickname. I rather like it. Every town, every place needs a postmaster, am I right? It's a new beginning. New identity. Aren't you the same, Townsend? You also have a new identity. Slaveowner and sugar planter."

Townsend didn't reply. This man horrified him, but he didn't want to reveal how upset he was. He was just beginning to understand Hutchinson's role in this conspiracy. This man must have known about the Secret Service agent who had been on board the *Southern Cross*. Hutchinson must have betrayed him and informed Hodge and Menéndez that they had a spy on their ship, and as a result they had brutally killed the man. Hutchinson must have been the inside man Secretary Seward was concerned about.

"When did you first start working for the syndicate, Major? When I saw you in Key West, were you working with Hodge?"

"You might say I had two jobs at that point. I had many contacts at Jenny King's place in New Orleans with useful information. The Army valued the intelligence I gathered, but so did the people I was spying on. I became quite useful to both. So, at the time of the hurricane, I was working with Hodge and Menéndez by creating doubts within the federal government about the validity of these kidnapping rumors. I will say, many officials seemed only too willing to turn a blind eye. No offense intended, Lieutenant, but I am grateful to you for handing over those charts and sketches from the *Hard Times*. That was damning evidence, indeed. I was able to keep it out of the official record."

The man winked and gave a half chuckle, half chortle, as if he'd just given Townsend some good-natured ribbing.

Townsend set his jaw and ignored the comment. "And when I saw you in Havana a little over a month ago?"

"I'd been able to find some major investors by then, and a list of plantation owners eager to get rid of their former slaves. It was those investors who handed me this opportunity. They gave me the money and made me the manager of this syndicate. That report about the Brazilian émigrés was my last job as Major Hutchinson."

"I see. And Hodge? What happened to him?" Townsend asked pointedly. He wanted to see if Hutchinson suspected anything.

"Unfortunately, he got caught by the Dagos in Havana harbor carrying out a little side smuggling business of his own. He had a load of pamphlets calling for a rebellion against Spain. I hear he says he was framed, but the Spanish don't believe him. He and his men are in the dungeons of El Morro. Not much chance of them being released. Shame to lose him, but we have other ship captains now. This operation is growing quickly."

Hutchinson stopped and cocked his head.

"But all that's history. The important question is, can we count you in for our next shipment? How many field laborers do you and your grandmother want for Mon Bijou?"

32

On the way back to Doña Julia's house, Townsend sat quietly in the *volanta* next to Emma, his mind troubled by what he'd heard. The kidnapping was no longer the work of a few angry ex-Confederates like Hodge. It was by all accounts a well-financed smuggling syndicate with hidden investors, a serious business enterprise. He'd already told Emma about Hutchinson and the *Suwannee*, and its secret cargo, both material and eventually human. He struggled to grasp the malevolence of the man. A double agent who had betrayed his government and hitched his wagon to what was in effect a new slave trade.

Emma broke the silence. "What do you intend to do?"

"Not much I can do. I had hoped to go to the *Guardia Civil*. Quiñones thought that was useless. He said the *Guardia* is only interested in uncovering any evidence of treason or dissent, only serious threats to the state."

"What about those coal torpedoes?" Emma asked abruptly as she stared at him with an iron calm.

"What about them?" Townsend asked.

"Aren't they the perfect weapon for an insurgency, impossible to trace, making them ideal for rebel groups?"

Townsend looked at her without saying anything.

"They can sink ships, yes? Why don't you tell the local commander of the *Guardia Civil* that you're concerned these nondescript bombs could easily fall into the wrong hands."

Townsend took in Emma's fiery face with that familiar look of determination. He thought she was prettier than ever.

"Spoken like someone who knows the tactics of Spain's enemies," Townsend said with a smirk. "Perhaps you could be an effective advisor to the *Guardia Civil*. Help them combat the rebels?"

"No, thank you," she snapped.

"Maybe you would like to come with me to the *cuartel?*" he asked nudging her.

"Not likely," she fired back. "Those animals might haul me back to that prison for abandoned women. Besides, I believe you are the one who offered to be the informant. I was never consulted."

Townsend dropped off Emma at Doña Julia's house. The two plainclothes officers were still standing there under the shade tree. He thought about approaching them but decided against it. It appeared they had their orders to watch Emma and that did not include talking with him.

It was dark when Townsend arrived at the prison-like headquarters of the *Guardia Civil*. He walked up to the guard standing outside the *cuartel* and gave his name and mentioned Major López Villanueva. He was prepared to use all the bluster and exaggeration he could muster to get inside but was surprised when a junior officer almost immediately appeared and escorted him through the corridors.

They passed by some men in chains and shackles who were being moved into a cell. He heard the clanging of metal and cursing, and then the crunch of military boots marching. He suddenly feared they were going to arrest him. He saw a squadron of uniformed *Guardia* drilling in a small parade ground. But instead of being thrown in a cell, he was taken through a large door. A man in a dark blue jacket with red trim and a wide belt with a brass buckle rose to greet him. The Spanish officer was well-coiffed and sported a slightly upturned stylish moustache. From his swagger and his smile, Townsend guessed that this was the commanding officer.

"Welcome, Lieutenant Townsend. *Soy el Capitán Luis Caicedo Guzmán. Es un gran placer.*"

Townsend was taken aback by the warm welcome but shook the man's gloved hand.

"We've been expecting you. My superior in Havana, Major López Villanueva, informed me that you were now working with us, and you might be stopping by."

Townsend swallowed his pride and said nothing.

"I understand you are completing a report on how to improve trade relations between the United States and Cuba. Is that correct? You and your fiancée la Señorita Carpenter Lozada? The Major says that your family owns an important sugar plantation in Matanzas? Do I have that right?"

Townsend nodded. He hadn't expected to hear such a thorough report on himself. He put on his best theatrical face and told the captain that he was pleased to help.

"I am so happy to know that we have friendly Americans who want to work to keep Spain's most faithful island safe and secure. So, tell me, what information do you have for us? My men are eager to strike a blow against these revolutionaries. They say they are fighting for independence and justice, but you and I know it's nonsense. *Pura tontería ¿verdad?*"

Townsend took a breath and plunged in, telling the officer about the *Suwannee* and the smuggled Confederate weapons he'd seen in the warehouse. He went on to describe the false labels and the all-too-cooperative police and customs officials.

The official sniffed, clearly not liking to hear any criticism of the local Spanish police.

"Interesting and troubling information," he said. "What makes you think that these weapons could be used against our government?"

Townsend reached inside the bag he was carrying and pulled out one of the coal torpedoes he had, four inches in size and weighing four pounds. The military officer grew quiet when Townsend opened the top and showed him the one and half ounces of black powder inside the fake piece of coal.

"Que horror!" he declared. "Insidious, but very effective, I imagine. Was this really used by the Confederates against US Navy ships?"

"Indeed, many times," Townsend replied as he embraced his new role as a Spanish informant. "Particularly in the last year of the war. There were many boiler explosions. One of them was the sidewheeler the USS Greyhound. That warship was consumed by fire in less than ten minutes."

Captain Caicedo Guzman studied the coal torpedo closely. "I must say I have to admire this engineering. It looks just like a piece of coal."

Townsend again tried to make his case. "As a friend of Spain, I'm afraid it's the *perfect* weapon for the revolutionaries. With these in the wrong hands, no Spanish Navy ship would be safe. The most frightening thing is, they leave no trace of their use."

"And you say our local police and customs are being lax in their inspection of this cargo?"

"It pains me to say so, but yes that's true. I would not speculate why. Perhaps they have their legitimate reasons. But as I explained earlier to His Excellency, Major López Villanueva, I will have to mention this activity in my report. I think you can understand how upsetting this would be to my government to learn of unreported supplies of Confederate weapons in Cuba. The American government views anything belonging to the Confederacy in Cuba as US property now. That includes blockade-running ships in Havana harbor and weapons."

"I see," Captain Caicedo Guzmán replied as he nervously twisted an end of his moustache with his left hand. Townsend could tell that the military officer wasn't certain what he should do.

"A further concern is where these weapons might end up. As you know, our government is keeping an eye on the renegade Confederate soldiers who never surrendered and took refuge in Mexico after the war. Some of those *desperados* reportedly harbor designs on convincing Emperor Maximilian to march north into Texas."

"I can assure you, Lieutenant Townsend, that a full investigation will be made, and a report will be sent to Havana. Thank you for coming in."

The man extended his gloved hand. Townsend immediately knew he had failed. Quiñones had been right. Captain Caicedo Guzmán might send someone to the ship, perhaps confiscate the weapons, but not much more. He was about to shake the official's hand when the same junior officer who had escorted him rushed into the office, saluting as he rushed up to the desk.

"My sincerest apologies, *Capitán*," he stammered, trying to catch his breath. "There has been an explosion in the harbor, right next to one of our Navy ships. The captain has ordered all hands to abandon ship and has requested our assistance. They aren't ruling out sabotage of some kind."

The captain, who had just moments before seemed so self-assured, now scrambled for his hat as he barked out orders to the junior officer to form a squadron and immediately march to the docks. He began yelling at his junior officers that he wanted the men on board the *Suwannee* arrested and the cargo confiscated.

February 24

For the next two days, Townsend kept a low profile, getting his news from the gossip at Mrs. Woodbury's boarding house. Everyone on board the *Suwannee* had been arrested and taken back to the *Guardia's* headquarters in shackles for questioning. Only one shot had been fired, and its target had been a dog that attacked one of the policemen. The initial story had been a barge fire, but Townsend learned that the first explosion was actually on board the Spanish Navy ship. Sparks from that fire had spread to the coal pile on the barge, which then began to sink. Spontaneous combustion of coal in the ship's coal bunkers was the official word.

Townsend said nothing but he kept remembering the way Quiñones had looked at that coal barge and the Navy ship. *What was it he'd said? Something about lack of guards on the barge, how it was low on the water.* Townsend knew it would have been a simple matter for him to row up in the dark and empty a sack of coal torpedoes near where the workers were loading up their buckets. Would the man take a risk like that? Maybe he'd decided this was the moment for him to join the fight.

When Townsend finally walked down to the docks, he stood looking out at the water's edge along with dozens of others. Out in the harbor, Spanish Naval Marines were boarding vessels from coastal patrol ships with bayonets attached to their rifles. A small fleet of tugboats circled the damaged Navy ship, which was listing to one side and was partially charred. The remnants of the barge were barely visible. Police kept onlookers at a distance. The entire waterfront looked like a military staging area with officers yelling out orders as newly arrived Army soldiers marched in from the train station.

Townsend walked over to the offices of Churchill, Brown & Manson. When he arrived at the counting house, he introduced himself to a young clerk, a pale New England boy who handed Townsend a letter. It was just a brief note. It said in English, "I hope you approve of my decision. It may prove to be mutually beneficial." The clerk then chimed in with a big smile on his face.

"Mr. Quiñones said he was sorry to miss you. He had to go to the interior to install a new steam engine for one of our customers. He wanted to make sure that I pass on his congratulations to you and your fiancée on your upcoming marriage."

February 25

Early the next morning Townsend and Emma rode together in a carriage on their way to Mon Bijou. They had all her luggage strapped onto the back of the *volanta*. The plan was to make their formal engagement known to Doña Cecilia and then immediately depart for Matanzas, taking the late afternoon train from there to Havana. Townsend wasn't sure how his grandmother would greet their news, but he wasn't optimistic it would be well received.

They both agreed that spending the night at Mon Bijou would be awkward for all.

The road out of town was dry and hard-packed. The *volanta* with its huge wheels bounced along over the ruts and the potholes with relative ease. Emma smiled up at him as she clutched his arm. Townsend could see that she was captivated by the views of the countryside with smoking chimneys weaving in between pastureland and open savannah. A few of the cane fields had already been plowed, and green shoots of young sugar cane were sprouting up like tiny asparagus, signaling a new season.

Over the last few days, they'd discussed their wedding and had settled on a plan. In Catholic Cuba, all Protestant services were banned. Townsend had inquired at the US Consulate and been told that a regular ordained minister of the Reformed Protestant Dutch Church was visiting the island from New York and would be willing to marry them there at the American Consulate in Havana. The Consul General would stamp the marriage certificate, thereby making it an official legal document.

Townsend was restless as his thoughts landed on his grandmother. Naturally she would be invited to the wedding, but he suspected she would not come. He dreaded talking to her about the future. He had to tell her that he was not going to stay at Mon Bijou. He and Emma had decided they would live in Havana. Emma would help her mother with the boarding house, and Townsend would work with Emilio to expand his Key West shipping business into the Caribbean, Mexico, and Central America by opening up offices in Havana. Emilio had told Emma he would be eager to have a partner like Townsend, to whom he owed such a big favor.

Townsend knew how much this would upset his grandmother. She would make him feel guilty. She would appeal to his sense of duty and obligation. He would have to tell her the truth—that he felt suffocated and trapped at Mon Bijou, and that he knew he would always be a stranger in a strange land at the plantation. He told himself he would say nothing about what he'd learned about her past. All of that would remain behind closed doors, even though he knew he would never be able to see her in quite the same way as before.

The winds were stronger than usual, stirring up clouds of dust behind them. To try to calm his nerves, Townsend took several deep breaths of the dry, salty air coming in from the Caribbean. He noticed how brown the sugar cane fields were becoming. The long leaves were curling to the ground, hanging limply in brown shreds like withering Spanish moss. The cutting of the cane stalks would soon end, and the cattle herd would be released into the fields to feed on the cane cuttings. He realized how quickly he'd learned about planting sugar cane in the short time he'd been in the Cuban countryside.

It was early that afternoon when they first smelled the smoke, as a tangy taste to the air. The postilion turned back to them and said, *"fuego de caña."* Emma looked at Townsend with some concern, but he assured her it was normal at this time of the year to have some fires. Within moments, he began to doubt his own words. Ahead, dense clouds of black smoke mushroomed upwards, not just in one area, but across either side of the road. In the far distance they could hear the loud clangs of several different plantation bells. Shouting and yelling, *"Fuego, Fuego"* could be heard faintly.

Townsend felt anxious, but he didn't say anything. The postilion looked back at him as if to ask for instructions. Townsend told him to press on. He guessed they were only eight miles from Mon Bijou. Ahead of them, the sky kept getting blacker in some sections and reddish orange in others. Black smoke, thick and oily, rose up around them. Each time a new field caught fire, bursts of flames shot upwards like angry, orange geysers, crackling and roaring. Workers, Black and white, had joined together, swinging their machetes, the blades glistening in the flames. Townsend could hear the shouts and orders of the overseers and the terrified whinnying of the horses.

Emma turned to him and said how unbearably hot it was. "Are we going to turn back? Surely we should."

"Absolutely not," Townsend said. "We're almost there."

As they got closer to his grandmother's land, Townsend noticed that the winds had switched from south to north. It seemed like a storm was brewing. The strengthening northerly wind was spreading the fire directly toward Mon Bijou. He yelled at the driver to push the horses to go faster into a canter. He now feared the worst. There was still so much dry cane that had not yet been cut, and the burning embers were flying into these new fields, causing the cane stalks to ignite in a rush.

His heart sank as they reached the outer edges of his grandmother's land. The fires had left behind a blackened ground with tiny pockets of flames here and there. On both sides of the road were some of the laborers who had fought the fire, their faces covered in dirt and black soot. They looked at him but did not seem to know who he was. Townsend felt a mounting wave of panic sweep over him, threatening to drown him. Down the driveway they galloped, past the scorched trunks of the royal palms. He braced himself for what he feared they would find.

33

In the distance Townsend could see the charred remnants of the sugar house. It looked like a bomb had gone off there. The huge copper sugar kettles had been blown into the yard like boulders from some prehistoric volcano. Flames still smoldered everywhere, snapping and hissing. Small Black children ran back and forth crying for their mothers. And then Townsend spotted what was left of his family home. Mon Bijou was nothing but blackened wood. The stone walls were still standing, but the roof was gone, along with everything inside.

The horses suddenly balked, rearing up in protest, refusing to go further. Townsend jumped out of the *volanta* and ran toward the house. He got as close as he could, calling out to the overseer, but there was no answer. He called out to his grandmother. There was only silence. He just stood there helpless and put his face in his hands. The heat from the fire was still too intense for him to get closer to the house.

The sky was now blacker than ever as the storm clouds mixed with the smoke, blotting out the sun. Townsend had no sense of time. He felt the comforting presence of Emma by his side. He felt a stinging cold rain on his face, and he heard the hissing on the hot ground from water hitting fire. A smoky haze now covered the black fields. He touched his beard and realized it had been singed. He rubbed the welcome rainwater into his sooty, burned face.

The next thing he remembered is hearing a voice calling out his name. He turned and recognized Julio, who was standing beside him with a horse.

"Where is everybody?" Townsend asked.

"Everyone is in the chapel. All the house servants went there when the fire broke out in the house."

"They're safe?"

Julio nodded.

"And my grandmother? Doña Cecilia. Is she there too?"

Townsend could see an anxious twitch in Julio's face, and he knew something was not right.

"What happened? Where is she?"

Julio's eyes were moist. He shook his head back and forth. "Your grandmother . . . *L'ama* . . . she didn't make it out of the house," he replied, his voice breaking. "I'm sorry. We all tried but we couldn't get her out. The roof fell in on top of her. Then she was lost in the flames."

Townsend had no words. He tried to speak but he couldn't. Finally, he yelled at the top of his voice, a scream of pain. He ran toward the house, but the heat was still too intense. Emma pulled him back to the safety of the carriage.

Julio got back on his horse and led the way to the chapel as the rain and the wind intensified. Once inside the small stone chapel, Townsend could make out the group of people, a mixture of the house servants and some of the carpenters and machinists. Someone brought a blanket, and Townsend covered Emma's shoulders. They were both soaked through. He inquired about McKintyre and was told that the Scotsman was still in the fields fighting the fires.

Townsend scanned the faces and nodded at those he knew, like Alejandro and his grandmother's serving maids, the two Marías. Julio led him over to where his mother was sitting, on a bench closer to the altar. Mercedes looked up at him with mournful eyes and stood up. He could see that she'd been crying. Her clothes were torn and black with soot. She'd taken off her colorful turban and wrapped it around one of her hands where she'd been burned.

"Are you badly injured?"

She shook her head. "A few burns and cuts. I've used aloe vera. Let me get some for you."

Before she could turn to fetch it—he reached out to hug her, and she broke down sobbing more heavily. He felt her shoulder blades shuddering, and he just let her shake and cry.

"Julio told me what happened," he said softly in Spanish. "Why didn't she leave earlier?"

"She did. She was safe. We were all safe. But then she cried out that she needed to go back. I grabbed her, but she broke free. She kept calling your mother's name, 'Esperanza, Esperanza.' I didn't know what she meant. Julio and I followed her into the house. There was nothing but smoke and flames in the parlor, and I could just barely see her. She'd grabbed hold of the painting of your mother that hung on the wall. You know the one. She loved that painting."

Mercedes paused as she wiped the tears from her eyes.

"She was on her way back toward me when one of the rafters fell down and struck her, crushing her to the floor. *Dios mío*, I pray that blow killed her. The heat was so intense. The smoke. There was no way to get to her . . . I tried . . . I tried . . . but I couldn't do anything and Julio pulled me back outside."

"Oh, my dear Lord," Emma said. "How horrible . . ."

Townsend didn't say anything. He felt his back and neck tightening, his stomach twisting and turning. He was not a religious man, but he looked up at the altar and made the sign of the cross the way his mother had taught him when he was a young boy. He felt his mother's presence. He bowed his head and said a prayer for both his grandmother and his mother. Then he put both his arms around Emma and Mercedes and pulled them close.

February 26

After a sleepless night in the chapel, the next day in the afternoon they held a funeral ceremony there. The local priest came as did many of the neighboring planters and the overseers. Other estates had suffered losses, but nothing like Mon Bijou. McKintyre was there with the plantation's sugar makers, slave drivers, carpenters, and machinists. Townsend made sure that the family servants were invited. He noticed that many of them had come, standing in the back of the crowded chapel. During the service, all Townsend was conscious of was the priest's deep purple robe and the smoking censer swinging back and forth to the steady rhythm of the chants.

The stray shafts of afternoon sunlight came shining through the small windows and rested on the small casket by the altar. Townsend had filled it with ashes from the part of the building where she had fallen. It was all he could think to do. They buried the ashes in a spot in the family cemetery next to her two daughters and her husband. Afterward, the nearby planters and some of the neighbors came up to him to pay their respects and to offer their help. Townsend felt touched by their kindness and generosity. He looked around at the land that his grandmother had so revered. What once looked like a rolling green carpet was now a dead, black landscape.

He watched the hunched shape of the Scottish overseer standing by the freshly dug grave. McKintyre was probably the closest to her of anyone on the plantation. Even though Townsend detested the man, he felt sympathy for him. He could see that this hulk of a man looked totally defeated, his spirit deflated like an airless balloon. The Scotsman had told him that morning the sad news that a great number of the four hundred slaves were unaccounted for. He speculated that many had probably run off, but some had been killed while fighting the fires. He'd told Townsend that they had lost the entire crop from not only the fire, but then the drenching rains that caused most of the cut cane to be sour and worthless. He said he would be leaving Mon Bijou and handed him his resignation.

After the funeral, Townsend rode around the property with Emma. He didn't need anyone to tell him that the losses were too great to contemplate doing anything but selling it. It was only worth whatever he could get from the land. He talked to Emma, and they both decided that he should immediately free the slaves who had remained, sell most of the sugar cane land to the neighbors, and parcel out the remaining land and proceeds for the slaves he'd freed.

He told Emma about his grandfather and how the family had embraced his dream that their land was in the beautiful Yumurí Valley. His grandmother had grown up with that story.

"My family lived with a fantasy, and it was this plantation. It was my grandmother's dream as well. It defined her. Gave her life meaning. Her views about slavery, the sanctity of the land, its ties to family, the importance of Spanish rule, all of that is what she believed in." He took a deep breath and sighed. "That was her reality, but it was also her fantasy. She chose not to see the ugliness and cruelty of slavery. It was how she saw the world. She loved that play by Pedro Calderón de la Barca from Spain's Golden Age, *La Vida es Sueño*. Life is a Dream. I intend to find a verse or a phrase from that play to put on her headstone. Perhaps something about how all life is nothing more than a dream within a dream. She would have liked that."

That evening, with the sun falling toward the horizon, Townsend pulled on the plantation bell and called all of Mon Bijou's workforce to the front of the house. Field hands, cooks, carpenters, domestic servants. Without any introduction, he shouted, "You are free, free as birds. *Libertos*, you are free men now!" he cried out. Their collective gasps and shouts brought tears to his eyes. "You do not have to work here or any plantation anymore unless you are paid." He then told the old Chinese man who had done the translating before to tell all the Chinese workers the same thing. They were no longer under any contract obligations.

The former slaves of Mon Bijou danced and sang while others kneeled and prayed. That night the drums beat and bonfires were lit. Townsend asked Mercedes what she wanted to do. She told him she would like to stay on the land. He said when he got to Havana and spoke with the lawyer there, he would make the arrangements so that she and Julio would be the owners of the chapel and some one hundred acres of land around it. He said he would also make sure that ten acres each went to those newly freed who had remained on the farm. A similar plan would be offered to the Chinese workers who had stayed. He then asked Julio to draw up a list of names of all the workers who had remained during the fire.

Townsend and Emma left the following day for Havana. He knew he would be dealing with the military police as well as his grandmother's lawyers and accountants as he tried to rid himself of the slavery that his mother had fled from. On the train, with the clattering of the wheels and the smell of cigar smoke, he began writing his report to Secretary Seward.

Hon. William H. Seward
Secretary of State
Washington, DC
February 27, 1866

Sir:

The most pressing information I have for you since I last wrote is that a New Orleans–based syndicate with hidden investors in New York and elsewhere is acquiring at least two new steamers to be used to carry hundreds of American freedmen to Cuba. I can relate to you that some key figures in this syndicate have been arrested in the town of Cárdenas and that their steamship, the *Suwannee*, was seized. The men on board reportedly have been charged with supplying weapons to the Cubans who are opposed to Spanish rule. Evidence seems to indicate that these weapons were once the property of the former Confederacy and had been abandoned in Cuba after the war. It should be noted that one of the men arrested was a former US Army major with the Bureau of Military Information by the name of Hutchinson, who appears to have played a central role as his assumed alias of Joshua Hawley.

Even though this is a positive development, I must warn you that the threat of more kidnappings will continue. This syndicate is reportedly well financed and has plans to carry over large shipments of freedmen on these American-flagged vessels. Plans have been set in motion to land these kidnapped freedmen on deserted islands on the north shore of Cuba. Once they arrive, there is little hope of rescuing them. The people in uniform locally—police and customs—are controlled by the island's slave interests and are paid to look the other way. To save face, the Spanish government will continue to deny any landings.

My time here in your service has convinced me that the plantations on this island are like castles, and even the Spanish government has no legal way of investigating what goes on behind their walls. The Spanish Captain General may know what is happening, but he doesn't dare challenge the interests of the planters, most of whom remain fearful of ending slavery. Cuba is an island saddled with repression and hobbled by talk of civil war. Quite simply, it is a tinderbox. Beyond fears of insurrection and the fight for independence from Spain lies the even thornier question of how slavery will end on this island that is so completely dependent on it.

It is my belief and humble opinion that unless the US government sends a strong signal to the Spanish government, a new slave trade could become a reality. As long as slavery exists here on this island, there will continue to be slave trading and the threat of continued kidnappings of American citizens. As a result, the US government may never know the full extent of this illicit trade.

I am, Sir, with great respect,
Your obedient servant,
Lieutenant Everett Townsend
USN
Havana, Cuba

Townsend put down his pen. Separately, he would write a more detailed report. He knew what he put on paper would never be part of the official records, but he felt he'd provided the Secretary with the firsthand information he'd requested. He also would write Mr. Rudd and notify him of the fire and the circumstances he now faced. His intention was to remain in Havana, awaiting word of his discharge from the Navy.

It was late when the train arrived at Regla on the opposite side of Havana Bay from the old city. The beam from the lighthouse at El Morro gleamed out to sea, beckoning all ships sailing south. He and Emma walked down to the waterfront and found a bungo boat for hire. The captain agreed to take them across the harbor to the main landing area by the Plaza de San Francisco. It was a full moon, and they could clearly see the skyline of the old city with its many domes and towers.

A wave of conflicting emotions swept over Townsend as he looked out at the harbor. He could still see his grandmother's pained face, his last memory of her before he had ridden away from the plantation. He had hoped to patch things up, but that was not meant to be. A pang of guilt now hit him as he realized in the wake of the fire that he felt a sense of relief. He knew that selling the plantation and freeing the slaves would free him now to follow his own destiny. His mother had fled but never been totally free of Mon Bijou. The fear he'd had of having to choose between taking over the plantation or leaving it behind was gone. That knowledge was like lifting a huge weight from his shoulders. Somehow fate had decided he had a different road to travel, yet to be revealed. He thought of his mother's words to him. "The world is constantly trying to make all of us into something other than what we are. Remember *mi hijo*, life is what you make it."

As the bungo boat began to heel over with the night sea breeze, he felt a light touch on his arm, and he looked over at Emma. Her upturned face caught in the moonlight, her hair falling down her back, the faint smell of lavender, all of that caused him to smile. The water alongside the boat was now gurgling and splashing spray on their faces. He suddenly felt a reason for hope. Emma was his family now. They were together finally. He grabbed her hand and drew her to him into a shadowy area in the bow of the little boat where it was more protected. The Cuban captain pretended to be looking at the sails and tending the sheets, but he finally muttered to them in Spanish that they should cover their heads to protect themselves from the moonlight.

THE END

Epilogue

There is no way of knowing the actual number of American freedmen who may have been kidnapped and taken to Cuba in the months and years following the Civil War. No credible investigation in Cuba was ever carried out. Rumors and reports continued throughout 1866. In the spring of that year, the Department of War seized two American steamships suspected of shipping freedmen from northern Florida to Cuba. No incriminating evidence was found, so the ships were eventually released.

At the same time, there were reports of several secret landings on the north coast of Cuba of what were presumed to be newly arrived African slaves, one of them near Sagua la Grande. In one instance, four hundred men were found stranded on an island off the coast of Cuba. They only spoke English, causing US consular officials to suspect that they could be kidnapped Americans. When questioned, Spanish authorities denied their existence, and said the reports were false.

Investigations and probes continued through 1869. But it wasn't until years later in the midst of the turmoil during Cuba's first War of Independence between 1868 and 1878 that an important testimonial was given. The story appeared in the *New York Tribune*. It was an account by a former Union officer who had met a runaway slave in Cuba who spoke only English and claimed he was an American. The man said he used to be a slave on a plantation in Louisiana near New Orleans called Fannie Place. This man said as a freedman after the war, he had been shipped to Cuba on an American ship in 1866 along with several others where he was enslaved on a plantation.

The man claimed he knew of other American Negroes in Cuba working as slaves on plantations and who had been brought there on American ships. This account by the former Union officer was given in an affidavit before the US Commissioner in Florida.

Author's Notes and
Acknowledgments

I would like to offer thanks to several people for their support, principally my wife, Tamara, who was generous with advice and encouraged me along the way with helpful suggestions and insightful edits. The unenviable job of reading the first draft fell to her, a thankless task for anyone. From the out-set, Alexandra Shelley helped me find the story's direction and launch the writing process, later giving me valuable advice at the halfway mark. Julie Miesionczek's thoughtful and thorough editing of the first complete draft smoothed out the many rough edges and helped to better define several of the characters.

This novel took shape in Key West after several visits there over the years. I am grateful for the generous help from Tom Hambright and his assistants at the Monroe County Library in Key West for giving me access to archival material there. Trips to nearby Fort Jefferson and the Marquesas left a strong impression on me. Key West had been the headquarters of the Navy's East Gulf Squadron during the Civil War, and the dismantling of the Naval base after the war interested me. While doing newspaper research, I discovered that a powerful hurricane had struck Key West in the fall of 1865, causing major damage to the Florida coast. This drama only made the setting of Key West more compelling to portray the outer edge of a country emerging from the shadow of war.

I first became aware of the story of American freedmen being kidnapped and taken to Cuba from an article in the *Florida Historical Quarterly* by James Cortada, "Florida's Relations with Cuba during the Civil War," 1980, volume LIX. This article speculated that the number of people kidnapped could range from forty to several hundred. Another important article on this topic was written by Jose Fernández and Jerrell Shofner, "Kidnapping of Freedmen from the United States for the Cuban Slave Trade" *Homenaje a Lydia Cabrera*, 1977. The book *Beyond Freedom's Reach* by Adam Rothman also deals with this subject, portraying the ordeal of a New Orleans former slave to free her three children who had been taken to Cuba and enslaved there.

For help with primary research on the kidnapping reports in the Gulf, I want to thank researcher Gail Lelyveld for gathering pertinent letters and reports written by the Army's office of the Provost Marshal General in New Orleans. These are stored in the National Archives. She also helped with the Library of Congress by retrieving the consular dispatches from Havana back to Washington in 1865 and 1866, the correspondence between Secretary of State Seward and the Spanish legation in Washington and a copy of the State Department report on the kidnappings delivered to the US Senate in early 1866. From all of these readings, I realized that this was a largely forgotten chapter in American and Cuban history that was still shrouded in mystery.

The works that were helpful in portraying Key West and Florida after the war were Lewis Schmidt's extensive volumes on the Civil War in Florida; Jefferson Browne's *Key West—the Old and the New*; Walter Maloney, *A Sketch of the History of Key West*; Whitelaw Reid, *After the War*; Laura Albritton and Jerry Wilkinson, *Hidden History of the Florida Keys*; Joe Richardson, "A Northener Reports on Florida: 1866," *Florida Historical Quarterly*, April 1962; and Antonio Rafael de la Cova, "Cuban Exiles in Key West during the Ten Years War," *Florida Historical Quarterly*, December 2011. Also recommended for the history of the Cornish Memorial AME Zion Church in Key West is the book *For a Great and Grand Purpose: The Beginnings of the AMEZ Church in Florida, 1864–1905*, by Canter Brown Jr. and Larry E. Rivers. Information on Naval Commander George Ransom is available at the William Clements Library in Ann Arbor, Michigan. The story of the Butler plantation in Georgia is described in the book *The Weeping Time* by Anne C. Bailey.

With regard to Sandy Cornish's language, I relied on a variety of sources, including Whitelaw Reid's published account of his encounter and conversation with Old Sandy in 1865. I attempted to get as close to the vernacular as I could by researching Zora Neale Hurston, who grew up in Eatonville, Florida, only a generation later. Unquestionably the different accents of African Americans at that time varied widely from region to region. To try and capture the slight West Indian accent of Levi Jacobs, I was again influenced by Hurston, but relied also on other linguistic sources.

To help portray Cuba at the time, some of the books that were helpful are Louis Perez, Jr., *Slaves, Sugar and Colonial Society*; Louis Perez Jr., *Cuba and the United States, Ties of Singular Intimacy*; David Murray, *Odious Commerce*; and Franklin W. Knight, *Slave Society in Cuba during the Nineteenth Century*. An article published in *Caribbean Studies* by Luis Martínez-Fernández, "Political Change in the Spanish Caribbean during the United States Civil War and its Aftermath," was extremely informative. The numerous travel journals, guidebooks, and memoirs written in the mid-nineteenth century about Cuba were invaluable. Some worthy of special mention are C. D. Tyng, *The Stranger in the Tropics*; Charles H. Dana, *To Cuba and Back*; Eliza Mchatton-Ripely, *From Flag to Flag*; Antonio Gallenga, *The Pearl of the Antilles*; Samuel Hazard, *Cuba with Pen and Pencil*; Joseph Dimock, *Impressions of Cuba in the 19th Century*; and Esteban Montejo, *The Autobiography of a Runaway Slave*. For information on the sugar trade in Cuba and the ties with American merchants, I would recommend the writings of Roland T. Ely: "The Old Cuba Trade," *The Business History Review*, 38, no. 4, 1964; as well as his book in Spanish, *Cuando Reinaba Su Majestad El Azúcar*.

For help with my use of the Spanish language, I want to thank Luis Martínez-Fernández and Sylvia Crane for their meticulous editing. Veteran ocean sailor and maritime author Donald Street was extremely kind to review my use of nautical terms on board a nineteenth-century schooner. Finally, I want to thank Florida researcher, Jan Campbell, the history department at Louisiana's Oak Alley Plantation, USN historian Anna Gibson Holloway, and Pastor Pearson-McEntyre with the Cornish Memorial AME Zion Church in Key West. A special thanks as well to Stacey Warner of Warner Graphics in Camden, Maine, who helped with the images in the book.